Praise for the novels of Sherryl Woods

"Sherryl Woods writes emotionally satisfying
novels about family, friendship and home. Truly
feel-great reads!"
> —#1 *New York Times* bestselling author
> Debbie Macomber

"During the course of this gripping, emotionally
wrenching but satisfying tale, Woods deftly
and realistically handles such issues as survival
guilt, drug abuse as adolescent rebellion, and
family dynamics when a vital member is suddenly
gone."
> —*Booklist* on *Flamingo Diner*

"Woods is a master heartstring puller."
> —*Publishers Weekly* on *Seaview Inn*

"Once again, Woods, with such authenticity,
weaves a tale of true love and the challenges that
can knock up against that love."
> —*RT Book Reviews* on *Beach Lane*

"Woods…is noted for appealing character-driven
stories that are often infused with the flavor and
fragrance of the South."
> —*Library Journal*

"A reunion story punctuated by family drama,
Woods's first novel in her new Ocean Breeze
series is touching, tense and tantalizing."
> —*RT Book Reviews* on *Sand Castle Bay*

"A whimsical, sweet scenario… The digressions
have their own charm, and Woods never fails to
come back to the romantic point."
> —*Publishers Weekly* on *Sweet Tea at Sunrise*

SHERRYL WOODS

West Texas Nights

mira

mira™

Recycling programs for this product may not exist in your area.

ISBN-13: 978-0-7783-8807-4

West Texas Nights

Copyright © 2020 by Harlequin Books S.A.

The Cowboy and His Wayward Bride
First published in 1999. This edition published in 2020.
Copyright © 1999 by Sherryl Woods

Suddenly, Annie's Father
First published in 1999. This edition published in 2020.
Copyright © 1999 by Sherryl Woods

This edition published by arrangement with Harlequin Books S.A.

For questions and comments about the quality of this book, please contact us at CustomerService@Harlequin.com.

Mira
22 Adelaide St. West, 40th Floor
Toronto, Ontario M5H 4E3, Canada
www.Harlequin.com

Printed in Spain

This one is for all the readers who've embraced my
characters and stories through the years.
You've been such a blessing in my life
and I treasure the friendship you've offered.

CONTENTS

THE COWBOY AND
HIS WAYWARD BRIDE

One

Pure, gut-deep exhaustion had settled over country-music superstar Laurie Jensen weeks earlier, and now it seemed she was walking around in a haze from dawn to dusk. A new baby who didn't know the meaning of a full night's sleep, a concert tour, publicity demands and the burden of keeping a secret from the one person in the world with whom she had always been totally, brutally honest—all of it had combined to take a terrible emotional toll.

She sat in her fancy dressing room long after her concert had ended and the fans had drifted away. With the sleeping baby nestled in her arms, her own eyes drifting shut, she relished the momentary silence, welcoming it just as she had the applause earlier.

Bliss, she thought. The quiet was absolute bliss.

Of course, it didn't last.

"Laurie, you ready?" her assistant called out in a hushed tone with an accompanying rap on the door. "The limo's outside to take us back to the hotel."

Even the soft tap and whispered reminder were enough noise to wake the always restless baby, who began to fuss, then settled into a full-throated yowling that gave Laurie a splitting headache.

"Shh, sweetheart. Everything's okay. Mama's here," she soothed, gathering up her purse and easing toward the door.

As the baby quieted and finally began to gurgle contentedly, Laurie did a quick survey of the room to be sure she'd left nothing behind, thankful once again for Val's efficiency. Her assistant handled everything from toting diaper bags to making complex travel arrangements with total aplomb. She'd even been known to tuck Amy Lynn into the crook of her arm and feed her while answering Laurie's fan mail with her free hand.

Often, observing her whirlwind assistant at work, Laurie wished she were half so competent, even a quarter so adept with the multiple demands facing her. There were times—and tonight was one of them—when she felt thoroughly overwhelmed, when she wanted nothing more than to run straight back to Texas and into Harlan Patrick's waiting arms. Assuming he was still waiting for her after all this time and after she'd made it clear that her singing career was what she wanted most in this world.

What was wrong with her? Was she completely out of her mind trying to tackle the demands of motherhood and a singing career all on her own? Especially when she knew with absolute certainty that the baby's father would have flown to her side in a heartbeat if only she'd told him about Amy Lynn?

But that was the trouble, of course. Harlan Patrick Adams would have taken the news that he was a daddy as reason enough to demand that she marry him at once, return to Los Piños, Texas, and be a rancher's wife. There would have been no ifs, ands or buts about it.

She'd known the man since she was in kindergarten. She knew how he operated. A bulldozer did gentle nudging by comparison. Oh, she knew Harlan Patrick, all right. They'd exchanged birthday presents at five, their first awkward dance at thirteen, their first real kiss at fifteen.

Harlan Patrick had flirted with typical Adams abandon with every girl in town, but there'd never been a doubt in anyone's mind that Laurie was the one he loved. With single-minded determination, he'd been asking her to marry him for years now. And she'd been saying no, while practically everyone in the universe told her she'd lost her mind.

Unlike the music business, Harlan Patrick Adams and his love were a sure thing, her mother had told her repeatedly. His family was the richest and most powerful in Los Piños, practically in all of Texas. He could give her stability, the kind of rock-solid future most women dreamed of, the kind her mother had always craved.

Unfortunately, Laurie's dreams tended toward a world that no one, not even an Adams, could guarantee. From the time she'd learned the words to an old Patsy Cline hit, she'd wanted to be a country-music sensation. God had blessed her with the voice for it. Whether it was the church choir or the school chorus, Laurie had always been the star soloist. The applause had been wonderful, but she would have sung for the sheer joy of it. And maybe, at one time, she would have been content with that.

But over the years Harlan Patrick had unwittingly fed her obsession by seeing to it that she saw concerts by every country superstar who appeared anywhere in Texas. He'd even wrangled a backstage meeting with a few. Laurie had discovered her destiny.

Somehow, though, he'd never taken seriously her desire to be up there on the stage, earning her own applause. For him, the gestures had been an indulgence. For her, they had been an inspiration. He'd thought time, a little coaxing and a few breath-stealing kisses would change her mind. She'd found his inability to recognize and accept her dream more annoying than her mom's.

After all, Mary Jensen had had a tough life. She was practical to the very core. Harlan Patrick, however, was supposed to be Laurie's soul mate, the man in whom she'd confided her hopes and dreams all her life. The discovery that he'd merely been indulging what he called "her little fantasies" had brought on one of the most heated fights they'd ever had.

Why hadn't he been able to understand that singing was simply something she had to do with the gift God had given her? He'd let her—*let her*, she thought indignantly—sing in the neighboring towns if that's what she wanted, but Nashville had been out of the question. His ultimatum had been phrased in a generous, condescending tone that had set her teeth on edge. As if the decision were his to make, she'd thought as she turned on her heel and walked out of his life for good.

In one way she was grateful. It had made it easier to say goodbye, to head for Nashville without looking back. She'd dug in her heels, too, even when the going had been tough and she'd been waiting tables to make ends meet. Knowing that he'd welcome her back with an I-told-you-so smile had driven her to stay the course.

It had been two long, lonely years before she'd been discovered by her agent, but then things had happened so quickly it had left her reeling. She'd captured the Horizon Award for up-and-coming stars with her first album, a Grammy and a CMA Award with her second. She'd gone from a show-starter for the superstars to a concert tour of her own that had broken box-office records. In no time, it seemed, every single debuted at the top of the charts and every album went gold.

Only then, with rave reviews and money in her pocket, had she gone back to Los Piños. It was the only time she'd seen Harlan Patrick in the five years since she'd left. She was home just long enough to discover that the chemistry between them was as explosive as ever and that he was every bit as bullheaded as he'd been the day she walked out. He'd actually thought that she'd be ready to walk away from it all now that she'd proved to herself she could do it, as if it had been some cute little game she'd been playing. The man could infuriate her faster than anyone else on earth.

Then, just a few weeks after their reunion, she'd discovered she was pregnant. From that moment on, all she'd been able to think about was keeping the baby a secret from Harlan Patrick. She'd been able to walk away from him not just once, but twice. Could she do it again, especially with a baby in the picture? She wasn't sure she'd have the strength or even the will.

For the first few months of her pregnancy, it had been simple enough to avoid his calls and keep the secret. She was either in Nashville or on the road and she was extremely careful that no one—not even the very discreet Val—had any idea she was going to have a child. Val knew only that she had no desire to speak to one Harlan Patrick Adams, which pretty much assured that there wasn't a chance in hell he'd get through to her. Eventually he'd gotten the message and given up. Not even Harlan Patrick was stubborn beyond all reason. Nor was he a masochist. It hadn't taken all that long for the Adams pride to kick in and assure her of a reprieve from his pestering.

When Laurie could no longer disguise her expanding waistline, she had scheduled five months in seclusion at her home on the outskirts of Nashville. She'd let Val and no one else in on the secret and let her assistant run interference.

"She's working on songs for her next album," Val had told any and all callers, including Laurie's agent. That had kept him, if not the media, satisfied.

Now she had Amy Lynn to remember her childhood sweetheart by, and it was both the most miraculous blessing on earth and a painful reminder of what might have been. When she thought of how Harlan Patrick would have adored their precious child, she hated herself for keeping silent. And yet, what choice had she had?

None, she assured herself. Handsome as sin, but stubborn as a mule, Harlan Patrick had given her none. The man didn't know the meaning of *compromise*. He'd made it impossible for her to do anything other than exactly what she had done.

After Amy Lynn's birth, she had scheduled recording sessions for the next two months. There'd been a short break, barely long enough for her to catch her breath while the album had been rushed to market, followed by the grueling pace of a concert tour set to coincide with the album's release.

By then, those closest to her knew about the baby, but they'd all been sworn to secrecy and they had united to protect both Laurie and the baby from the glare of the spotlight. It couldn't last forever, but it had to last long enough that Harlan Patrick wouldn't connect her child with that last visit to Los Piños.

It meant sneaking in and out of concert halls and clubs, using hotel back doors and heavily tinted limo windows, but the worst of it was over. One more month, mostly in small towns and out-of-the-way clubs to which she owed a debt, and they'd be home again. She could drop out of sight completely there, live in seclusion with her daughter. Just thinking of it was enough to have her sighing with relief.

They were halfway down the hall when Val muttered a curse. "I left that package of autographed pictures in the office. Wait for me at the back door, and I'll check the alley before you go out."

It was an established routine. When Laurie had the baby with her, Val always preceded her to make sure the coast was clear, that there were no paparazzi or overly zealous fans lurking in the shadows. Sometimes it was Val who carried Amy Lynn tucked in her arms as if the baby were her own.

Tonight, though, Laurie was thinking only of crawling into the back of the limo, resting her aching head against the smooth-as-butter leather and catching a ten-minute nap on the way back to the hotel. That was how bad it had gotten. Even ten minutes of uninterrupted sleep sounded heavenly.

She was so anxious to reach the car and settle in that she opened the door of the auditorium without waiting for Val. The instant she did, a photographer's flashbulb exploded in her face. Panic had her whirling to shield the baby, but she knew in her heart it was too late. The man had had a clear shot in that instant before she'd been aware of his presence and time to click off a few more shots while she'd been temporarily blinded by the first brilliant flash of light.

"Oh, God, no," she murmured, imagining the picture splashed across the front of every tabloid in the country. Tears slid down her cheeks even as Val exited the building, saw what was happening and took off after the photographer with fire in her eyes.

To Laurie's relief, Val caught him at the end of the

alley, but all of her pleading and cajoling could not make him relinquish the prized roll of film. Nor could the swift kick she aimed at his shin or the knee she tried to place deftly in his groin, but Laurie had to admire her courage in trying. She vowed to give the woman a raise for going way above the call of duty, even if her efforts had failed.

Defeated, Val returned to the limo. "I'm sorry," she whispered. "I should have checked the alley."

"It's not your fault," Laurie reassured her wearily. "I should have waited. I was just so tired."

"Maybe he was just some local guy and the picture won't make it beyond here," Val suggested hopefully.

"Ever heard of wire services?" Laurie inquired, wishing she could believe Val, but knowing that she was doomed. Harlan Patrick was going to see the picture. Sooner or later someone would bring it to his attention, and then, no matter what conclusion he reached when he saw it, it was going to rip his heart in two.

Then, she thought with a sinking sensation in the pit of her stomach, all hell was going to break loose. It was just a matter of time.

"I say we buy up all the copies in town and burn them," Sharon Lynn said vehemently, tossing the offending tabloid onto her parents' kitchen table. "If Harlan Patrick sees this, he's going to freak out."

This was a half-page picture of country-music superstar Laurie Jensen with "Her Secret Love Child."

"He's finally over her," Sharon Lynn said of her brother. "He's not even playing her songs on the new jukebox down at Dolan's anymore."

"No, now he plays them on that boom box he carries with him everywhere he goes," her mother said. "We have to show it to him. Maybe this will finally close that chapter in his life. He'll have to move on once he sees she has a child."

Harlan Patrick stood outside the kitchen door and listened to the whole conversation. His stomach had clenched and his hand had stilled on the screen door the instant he'd realized the topic. The merest mention of Laurie was all it took to get his heart to thudding dully and his forehead to break out in a cold sweat.

How the hell was he supposed to get over Laurie when she was a part of him, as vital to him as breathing? Losing her had made him question everything, every choice he'd made, even his commitment to the family ranch. There were times when the weight of the family's expectations and his sense of his own destiny almost combined to crush him.

With his grandfather in his eighties and his father, Cody, getting older, the fate of White Pines was all but his. Ranching was in his blood; it defined who he was, but that didn't make it any less of a burden at times. Day in, day out, 365 days a year, the demands were unceasing. The damned ranch was what stood between him and Laurie, and yet, when the chips had been down, the ranch was what he'd chosen, just as surely as she'd chosen her music over him.

His heritage over his heart. It was pitiful enough to be the heartbreaking theme of a country-music megahit. He was surprised Laurie hadn't written it herself. She'd turned everything else they'd shared into top-ten hits. There was something downright eerie and irritating about hearing his life played out on the radio.

Thinking back, he realized that maybe he'd made the decisions he had because he hadn't believed for a minute that she'd really leave. Despite repeated warnings from his sister, his cousin Justin, his grandfather, just about everyone, he'd trusted that their love was stronger than anything else on earth. By the time he'd recognized his mistake, it was too late. Laurie had been gone and with her, his soul.

Ironically he'd gotten another chance a little over a year ago, but his pride had kicked in with a vengeance and he'd watched her run out on him all over again. Pride, as his granddaddy had told him more than once, made a mighty cold bedmate. Even knowing the truth of that, he still hadn't been able to make himself go after her. He'd called for a while, but when those calls hadn't been returned, he'd cursed her every which way and given up.

Okay, so he was a damned fool. He admitted it. She'd made things clear enough the last time he'd seen her. She'd told him flat out that she still loved him, just not enough to come home and be his wife. He'd accepted her decision. What choice did he have? He couldn't go chasing halfway around the world to be by her side, could he? What was he supposed to do? Run White Pines long-distance?

But he hadn't forgotten about her, not for a single second. Now she had a child? He didn't believe it, couldn't believe that some other man had shared her bed, not when she'd so fiercely declared that she was still in love with him. Theirs simply wasn't the kind of love that died overnight, no matter how badly they'd mistreated each other. No one had replaced her in his heart or even in his bed. He'd managed to convince himself that she'd do the same. Apparently that was just one on a whole long list of delusions he'd held about Laurie.

He yanked open the screen door, then let it slam behind him as he stared into two shocked, guilty faces. "Let me see it," he demanded, his voice deadly calm.

Sharon Lynn moved between him and the table, blocking his view of the paper. "Forget about it," she said. "Forget about her."

He watched as her sense of indignation and family loyalty kicked in and loved her for it. His big sister had a mile-wide protective streak. All of the Adamses did.

"Laurie Jensen isn't worth one more second of your time," Sharon Lynn declared. "She's never been any good for you, and this proves it."

"I know what you're trying to do, sis, but you and I both know that Laurie is the only woman for me."

Sharon Lynn blushed. "Okay, I'm sorry. It just makes me so mad the way she keeps walking out on you."

He decided not to remind her that that was only half of the story. The first time Laurie had gone, Sharon Lynn had actually taken her side, accused him of being a shortsighted jerk for not going after her, for not trying harder to become a part of her new life, maybe using his business degree to become her manager or something. When Laurie had gone this last time, Sharon Lynn had positioned herself staunchly behind him. Rarely did a kind word about Laurie cross her lips. The rest of his family tried never to mention her at all.

He scowled at Sharon Lynn. "Just hand over the paper, okay?"

His sister wasn't quite finished. Once she got wound up, it was impossible to slow her down. She gave him a defiant look. "You have to forget about her, Harlan Patrick. Move on. There are a zillion women in Texas who'd love to be with you. Pick one of them, one who'll treat you right instead of running out on everything you have to offer."

"Easier said than done," he said.

He ought to know. He'd cut a wide swath through the

available women in three or four counties after Laurie had
left the first time. He hadn't had more than a date or two
with any of them then and he hadn't bothered to call even
one of them after Laurie had left this last time. He'd accepted the possibility that no one would ever measure up.

"Sis, I appreciate your loyalty. I really do," he assured
her, then glared. "Now let me see the blasted paper, unless you'd prefer to have me drive all the way into town
to pick one up. Do you want me to be standing in the su-
permarket with half the town gawking at me when I read
it? That ought to keep the gossips busy for a while."

His mother, who'd been letting the two of them battle
it out up until now, sighed. "Let him see it, Sharon Lynn.
The horse is out of the barn anyway."

His sister handed him the paper with obvious reluctance. The front page was folded in two. He opened it
slowly, regretting that he had even his mother and sister
as his audience.

The sight of Laurie, all done up in her fancy, rhinestone-
studded cowgirl stage costume, brought his pulse skidding
to a halt. No matter how many times he saw her picture,
he never got over the wonder of her beauty—the thick
chestnut-colored hair, the dare-you curve of her smile, the
sparkle in her eyes. Despite the fancy getup, there was no
artifice about her. She didn't need a lot of makeup to en-
hance what nature had given her.

He'd pretty much stopped looking at these rags, because the sight of her always had the same effect and he
figured sooner or later it was going to turn deadly. How
many times could a man's heart grind to a halt before it
stopped pumping altogether?

This time, though, the photographer hadn't done her
justice. There was no glint in her eyes, no smile on her

lips. He'd caught her in an instant of stunned disbelief, one hand held up, futilely trying to block the lens, while she turned to try to shield the baby in her arms.

She'd been too slow. The baby was in perfect focus, round faced, smiling, with a halo of soft brown curls and blue, blue eyes sparkling with pure devilment. Adams eyes, Harlan Patrick thought at once, unmistakably Adams eyes. There was a whole mantle full of baby pictures just like this up at Grandpa Harlan's. He was surprised his mother and Sharon Lynn hadn't guessed the truth—but then they hadn't known about that last meeting—the one where he lost his head and made love to her one last time.

This time it wasn't love or even lust that kicked his pulse into overdrive. It was fury. The suspicion that had been nagging at him from the moment he'd heard his mother and Sharon Lynn talking was all but confirmed. Laurie Jensen had had his baby and kept it from him. Betrayal cut through him like a lance. He was surprised he wasn't bleeding from the wound.

In less than an instant, fury was replaced by icy resolve. He whirled around and without a word went out the way he'd come in, slamming the door behind him, the tabloid crushed in his hand.

"Oh, my God," Sharon Lynn murmured. "Did you see his face?"

"I saw," his mother said, racing out the door after him. "Harlan Patrick, get back here!"

He ignored the command and headed straight for his pickup. A half hour later he was at the airstrip with Uncle Jordan's corporate jet fired up and waiting for him.

He was going after Laurie Jensen and his baby and when he found them, there was going to be hell to pay.

Two

Laurie had been heartsick ever since her manager had shown her the tabloid a week after that fateful night outside a Kansas concert hall. From that moment on she had prayed over and over that Harlan Patrick would never see it. Whether he recognized the baby as his or not, the picture was going to break his heart. She'd vowed the last time she'd seen him not to ever do anything to hurt him again. As it was, she'd broken his heart more times than she could count.

She'd tried to prepare for the possibility that her prayers wouldn't be heard. She'd warned everyone in her agent's office that her schedule was not to be given to anyone, no matter what name they gave, no matter what ruse they used. She had described Harlan Patrick to Nick's secretary from his thick, sun-streaked hair, to his laser blue eyes and angled cheekbones.

"And you *don't* want this man to find you?" the woman had said incredulously. "Are you nuts?"

"There are those who'd say I am," she agreed. "And, Ruby, let me know the instant he shows up, okay? I need to know what kind of mood he's in."

"Fit to be tied would be my guess," Ruby said bluntly. "Can't say I blame him, either. It's a hell of a way to find out you're a daddy."

"Ruby," Laurie protested.

"Okay, okay, I'm just the hired help around here. You don't want the man to find you, I'll make sure the man doesn't find you, at least not with any help from me. Just don't forget, honey, you're the kind of woman who tends to make news, especially in this business. *Entertainment Tonight*'s scheduled to shoot that club date in Montana. It's way too late to back out. Nick would have a cow. He worked like crazy to get it set up."

"It won't matter. By the time it airs, I'll be on the road again. With any sort of luck at all, Harlan Patrick will be one step behind me."

"Maybe you ought to slow down and let him catch up," Ruby suggested one more time. "Have it out and get it over with. Hiding's no good, not in your profession. This was bound to happen sooner or later. And, forgive me for saying it, but that little girl of yours has a right to know her daddy. This plan of yours to keep 'em apart seems a tad selfish to me."

Laurie winced. Ruby was young, but she had terrific common sense and a mile-wide streak of decency. A part of Laurie wanted to follow her advice, but another part wasn't at all sure she could cope with one more battle with Harlan Patrick, not with the stakes as high as they were.

"I know," Laurie conceded. "But I can't deal with him yet. I just can't. You'll see what I mean if he shows up there. It's like trying to talk sense with a bulldozer that's rattling toward you in first gear."

Of course, she consoled herself, there was always the outside chance that Harlan Patrick had never even seen

the tabloid. Maybe he hadn't been anywhere near a super-
market checkout stand. Maybe the entire shipment to Los
Piños had been lost in transit. Maybe the delivery truck
had caught fire. Maybe…

Dammit, she had to know. She had to find out if he'd
seen it and what his reaction had been. She had to be prepared, in case he was coming after her. For all of her attempts to cover her tracks, she knew Ruby was right. If
Harlan Patrick wanted to find her badly enough, he could.
Ruby and Nick could only stall him for so long. Any private eye worth his license could pinpoint her location
quicker than that photographer had snapped her picture.
The only real question was whether Harlan Patrick was
furious enough to come chasing after her or so hurt he'd
written her off once and for all. If he'd recognized that
baby as his, she was pretty sure which it would be. He'd
be mowing down any obstacle in his path to get to her.

She could call her mother, but her mom almost never
crossed paths with Harlan Patrick's family. She could call
Sharon Lynn, but after this last visit, Harlan Patrick's protective older sister had all but written her off. Sharon Lynn
had told her more than once that she was a selfish fool for
running off and leaving the best man in the whole state
of Texas pining after her. His parents had never echoed
the same sentiments in so many words, but they clearly
hadn't been her biggest fans. When she'd come back this
last time, they'd regarded her with suspicion at worst, caution at best. The attitude had hurt, because once they'd
considered her another daughter.

That left his grandfather. Harlan Adams was a wise
man, a fair man. He'd protect his family with his dying
breath, but he also had the ability to see that there was
more than one side to most stories. He'd always treated

Laurie with kindness, and there'd been no judgment in his eyes when she'd left yet again, only sorrow. He would tell her what she needed to know and he wouldn't pull any punches.

It took her most of the day to work up the courage to call White Pines. She told herself it was because she wasn't likely to find Harlan Adams at home much before nightfall. Despite his age, he still worked the ranch as best he could. And when his aches kept him off a horse, he was busy meddling in everyone's lives.

The truth, though, was that she was scared to hear whatever he had to say, even more afraid that this time he wouldn't be so kind at all if he thought she had betrayed his grandson.

She shouldn't have worried. Either he didn't know about the baby or he'd taken it in stride. At any rate, he greeted her with his usual exuberance.

"Laurie, darlin' girl, how are you? Pretty as ever, I know, because I see your picture in the paper and on TV all the time. You still singing up a storm?"

"I'm busier than ever," she told him. "I'm right in the middle of a concert tour now. I won't be back in Nashville for another month." She figured it wouldn't hurt to reiterate that, in case the conversation was repeated to Harlan Patrick. Maybe he'd stay away from Nashville if he knew she wouldn't be there.

"And you enjoy all this wandering around, instead of taking the time to sit a spell in one place?" Harlan Adams asked.

"Most of the time," she admitted. "It's part of the job."

"Tell me about the next album. You finished it yet?"

"No. I haven't even started. This one's only been out a couple of months now. I probably won't get back into the studio until a few months after I get back to Nashville. It's a good thing, too. I've been scribbling down a few things, but I still haven't settled on the last two songs."

"You still writing them all yourself?"

"Most of them."

"You always had a way with words. I still remember that song you wrote and sang for me when I turned eighty. Not a dry eye in the place when you were done singing. I knew then you were going to be a superstar."

"That's more than I knew then."

Silence fell, and it was Harlan who finally broke it when Laurie couldn't find the words she needed.

"So, darlin' girl, you just calling to say hi, or is something on your mind?" There was a sly, knowing tone to his voice.

Just say it, she instructed herself firmly, then swallowed hard. "Actually, well, I was wondering about Harlan Patrick. He's been on my mind a lot lately."

"I see."

Clearly he didn't intend to give away a thing without her asking a direct question. "How's he doing?" she asked finally.

"Still misses you, if that's what you're asking. I suspect he always will. Never seen a man as lovesick as he was from the minute you left town."

That wasn't what she'd been asking, but in some tiny corner of her heart, she was glad to hear that he hadn't forgotten her. Talk about conflicting emotions. Her life was riddled with them.

"You've seen him in the last couple of days?" she asked, broaching the subject of his whereabouts cautiously.

Harlan hesitated. "Now that you mention it, his daddy did say that the boy had taken off unexpectedly. Never did mention what it was all about, though. Business, I suppose. You want me to have him call you when he gets back?"

Laurie sighed heavily. She had a feeling there would be no need for that. The timing of his unexplained departure had to be more than coincidence. If she knew Harlan Patrick, she'd be seeing him any day now, as soon as he could get someone to give him her concert itinerary.

"That's okay," she said, then added quietly, "thank you."

"Thanks for what?"

"For not hating me."

"Oh, darlin' girl, I could never hate you," he said, his tone sympathetic. "There was a time when you were practically family. As far as I'm concerned, you're as good as that now."

"But I brought so much pain into Harlan Patrick's life."

"And so much joy, too," he reminded her. "Don't forget that. Sometimes the best you can hope for in life is that it all evens out in the end. You take good care of yourself and come see me next time you're home. I'll get the piano tuned, and we'll have an old-fashioned sing-along. I can't carry a tune worth a hoot, but it'll be fun all the same."

"I will," she promised. "Give Janet my love, too, will you?"

"Of course I will. You take good care of yourself, Laurie. Don't forget all the folks back here who love you."

As if I could, she thought, but didn't say. "Goodbye, Grandpa Harlan. I miss you."

Only after she'd hung up did she realize there were tears streaming down her cheeks. For the first time in more than six years, she realized just how much she missed home. And when she thought of it, she didn't remember the little house in which she'd grown up, didn't even think of her mother, though she loved her dearly. No, she remembered White Pines and the close-knit Adamses, who back then had been more than willing to accept her as one of their own.

And she remembered Amy Lynn's daddy and the way she'd always loved him.

He might as well have been traveling in a foreign country, Harlan Patrick thought on his first day in Nashville. He'd taken off without thinking, without the slightest clue of how to go about tracing a woman who didn't want to be found.

On the flight, which he'd piloted himself, he'd had plenty of time to try to formulate a plan, but images of Laurie and that baby had pretty much wiped out logic. All he'd been able to feel was some sort of blind rage. Aside from a friendly tussle or two with his cousins growing up, he wasn't prone to violence, but for the first time in his life he felt himself capable of it. Not that he'd have laid a hand on Laurie, but he couldn't swear that her furniture would be safe. Smashing a few vases and chairs might improve his mood considerably.

Then again, it probably wouldn't. Satisfaction probably couldn't be had that easily.

After landing, he rented a car and drove into downtown. He found a hotel smack in the center of things and dragged out a phone book. It was then that he realized just how little he really knew about Laurie's life in the past few years. An awful lot of it had been played out in public, of course, but that wasn't the part that would help him now.

"Well, damn," he muttered staring at the Yellow Pages and trying to figure out which talent representative or which recording studio to call. He couldn't even remember which record label produced her albums, even though he had CDs of every single one of them. It was hard enough listening to her songs without learning every little detail of the life that had stolen her from him.

He plucked a scrap of paper out of his pocket and glanced at the number, then dialed her house first, though he recognized it was a long shot. She was on the road and she'd told him that she'd never gotten around to hiring a housekeeper because she wasn't comfortable with somebody else doing cleaning and cooking she was perfectly capable of doing for herself.

When no one answered at the house, he searched his memory for some offhand reference she'd made to the new people in her life. Unfortunately, though, the few days they'd had together just over a year ago hadn't been spent doing a lot of talking, at least not about the things that hadn't mattered. That baby was living evidence that they'd spent most of the time in bed, remembering just how good it felt to be in each other's arms.

"Okay, Harlan Patrick, think," he muttered under his breath.

For all of its skyscrapers and new construction, Nashville was still a small Southern town in some ways. Surely the music industry was tight-knit enough that everyone would know everybody else's business. He picked a talent agency at random and dialed.

"Hi, sweetheart," he said to the drawling woman who answered. There was enough sugary sweetness in her voice to make him feel right at home with a little flirting. He had her laughing in a matter of seconds.

"You are sooo bad," she said in response to his teasing. "Now, tell me what I can do for you."

"Actually I've got some business to do with Laurie Jensen. Any idea how I can get in touch with her?"

"Laurie Jensen?" she repeated, her voice a degree or two cooler. "I'm sorry. We don't represent Miss Jensen."

"Could you tell me who does?"

"What kind of business did you say you were in?" she asked. This time her tone was downright chilly.

"I didn't, darlin', but it's an ad campaign. We were hoping to get her to do the spots for us."

"I see," she said. "Well, maybe you ought to have your ad agency contact her people. That's the way it works."

Harlan Patrick tried to hold on to his patience. "Don't you see, sugar, that's the problem. I don't know her people."

"Any reputable ad agency will," she said, and hung up in his ear.

Harlan Patrick stared at the phone, stunned. Then he sighed ruefully. Obviously he wasn't the first person to try a ruse to get to a Nashville superstar. He resigned himself to an afternoon spent working his way through the phone listings.

He didn't waste time trying to wrangle information from unwilling receptionists. The minute he discovered the agency didn't represent Laurie, he moved on to the next. It was after six when he finally struck paydirt—or thought he had.

"Nick Sanducci's office."

"Yes. I'm trying to arrange a booking for Laurie Jensen. Can you help me?"

"Who are you with, sir?"

"Does Mr. Sanducci represent Ms. Jensen?"

"He does, but—"

"Thank you." He hung up and grabbed his hat. Clutching the page from the phone book and scribbled directions from the hotel desk clerk, he drove to a quiet street that looked more residential than commercial. A block or so from the address for Sanducci's office, he noted the discreet signs on the lawns of modest-sized homes that appeared to have been built around the turn of the century. Law offices, talent agencies, even a recording studio had been tucked away here before skyscrapers had lured most of the business into downtown.

Harlan Patrick pulled into a circular driveway just as a fancy sports car shot out the other side. One car remained in front of the house, a minivan with a child's seat in the back and toys scattered on the floor. He doubted it belonged to Mr. Nick Sanducci.

He strolled through the front door and wandered into a reception room that had obviously once been the house's living room. The walls were decorated with gold records and photos of a half dozen of the hottest names in country music, including a blowup of Laurie that could make a man's knees weak. That wall of photos and records was the only testament to the nature of Mr. Sanducci's business, however.

Harlan Patrick had to admit the man had excellent taste. The place was crammed with exquisite, expensive antiques. There were some just as valuable up in Grandpa Harlan's attic, where they'd been stored after Janet had gone through and turned White Pines from a hands-off showplace into a home.

The reception desk was neat as a pin and, with no one seated at the chair behind it, more temptation than he could resist. He edged a little closer, noting that the desk belonged to one Ruby Steel, according to the nameplate that was half-buried in a stack of papers.

He surveyed the rest of the desk with interest. That big old Rolodex probably had phone numbers on it that could do him a whole lot of good. And that bulging desk calendar probably contained all sorts of concert dates, including Laurie's.

He was about to make a grab for it when a lazy, sultry voice inquired with just a touch of frost, "Can I help you?"

He turned slowly and offered the sort of grin that had gotten him out of many a scrape over the years, at least if there was a female involved. Ruby was young enough to look susceptible, but her frown never wavered. Obviously a woman who took her last name—Steel—to heart.

"Hey, darlin', I was just wondering where you'd gone off to."

"And you thought you'd find me under the desk?" She gave him a thorough once-over that could have served her well at a police lineup. "Let me guess. You're the one who called wanting to book Laurie Jensen."

He could have lied, probably should have, but something told him the truth would get him what he needed a whole lot faster.

"You've got a good ear for voices, sugar."

"And I've got the good sense not to go giving out information to strangers," she said in a tone that warned him not to waste his time trying to wheedle anything out of her.

Harlan Patrick was undaunted. He pretended he hadn't been close enough to discover the nameplate and asked, "What's your name, sugar?"

"My name's Ruby, cowboy, and there's no need telling me yours, because it doesn't matter. I can't help you."

His gaze narrowed at that. Something told him that

Laurie had given this woman very clear and specific instructions where he was concerned.

"Now, why is that? Aren't you in the business of getting work for your clients?"

"Nick is. My job is protecting them."

"Then maybe I ought to talk to Nick."

"You can't. He's gone."

The fancy sports car, Harlan Patrick concluded. "When will he be back?"

"Hard to say. Nick's unpredictable."

"Tonight?"

"I doubt it."

"Tomorrow morning?"

"Possibly. Then again, he could get a call from one of his clients and have to take off in the middle of the night."

Harlan Patrick hid a grin. Ruby was tough, all right. "How often does that happen?"

"You'd be surprised."

"I don't suppose you'd like to go out for a drink?"

She waved her left hand under his nose. A wedding ring and diamond flashed past. "I don't think so, cowboy. And you could get me drunk as a skunk and I still wouldn't tell you how to find Laurie."

"Because she told you not to," he guessed aloud.

Ruby hesitated for just an instant, then nodded. "Because she told me not to and because I protect the privacy of all our clients. I value their trust."

"What if I told you I was her old childhood sweetheart?"

"I'd ask how come she left you behind if you were all that special."

The barb hit its mark. "Now, darlin', that is the sixty-four-thousand-dollar question." He regarded her thoughtfully. "You know, don't you?"

For the first time, little Miss Ruby squirmed. "Know what?"

"That I'm the daddy of that baby of hers."

"I don't know any such thing," she retorted, but there was a telltale flush in her cheeks.

He kept right on. "And you don't believe that a daddy should be separated from his child, do you, Ruby?" He recalled the baby seat in the van outside. "You're a mama yourself. You disapprove of what Laurie's done to me. I could see it in the way the corners of your mouth turned down when I mentioned that baby."

She ducked her head. "It doesn't matter what I think."

"Because your duty's to Laurie."

Her chin came up, and she shot a defiant look straight at him. "Exactly."

They stood there, facing each other, neither of them saying a word, until finally Harlan Patrick sighed.

"Would it matter if I told you I love her?"

Her expression softened. "It might to me, but I'm not the one who needs convincing, am I?"

He grinned. "No, but you are the one who stands between me and her."

She grinned back. "You are a sneaky, persistent devil—I'll give you that."

Harlan Patrick felt a faint stirring of hope. "Will you help me, Ruby?"

Still smiling, she looked him straight in the eye and said, "No. Now, scoot along out of here, cowboy. I'm closing for the day."

"I'll be back in the morning," he promised, taking the defeat with good grace. Ranting and raving wouldn't work with a woman like Ruby, but he had a hunch that he could wear her down with charm and a few more reminiscences about the old days he'd shared with Laurie.

"Suit yourself, but the answer won't be one bit different tomorrow."

"We'll see," he said, and tipped his hat. "It's been my pleasure, darlin'."

She gave him a stern, no-nonsense look. "I can't imagine why. You look like a man who's all too used to getting his own way."

He winked. "I am. That's why it's fascinating to run into a worthy challenge every now and again."

He slipped out the door before she could respond to that. He drove down the block and parked around the corner. He didn't doubt for an instant that Ruby would be on the phone to Laurie the moment he was out of sight.

And the moment Ruby was gone for the night, he intended to sneak back into the office, punch Redial and discover for himself exactly where Laurie Jensen was holed up with his baby girl.

Three

Going back into Nick Sanducci's office and checking the phone had been a good idea. Maybe even a great idea, Harlan Patrick thought ruefully. Unfortunately Ruby was either on to him and hadn't used the office phone to call Laurie or had simply made another call after that. He'd managed to slip back into the building easily enough—the locks were downright pitiful—but when he'd pressed the Redial button, a very cranky man had growled hello, then slammed the phone down when Harlan Patrick had been too stunned and disappointed to speak.

His reaction proved what a lousy detective he'd make. Only afterward had he considered all the possible explanations for who that man might have been. It could have been someone answering for Laurie herself. Or it could have been her agent, Nick Sanducci, he concluded belatedly, regretting his silence. But even if it was the illustrious, high-powered agent, he was clearly in no mood to indulge Harlan Patrick's request for information about Laurie. He resigned himself to waiting for morning and another round with Ruby.

Back in his hotel room after a steak dinner that had

tasted like sawdust, he was able to think rationally. He recognized that he ought to be grateful for the delay. In her own way Laurie was every bit as stubborn as he was—to say nothing of unpredictable. She had the financial wherewithal nowadays to simply disappear, taking his daughter with her. Obviously, confronting her when he was ready to commit mayhem was no way to get what he wanted.

Whatever that was, he amended with a sigh. It occurred to him that he ought to figure that much out at least before coming face-to-face with the woman who generally rendered him tongue-tied and weak-kneed.

Did he just want to see his child? Did he want to exact revenge on Laurie for deceiving him? Or did he want what he'd always wanted, to take both of them home with him, to have a family with Laurie Jensen?

One thing for certain—he needed to figure all that out before he blasted his way back into her life. He needed to be seeing things clearly and thinking straight, or she'd waltz right out of his life one more time. Something told him this was their very last chance to get it right.

He spent two frustrating days thinking about Laurie, the baby and their future, while trying to convince Ruby to divulge Laurie's itinerary to him. Nick proved as elusive as a stray calf loose on ten thousand acres of pastureland, but Ruby was mellowing. Harlan Patrick had been plying her with chocolate-covered doughnuts and compliments and he was pretty sure she was weakening. She'd actually tossed a handful of newspaper clippings at him that morning and told him to figure out Laurie's whereabouts for himself.

"You're a clever man. See what you can make of these," she'd challenged.

There was plenty of information to be had in those clippings, bits of rave reviews, comments on her new album's fast rise in the music charts. It was plain that Laurie Jensen was hot news in Nashville. The only trouble was that that news was a day too late to help him find her. By the time Ruby handed over the clippings, even the most recent ones, Laurie was already moving on.

He was back at the agent's office for the third straight day, when a teenager who was working part-time finally took pity on him and slipped him a copy of the concert schedule. He had a feeling Ruby had looked the other way—or maybe even instigated it, but he was careful not to let on what he thought. Ruby plainly felt her integrity was on the line, but just as plainly she felt that Laurie's baby deserved to have a daddy in her life. She'd all but admitted that to him on several occasions.

Clutching the itinerary in his hand, he grabbed his bag from the hotel and headed for the airport, where once again Jordan's jet was fueled up and waiting. Laurie was scheduled for a stop in Montana, then a hop over to Wyoming, a jog back to Montana, then after a two-day break, the Ohio State Fairgrounds. Columbus was closest, but he didn't want to wait another minute, much less several days. Too much time had been wasted already. He calculated the flying time and figured he could make that first Montana stop in time for her closing set.

An icy calm settled over him as he flew, but as he drove to the country-western bar where she was singing, an old, familiar sense of anticipation began to build. It was doggone irritating that she could still have that effect on him, especially under these circumstances when he very much wanted to wring her neck. His pulse was zipping with lust, not adrenaline.

He found the bar after a few wrong turns. It was bigger than some he'd seen, but smaller than he'd expected a star on the rise to be playing. In fact, the End of the Road back in Garden City had been a step above this place. He found that irksome, too. She could have stayed in Texas and done this well for herself.

Then he recalled what he'd read in one of the clippings, that part of this tour had been arranged to settle old debts to club owners who'd given her a break. Typical of Laurie. She was loyal and generous. If it hadn't been for him, she'd probably have played the End of the Road on this tour as well. If he'd had a lick of sense or any foresight, he'd have had the owner ask and then Laurie could have come to him, instead of the other way around. Of course, because of the baby, she probably wouldn't have set foot near the place. But that was water under the bridge anyway. He was here now, and Laurie was only a hundred yards away or less.

With the bar's front door ajar on the warm night, the sound of her voice washed over him as he walked from the parking lot toward the neon-lit building. She had the kind of voice that made a man think of sin, no matter how innocent the words. It was low and sultry and filled with magic.

How many nights had he lain awake remembering the whisper of that voice in his ear? How many days had he played her albums as he worked around the ranch? Enough that he and most of the hands knew the lyrics of her songs by heart. One daring newcomer, who didn't know their history, had made a suggestive remark about Laurie, only to have Harlan Patrick yank him out of his saddle and scare him half to death before reason kicked in.

Heaven knew, the woman could sing. He grabbed hold of the door and braced himself to enter, reminding himself to stay calm no matter what. Only after he walked inside the bar did he realize that what he'd heard had come from a jukebox, while the impatient audience waited for the second set to begin. Harlan Patrick slipped into the shadows in the back, ordered a beer and waited.

A few minutes later Laurie emerged amid a flash of red, white and blue strobe lights, the beat of the song fast and hard and upbeat. The wall-to-wall crowd was on its feet at once, and the whole place began to rock with the sound of her music and wild applause. She kept up the fever pitch through one song, then two, then a third. Just when Harlan Patrick was sure half the room was going to pass out from the frenzy, she turned the tempo down and had them swaying quietly to a tune so sad and soul weary, he almost shed a tear or two himself.

A cynic might have said she was manipulative. A critic would have said she had the crowd in the palm of her hand. Harlan Patrick simply wondered at the mixed emotions he felt listening to the woman he loved captivate a whole roomful of strangers. He'd had her to himself for so many years. Was that the real problem, that he didn't want to share her with the world? Was it selfishness, as much as cussedness, that had made him refuse to search harder for a compromise?

The thought that possessiveness might be the root of their troubles made him too uncomfortable to stay in the room a moment longer. While the show went on, he slipped out the door and made his way to the club's back entrance, which was also standing open to permit the night's breeze to drift inside the overheated club.

Harlan Patrick had no trouble slipping past the bulky, fiftyish guard. The man was too busy gazing at the woman on stage, his foot tapping to the beat of her song, a smile on his lips and a yearning in his eyes. That was when

Harlan Patrick realized that part of Laurie's success was her ability to touch hearts and inspire dreams, even the impossible ones.

The backstage area was cramped, with barely enough room for an office, a storeroom and one remaining room that had to be Laurie's dressing room. He opened the door, saw the tumble of clothes and cosmetics and smiled for the first time in ages. Laurie never had been much for picking up after herself.

It was a no-frills dressing room, with a metal rod for a clothes rack and bare bulbs around a square mirror. The chair in front of the dressing table was molded plastic, but the bouquet of flowers beside the scattered makeup was lavish enough for the biggest superstar.

While he waited, he tidied up, folding this, hanging that on the bare metal rod stuck in an alcove. He lingered over a scrap of lace and prayed to heaven no man had ever seen her wearing it. He'd have to rip his eyes out. Finally he tucked the panties into the suitcase sitting on the floor in the corner and pulled out the room's only other chair—a straight-backed monstrosity with a seat covered in tattered red plastic. He turned it around until he could straddle it and face the door.

He heard the last refrain of the encore die down, then the thunder of applause, then the sound of laughter in the corridor and boots on the hardwood floor outside the door. His pulse thundered as loudly as a summer storm.

The door swung open and there she was, pretty as ever, with her color high and her long, chestnut brown hair mussed and glistening with glints of gold and damp with perspiration. He'd seen her looking just like that after sex, only without so many clothes on.

Her mouth formed a soft "oh" of stunned dismay. The

color washed out of her cheeks, and for just an instant he thought she might faint, but Laurie was made of tougher stuff than that. She squared her shoulders and met his gaze evenly.

"Hey, darlin'!" Harlan Patrick said in his friendliest tone. "Surprised to see me?"

Laurie's pulse was racing so fast, she was certain she was only a beat or two shy of a medical emergency. She'd guessed Harlan Patrick would hunt her down—*known* he was coming, thanks to Ruby's warning call—but seeing him here, so at home in her dressing room, had caught her off guard.

How many times had she found him waiting for her just like this in the old days? How many times had she come offstage, giddy with excitement, and rushed into his waiting arms to be twirled around until her head spun? Of course, there was no crooked grin tonight and his arms were crossed along the back of that pitiful chair, not waiting to catch her up in an exuberant hug.

Lordy, he was gorgeous. Under other circumstances her pulse would have been scrambling from pure desire, rather than panic. The Adams genes were the best in Texas, maybe the best on earth. Even travel weary, Harlan Patrick was pure male, from that angled jaw to his broad shoulders and right on down to the tips of his dusty boots. The sensual curve of his mouth was a reminder of deep, hot kisses that could rock her to her soul.

But the look on his face, so cool and neutral and composed, was worrisome. Harlan Patrick's emotions were usually right out there for anyone to see. Only when she looked into his eyes did she detect the fire of complete and total fury. That's when she knew that not only had he seen the tabloid, but he'd also realized that Amy Lynn was his.

That left her with a quandary. She could fold right now and throw herself on his mercy or she could stand up to him the way she'd been doing since their first playground scuffle so many years ago. Her first rule in dealing with him had always been to get the upper hand and hang on for dear life. It was the only way she knew to deal with a steamroller.

"How did you get in here?" she demanded, every bit the haughty superstar.

"Unfortunately for you, the security guard's a fan. He never even noticed me. Be glad I wasn't a stalker, sugar, or you'd be in a heap of trouble."

She had a feeling in his own way, Harlan Patrick was every bit as dangerous as any stranger about now. "I could have the guard in here in a flash if you start stirring up trouble," she threatened. "Nobody gets backstage without a pass, and Chester has a very jittery trigger finger."

"Now, darlin', why would I want to stir up trouble for you?" he asked in a patient tone belied by that hard glint in his eyes.

She refused to be taken in by the deceptively mild question. Skepticism lacing her voice, she asked, "Then this is purely a social call? You just happened to be in Montana and thought you'd drop by to catch the show? We're just a couple of old friends getting together to catch up?"

"Could be."

"Why don't I believe that for a minute?"

"Guilt, maybe?"

He looked her over so thoroughly, so knowingly, that it took everything in her not to bolt or spill her guts, pouring out the whole story behind her decision to keep Amy Lynn a secret from him. She forced herself to wait him out.

"So, tell me, Laurie," he began eventually, "anything new in your life?"

Oh, he knew, all right, she thought, listening to this cat-and-mouse game of his. She could have strung him along for another minute or two, maybe more, but why bother? Now that he'd found her, they were going to hash this out sooner or later. Hopefully they could get it over with right here in her dressing room. It was a hell of a lot better than having it out at the hotel, where Amy Lynn was already fast asleep with Val watching over her.

She looked him straight in the eye and forced his hand. "Come on, Harlan Patrick, spit it out. You saw the tabloid, didn't you?"

His gaze locked with hers. "I did."

There was that neutral tone again. It was maddening. "And?" she prodded.

"And I want to know why the hell you kept my daughter a secret from me?"

There was the blast of temper she'd been expecting, the confirmation that he'd guessed it all. Laurie didn't bother trying to deny the truth. In fact, she was glad it was finally out in the open. The secret had been weighing her down for months now, ever since the home pregnancy test she'd taken had turned out positive. She hadn't been able to go near Los Piños so her mama could see the baby for fear of Harlan Patrick finding out that she'd deceived him. At last she could put all of that behind her. She told herself she should be grateful, but all she felt was a gut-wrenching sense of fear.

"I made a choice," she told him quietly. "You and I had said our goodbyes. We had finally admitted once and for all that it wouldn't work with me being on the road all the time and you chained to that ranch you love so much. How could I tell you that there was a baby on the way?"

"How could you not tell me?" he countered in that same patient, lethal tone. "Did you think for one second I wouldn't want to know, that I didn't deserve to know?"

"No, of course not, but—"

He was on his feet now, pacing, agitation replacing patience and calm.

"But nothing," he said, whirling on her.

He grabbed her arms, clearly fighting the urge to shake her. With any other man she might have been afraid of the look in his eyes, but she knew Harlan Patrick as well as she knew any human on earth. There wasn't a violent bone in his body. Even now, he had a tight rein on his temper.

Then again, as far as she knew, he'd never been tested like this before.

She looked into his eyes and saw beyond the outrage, saw the genuine hurt and anguish, and that was her undoing. Tears spilled down her cheeks.

"I'm sorry," she whispered. "I'm sorry. I didn't know what else to do."

He regarded her incredulously. "Couldn't you have called me, talked to me? There was a time when we brought all our problems to each other. We could have worked something out."

"We'd said our goodbyes," she repeated. "I couldn't go stirring things up again, not when there were no easy answers. It wouldn't have been fair."

"Fair?" he all but shouted. "What was fair about not telling me I had a baby on the way? What was fair about you going through a pregnancy all alone? What was fair about letting our little girl start her life without a daddy?"

"I did what I thought was best for all of us," she insisted.

"What *you* thought was best," he mocked. "You didn't even give me a chance to come up with a solution."

"Why should it have been your problem, your solution? I was the one who was pregnant."

"With my baby, dammit!" He closed his eyes, drew in a deep breath, then said more calmly, "We could have figured it out together."

"And done what? You'd be miserable away from White Pines. And I can't live there. It was as simple as that."

"We could have worked it out," he insisted with the stubborn conviction that was pure Adams. It didn't matter that they'd run into the same brick wall a thousand times before.

"And they're always telling me I'm the romantic," she said with a rueful sigh. "This time there wasn't a happy ending, Harlan Patrick. Trust me."

"Trust you," he hooted. "That's a laugh."

He regarded her evenly and took a step closer. He was near enough that she could feel the heat radiating from his body, smell the pure masculine scent of him. He reached out and ran his knuckle along the curve of her cheek, setting off goose bumps. She hated that he could make her react like that with just the skim of his fingers.

"Darlin', we've got a whole passel of passion, no question about that," he said. "We might even have a little love left. But I'm afraid trust is the one thing we'll never have between us again. You've pretty much seen to that, haven't you?"

Something died inside her at the cold, hard flatness of his words, but she knew it was the truth, had known it way back when she'd made the decision to keep the secret. Staying silent was going to cost her eventually. Now it had and it hurt more than she'd ever imagined.

"I'm sorry," she said again.

"*Sorry* won't cut it this time. Now how about getting this stuff together and taking me to see my daughter?"

It was a command, not a request, and it sent a jolt of pure fear shooting through her. "Tonight?"

"I think it's time, don't you? Way past time, in fact."

"She'll be asleep," she protested, trying to buy time. An hour from now she could bundle Amy Lynn up, wake the band and be on the bus heading for the next stop. No one would question the abrupt, middle-of-the-night departure, not aloud at any rate, and definitely not once they'd heard about Harlan Patrick's untimely arrival.

He gave her a look that suggested he saw straight through her. "I'll be quiet as a church mouse," he countered. "And if she happens to wake up, well, I'd say a momentous occasion like this is worth losing a little sleep over, wouldn't you?"

Laurie couldn't think of a single argument that could possibly counter the bitter logic of that. "Give me five minutes," she said tightly, then waited for him to leave the room.

He didn't budge. Regarding her evenly, he said with wry humor, "You surely weren't thinking I'd wait outside, were you? With that big old window right over your dressing table? I don't think so. As I recall, climbing out windows in the middle of the night used to be one of your specialties. That's how we got around your curfew way back when we couldn't keep our hands off each other."

"I was a kid back then," she protested, then gave up. He was sticking to her like glue, and that was that. "Okay, then, at least turn your back."

"Laurie, there's not an inch of bare skin on your body I haven't seen with my own eyes. It's a little late to turn all prim and proper on me."

She thought she detected a faint hint of laughter in his voice, and that alone was enough to give her hope that they could get through this mess tonight and go on with their lives. This was Harlan Patrick, after all. He'd always been quick to anger, but just as quick to forgive. He'd see Amy Lynn, satisfy himself that she was okay and go back to Texas. That would be that, she thought optimistically.

One glance at his expression told her she was delusional. Harlan Patrick wasn't going anywhere. And once he'd seen Amy Lynn, what then? Would he really be able to walk away, or would that just be the beginning of her worst nightmare? Mad as he was, she couldn't envision him demanding marriage at the moment. Would he try to take her baby? It was a distinct possibility.

Already gearing up for the fight, she scowled at him. "Oh, for heaven's sakes," she said, "if you're so hard up you have to sneak a peek at my bare breasts, then have yourself a ball."

She stripped out of her damp stage clothes and reached for fresh underwear. Only then did she notice that it wasn't strewed all over the room the way she'd left it.

Without bothering to cover herself, she turned to him, laughter bubbling up. "You straightened up in here, didn't you?"

He shot her a defiant look. "So what if I did?"

"Harlan Patrick Adams, I'm surprised at you. I thought you were long past tidying up my messes."

"Old habits die hard, darlin'," he said in a tone rich with hidden meanings. "Maybe you should remember that."

Four

Seeing Laurie again stirred up all the old feelings for Harlan Patrick. From love to hate, from bitterness to joy, his emotions went on a sixty-second roller-coaster ride, leaving his palms sweaty and his belly in knots. After that things only got worse.

Pure lust slammed through him the instant she walked in that dressing-room door. No woman had ever been her equal for making his temper hot and his body hotter. Having her stare him down with hardly a stitch of clothes on had just about broken his resolve to keep his hands to himself until they had this whole sorry situation straightened out. He was just itching to kiss her senseless, to lose himself in her warmth and her scent, to prove to himself that at least one thing hadn't changed between them.

There'd been a time when he'd have gone for it, taken the immediate satisfaction, reveled in the sensory explosion without a thought to the consequences. A few years of loneliness and loss had made him more cautious, maybe even more mature. In one tiny corner of his brain, it registered that sex wasn't the answer.

For once he jammed his hands in his pockets and stayed

as far away from her as it was possible to get in that itty-bitty dressing room. It wasn't quite as far as good sense called for, but it was as far as he dared given the likelihood that she'd run out on him at the first opportunity. It had taken too long finding her for him to risk losing track of her again. He wasn't going anywhere until he'd seen his daughter and he and Laurie had made some decisions about the future.

Not that she was in much of a decision-making mood. In fact, he suspected she was going to be thoroughly unreasonable, just the way she'd always been when she'd been cornered. Normally he'd spend a lot of time trying to coax her into a better frame of mind, but there wasn't time for that, either. She and his baby girl were likely to slip right through his fingers before he could blink if he didn't stay right on top of Laurie every second, if he didn't make it perfectly clear what his own expectations were.

"I'm ready," she announced, drawing his attention.

She'd wiped away the last traces of stage makeup, leaving only a touch of lipstick. The glittery outfit she'd worn had been replaced by worn jeans and a T-shirt. She'd scooped her hair up into a careless ponytail, just as she had as a girl when the heat of a Texas summer afternoon got to be too much. His fingers itched to pull away the band holding it, allowing it to fall free again, the way he liked it.

Finally, though, he thought, she looked like his Laurie, approachable and unassuming, the girl next door. In some ways that was more dangerous than the sexy woman who'd walked into the dressing room a half hour before. He'd fallen in love with the girl from his old hometown, not the superstar image. He'd convinced himself that Laurie, wide-eyed with wonder, had gotten lost.

Of course, the change was superficial, all about appearances. Try as he might, he couldn't tell yet how deep the changes ran, if there was anything of the old Laurie in her heart.

He stood up and took her small suitcase. It weighed a ton. He grinned. "Still don't have a clue how to pack light, do you? What's in here? Rocks?"

"If you're going to complain all the way back to the hotel, I'll carry it," she said, reaching for it. "I've been on my own a long time, Harlan Patrick. I don't need you."

He grinned at the quick flare of temper. "You must be out of sorts if you can't take a joke."

"I lost my sense of humor when I found you in my dressing room."

He laughed at her disgruntled expression. "Careful, darlin', or you'll hurt my feelings."

"Not with your thick hide," she muttered under her breath as she sashayed past him.

"I heard that."

She ignored him and gave the guard a quick hug. "Thanks for everything, Chester."

The red-faced guard gave her a smile and Harlan Patrick a suspicious look, clearly wondering how he'd turned up in her dressing room. "Is everything okay, Laurie?"

"Everything's fine, Chester. This is an old..." She hesitated as if she couldn't quite decide how to describe Harlan Patrick. "Friend," she said finally. "Mr. Adams is an old friend from Texas."

The guard accepted the explanation readily enough and beamed at him. "Well, then, it's a pleasure to meet you, sir. I'll bet you're proud of our Miss Laurie."

"I am indeed," Harlan Patrick said.

After they'd left the building, Laurie glanced up at him. "You almost sounded as if you meant that."

"I did," he said simply, then sighed. "Even though your career came between us, I'm glad you made it because it's all that ever mattered to you. I'd hate to think you gave up all we had and had found nothing to replace it."

"It didn't replace it," she countered. "You mattered to me, Harlan Patrick. You still do."

"Just not enough," he said bitterly.

"Please, it wasn't like that. If there'd been another way…"

"You mean like me giving up White Pines."

"No," she retorted, then she was the one who sighed. "Yes, I suppose that was the only other alternative, at least at the beginning. Can you see now why I said it would have been impossible for us to find a solution when I got pregnant? We live in two different worlds, Harlan Patrick, literally."

"Two different cities," he corrected as if the distinction made a difference, knowing it didn't.

"Whatever. You have to admit it was an impossible situation."

"No. What I see is that our baby wasn't important enough for you to even try."

Her hand connected with his cheek before he even realized what she intended. "Don't you ever say something like that, Harlan Patrick Adams. Not ever. Our baby is the most important thing in my life."

Harlan Patrick rubbed his cheek, but he didn't back down. "What would happen if it came to a choice between her and your music, Laurie? What then? What happens when it's time for her to go to school? Will she lose then the same way I did? Will you shuffle her off to some boarding school?"

He let those words hang in the air as he opened the

rental-car trunk and tossed her suitcase inside. He noticed that she was very subdued as she joined him. She got into the car without a word and, aside from giving him directions, she remained silent all the way to the hotel.

It was an old hotel, three stories high with a creaky elevator and a half-asleep clerk behind the desk. In the lobby Laurie paused. "Please wait until morning to see the baby," she pleaded for the second time that night.

Harlan Patrick met her gaze evenly, then slowly shook his head. "I can't."

"Because you don't trust me to be here in the morning."

"That," he agreed, "and because I can't wait any longer. I want to see my daughter, Laurie. I want to hold her and discover whether she smells like talcum powder the way all the Adams babies do. I want to look into those blue eyes of hers and see if she instinctively recognizes her daddy. You owe me that."

She gave in then without another argument and led the way to her suite on the second floor. He didn't doubt that it was luxurious by the hotel's standards, but the two rooms were probably half the size of what she was used to and furnished in an eclectic mix of styles that aimed for comfort, not fashion.

There was a young woman curled up on the chintz-covered couch with an open book in her lap. One look at Harlan Patrick and her mouth gaped. Her gaze snapped from him to Laurie and back again.

"Uh-oh," she murmured as she stood up. Her worried gaze landed on Laurie again. "Is there anything you'd like me to do?"

Harlan Patrick grinned at the unspoken willingness to call out the security troops if need be. Laurie shook her head.

"It's okay, Val. I can manage Mr. Adams."

Val looked skeptical. "If you say so." She edged toward the door with obvious reluctance. "If you need anything, anything at all…"

"I know where to find you," Laurie replied. "Thanks. Is the baby okay?"

"Sleeping like a little angel," Val assured her. "She had a bottle about an hour ago and drifted right off." She cast one last worried look at him, then shrugged. "I'll see you in the morning, then."

Laurie nodded. "Good night, Val."

When Val had gone, Harlan Patrick studied Laurie. "Are all of your employees willing to go the extra mile for you?"

"Pretty much." A smile hovered on her lips. "Some of the guys in the band can swing a mean guitar and they do love a brawl. You might want to remember that."

The echo of his earlier taunt hung in the air. Finally he nodded his agreement. "Duly warned."

Now that they were actually in her room, she seemed at a loss. Clearly she wasn't going to take him to his daughter without more prompting.

"Where is she?" he asked finally, then gestured toward what seemed likely to be the bedroom door. "In there?"

Laurie looked as if she'd like to deny it, but she finally shrugged. "Yes." She rested a hand against his sleeve. "Please, Harlan Patrick, don't wake her."

"I told you I wouldn't." He headed for the bedroom, then stopped when he realized she wasn't following. "Aren't you coming with me? Or don't you want to be around when a daddy sees his baby for the first time? Can't say I blame you. It could set off a whole streak of guilt."

Tears welled up in her eyes at that, and he wondered if he'd pushed her too far with his sarcasm and anger. He wanted to hurt her, though, wanted her to know the kind of pain he'd been suffering from the moment he'd seen that baby's picture on the front page of that tabloid.

He turned away from her tears and strode into the bedroom, halting at the sight of a crib that had been set up in a corner. The puffy yellow gingham comforter with its design of daisies and ducks wasn't hotel issue. He was sure of that. Nor was the host of stuffed animals stuck around the sides like padding.

A huge lump formed in his throat as he crept closer. He felt the salty sting of tears as he caught his first glimpse of her with her diapered bottom poked in the air.

His first child, he thought, his throat choked with emotion. *His.*

By his calculations she was just over six months old now, a little plump and an Adams through and through. Bubbles formed at the corners of that little rosebud mouth, and her skin looked soft as satin. She was sleeping on her tummy with her still-damp thumb just a fraction of an inch from her mouth.

Words failed him. He just stood beside the crib and stared, stunned to discover that tears were welling up and overflowing. He was swamped by a feeling of protectiveness so deep, so powerful that it was all he could do not to grab her up and run with her back to White Pines where he could keep her safe always.

Instinctively he reached for her, then stopped himself as he remembered his promise not to wake her. But, oh, how he wanted to hold her, wanted to feel the weight of her in his arms, skim a knuckle over the delicate curve of her cheek. She was his precious first-born, and he didn't even know her name.

Realizing that brought back the anger, but he held it in check. Later there would be plenty of time for more recriminations. Right now he wanted only to drink in the sight of this tiny baby who was a part of him.

A part of him and Laurie, he reminded himself. This should have been something they shared from beginning to end. He should have been there to see her body swollen with his child. He should have been able to place his hand on her belly and feel that first miraculous stirring of life inside her. He should have been in the delivery room, holding her hand, coaching her through every stage of her labor, watching their baby enter the world.

That was the way he'd always planned it. He'd envisioned the two of them together till the day they died, surrounded by kids and, later, grandkids, maybe even great-grandkids, just the way Grandpa Harlan was, with White Pines as the center of their universe.

It wasn't supposed to be like this, with Laurie off on her own, pregnant, then having a baby in secret with no one by her side to share the joy. He wasn't supposed to be finding out he was a daddy from a blasted newspaper, then chasing all to hell and gone to find his child.

With his hands clenched into white-knuckled fists, he sensed Laurie beside him, but she hadn't said a word. As if she understood his turmoil, though, she reached out and tentatively covered his hand with her own. Almost despite himself, he relaxed at the touch, folded his fingers around hers.

"She's beautiful," he said finally, his voice choked with wonder.

"She is, isn't she?" she said with evident pride.

"What's her name, Laurie? I don't even know that much."

"Amy Lynn."

"Amy Lynn," he repeated in a whisper, his gaze on the baby. As the name sank in, he smiled. "Just like we planned." He faced Laurie. "You remembered that, didn't you? You remembered we talked about naming our first baby Amy Lynn if she was a girl. Amy because it was from your favorite book, *Little Women*, and we both liked it, and Lynn after my sister."

"And Cody if he was a boy, after your dad," she said.

Harlan Patrick closed his eyes against the fresh tide of memories that washed over him. So many dreams, so many innocent plans lost, and all because he and Laurie had never learned the meaning of compromise.

"Tell me everything," he pleaded. "From the minute you found out you were pregnant, I want to hear it all."

She shot him a rueful look. "Including all the gory morning-sickness details?"

"Everything," he said adamantly. "I figure I've got a lot to catch up on, better than a year."

Laurie regarded him with a resigned expression. "Then we'd better go into the other room and order up coffee. It's going to be a long night."

Harlan Patrick didn't care how long it took or how exhausted he was. Two pots of coffee made him jittery, but the details Laurie provided only made him want to know more. He listened and kept silent for hours on end, ignoring the sharp pangs of anger that rose up again and again as she described moments that could never be recaptured. Regrets piled up over what he'd missed through no fault of his own.

"Are there pictures?" he asked finally. "Of when you were pregnant? Of the baby when she was born?"

"Yes. Back in Nashville. There are several rolls of film from this trip that need to be developed. We just haven't been any place long enough to take it in."

He would have to be patient, but he would see them eventually, and then maybe some of this sense of loss, this feeling of having missed out on so much, would diminish. He wondered, though, if any scrapbook could ever take the place of real memories.

"Is she a good baby?"

"The best. She loves all the attention from the band and she doesn't even mind all the traveling. In fact, riding on the bus seems to lull her to sleep."

"Are you sure the bus is well ventilated?" he fretted. "Maybe there's carbon monoxide leaking in, maybe that's why she sleeps so well."

Laurie shook her head at the leap his imagination had taken. "The bus is fine, Harlan Patrick. I'm not going to do anything to endanger the baby's life."

"Maybe you shouldn't even be on a bus. Maybe it would be better if you flew."

"The bus is equipped with every convenience imaginable," she protested. "Besides, I like traveling with Val and the whole band. I get some of my best songs written while we're on the road."

His temper flared again. "It's always about you, isn't it? What about what's best for the baby?"

Clearly undaunted by the accusation, she regarded him evenly. "That's not fair and you know it."

"No," he said, just as calmly, "I don't. I haven't been a part of your life for a very long time, but that's about to change."

There was a flicker of panic in her eyes then, but her voice was steady. "Meaning…?"

"What the hell do you think it means?" he asked heatedly. "It means that as of now I'm sticking to you like glue. Forget about running. Forget about hiding."

She winced. "I can see I was right about one thing."

"Which is?"

"I see where Amy Lynn got her temper. She's definitely her daddy's girl. She already has the family stubborn streak. Most babies don't learn to say no until they're two. Amy Lynn may not be able to say it yet, but she sure can make her preferences known." She gave him a pointed look. "I'm not sure it's a legacy you ought to be proud of."

Maybe he deserved the censure. He was stubborn. He was an Adams. It came with the genes and from his perspective, it wasn't a bad trait to inherit. Call it stubbornness or persistence—to his way of thinking it was the same as commitment and staying power. He wasn't about to let Laurie's accusation throw him off course.

Facing her, he said fiercely, "I want my daughter to be a part of my life, Laurie. I want her to know she's an Adams. I'll fight you for that if I have to."

He saw the tumble of fear, followed by resignation in her expression. Clearly she'd been anticipating something like this ever since he'd turned up.

"I won't fight you," she said quietly. "We'll work something out. When she's a little older, she can come to the ranch as often as you'd like."

And have his daughter think of him as a distant stranger? There was no chance in hell he'd buy a plan like that. He scowled at Laurie.

"I mean starting now," he said, his tone implacable.

"But she's just a baby," Laurie protested.

"And I'm every bit as capable of caring for her as you are. More capable, in fact. At least I have a home I stay in, instead of moving from hotel to hotel. She wouldn't be turned over to nannies. She'd be surrounded by family, including your own mother, I might add." He regarded her pointedly. "Best of all, she wouldn't be getting her picture plastered all over the front of the tabloids."

Laurie flinched at that, but came back fighting. "That picture was what brought her to your attention," she reminded him. "Maybe you ought to send a thank-you note to the photographer."

"You mean you haven't already had him strung up for giving away your little secret?"

"Believe me, if I'd had any recourse at all, I would have taken it," she said fervently. "No one wanted you to find out about Amy Lynn this way, least of all me."

"No," he agreed quietly. "You never wanted me to find out about her at all."

He noticed she didn't try to deny it. Instead, she rubbed her eyes in a gesture that was as familiar to him as the feel of her skin. Laurie'd always stayed awake past exhaustion because she never wanted to miss a thing. If he'd been in a kinder frame of mind, he'd have seen it earlier and insisted that they both get the sleep they sorely needed. He did suggest it now.

"Go to bed, Laurie. We'll finish this conversation in the morning."

He caught the quick flash of relief in her eyes and guessed exactly what was on her mind. "You aren't thinking of skipping out during the night, are you, darlin'?"

Color tinted her cheeks pink. "Of course not," she denied a little too hastily. "I'll be right here when you get back in the morning. I promise."

He smiled at the solemn vow. He figured it wasn't worth spit. "Of course you will be," he said agreeably. "And I'm sure you won't mind if I just take a precaution or two."

"Such as?"

"Well, for starters, I'll be sleeping right in there next to you."

She swallowed hard at that. Color flamed in her cheeks. "I don't think so."

"You don't have any choice in the matter."

"It's a bad idea," she insisted.

"Why? Afraid you won't be able to resist me?"

"*That* is not the issue."

"Then what is?"

"It's just wrong, that's all."

"You'll have to do better than that, darlin'. You've had my baby. It's a little late to get all prissy about sharing a bed with me."

She opened her mouth, then snapped it shut again. As regally as any queen, she rose from the sofa and headed for the bedroom. She was almost at the door when Harlan Patrick realized that if he didn't hightail it across the room, she'd have that door slammed and locked before he could blink. As it was, he barely got his foot wedged into the crack when she tried to close the door in his face.

"Nice try," he enthused as he waltzed into the bedroom behind her.

Her shoulders slumped. "Oh, have it your way. If you'll feel better forcing your way into my bed, then so be it."

Her phrasing rankled, but Harlan Patrick didn't back down as she'd obviously hoped he would. He tugged off his boots, then stretched out on top of the covers.

"See, darlin', my intentions are honorable. I'm not even shucking my jeans."

"What a saint."

He leveled a smoldering look at her then. "Not a saint, Laurie. You'd be wise to remember that before you start testing me."

"I have no intention of testing you," she insisted, giving him a haughty look before going into the bathroom and closing the door emphatically behind her.

When she came out again, she was wearing a too-big Dallas Cowboys T-shirt that reached to midthigh and brought a smile to his lips. If he wasn't very much mistaken, it was the very same shirt he had given her on her last visit to Texas, a shirt he'd worn until it was faded and one she'd loved because it carried the scent of him. He wondered if she remembered that when she'd put it on or if she'd simply hoped that he'd forgotten.

She turned out the light on her way to the bed, then slid beneath the covers. The mattress wasn't what it could have been. It sagged under his weight, which eventually caused her to roll toward him despite her best efforts to cling to her own side.

Harlan Patrick was still wide awake when she settled against him. He heard her soft exhale of breath and felt her snuggle just a little tighter. That was the second time in twenty-four hours when it took every ounce of willpower he possessed to keep his promise and keep his hands off of the woman he loved.

Five

A baby's soft whimpers jarred Harlan Patrick out of a restless sleep that had lasted all of a half hour. For a minute he had no idea where he was or why a baby might be nearby. Then he felt the once familiar whisper of Laurie's breath fanning across his cheek, felt the weight of her arm resting on his chest, sniffed the rose-petal scent of her perfume.

It all came flooding back to him then, the tabloid, the trip to Nashville, the rush to Montana. Those whimpering cries, which he judged from experience with what seemed like a zillion nieces and nephews and second cousins, were about to turn into a full-throated yowling.

Miracle of miracles, he recognized that those cries were coming from his daughter. *His daughter.* What an unexpected blessing.

He eased out of the bed and padded over to the crib. At his arrival the baby seemed to take a deep breath and wait, as if trying to decide whether the whimpers had accomplished her goal or if more-strenuous cries were necessary. Blue eyes, shimmering with tears, stared solemnly back at him. He felt his heart turn over in his chest.

"Don't cry, precious girl. Daddy's here," he whispered as he picked her up and cradled her in his arms.

"Daddy's here," he said again a little more emphatically as he carried her into the living room of the suite and settled into a chair with her, awestruck with the wonder of holding his own child in his arms.

The whimpers subsided the instant he picked her up, but he figured it wouldn't be long before they started up again unless he figured out what had brought them on in the first place. Again years of experience with other people's kids kicked in.

"So, what's the deal?" he asked. "You wet? Hungry? Maybe both?"

She seemed to study him quizzically, either trying to make sense of his words or trying to weigh whether or not to trust him. Suddenly that little rosebud mouth tilted into a crooked smile that came pretty darned close to breaking his heart.

"Did I guess right?" he asked conversationally. "I'll bet there's a diaper bag around here somewhere, but what about a bottle? Any ideas?"

She gurgled at him happily, as if imparting the information he'd requested. Unfortunately he didn't have a clue how to interpret it.

Tucking her against his shoulder, he searched for supplies. As he'd anticipated, the diaper was easy enough to come by and no challenge at all to put on. The bottle had him stymied. He wondered if room service was up to the challenge, or was this something for the invaluable Val, whose last name and room number he didn't know?

When he was about to concede that he was going to have to wake Laurie, he was struck by an inspiration. There was a tiny refrigerator in the room. Under normal circumstances it would be stocked with sodas and liquor and overpriced snacks, but maybe Laurie Jensen would rate a selection of baby bottles instead. He used the key that had been left lying on top of the refrigerator. Sure enough, there was a handful of bottles tucked inside.

"See there, darlin', Daddy's not going to let you down. We just have one little problem left. Something tells me you won't like this stuff if it's cold as ice."

He glanced around, but there was no sign of a microwave. He could think of only one alternative. "Shall we take a little stroll down to the hotel kitchen and have it heated? I know it's barely daybreak, but surely someone will be stirring down there."

Amy Lynn gurgled in apparent agreement.

He propped the baby against a nest of pillows while he paused to tug on his boots. Even the momentary abandonment almost brought on a fresh bout of tears. The instant he had her back in his arms, she beamed at him approvingly, clearly pleased that he was catching on. He slipped quietly out of the room and carried her and the bottle downstairs.

The only waitress on duty in the hotel restaurant at that early hour took one look at the two of them and rushed to help.

Harlan Patrick held out the bottle. "Help? I know you're probably not quite ready to open, but we have a little emergency here."

"No problem. I'll have that heated right up for you," she said, taking the bottle and giving him a less than surreptitious once-over. "Just have a seat at that table over there by the window. It's got the best view in the room. The sun ought to be sneaking up over the mountains any minute now. You want a cup of coffee when I come back, sugar? It should be just about ready by now."

Harlan Patrick thought of the acid already churning in his stomach from last night's caffeine overdose and shook his head. "Maybe a big glass of orange juice and some toast, if it's not too much trouble."

"Coming right up," she promised.

She was back in no time with the juice, the toast and the heated bottle. His daughter took the bottle and began sucking lustily. He grinned at her enthusiasm. "Most definitely an Adams," he observed. "We all have healthy appetites."

"She's a beautiful baby," the waitress said.

"Isn't she?"

"And you're a natural with her. She's a lucky kid."

Harlan Patrick grinned. "Thanks."

"You give a holler if you need anything else."

He glanced at his daughter. "Oh, I think we're all set now."

After the waitress had gone, he held Amy Lynn contentedly while she finished the bottle, staring at her in awe, still unable to believe he'd had a part in creating anything this perfect, this fragile. This time alone with her reassured him that his determination to make a place for himself in her life was well-founded. He'd always wanted kids, but it had been an abstract kind of longing, something he pictured in his future with Laurie. Amy Lynn was real, and the protective paternal sensations she stirred in him were overwhelming.

Just when he was finishing up his juice and thinking it was time to go back upstairs, all hell broke loose. Security guards, trailed by a frantic Laurie, still wearing only the Dallas Cowboys T-shirt, along with Val and several men

Harlan Patrick guessed were members of the band came charging into the dining room.

"There," Laurie shouted, pointing at him and practically quivering with outrage. "There he is. He's trying to steal my baby."

Harlan Patrick reacted with stunned silence to the outrageous accusation.

Even before the guards could react, Laurie rushed across the room and tried to snatch Amy Lynn from Harlan Patrick's arms. He stared at her and held the baby out of reach.

"Have you lost your mind?" he asked Laurie in a deceptively mild tone as men surrounded him.

"You took her," she accused. "You took her without my permission."

When one of the guards reached for him, Harlan Patrick shot a quelling look in his direction that instantly had the man backing off.

"Ms. Jensen, it looks like your baby's just fine," one guard suggested quietly. "He hasn't gone anywhere with her."

"He just brought her down for a bottle," the waitress chimed in. "What in heaven's name is all the fuss about?"

"He took her from my room," Laurie whispered, sinking onto a chair beside him as the fight drained out of her. "I woke up, and my baby was gone."

Harlan Patrick finally understood her hysteria. In a fleeting, half-awake daze, she had thought he'd taken off with the baby. It was ironic given his own fears that she'd do the very same thing if given a chance. Still, he cursed himself for not thinking to leave a note. He'd never meant to scare her to death. He'd just assumed she wouldn't awaken before he returned.

"Darlin', you knew she was with me," he reminded her quietly. "You had to know no harm would come to her."

"Don't you see?" she replied in a choked voice. "That's why I was so terrified."

"You thought I'd run off with her," he said, voicing his earlier assessment of her overreaction.

She nodded, and this time when she reached for Amy Lynn, he placed the baby in her arms. Then he tucked a finger under Laurie's chin and forced her to face him. Her eyes shimmered with unshed tears, and her chin wobbled.

"Listen to me," he commanded gently. "No matter what happens between us, no matter how angry I get or how frustrated, I will never just walk away with Amy Lynn. You have my solemn vow on that. Whatever happens, the two of us will decide it together, okay?"

Her gaze locked with his. "You swear it?"

"On my honor."

A sigh shuddered through her then. One glance at Val was all it took for the security guards and the band members to melt away, leaving the three of them alone—Harlan Patrick, Laurie and the baby. Even the friendly waitress seemed to know enough to steer clear.

"You okay?" Harlan Patrick asked eventually.

Laurie gave him a halfhearted smile. "Just embarrassed over the fuss I caused."

He grinned. "If you're feeling that way now, then there's no telling how you're going to react when you realize you're in the middle of a public restaurant wearing nothing but a big ol' T-shirt."

She glanced down at herself and moaned. Then she scowled at him. "This is your fault, you know."

He nodded solemnly. "I know. And I am sorry. The baby was hungry and I wanted to get her fed without waking you. I thought I was being clever to think of coming down here to get her bottle warmed."

"A noble intention," she agreed, "but then yours usually are. That's never meant you couldn't find some way to turn my life upside down in the process."

He nodded at that, too. "It's been my pleasure," he said with a grin. "Yours, too, if I remember correctly."

"Sometimes," she conceded. "But we're supposed to be responsible adults now. We have a child, for goodness' sakes."

It was exactly the opening he'd been waiting for. "I'm glad you can see that. I have a suggestion."

"What's that?"

"Let's prove just how responsible we are. Let's get married."

The suggestion was made impulsively. Harlan Patrick had no idea when he'd reached any decision that marriage was the route they should take. If he was startled by the words coming out of his mouth, though, Laurie looked as if he'd suggested they go snowboarding stark naked.

"Oh, no, you don't," she said, hitching her chair backward to get away from him as if his very nearness was somehow threatening.

"Don't what?"

"You are not going to manipulate me into marrying you, Harlan Patrick Adams," she said with fire in her eyes.

"I wasn't aware I was manipulating. I thought I was proposing."

"In this case, it's the same difference."

"And you say the stubborn genes are all on the Adams side," he taunted. "Laurie, let's be logical for a minute. Amy Lynn is mine. I want her to have my name."

"She already does," she confessed in a whisper.

This time he stared. "What?"

"I put your name on the birth certificate. I never wanted there to be any doubt about that, at least. So, you see, marrying me would be superfluous."

He grinned at the airy declaration. "Is that what you call being my wife? I could take offense."

"You know what I meant," she retorted with a defiant jut of her chin.

He debated arguing with her, then decided to leave well enough alone. He might have lost the battle, but the war could be won another day.

"Okay," he conceded. "I can see I'm not going to get anywhere this morning. Just think about it. We have plenty of time to decide. I'm not going anywhere." He shot her a wicked look. "You, however, might want to find out if there's a back way out of here. Otherwise the next tabloid picture you're in is likely to be a whole lot more revealing than either of us would like."

Laurie's nerves didn't settle down until after she was back in the suite and had spent an hour with Amy Lynn tucked securely in her arms. Those few minutes before she'd found the baby downstairs with Harlan Patrick had been the most terrifying of her life. Even though she knew him as well as she knew herself, she had wondered for just an instant if he was so furious with her that he'd be capable of kidnapping their baby.

Not that it would have been all that hard to trace him, she admitted. There wasn't a doubt in her mind that he would make a beeline for White Pines to show his daughter off to his family.

His proposal on the heels of that upset had been enough to thoroughly shake her. It was difficult enough to cope with Harlan Patrick when he was angry and unreasonable. It was even more difficult to fend him off when he was being quietly reasonable and persistent.

Of course, this was hardly the first time the question of marriage had come up between them. She smiled as she recalled the first time he'd asked, way back in high school on the night of his senior prom. They'd been in the back seat of a convertible, staring up at the stars. She'd turned him down then and every time since.

Even in high school, when she had been starry-eyed and madly in love with him, she had known instinctively that she would never be content as his wife unless she had really tried to make a career out of her music. He had never understood how much it meant to her, nor why she couldn't be happy just singing in a local club every now and then or maybe just with the church choir. He simply hadn't comprehended her ambition and her desperate hunger for success.

Sometimes she hadn't fully understood the need herself, though she suspected it had a lot to do with the hand-to-mouth existence she and her mother had led. She'd wanted to be independent enough to survive on her own without relying on the whims of a man—even Harlan Patrick—to provide for her needs.

Harlan Patrick had everything in the world he wanted right there in Los Piños, Texas. His ranch. His family. She wanted the world and the reassurance of having her own bank account, piled high with money she'd earned herself, money she knew she could replace herself if the need arose.

She glanced across the room to find his gaze on her. He was sprawled in a chair, his expression speculative, as if he were trying to puzzle out which buttons to push to get her to come around to his point of view. It was disconcerting, because she knew that sooner or later he would figure it out. He always had. The only time she'd ever said no to him and stuck to it was on the subject of marriage. With Amy Lynn to consider and more money in the bank than she could ever spend, she wasn't sure how long it would be before she gave in on that, as well.

"You still mad at me?" he asked finally.

"No."

"I really didn't mean to frighten you."

"I know that."

"So, what's on the agenda for today?"

Laurie glanced at her watch. "We need to pack up and be on the bus in an hour. The club I'm playing tonight is a couple of hours from here. That'll give us time to get there, set up, test the sound system and rehearse for an hour or so." Even though she suspected she already knew the answer, she asked, "What about you?"

"Where you go, I go."

She sighed. "For how long, Harlan Patrick?"

He gave her an all too familiar stubborn look. "As long as it takes."

"What about the ranch?"

"Daddy's there and Grandpa Harlan. They can get by without me for a while."

She hesitated, then said, "I spoke with your grandfather the other day."

His eyes widened with surprise. "How did that happen?"

"I called to see if you knew about the tabloid," she admitted ruefully. "Based on what he said about you taking off for parts unknown, I gathered you did, but he didn't."

"He probably does by now. He probably started asking

questions the instant he hung up. Mama and Sharon Lynn no doubt gave him an earful."

"They know, then?"

"Oh yeah, they know. Sharon Lynn was the one who brought the paper out to the ranch. They were scheming to buy up every copy in town and burn them, when I walked in."

"Your sister used to tolerate me well enough because she knew you cared about me, but she must really hate me now," Laurie said with unmistakable regret. For so many years all she had wanted was to fit in, to be accepted by this wonderful, loving family.

"Let's just say I'd be careful about ordering any food from her next time you stop by Dolan's," Harlan Patrick told her with a crooked grin exactly like the baby's. "Big sisters have a way of carrying loyalty to extremes."

"I wouldn't know," she said, unable to hide the trace of envy in her voice. "No sisters, no brothers. That's why I always loved going to the ranch with you. Even though it was just you and Sharon Lynn in your family, the extended Adams family was so huge and rambunctious."

"That's Grandpa Harlan's doing. He's not happy unless the place is crawling with family. He likes to think of himself as head of a ranching dynasty."

"He was very kind to me when I called. I doubt he will be the next time I show my face in Los Piños."

"Oh, darlin', you've got to be kidding. You're the mama of yet another great-grandbaby. You'll be welcomed with open arms. In fact, don't be surprised if he doesn't greet you, then introduce you to a minister and hand me a couple of gold bands."

"Now, there's a reason to stay away," she murmured.

Harlan Patrick chuckled. "I never took you for a coward. You don't have a bit of trouble saying no to me. Are you saying you won't be able to resist granddaddy's matchmaking?"

"You know I've always respected your grandfather."

"And?"

"And yes, it would be hard to ignore his wishes. I would hate to have him think less of me."

"Guess that tells me where I rank in the Adams hierarchy."

"Don't pout, Harlan Patrick. When you're eighty, I'll probably listen to you, too."

"In the meantime you've just given me a tremendous incentive to lure you back to Texas."

She regarded him with a stubborn lift to her chin. "I am not going anywhere near Texas, so you can just forget about that."

He shrugged. "Then I'll just have to figure out how to be more persuasive in Montana, Texas, Tennessee or wherever else you intend to run to hide out."

"I'm not hiding out. I'm working."

"From where I sit, it looks like the same difference."

Laurie couldn't take any more. The worst part about Harlan Patrick's accusation was that it was true. The further she ran, the busier she stayed, the less she had to think about Amy Lynn's daddy and the sneaky way he had of stirring up vivid memories and wicked sensations.

The instant she stood up, though, the baby began to cry. Harlan Patrick was on his feet in a heartbeat, reaching for Amy Lynn and murmuring soothingly until she quieted at once in his arms. Laurie scowled at the two of them—one a persistent, clever devil, the other a tiny traitor.

"I'm going to go in and pack," she said, and whirled around to leave the room. If she spent too much time witnessing the wonderful, instantaneous bonding between Amy Lynn and her daddy, she would never in a million years be able to keep Harlan Patrick on the fringes of their lives.

At the doorway to the bedroom, she glanced back to find Harlan Patrick totally absorbed with his daughter. He was regarding her as if she were the most magnificent, mysterious creature on earth. Which, of course, she was, Laurie conceded with motherly pride.

Watching the two of them, she realized that in less than twenty-four hours the plan she'd had to keep Harlan Patrick at bay had totally and thoroughly unraveled. She would never keep him on the fringes of their lives as she had hoped just moments ago. He was already smack-dab in the middle of their world. And one thing she knew about Harlan Patrick—about any Adams—was that budging him once he'd gotten so much as a toehold was all but impossible.

For better or worse, Harlan Patrick was in their lives to stay.

Six

Once he'd lost the first round in his fight to claim Laurie as his wife, Harlan Patrick didn't even have to think twice about what he was going to do. For as long as it took to win them over, he intended to stick to Laurie and Amy Lynn like glue.

First he called Jordan and made arrangements to have his uncle's plane picked up in Montana and flown back to Texas. Next he called his father and arranged for an extended vacation from the ranch. He'd expected an argument and was surprised when he didn't get one. He was even more surprised when his father began to probe more deeply into his reasons for staying away.

"Do you still love her?" Cody Adams asked him point-blank, proving that the family grapevine was in fine working order and engaging in a whole lot of speculation.

He hesitated, then admitted, "Right now a part of me is still furious with her, but yes, I love her. I always have."

"And you're happy about being a daddy?"

There wasn't even a split second of hesitation before he responded to that one. "It's amazing, Dad. I've never felt anything like it. Just wait till you see Amy Lynn," he said. "She's a little angel. How could I be anything but happy about her? She'll steal your heart, too."

"Then take my advice, son. Don't take no for an answer. They're your family. You fight for them any way you have to."

"Even if I have to play down and dirty?" he inquired lightly, thinking of how he could always bend Laurie to his will with a couple of well-timed kisses.

"Whatever works," his father agreed. "I pulled out all the stops with your mama and I've never regretted it. The situations are not all that dissimilar, you know. She'd had your sister without telling me, and I came back to Texas to discover I had a ready-made family. I was furious, but once I got beyond casting blame I did everything except stand on my head and whistle the wedding march to get through to her. I'd have tried that, too, if I'd thought it would work."

"What did work finally?" he asked his father, not too proud to seek advice that might make a difference in his campaign to win Laurie.

His father laughed at his eagerness for surefire answers. "You'd have to ask your mother that, but if I had to guess, I'd say it was the fact that I never gave up, that I stuck around even when she was being the most contrary female in all of Texas. She finally had to take me seriously." He chuckled. "Of course, she did wait till they were wheeling her into the delivery room to give birth to you before she finally gave in. I suppose she figured with two babies of mine, she didn't have a chance in hell of ever shaking me."

Harlan Patrick had heard the tale a thousand times before, but this time he was hearing it in a whole new light. This time it wasn't just a humorous family legend. It was inspiration for his own battle to win Laurie's heart and claim his family. If persistence was what it took, then he was already on the right track.

"Thanks for reminding me of that," he told his father.

"You just bring those two back home with you. They're what's important in your life right now. Family matters more than anything else, son, this ranch included. Your granddaddy would be the first to tell you that, and you know how he feels about this place. In the meantime he and I can manage the ranch. There are plenty of others in the family who'll pitch in if we need them to."

"Just don't forget that I'm the one who's going to get the place one day. I don't want you running it into the ground while I'm not looking."

"Very funny," his father said dryly. "Besides, with your granddaddy around, I don't think there's much chance of that. As old as I am, he'd still tan my hide if he thought I was messing with his legacy to all of you. Take care, son, and good luck with Laurie. If she's the woman you want, then I wish you only the best in getting her."

Harlan Patrick knew what it had cost his father to wish him luck. He'd been blaming Laurie for a long time now for mistreating his only son. Forgiving her would take some time, but Harlan Patrick didn't doubt that in the end his father truly did wish them well.

"Thanks," he said. "Something tells me I'm going to need all the luck I can get."

As he hung up, he realized that Laurie was standing in the doorway.

"Your father?"

"Yep."

"How is he?"

"Fine. He sends his regards."

She looked skeptical. "Is that so?"

"He told me to hurry up and come home with you and Amy Lynn."

She frowned. "Now, Harlan Patrick—"

He cut her off. "I know. You haven't agreed to go anywhere with me. I guess that leaves me with just one alternative."

"Which is?"

"I'll go with you."

Laurie looked shaken by the announcement, even though she had to know that it was what he'd intended all along. "With me?"

Harlan Patrick grinned. "That's right, darlin', when that big ol' bus of yours pulls out of here, I'll be sitting in there right alongside you."

"But the ranch…" she began hopefully.

"Covered."

"Didn't you say you flew here in Jordan's plane?" she asked with a note of desperation in her voice.

"I did. He's sending someone to get it."

Her expression fell. "I thought maybe you'd just fly to the next stop or rent a car or something."

"Not a chance."

"You'll hate being all cramped up on the bus."

"You like it, don't you?"

"Yes, but—"

"I'll manage, Laurie. If it's good enough for you and Amy Lynn, then it's good enough for me."

She stared at him silently, then asked, "You're going to pester me until you get your way, aren't you?"

He chuckled. "You've got that right. I gotta say I'm looking forward to it, too. Always did love a challenge."

"Does it matter at all to you that I am not looking forward to it?"

He regarded her solemnly. "Well, of course, it troubles me that you'd like to be rid of me, but if you're asking if that means I'll give up, the answer is no."

She sighed heavily. "I was afraid of that."

They sat across from each other in silence. Harlan Patrick knew from her irritated expression that Laurie was wrestling with herself, trying to decide whether she could get away with banishing him from her bus. He was confident she'd reach the right decision, so he didn't waste his energy trying to start a debate with her.

When the quiet had dragged on too long, he grinned. "Give it up, Laurie. You can't think of any way to get rid of me short of having a security guard hold me down while the bus drives off."

For an instant her expression brightened.

"Don't even think about it," he warned. "I'll just keep turning up like a bad penny, and my mood won't improve if you make it difficult for me."

"Why? Doesn't it matter that I don't want you around?"

The remark stung, though it shouldn't have, especially since he knew for a fact it wasn't true. She didn't really want him to go away. She was just scared that having him around would weaken her resolve, that she'd give in and marry him. She was probably right to be terrified of that, because making her his wife was exactly what he had every intention of accomplishing.

Reacting without thinking, he crossed the room and pulled her up and into his arms. His mouth found hers just as it opened to form a protest. The kiss went from an intended brush of his lips across hers to a deep, soul-searing possession in seconds. She tasted of minty toothpaste and surrounded him with some sweet, fresh scent from her morning shower, unadorned by the rose-petal perfume she favored. This was Laurie at her most basic—innocently alluring, unconsciously seductive.

His pulse pounded as tongues met and danced an old, familiar duel. His skin was on fire where her hands finally settled after an instant of protesting reluctance. His body throbbed with need as her hips cradled his arousal. He threaded his fingers through her hair, tangling in the long strands of silk. He withdrew from the kiss, gazed into her dazed eyes and went back for more.

But that brief hesitation had been enough to break the spell, long enough for her doubts to come flooding back, apparently, because she gave him a shove that took him by surprise and had him staggering back a step before he recovered.

There was fire sparkling in her eyes and a don't-you-dare expression on her lips when he grinned at her. "That's okay, darlin'. I think I proved my point."

She scowled. "And what point would that be?"

"That you're not immune to me, even after all this time. You just wish you were."

"Oh, go to blazes, Harlan Patrick," she all but shouted just as someone knocked on the door of the suite. Laurie raced to open it.

Harlan Patrick spotted Val on the doorstep and concluded that the kissing and the argument were at an end for now. Laurie wouldn't pursue either with an audience.

"You all set?" Val asked Laurie, though her speculative gaze was fixed squarely on Harlan Patrick.

Laurie nodded. "I'll get the bags."

"Want me to get Amy Lynn?" Val asked.

Harlan Patrick interceded. "I'll be bringing her," he announced, seizing the carrier in which the baby had been napping, along with his own bag.

Val's gaze shot from him to Laurie and back again. "You're coming, too?"

"I am," he confirmed.

She looked to her boss. "He is?"

Laurie shrugged. "Apparently so."

Val edged closer to her boss and lowered her voice. "How do you feel about that?"

"She's mad as a wet hen," Harlan Patrick supplied cheerfully.

"I asked her," Val noted.

Laurie glowered. "He has it right."

"I could make him disappear," Val offered. "All it would take would be a word to security."

"Don't waste your time," Laurie said with regret. "You might slow him down, but you won't get rid of him."

"But it's your bus, your tour," Val argued. "He has no right—"

"Now, that's where you're wrong," Harlan Patrick corrected mildly. He hoisted the baby carrier to draw attention to it. "This little girl gives me all sorts of rights."

To his satisfaction that seemed to be enough to silence both women. He doubted, though, that he'd heard the end of it, especially from Laurie.

On the bus Laurie headed straight for the back, hauling Val right along behind her and all but shoving her into one of the two custom-made lounge chairs that had replaced the half-dozen regular seats in the back to create a comfortable lounge. There was a table between the two seats with cup-holders built in. A small refrigerator had been tucked in on one side with a microwave atop it for heat-ing Amy Lynn's bottles or the coffee the band consumed by the gallon. There was a built-in crib, as well, a recent addition that had been installed right after she gave birth. Laurie's guitar cases rested in a pile behind the seats.

Satisfied that Harlan Patrick was several rows in front of them with the baby's carrier seat-belted in beside him, Laurie sank down.

"Do you want something to drink?" Val asked, regarding her worriedly.

"Bottled water," Laurie said. "And a couple of aspirin."

"I imagine fending him off would be enough to give you a whopper of a headache," Val agreed, handing her the requested items. "He's a persistent guy, isn't he?"

"You don't know the half of it," Laurie muttered.

"Sexy, too."

"Are you planning to enumerate all of his attributes?" Laurie inquired testily.

Val grinned. "Nope, I think I'll just linger awhile on sexy. I haven't seen a man that gorgeous up close in a long, long time. You must have astounding willpower to have turned your back on him."

Laurie waved her off. "If you find him so blasted fascinating, you can go on up there and sit with him," she suggested. "Look to your heart's content. Keep him distracted."

"You wouldn't mind?" Val asked, sounding just a tad too eager.

"No. I've had a song buzzing around in my head for the past couple of hours. Maybe I can get some of it down."

"Something to do with cowboys and Texas, I'll bet," Val commented with a wink.

"No," Laurie denied. "Something about murder and mayhem on a country singer's tour bus."

That was enough to encourage Val to scoot out of the line of fire. She settled into a seat across the aisle from Harlan Patrick and attempted to engage him in conversation. Even though Val's move had been her idea, Laurie found she couldn't concentrate knowing that the two of them were chatting. When she heard Harlan Patrick's low, seductive laugh, her stomach knotted. When he leaned halfway across the aisle to whisper something to Val, it took all her willpower to stay in her own seat.

She was jealous, she realized with astonishment. In all the years she'd been in love with Harlan Patrick, he'd never given her cause to be jealous. Though plenty of girls in high school had chased after him, though he'd been a natural flirt, she'd never felt so much as a twinge of jealousy because she had always known that he was hers.

He claimed the same thing was true now, but just how long would he remain loyal with her pushing him away and declaring that she didn't want him back? Did it even matter, when nothing had changed? She lived half her life on the road. He was the ultimate homebody.

But he was here now, a nagging little voice reminded her. He had walked away from White Pines in the blink of an eye when he'd discovered he had a daughter. Could he walk away for good? She doubted it. This was temporary. He was just staking his claim, trying to get her to marry him and go back to Texas with him. He'd said nothing at all about making a long-term change in his life-style. The impasse was as overwhelming as ever.

Gary Whitakker, her lead guitarist and one of the kindest, gentlest guys she'd ever known, edged down the aisle and dropped into the seat Val had vacated. There'd been a time when she'd considered the possibility of a romance with him, but memories of Harlan Patrick had intruded every time the man had tried to kiss her. Eventually they'd settled for being friends.

"You doing okay?" he asked, searching her face for signs of distress.

"I've had better days," she admitted.

Gary glanced toward the row of seats in front of them. "He seems like a nice guy."

"He is."

"I saw the way he was looking at Amy Lynn when we found them in the hotel dining room. He already adores that baby girl. He's not going to walk away without a fight."

"I know."

"He looks at you the same way."

She gave him a rueful look. "I know that, too."

"He's the reason nothing ever happened between us, isn't he?"

She nodded.

"If you're so crazy about him, I'm not sure I see the problem."

"He's in Texas. I'm not."

To her irritation, he grinned. "Did you run out of cash for plane tickets?"

Laurie scowled. "You know, Gary, these pithy little observations of yours are getting on my nerves. Do you have any solutions?"

He had the audacity to chuckle at her display of temper. "In the words of a country-music superstar I know, you might try listening to your heart."

Good advice, Laurie conceded, but she couldn't risk taking it. Her heart's message was clear as a bell, but there were far-reaching implications that she simply couldn't deal with.

"Grab your guitar," she instructed instead, reaching for her own. "I've got a new song I want to play around with."

Like all of her musicians, Gary's eyes lit up at once at the prospect of creating another megahit. He listened as she strummed a few chords and picked up on her rhythm with the instinct of someone who'd grown accustomed to her creative process.

Laurie jotted down a few words, hummed a few bars, then tried the words aloud. It didn't take long before a few of the others were joining in and the bus was filled with the country-pop crossover sound that had taken her to the top of the charts.

She felt Harlan Patrick's eyes on her as her voice rang out and wondered if he guessed that he was behind the heartbreak in the lyrics. She lifted her gaze and met his. All at once she was lost in those deep blue eyes, eyes that reflected understanding and love, so much love that it was all she could do not to weep.

Why was it, she wondered as she strummed the last chord and then fell silent, that sometimes love simply wasn't enough? Leaving Harlan Patrick not once but twice had hurt. She had anguished over it both times.

But having him back in her life again, having him so near and knowing that another parting was inevitable, was tearing her apart.

She heard Amy Lynn whimper and was half out of her seat in the blink of an eye. Harlan Patrick's gaze remained steady on hers for another instant, and then he broke eye contact and reached for the baby—their daughter, she reminded herself as tears stung her eyes, as much his as hers, though she'd tried to deny that for months now.

Sinking back into her seat, she watched father and child, unable to tear her gaze away from the adoration in Harlan Patrick's eyes. Already Amy Lynn seemed to recognize her daddy. She accepted his comfort, settled down at once in his arms. They were bonding, and she knew without a doubt that the ties forming now would be impossible to break.

"Mind a word of advice from a friend?" Gary inquired lightly, drawing her attention away from the scene being played out up the aisle.

"What?"

"Find a way to make it work."

"It's impossible," she said, unable to hide the despairing note in her voice.

"Nothing's impossible if you both want it badly enough."

She seared him with a look. "Let me ask you this. Would you give up everything we've accomplished the past few years and go back to singing backup in advertising jingles just to be with the woman you love?"

"You seem to forget, I've been divorced three times. I'm not sure I've ever had the kind of love you two have. For a love as powerful as what I'm witnessing right here, right now, yeah, maybe."

"I don't believe it for a minute," she countered. "You of all people know what it takes to get the kind of breaks we've had, to reach this level. You'd never throw it away, not for any reason."

He gave her sad look. "Yes, I would. For just one glance like the one you've been casting toward him, I'd walk away from anything."

It wasn't the first time that Gary had hinted that he was half in love with her himself, but he'd long since accepted that her heart belonged to someone else. He leaned down now and pressed a brotherly kiss to her cheek.

"Think about it," he advised. "We've known each other a long time. I can read you like a book. You'll never be thoroughly happy or alive if you don't find some way to keep that man in your life."

"But how?" she whispered as Gary walked away without answering.

How could she keep Harlan Patrick in her life and have a singing career, too? If she made a choice, either choice, would she be able to live with it, or would resentment destroy whichever one she chose?

No sooner had Gary left than Harlan Patrick rose with the baby in his arms and came back to join her.

"I think it must be close to lunchtime for the little one," he said quietly. "She's been fussing for a few minutes now."

"I'll fix her bottle," Laurie said, glad to have something to do.

"I liked the song," Harlan Patrick said as she heated the baby's milk.

"It's still a little rough, and the last verse sucks."

He grinned. "You're never happy till it's perfect, are you?"

"Of course not."

"You know, it seems to me that perfection might be fine to strive for when you're writing a song, but it's not real practical when it comes to life."

Her hand stilled as she reached to take the bottle from the microwave. "Meaning…?"

"There might not be a perfect solution to our dilemma."

She sighed, accepting the truth of that. "But there has to be something better than what we've come up with so far, don't you think?"

"Darlin', I'm not even sure what we've come up with,

unless you count you being on the road and me being in Texas and both of us being miserable. That's not a solution. That's settling for the easy way out."

"It hasn't been easy," she objected.

"Okay, not easy. Convenient, then. Or maybe cowardly. Neither one of us has had to make any tough choices. We haven't even considered compromise."

She grinned at him and pressed her hand over her heart in a gesture of shocked disbelief. "I never thought I'd hear that word cross your lips."

He grinned back. "It's a new one, all right. You game to discuss it?"

"Oh, Harlan Patrick, can't you see? Discussing it's easy. It's living it that's impossible."

His jaw set. "Anything's possible if we both want it badly enough."

Pretty words, Laurie thought, but that's all they were: words. Their history told another story. It was Harlan Patrick's way or no way.

With Amy Lynn's future at stake, to say nothing of her own happiness, she would meet him halfway, though. "We'll talk about it," she promised.

"When?"

"Tonight, after the show. You can take me out to a late supper, since tomorrow's not a travel day."

"Why, Laurie Jensen, are you asking me out on a date?"

"I am," she agreed. "And I hope you've got your credit cards, because my tastes have gotten a whole lot more expensive. You're not going to get away with a hot dog and some cotton candy."

"Steak and champagne?"

She nodded. "For starters."

"Exactly where do you go next and when do you have to be there?"

"Ohio and not till the middle of the week. Why?"

"Just wondering," he said, and excused himself.

"Where are you going?" she demanded.

He gestured toward his seat. "Not far. I've got some arrangements to make."

"What kind of arrangements?"

"You'll see."

She didn't like the gleam in his eyes one little bit. Nor was she crazy about the way he and Val had their heads together for the next half hour whenever he wasn't on his cellular phone. Something told her she'd started something when she'd agreed to have dinner with him to talk about the future. He seemed to have taken it as a challenge. And just as he'd said earlier, one thing she knew for certain about Harlan Patrick was that the man did love a challenge.

Seven

Harlan Patrick knew he was taking a huge risk even as he made the plans for his first date with Laurie in years. He had no idea how she'd react when she discovered they weren't going out for a simple postperformance dinner.

For the first time in his life, he was truly grateful for the financial resources at his disposal. He discovered that money could make a lot happen in very little time. The hardest part was trying to explain to his uncle why the plane he had just sent back to Texas needed to be piloted right back out again.

"Harlan Patrick, are you sure you know what the devil you're doing?" Jordan inquired with an impatient edge to his voice. "I held my tongue when you took off with the corporate jet without a word to me. I sent my pilot to Montana to retrieve it without a single complaint. And now you want him to pick you up? I'm not running a blasted air shuttle. If Laurie's got you this tied up in knots, maybe you ought to get back home and think things over."

"In a way that's just what I intend to do," he said, taking the well-deserved criticism without flinching. He knew he'd tested Jordan's patience to its limits, but he was also counting on the fact that his uncle still had at least a tiny touch of the Adams love of romance in his soul. After all, the tales of Jordan's elaborate attempts to convince Kelly to marry him were legendary. The current generation had made use of a few of them.

"Meaning…?" Jordan asked.

"I'm coming home and I'm bringing Laurie and the baby with me."

Silence greeted that announcement, followed by a sigh. "Are you sure that's wise? You know the kind of questions you're likely to face here, the pressure from your grandfather to marry."

Harlan Patrick matched his uncle's sigh. "I know, but I can't think of any other way to make her remember what we had. I want her to see what we could have again, if only she'd be reasonable."

"I sympathize with the position you're in, I really do, but I seem to recall that Laurie's got a mind of her own, to say nothing of a temper. This is a whole lot more complicated for her than you're making it out to be. The fact that you're saying she's the one who needs to be reasonable tells me you don't fully understand her position."

"Dammit, I do know it's complicated," Harlan Patrick replied.

"Do you really? It seems to me your first mistake was not taking her seriously enough years ago. Are you absolutely sure you can see her point of view now?" He waited, then asked, "Or are you just trying to bulldoze right on over her the way you always did?"

Harlan Patrick wasn't entirely comfortable with the question. He supposed he did have a tendency to get a notion into his head and then run with it, regardless of the other person involved. Some might say he was selfish and bullheaded. He preferred to think he was simply fighting for what he believed in.

"You haven't answered me," his uncle persisted.

"Dammit, we have a baby," Harlan Patrick retorted. "That's what's important. Not my feelings or Laurie's. I want that baby to be a part of my family."

"Well, of course you do," Jordan soothed. "But tricking Laurie into coming back to Texas when she's made it clear she doesn't want to be here seems like the wrong way to go about it. Why not just ask her to come?"

"What makes you think I'm tricking her?" Harlan Patrick grumbled defensively. "Maybe I have asked her."

"Then why are you whispering? That's a surefire indication that she's close by and you don't want her to know what you're up to."

"Maybe it's just a surprise. What's wrong with that?"

Jordan chuckled. "Depends on whether it's the sort of surprise the recipient will appreciate. Not all of the surprises I tried out on your aunt Kelly went over that well, as I recall. You know," he added thoughtfully, "there are some similarities. My business was in Houston then, and Kelly wanted to stay right here in Los Piños on her ranch. We fought about it tooth and nail for a while."

"And you were the one who gave in. Okay, okay, I hear you," Harlan Patrick conceded reluctantly. "Are you saying you won't send the plane back? If you are, I understand. I'll arrange for a charter."

"Forget chartering another plane," Jordan said impatiently. "I can just imagine what your granddaddy would have to say if I did that. If you need the plane, it's yours. You let me know what time you want the pilot ready to bring you back here, and he'll be waiting at the closest airstrip."

"Thanks, Uncle Jordan."

"Don't thank me yet. I'm still not convinced you're not making a huge mistake."

When Harlan Patrick hung up, he tried very hard not to think about his uncle's reaction. What if Jordan was right? What if Laurie was infuriated by his scheming? What if this plan of his backfired?

But how could it? He was just trying to assure that Laurie remembered the good times, so she could weigh them against what she had now.

He glanced around at the lavishly appointed custom interior of her touring bus, then recalled the club date she'd played the night before with its standing-room-only crowd and wild applause. How would a quiet stay in Los Piños stand up against that? Would it be a welcome respite or a stark contrast that couldn't measure up? What about the men she'd met? Were they more exciting than a simple rancher from Texas?

"How are those plans coming?" Val asked, leaning across the aisle and breaking into his gloomy thoughts. "Everything falling into place?"

"Pretty much. Thanks for going along with this and for agreeing to come to Texas with us." He studied Laurie's assistant with her short blond curls and deceptively innocent expression. No one knew better than he just how fiercely loyal and efficient this woman could be. "Tell me something, Val."

"If I can."

"Is Laurie going to go through the roof when she figures out what I have in mind?" It bothered him more than he wanted to admit that this comparative stranger might know Laurie—today's Laurie—better than he did.

Val grinned. "Very likely."

He winced. "Why doesn't that seem to bother you?"

"Because she needs shaking up. She needs to take a long hard look at her priorities. She's got a handsome man—the father of her baby—absolutely wild about her and she'd rather sing songs to strangers night after night."

She gave him a solemn look. "Now don't get me wrong. I'm not saying she shouldn't sing if it matters to her. Millions of people would go nuts if she even thought about quitting. I'm just saying she needs to get some balance back in her life. She seems to think it has to be one way or the other." She tilted her head and regarded him quizzically. "Wonder where she got an idea like that?"

Harlan Patrick sighed. "Probably from me."

"You still feel that way?"

He searched his heart and had to admit that a part of him did still want her home with him a hundred percent of the time, especially now that they had a daughter. For all of his crazy and impulsive exploits, it seemed he was just an old-fashioned guy at heart.

"You do, don't you?" Val guessed without him saying a word. "No wonder the two of you butt heads. You've both got a mile-wide stubborn streak, don't you?"

"Maybe so," he conceded. "But I'm working on it."

She looked skeptical.

"I am."

"I hope so, but we'll see, cowboy. We'll see."

Laurie was exhausted by the time she left the stage after her last set. It was ironic, really. She'd reached a point in her career when she could perform for an hour or ninety minutes before thousands in the country's biggest concert halls and stadiums and she'd chosen to do twice that much singing in clubs that could barely hold a hundred.

But these were the clubs that had given her a break. When she'd been a struggling nobody, these out-of-the-way club managers had offered her a chance to hone her act and build a following, and she believed in paying back old debts. She could have insisted on a single seating, just one show a night, but she wasn't about to shortchange either the clubs or her audience. She did two performances nightly and she sang her heart out.

By the time she retreated to her dressing room after the second show, she wanted nothing more than a hot shower, something cold to drink and a good night's sleep. Instead, she found Harlan Patrick waiting for her, straddling a chair just the way he had been when she'd first discovered him in her dressing room the night before.

Had it only been twenty-four hours since he'd walked back into her life? It felt as if he'd been back forever, stirring her up, making her long for things she'd resigned herself to never having.

"You look all done in, darlin'."

"Now, that is just what a woman wants to hear," she grumbled as she sank onto the chair in front of her mirror and methodically wiped off her stage makeup. "If you can't say something nice, go away."

"Have you forgotten? We have a date."

She groaned. She had forgotten. Well, almost forgotten. It was pretty much impossible to forget entirely about Harlan Patrick and his expectations.

"Not tonight, please. I was awake most of the night, thanks to you. I'm exhausted. I'll be lousy company. All I want is a good night's sleep."

"You could never be lousy company. Besides, you promised me an evening out," he reminded her. "Don't worry. You'll have time to catch a little catnap on the way."

Her gaze narrowed at the gleam in his eyes. "On the way to where?"

"Dinner, of course."

She met his gaze in the mirror, didn't like what she saw and turned around. "What are you up to, Harlan Patrick?"

"Just think of it as living out a fantasy."

"Oh, no," she protested. "I don't like the sound of that."

He grinned. "Everybody has a fantasy, darlin'."

"Yes, but yours and mine can sometimes be worlds apart."

"Trust me."

She was troubled by the soft-spoken plea. Harlan Patrick had a way of asking her to trust him, then leading her straight into a whole mess of trouble. He'd been doing it forever.

There'd been more than once when he'd lured her out her bedroom window to go skinny-dipping in the creek out at White Pines. There'd been the time he'd insisted they both needed hot-fudge sundaes at midnight and broken into Dolan's to get them. When they'd been caught, he'd counted on Doc Dolan's high tolerance for Adams shenanigans to get them out of the fix they were in. Heck, he'd even told her he had protection the night Amy Lynn was conceived and he had. It was just that their passion had outlasted his supply.

"Harlan Patrick, read my lips," she said quietly. "I do not trust you."

He seemed stunned by her response, but as always, his eternal optimism and supreme self-confidence kicked in. "Give it time, darlin'. You did once and you will again."

"You make it sound so simple."

"It is simple."

"No, it's not. It has never been simple between the two of us."

That square-cut Adams chin jutted up in defiance. Blue eyes challenged her. "We've loved each other forever. What could be simpler than that?"

"We've also broken each other's hearts. If you ask me, that complicates things."

His expression wavered just a little at that. "Okay, you have a point. Let's not try to solve everything in one night. You'll come with me tonight, have a nice dinner, some quiet conversation and we'll see where it leads."

He made it sound so easy, so nonthreatening, when his very presence in her life was a danger. With his glib tongue and determination, he could make her believe in anything, even the two of them.

"I don't know, Harlan Patrick. Another night would probably be better."

His eyes caught hers, held. "Please."

In all the years she'd known him, she couldn't remember him ever using that word before. With strangers, maybe. His family, definitely. But not with her. With her he teased. He cajoled and coaxed. He commanded, but a simple *please* had always seemed beyond him.

In the end that was what got to her. It hinted at his desperation, maybe even at his willingness to change if that's what it took to get her back.

"Okay," she said finally. "I did make a promise. But it can't be a late night, Harlan Patrick. Val's with Amy Lynn now, but I can't ask her to baby-sit half the night. She already works way too hard."

"Deal," he said at once. "Now, shake a leg, darlin'. We've got places to go, things to do."

"In the middle of nowhere?" she said, shooting him a

wry look in the mirror. "We'll be lucky if there's a fast-food restaurant open."

"I can do better than fast food," he assured her. "You just wait and see."

Harlan Patrick packed while she finished dressing. She hid a grin at the sight of him folding everything and tucking it into her bag in nice, neat piles. She would have been satisfied to stuff it all in helter-skelter and worry about the wrinkles later. The man did have a thing about neatness, especially when it came to clothes. Except when he worked, his were always impeccable. His blasted jeans had precise creases in them. It was just another contradiction between them.

"All set?" he asked when he was finished.

She regarded him with amusement. "I've been ready. You're the one who's been dillydallying over the packing. What is this obsession of yours with neatness?"

He scowled. "It's not an obsession. If you have things, you take care of them. That's all."

"Did that come from your father and grandfather teaching you to take care of the ranch?"

"The ranch, family, whatever."

They were waltzing close to dangerous territory now. Laurie regarded him cautiously. "In other words you protect what's yours?"

"Something like that."

She concluded there was a point that needed making. "Clothes are one thing, Harlan Patrick. I'm another. It's not your job to protect me."

"I think it is. You and Amy Lynn are my responsibility," he insisted emphatically. "Just because you ducked out on me and hid Amy Lynn for months doesn't make it less so now that I've found you."

She winced at his stubborn expression. "Forget it. I am not having this conversation with you, not tonight."

"Wise decision," he commented as he ushered her out of the club and into a waiting car. "It's an argument you can't win. Now just sit back, close your eyes and rest till we get where we're going."

"Oh, no," she retorted. "I'm not closing my eyes or turning my back on you for one single second, Harlan Patrick Adams."

He grinned. "Suit yourself."

But despite her vehement protest, Laurie felt her eyes drifting shut within a matter of minutes. Lulled by the car's motion, she was sound asleep in no time.

When she eventually awoke again, she had no idea how much time had passed. Her eyes snapped open as she realized that the sound she was hearing couldn't possibly be a car's engine. One glance around confirmed that she was riding in an airplane—Jordan's corporate jet, unless she was very much mistaken.

"Harlan Patrick!" she bellowed when she didn't spot him right away.

He poked his head around the back of her seat. "Hush, darlin'. You're going to wake the baby."

"I'm going to do more than wake the baby," she threatened. "I am going to wring your sneaky, conniving neck, right before I toss you out of here. Where are we and where are we going?"

"We're in a plane."

"That much is clear."

"Jordan's plane."

She sighed heavily. "I thought so. I thought you'd sent it back to Texas."

"I had."

"Your uncle must be thrilled with all the use his jet is getting these days."

"Let's just say he's resigned to it."

"Let's move on to the other question I asked. Where are we going?"

He met her gaze evenly. "Home, darlin'. We're going home."

Laurie felt her heart begin to thud dully. "Home," she repeated in disbelief. "You've kidnapped us and you're taking us back to Texas?"

"I haven't kidnapped you," he insisted, looking offended.

"What would you call it?"

"You agreed to come to dinner. I picked the place. Mine."

"I'm in the middle of a concert tour. I can't go to Texas," she protested.

"Of course you can," he contradicted. "You told me yourself, you have a couple of days off before you're due in Ohio. We'll fly up day after tomorrow. The band will meet you there."

"And you took care of all these little logistical details yourself?" she asked skeptically.

He looked vaguely uneasy. "Not exactly."

To Laurie's astonishment, Val popped up just then.

"I helped," she announced unrepentantly.

"You?" Laurie asked incredulously. "Might I point out that I am the one who pays your salary. I'm the one who should be giving the orders."

Val grinned. "You pay me to make things happen. I made this happen."

"But I didn't want this to happen," Laurie all but shouted.

"Sure, you did, darlin'. You just didn't know it," Harlan Patrick responded in a low, soothing tone. "Don't blame Val. It was my idea."

"Oh, I am very sure of that," she agreed. "I'll deal with you in my own good time."

Despite the threat and her scowl, apparently he concluded it was safe enough now that the initial explosion was over, so he slid into the seat next to her. She glared at him. He smiled right back at her.

"I ought to hate you for this," she said.

"But you don't," he said confidently. "Do you?"

"I'm still debating."

"Laurie, face it. You couldn't hate me if you tried. Not really."

"You know, Harlan Patrick, one of these days someone's going to come along and bring you down a peg or two. Not everyone finds your inclination to control things amusing."

He chuckled at that. "Maybe so, but it won't be you."

"Don't count on it," she said grimly. "This little jaunt may prove to be just the incentive I needed to change my ways where you're concerned."

She folded her arms across her middle, settled back in her seat and prepared to endure the rest of the trip. As she stared out the window into the inky black sky with its dusting of stars, she reached a decision. Harlan Patrick might have won this battle with his clever little scheme, but the night wasn't over yet. She could turn the tables on him when they landed. In fact, she had the perfect scheme in mind.

A half-hour later they were on the ground at the tiny Los Piños airstrip. Harlan Patrick had a car waiting for them. Laurie gazed into his triumphant eyes and felt a moment's unease. He was going to be really, really unhappy when he realized what she intended.

So what? she consoled herself. He was the one who'd dragged her back here without asking. He was the one who was so hot to recapture the past. She'd take him back a few years, all right. Right down memory lane. There was one person on earth who'd never been charmed by Harlan Patrick, one person who'd been able to keep him in his place.

She turned and regarded him innocently. "Swing by my mom's, okay?"

"Now? It's the middle of the night."

"She's never seen Amy Lynn," Laurie explained, keeping her tone innocent.

"She can see her in the morning," he countered.

"Indulge me."

"Oh, for heaven's sakes," he muttered, but he turned the car toward town.

There wasn't a lot of sight-seeing to be done between the airstrip and Los Piños and it was too dark to see anyway, but with every mile they covered, Laurie felt herself drifting back to another time in her life. She was a teenager again, and a reluctant Harlan Patrick was driving her home from a date.

He pulled into her mother's driveway just moments later, and Laurie got out, along with Val and the baby. Harlan Patrick followed, feet dragging now that he'd lost control of events.

"You're going to scare her to death turning up here like this," he warned as Laurie rang the bell, rather than using the key she still had in her purse.

"Whose fault is that?" she countered.

Lights began coming on all through the house as her mother made her way to the door. Then it was open, and her mother's bemused, worried expression turned to pure joy when she saw the little crowd on her doorstep.

"Hi, Mama," Laurie said, walking into her tearful embrace. "I'm home."

"Oh, you beautiful child, come in here. Come in here right this minute. And you must be Val. I've heard so much about you. Now let me see that precious granddaughter of mine," she said, reaching for Amy Lynn and taking her from Val's arms.

"Oh, my, she is beautiful," she whispered. "She reminds me of you when you were a baby, Laurie."

Her gaze fell on Harlan Patrick then, and she beamed at him, too, obviously feeling more benevolent toward him tonight than she usually did.

"You did this, didn't you? You brought our girl home again. I can't thank you enough. You just carry her bags right on up to her old room and don't pretend you don't know which one it is, because I remember all too well how many times you climbed that tree outside her window."

Harlan Patrick stared at her, clearly flabbergasted by the unexpected turn of events. "But—" he began.

"Go on, Harlan Patrick. Do as Mama said," Laurie said, shooting him a triumphant grin.

"This isn't what was supposed to happen," he muttered under his breath.

Her grin widened. "No, I'm sure it isn't."

He scowled at her. "You will pay for this, darlin'."

"I'm sure you'll try to see to it that I do," she agreed. "You might want to remember, though, that when it comes to being sneaky, I learned from a master."

Eight

She had bamboozled him! Harlan Patrick drove out to White Pines still cursing the fact that Laurie had actually managed to trump him at his own game.

He couldn't very well stand in Mrs. Jensen's living room and demand that Laurie, Amy Lynn and Val leave with him. For one thing the woman was so clearly ecstatic about having her daughter home again. For another, Mary Jensen was no pushover. She had very strict ideas about morality. She would have managed to shame him for even thinking of taking Laurie to his home, when the two of them weren't married. Never mind the fact that they had a little girl as proof that their relationship had ventured beyond hand-holding.

Oh, Laurie was a sneaky one, all right. She had known just what would happen when she walked through that front door. She had also known that he would indulge her whim to stop by, because he had always given her everything she'd ever wanted.

She would pay for it, though. She would pay the minute he could think of something devious enough to get the upper hand again.

A half-hour later he walked into his small house on a far corner of Adams land and slammed the door behind him. The thud gave him a moment's satisfaction, but he wouldn't be truly satisfied until he had his daughter and Laurie under this roof with him.

If there'd been any choice at all, he would never have left them in town where they were free to sneak off the instant his back was turned. He'd just have to trust that Mrs. Jensen would be no more anxious than he was to let them go or that Val was strong-willed enough to rat out her boss if Laurie got a notion to run. That was an awful lot of blind faith for a man who'd had some lousy lessons in broken trust lately.

He sank down on the sofa, too exhausted to even bother with taking off his boots or hauling himself up to bed. Besides, he'd had too many very erotic images the past couple of days of Laurie being back in that bed with him to want to climb into it alone.

Why did he have to want her so damned much? Life would have been a whole lot less complicated if his daughter were the only one who mattered to him. He could battle to get custody of her and forget all about her mama.

But that wasn't possible. He might have been furious with her, but one look at Laurie up in Montana and he'd known that he was going to have to fight tooth and nail for both of them. He was as captivated by Laurie as he'd ever been. She enchanted him as much as she infuriated him, a mix that had been dangerous to a man forever.

Anger, rage, betrayal all paled beside the white-hot need to hold her in his arms again, to bury himself deep inside her and hear her cries of pleasure mounting with every thrust of his body. Images hot enough to singe burned behind his eyelids and kept him restless.

When daybreak came, he hadn't slept a wink. He was in no mood at all for the pounding on his door that had him dragging his butt off the sofa.

"All right, all right," he muttered as he yanked open the door to find his father on his doorstep.

"So, you are here. Your mother told me she'd seen you come flying by in the middle of the night," Cody Adams said, scowling at him. "I told her she had to be wrong, that it must have been one of the hands coming in late. Aren't you supposed to be in Montana with Laurie?"

"It was four o'clock in the morning," Harlan Patrick grumbled, ignoring the reference to Laurie. He figured they'd get back to her soon enough. "What was Mom doing up?"

"She never sleeps well when one of her chicks is far from the nest. She figures Sharon Lynn has Cord looking out for her now, so she can concentrate on you."

"Heaven help me," Harlan Patrick said fervently.

His father grinned. "You could go a long way toward settling her down if you brought Laurie and Amy Lynn back with you. Are they here? Did you convince them to come home?"

"More or less. I'm surprised Uncle Jordan didn't fill you in."

"What does that mean? What does Jordan know that I don't?"

"It means I pulled a fast one to get them back here and they wound up in town with her mother," he admitted reluctantly.

His father's infamous grin broadened. "Not what you had in mind, was it?"

"No. That woman's sneakier than Grandpa Harlan."

"I doubt that," his father said. "You'd better hope he

hasn't gotten wind that Laurie's back or he'll be meddling in your life, too."

If turning the matchmaking over to his grandfather would have worked, Harlan Patrick was just about desperate enough to try it, but he wasn't prepared to admit that to his father.

"I haven't spoken to Grandpa Harlan since I left," he said.

"But Laurie has," his father reminded him. "He told me all about it. That conversation got his hopes for the two of you up real high, and that was before he found out about the baby."

"He knows about Amy Lynn?"

"Oh, yeah. We tried to stop it, but that tabloid has made the rounds. Janet finally decided it was pointless trying to keep it from him."

"How'd he take it?"

"Needless to say, he'd be down here himself building a nursery, but Janet won't let him do it since he came close to breaking a hip the last time he climbed up on a ladder. Don't be surprised, though, if a whole crew shows up here later today with lumber and baby supplies. You know your grandpa once he gets a notion into his head."

Harlan Patrick studied his father intently. "For a man who recently claimed he didn't like Laurie, that she wasn't good enough for me, you seem mighty amused by all of this."

"It's your opinion of her that counts. As for me, I'm reserving judgment on Laurie for the moment. Meantime, I have to admit, there's nothing I like better than watching your granddaddy stir things up. Keeps him young."

Despite the levity, something in his father's voice stirred alarm. "He's okay, isn't he?" Harlan Patrick asked.

"He's fine. You know your grandfather. He's a stubborn old cuss. He'll probably outlive us all, especially if there's another grandbaby or great-grandbaby he feels the need to see settled in life. You're his number-one project these days, so consider yourself warned." His expression sobered. "You planning on coming back to work today? We could use the help."

Guilt washed over Harlan Patrick. He'd left the ranch in a bind when he'd taken off, though his father had been gracious enough not to belabor the point. Still, he couldn't just get back on his horse and ride off on some chore when his whole damned life was so unsettled.

"Never mind," his father said before he could reply. "We'll manage. You won't be worth a hoot to us as long as Laurie's on your mind. Just do me one favor."

"What's that?"

"Stop by the house and see your mother. She's worried about you. Has been ever since you took off. She and Sharon Lynn were carrying on the night you left, blaming themselves for your going, for letting you get a glimpse of that picture. She won't rest easy till she sees with her own eyes that you're doing okay."

"I'll go by for breakfast on my way into town," Harlan Patrick promised.

"That'll make her happy. She'll start the waffle iron the minute I tell her. From the day she married me and stopped working at Dolan's, she's happiest when she's serving up a big breakfast. If we hadn't had you kids, she would probably have taken over that lunch counter the way Sharon Lynn has done."

"Surely you're not complaining," Harlan Patrick teased. "Seems to me nobody likes breakfast better than you, especially when you get a chance to sneak a kiss whenever

Mom passes by the table. Better than sugar, you used to tell us."

His father grinned. "It was and is."

"Spare me the details," Harlan Patrick replied. "Just tell Mom to make those waffles blueberry."

"As if she'd make anything else but your favorite when she's feeling a need to baby her youngest." He put his hand on Harlan Patrick's shoulder and gave it a squeeze. "You bring those gals of yours by when you can. I have to admit, I'm a little anxious to see my granddaughter, too."

"I'll have 'em out here just as soon as I can," Harlan Patrick promised.

It was one vow he intended to keep before the end of the day. Whether he could get them to stay, though, was another matter entirely.

Harlan Patrick consumed a plateful of waffles and let his mother fuss over him for the better part of an hour before he insisted on getting into town to check on Laurie. The minute he was out of sight of the house and his mother's watchful eyes, he hit the accelerator and drove into town at a pace all but guaranteed to have the local sheriff on his tail. Fortunately the local sheriff was his cousin Justin. He grinned when he saw the flashing lights behind him.

"Dammit, Harlan Patrick, you keep driving like that and I won't have any choice except to give you a ticket," Justin grumbled. He waved his citation book under Harlan Patrick's nose before stuffing it back in his pocket. "Where's the fire?"

"I'm going to see Laurie."

His cousin's expression turned sympathetic. "Ah, I see."

"I don't see why you say it like that."

"Because you never knew any way to chase after Laurie except full speed ahead."

"And the problem with that would be…?"

"She always knows exactly what to expect. In fact, she probably counts on it."

Harlan Patrick didn't like what Justin was suggesting. "Are you talking in general here or are you referring to that tabloid picture?"

"It is possible she planned it," Justin mused. "Who'd know better how to plant publicity designed to catch your attention?"

"She was trying to block the baby from view. Anybody could see that."

"She didn't do a very good job of it, though, did she? That baby of hers was in plain view."

"You're spending too much time around the criminal element. You're starting to see conspiracies everywhere you look."

"I'm just saying the woman had to know that you'd come hightailing it after her, the minute you saw that picture." Justin regarded him intently. "She was expecting you, wasn't she?"

"Of course not," Harlan Patrick retorted, then thought of all the roadblocks Laurie had put in his path. Half of Nashville had been warned to keep her whereabouts secret. "Okay, she assumed I'd come running, but she didn't want to be found. In fact, she did everything she could to see that I couldn't find her."

Justin gave him a pitying look. "Oh, please, Harlan Patrick. Who knows better than Laurie how you respond to a challenge. The more difficult she made it for you, the more determined you'd be to track her down. That's your nature."

"Am I that predictable?"

"You are where Laurie Jensen is concerned. Maybe you ought to think about being the one to turn your back this time. Let her do the chasing."

The idea held a certain appeal. Unfortunately he and Laurie weren't the only ones whose fate was at stake. "You're forgetting about Amy Lynn."

"No, I'm not. It is precisely because of your daughter that I want to see the two of you get it right. Let Laurie find her way back to you, Harlan Patrick. Maybe she needs a challenge in her life, too. If you don't believe me, just look at how hard she worked to become a superstar, when she could have done nicely as a singer right here in Texas. Every time you mentioned a roadblock to her back then, she found some way to scramble over it."

What his cousin said made a lot of sense, but Harlan Patrick pictured Amy Lynn, imagined losing her if he made the wrong decision. "I can't turn my back on them," he said finally. "I can't take that chance."

"I know it would be hard," Justin said sympathetically. Then his eyes lit up, and he grinned. "Remember that little bird we found when we were kids, the one that had fallen out of its nest?"

"Are you sure you're not confusing me with Dani? Your sister is the vet in the family."

"Think back. We were maybe five or six. We nursed that little bird for a week or more, fed it what seemed like a hundred times a day."

Slowly a dim memory began to take shape. "It was a scrawny little sparrow, wasn't it? I kept wanting it to be a baby eagle."

Justin's grin spread. "You were delusional. Anyway, remember when it was strong enough and Grandpa Harlan told us it was time to set it free? You'd gotten real attached to that bird by then and didn't want to let it go. You said you loved that little bird, and it loved you."

It all came back to him then, the feeling of panic that had come over him at the thought of letting the tiny creature fly away. "I remember," he said quietly.

"Do you also remember what Grandpa Harlan told us? He said when you love something, you have to let it go, that it's only when it comes back to you of its own free will that you can truly know the meaning of love."

The parallels to his current situation were obvious. Harlan Patrick sighed. "Quite a philosopher, our grandfather. He has a nasty habit of being right most of the time, too."

Justin grinned. "Don't look so downcast. Do you remember what happened with that sparrow once Grandpa Harlan convinced you to set it free? It came back and sang its little heart out for us all summer long."

Harlan Patrick's spirits lifted. "Yeah, it did, didn't it?"

"And the moral of this story is…?" Justin prodded.

"Okay, okay, I get it. You don't have to whack me over the head with it."

"Then I'll be on my way," Justin said. He'd walked only a couple of steps before turning back. "By the way, cousin. If I catch you going so much as one mile over the speed limit, there won't be enough money in the family coffers to bail you out of my jail."

Harlan Patrick laughed, which put a scowl on his cousin's face.

"I'm dead serious."

"I know you are. That's why it's so funny. You can lock me up and throw away the key, but I flat out guarantee you that granddaddy will have your badge for it. Weigh that while you're chasing me down."

He let that warning hang in the air as he put the car into gear and took off, kicking up a trail of dust just to taunt Justin. The man really did need to loosen up. He'd hoped marriage to Patsy would do the trick, but it hadn't. Therefore Harlan Patrick considered it his personal—if not his civic—duty to see to it.

Laurie expected Harlan Patrick to show up at her mother's again before dawn. When he still wasn't there by nine, she began to wonder what he was up to. As the morning dragged on with no sign of him, her gaze kept straying toward the window.

"Expecting someone?" Val inquired as she sipped another cup of coffee.

Val had settled into Laurie's mother's kitchen as if she'd been visiting there for years. She'd appropriated the portable phone to follow up on publicity arrangements for the final stops on the tour. She had papers spread all over the Formica-topped table. One thing Laurie had to say for her: Val could work efficiently just about anywhere. She didn't require the trappings of an office.

Val continued to regard her with amusement. "Not answering, huh? Must mean the answer's yes."

"Just how furious do you think he was when he left here last night?" Laurie asked.

"Who?"

"Who do you think?" Laurie growled. "Harlan Patrick was the only man who left here in the middle of the night, wasn't he?"

"As far as I know," Val said evenly. "I'm just surprised it matters to you. You seemed mighty anxious to see him go. You were looking downright pleased with yourself when he walked out the door."

"I wasn't anxious for him to go," Laurie protested. "I was just trying to make a point."

Val tried unsuccessfully to smother a grin. "Well, I guess you succeeded, then, didn't you? He knows now that you are even trickier than he is."

"Do you suppose I should call him?" Laurie fretted.

"If you want to."

"I don't want to," she snapped.

"You just said—"

"I'm just worried that something might have happened to him. It was awfully late. He was ticked off at me. He was probably driving too fast the way he always does. The roads out here are dark as sin. What if his car's in a ditch or something? Who besides us would know to go looking for him?"

"Worried about me, darlin'?" the very man in question inquired from behind her.

Laurie almost jumped out of her skin at the sound of his voice. She whirled around and glared. "Don't you sneak up on me."

"I thought you'd be relieved to hear my voice. Weren't you picturing me in a ditch?"

"With pleasure," she retorted.

His crooked smile mocked her. "Liar, liar," he taunted.

"Well, you're just fine, aren't you, so it hardly matters what I was thinking."

He gave Val a wink, then bent and brushed a light kiss across Laurie's lips. "Glad to know you missed me."

"I never said I missed you," she said, though an unmistakable shiver had washed through her at the touch of his lips against hers.

"Didn't have to," he said, helping himself to a cup of coffee. "That blush tells the story."

"I do not blush, Harlan Patrick."

He cast a look toward Val. "What do you say? Did her cheeks turn pink just now or not?"

Val held up a protesting hand. "Leave me out of this. The woman pays my salary."

"If she fires you, I'll hire you," Harlan Patrick promised. "We can always use a whiz like you out at White Pines."

Laurie tried to stop herself, but she couldn't help it. She chuckled at the image of the dainty whirlwind before her herding cattle. "Somehow I don't see Val on a ranch. Getting up close and personal with a cow is not her style."

"We have an office, darlin'. We have books to keep, logistics to plan. Something tells me Val could grasp the details in no time."

"But she'd hate it," Laurie countered. "Val likes the world of country music, don't you, Val?"

"All that singing about heartache and cowboys and you don't think she'd like to meet the real thing," Harlan Patrick retorted before Val could reply. "I say we take her on a tour and let her decide for herself."

Laurie's gaze narrowed. "This is just your sneaky way of getting us out to White Pines, isn't it? You're just itching for the family to get a look at your daughter."

"Well, of course I am," he agreed. "Nothing says we can't include a little sight-seeing for Val along the way."

"Val has things to do."

Harlan Patrick turned to her assistant. "Is that right? Are you too busy to pay a visit to the ranch?"

Val heaved an exaggerated sigh of relief. "Finally. I am so glad that somebody noticed I was still in the room." She shot a defiant look toward Laurie. "And I would absolutely love to see the ranch." She stood up. "I'll get

Amy Lynn ready to go, if I can pry her away from your mama, that is."

She scooted out of the room in the blink of an eye, leaving Laurie alone with the most impossible man on earth.

"How is it that you have managed to twist that woman around your finger already?"

"Charm, darlin'. It used to work on you, too."

"That was before I knew you better."

"You really are going to have to do better than that, if you intend to insult me."

She regarded him curiously. "You really do let my barbs roll right off your back, don't you?"

"Most of them," he agreed. His expression sobered. "Not all."

"Funny," she observed. "I never thought I got to you at all."

"Except by leaving," he said quietly. "You knew that one was a real killer, didn't you?"

Laurie was startled by the genuine pain in his voice, the flash of vulnerability in eyes that normally twinkled with mischief. The accusation stung because it implied that she'd gone only to hurt him.

"I didn't leave to make you miserable, Harlan Patrick. Surely you've figured that out by now. Or do you still think my music is some clever little game I play, a nasty habit you're forced to tolerate?"

He sighed and raked a hand through his hair. "No. I know how important your music is. I ought to. You've chosen it over everything else in your life."

She frowned. "I won't have this conversation with you again. It never changes. You try to make me feel guilty for loving what I do. I blame you for trying to take it away from me, for making me choose. What's the point, Harlan Patrick? We always end up right back where we started."

"Amy Lynn's the point."

"Amy Lynn is doing just fine with the things the way they are."

"Now, maybe," he conceded grudgingly. "She's a baby. What happens when it's time for her to go to school? You planning on dragging a tutor along on tour with you? Or do you intend to shuffle her off to some boarding school?"

"For heaven's sakes, Harlan Patrick, it'll be years and years before she goes to school," she protested impatiently. "When the time comes, I'll make whatever arrangements are necessary."

"What about friends? How's she supposed to have friends if she's always on the go? A kid needs a home, roots, family, just the way you and I did."

"You had that, not me," Laurie countered. "I had a mother who struggled every day of her life to keep a roof over our head. That's it. Talk about living with insecurity. Been there. Done that."

She stared at him defiantly. "And I survived. It certainly wasn't the same as you living all safe and secure out at White Pines, surrounded by family."

"All the more reason why you should want what I had for Amy Lynn."

"Who knows better than I do that you can get by with less?" she countered, even though the truth was that not a day of her youth had gone by that she hadn't envied what Harlan Patrick had. Not the money so much, but the ranch and what it represented—history and family.

"And that's what you want for Amy Lynn?" he inquired softly. "Less than the best?"

"That is not what I meant," she said, shoving her chair

back and leaping to her feet so she could pace in the small kitchen. He was twisting her words, trying to instill enough guilt so she would cave in and let him have his way. Once he would have gotten away with it, too, but she was stronger now, tougher and smarter. She could see right through him.

"That's what you said," he insisted.

"Only because you make me so crazy I don't know what I'm saying half the time," she said, pausing to glower at him. "Besides, thanks to my career, I can provide Amy Lynn with all the financial security she'll ever need and then some. We don't need you."

That claim was meant to rile him, and it did. His eyes glittered dangerously. She tried to make a clean getaway, but he snagged her hand as she whirled around. Before she knew it, he'd hauled her into his lap.

"Let me up," she demanded, shoving ineffectively at his chest.

"Not till you admit I'm right," he said, a teasing sparkle replacing the fury that had put fire in his eyes only seconds earlier. "Not till you admit you need me."

"When hell freezes over," she retorted.

"Admit it," he commanded.

"Never."

"Say it or I will…" His gaze clashed with hers, held. The silence built. Tension shimmered in the air.

"Or you will what?" she asked, her voice suddenly shaky.

"This," he whispered just before his mouth claimed hers.

His fingers tangled in her hair as he coaxed her lips apart. His tongue dipped, tasted, savored. Then hers did the same. The kiss stirred her blood, stirred memories.

He tasted of coffee and just a hint of maple syrup. Laurie rocked back in his lap and grinned.

"Your mama made you waffles this morning, didn't she?"

"What if she did?"

"The woman spoils you rotten. No wonder you're so impossible."

"I'm not impossible, darlin'." He shifted her ever so slightly so she could feel the hard shaft of his arousal. "When I'm with you, I am always very, very possible."

She sighed and buried her face against his shoulder, relaxing into the wondrous sensation of having his arms tight around her again. Last night, walking into her mother's house again after being away for so long, had been incredible, but this? This was what it felt like to come home.

"Oh, Harlan Patrick," she murmured. "If only everything were as easy as you make it sound."

"It's as easy or as complicated as we make it."

"Then why do we insist on making it so complicated?"

"Damned if I know," he said ruefully. "Maybe that's just how it has to be, so we'll appreciate what we have when we finally work it out."

She pulled back and gazed into his eyes. "I hope you're right. I really do."

He smoothed her hair back from her face and smiled, a sad, wistful little smile. "I hope so, too, Laurie. I truly do."

Nine

A knot of dread formed in Laurie's stomach as they got closer and closer to White Pines. Once this ranch had been like a second home to her. She and Harlan Patrick had explored every acre of it on daylong horseback rides and picnics. She'd been welcome at family gatherings, included on special occasions, all because everyone had assumed that one day she and Harlan Patrick would marry.

She wondered what they thought of her now. Oh, she knew what Harlan Patrick had told her, that everyone, including his grandfather, cared only that she'd given him a daughter. That might be what they told him, but she had little doubt that resentment would be simmering below the surface. How could it not be? He was an Adams, and she had betrayed him.

Hands clenched, she stared out at the rugged, familiar terrain and tried to see the beauty in it that Harlan Patrick saw, tried to feel the same connection to the land. All she felt was uneasiness and the same restless urge to wander that had driven her away from Texas years ago.

As much as she loved the people here—as much as she loved one particular person here—it hadn't been enough.

She had desperately wanted a singing career. She had needed to be somebody, on her own, not just because she married into the wealthiest family in town. Marrying a man like Harlan Patrick would have been blind luck, not an accomplishment she could claim.

"You okay?" Harlan Patrick asked, giving her a sideways glance as he turned into the long driveway leading up to the sprawling house that had been built as a replica of the home his Southern ancestors had lost in the Civil War, then recreated after moving west.

"Sure."

As if he could read her mind, he said quietly, "Nobody here hates you, Laurie."

"Then why do I feel as if I'm on my way to my own hanging?"

"Don't go blaming me for that," he said less sympathetically. "I'm not accountable for whatever guilty thoughts you're having."

She scowled. "I have absolutely nothing to feel guilty about."

"Then stop agonizing over what's to come. You're going to visit a few old friends, show off our beautiful daughter. What's the big deal?"

"The big deal is that I kept Amy Lynn from you. Don't you think I know how that will make me look in everyone's eyes, especially your sister's? Sharon Lynn and I were friends once, but when I walked out on you, it changed things between us. This will only make the tension worse."

He braked to a stop on a curve in the lane and faced her. "The only person whose opinion really matters here is me, Laurie."

"Okay, then," she said, accepting the truth of that. "What about you? Have you forgiven me?"

He hesitated at the direct question, then sighed. "No, but I'm working on it."

That sinking sensation returned to the pit of her stomach. "Thanks. That really helped," she said sarcastically.

He reached over and touched her cheek. "I love you just the same as I always did. The rest will come."

In the back seat, Val cleared her throat loudly. "Excuse me for interrupting, you two."

"What?" Laurie and Harlan Patrick asked in a startled chorus.

"Don't look now, but there are several huge beasts ambling this way. Is that significant?"

Harlan Patrick glanced in the direction Val indicated and chuckled. "They're just cows coming to see what's going on over here. They're hoping we might be planning to drop some feed over the fence."

"And if we don't?" Val asked, eying them warily.

"They'll wander away."

"No retaliation? No stampede?"

Laurie laughed at her assistant's vivid imagination. "You almost sound disappointed. Were you hoping for a tale of danger you could repeat all over Nashville?"

"Sure," Val said with a nervous chuckle. "It would be great publicity, you know." She paused, her expression thoughtful, then added, "As long as you don't get trampled."

"Yeah," Laurie said dryly. "That would be a bummer."

"Everybody settled down and ready to move on now?" Harlan Patrick asked.

"More than ready," Val replied.

"As ready as I'll ever be," Laurie said grimly.

In the back Amy Lynn gurgled and waved her tattered stuffed bear in enthusiastic agreement.

"I guess that's everybody, then," Harlan Patrick said, watching his daughter in the rearview mirror, his expression amused. "Okay, baby girl, let's go home."

His tone was lighthearted but the statement was laden with hidden meanings that immediately put Laurie on edge all over again. This was not Amy Lynn's home. Her home was hundreds of miles away in Nashville. She wondered, though, if there was anything she could say or do to get that through Harlan Patrick's thick skull.

Harlan Patrick bypassed the turn that would have taken them to his own home or his parents' and headed straight for White Pines itself. He'd called his mother from Laurie's and told her to meet them at the main house. He figured it would be easier on everybody if there was one big welcome, rather than having to go through reunion after reunion, especially when some were bound to be uncomfortable.

Laurie's obvious case of nerves was beginning to get to him. He suspected even Amy Lynn could sense her mother's mounting tension. She'd begun fussing just as they reached the house, and nothing Val could do seemed to soothe her.

"I'll take her," Laurie said, leaping out the instant he cut the engine. She rushed around to the other side and practically snatched Amy Lynn from her car seat as if she needed to stake her claim before anyone else did.

"Planning to use her as a shield when you enter the enemy camp?" Harlan Patrick inquired lightly.

"I'm trying to get her to settle down," she countered defensively. "She probably needs changing, and it's almost lunchtime. We should have waited until another time to do this. I wasn't thinking."

"You've been doing that a lot lately," he observed.

Her eyes glittered dangerously. "What?"

"Not thinking."

She frowned. "Don't you dare do this," she warned in a low tone. "Don't you dare try to start something with me just as we're going in to see your family."

Was that what he'd been doing? More than likely, he was forced to admit. "Sorry. I didn't mean to make this any more difficult." He reached for the baby. "Let me carry her. She's too heavy for you."

Laurie held Amy Lynn a little tighter. "She's fine."

"Okay, then, let's go. Val, you all set?" he asked as she lagged behind them.

"I think maybe I should stay out here for a bit, maybe take a walk. I don't belong in there right now."

"Of course you belong," Laurie said at once. "You're my friend."

"And mine, too, I hope," Harlan Patrick said. "Though I can understand why you might prefer to stay out of the cross fire. If you'd rather go for a tour, I can get one of the hands to take you around."

She nodded eagerly at that. "Yes. That would be wonderful."

"Wait here. I'll see who's around."

As he headed for the stables, he saw the newest hire bringing a horse into the paddock. Slade Sutton was an embittered ex–rodeo star, barely into his thirties, who'd been brought aboard to work with the horses and to start a breeding program. With his taciturn demeanor Sutton wouldn't have been his first choice for tour guide, but

Harlan Patrick suspected his choices were going to be limited at this time of day.

"Hey, Slade, you got a minute?"

The no-nonsense man scowled predictably at the interruption and limped over. "Just about that. No more."

"I need you to do something for me," Harlan Patrick said, ignoring the man's testiness and his obvious reluctance to be drawn into any task that didn't involve the horses.

"What's that?"

"I've got a real tenderfoot out here who needs a tour. I wouldn't ask except the next hour or so is going to be tense inside and there's no need for her to be a part of that."

Slade's scowl deepened. "You didn't hire me to play tour guide. I've got horses to work with."

"Then let her watch. She'll be content with that, as long as you manage to throw a smile her way every now and again, along with an explanation of what you're up to. I'd be grateful if you'd help me out."

He walked off to get Val before the man could protest again. When he came back with her in tow, Slade didn't even bother to look up from his work until Harlan Patrick called his name insistently.

"Slade Sutton, this is Val Harding. She's Laurie Jensen's assistant."

There was a brief flicker of recognition and surprise at the mention of Laurie's name, but no more. Slade tipped his hat and went back to using his pick to clean the caked-up dirt in the horse's shoe.

"Slade doesn't say much, but most of what he does say is profound," Harlan Patrick told her, drawing a sour look from the man in question. "I'll be back for you when the fireworks are over."

"I'm sure I'll be fine," Val assured him, proving that she would rather be any place on earth than inside White Pines. She sent a beaming smile toward Slade. "I'm sure Mr. Sutton and I will get along very well."

Harlan Patrick was pretty sure he heard Slade mutter a contradictory response under his breath, but he let it pass. As cantankerous as he knew the man to be, he also knew he would never be overtly rude to a woman. Silent, maybe, difficult definitely, but not rude. Sutton prided himself on being a cowboy through and through, and basic courtesy was ingrained. It might be interesting to see how the ever cheerful Val handled him, but unfortunately he couldn't stick around to watch. He had his own awkward situation to deal with.

Naturally, by the time he walked back to the front of the house, everyone had poured into the yard and Laurie and his daughter were surrounded. She might have feared being cast as the bad guy, but at the moment she appeared more in danger of being smothered by eager Adamses, anxious to get a look at the newest addition.

"Hey, give the woman some room," Harlan Patrick called out. "Otherwise, she'll make a break for it the first chance she gets."

There was more truth than jest in his words, and everyone there seemed to know it. They backed off instantly, everyone except his grandfather. He stood his ground, his gaze on the little girl in Laurie's arms.

"She has Adams eyes," he noted with pride. "And an Adams chin." He held out his arms. "May I?"

Laurie never hesitated. "Of course. Sweetie, this is your great-grandpa Harlan," she said as she handed the baby over.

"Oh, darlin' girl, I'll bet you are a handful," Grandpa

Harlan said with tears shimmering in his eyes. "Come along with me and I'll tell you all about being an Adams, then I'll explain how I'm going to go about spoiling you rotten."

"Oh, no, you don't," Harlan Patrick's father contradicted, all but snatching the baby out of his arms. "That's my job now."

"Don't fight over her," Janet chided her husband and stepson. "Honestly, you'd think the men in this family had never had an heir before, the way they carry on over every baby."

"You're just mad 'cause you're not getting a turn to fuss over her," Grandpa Harlan retorted, linking arms with his wife. "Come on, everybody. Let's go inside, so we can be comfortable."

Laurie hung back as the others climbed the steps. Harlan Patrick lingered beside her.

"Feeling better now?"

She gazed up at him, and to his amazement there were unshed tears welling up in her eyes. "They love her," she whispered. "Just like that, she's one of them."

"Well, of course she is. No matter how things stand between you and me, she's my daughter. Did you think for one second they wouldn't accept her?"

"No, but…" Her voice trailed off, and she looked away.

"But what about you?" Harlan Patrick suggested quietly. "Is that what you were going to say?"

She nodded. "They barely even looked at me."

"Darlin', that's not a reflection on you. Haven't you been around this family long enough to know that any new baby stirs everybody up? The mom and dad tend to get lost in the shuffle until the novelty wears off. Would you have preferred it if they'd laid into you right off for hiding Amy Lynn away these past months?"

"No, of course not."

"Well, then, be grateful to our little girl for taking the heat off us for the moment."

"I suppose you're right."

"I know I am. Once the questions start, you're going to wish they were back to ignoring you."

She managed a shaky smile at the reminder. "I *know* you're right about that. By the way, how's Val?"

"I left her with an ex–rodeo star."

Laurie grinned. "That ought to make her day."

"It might if he ever says more than two words to her. Slade's not the talkative type."

"That's okay," she said with a grin. "Val is. She'll have his life story out of him before he can blink."

"Now, that would be worth paying to see. He's been here two months and none of us knows more than his rodeo history and his way with horses."

"We could sneak around back and watch," Laurie suggested, gazing wistfully in that direction.

"Oh, no, you don't. We belong inside, and inside is where we're going." He captured her hand in his and found it icy cold. "Still nervous?"

"Wouldn't you be if you had to face the inquisition I do?"

"I do have to face the inquisition you do," he reminded her. "I'm not off the hook here, sweetheart. I do know one thing that might take your mind off of it, though."

"What's that?" she asked suspiciously.

"This."

He lowered his head and settled his mouth across hers. If the kiss earlier had stirred temptation, this one set off skyrockets. Nothing on earth could fire his blood the way the simple touch of Laurie's lips could. The woman's mouth was magic, soft as satin and clever as the dickens. She could turn a nothing little kiss into pure sin.

By the time the kiss ended, he was sucking in great gulps of air and trying to ease the pressure of denim on a very sensitive part of his anatomy. Every shift in movement, though, was torture.

"I want you so bad, my whole body aches with it," he murmured against her ear as he held her loosely in his arms. "Maybe we could sneak away to my place."

"Not five seconds ago you were insisting we had to go inside," she reminded him.

"That was before."

"Before what?"

"Before I remembered what it was like to feel you up against me. You could drive a man crazy."

"And that's a good thing?" she asked doubtfully.

"Oh, yeah, that is a very good thing."

"You were singing a different tune when you showed up in Montana. Chasing after me drove you crazy, and you weren't one bit happy about that."

"We're talking about two very different things here."

"Lust being one," she guessed. "And the other?"

"Life, love, getting along, whatever you want to call it."

She nodded. "I think I get it now." With that she poked him sharply in the ribs. "And I do not like it, Harlan Patrick. You're saying I make you crazy physically, so you want to sleep with me, but beyond that, I just plain drive you crazy."

"More or less," he admitted, gingerly rubbing the spot she'd punched. "Did you want me to lie about it?"

"That depends."

"On?"

She grinned at him then. "Whether you ever want to sleep with me again."

"Oh, I do, darlin'. I surely do."

"Offhand, I'd say your chances right now are about that of a snowball's in hell."

With that she whirled around and marched up the steps and into the house, leaving him to ponder the wisdom of telling the truth over uttering a more diplomatic little white lie. Short-term, the truth clearly had its drawbacks. Long-term, well, that remained to be seen, he concluded as he followed her inside.

Laurie stood in the doorway to the living room and drew in a deep breath. Half the adults were down on the floor with Amy Lynn, who appeared to be ecstatic at all the attention. The child was showing off her first teeth in a grin that had everyone cooing at her. She crawled from one new relative to another and offered smacking kisses.

"Quite the little charmer, isn't she?" Harlan Patrick said proudly.

"Like her daddy," Laurie observed with less enthusiasm.

"Seems to me she's more like her mama, enjoying being the center of attention."

"Don't start with me, Harlan Patrick."

"That wasn't a jab," he insisted.

"Sounded like one to me."

He frowned. "Does every conversation we have have to disintegrate into an argument?"

"Seems that way."

"I'm tired of it, Laurie. I'm tired of the sparring. Aren't you?"

"Yes," she conceded.

"Then let's make a pact," he suggested. "Let's declare an honest-to-God truce. Let's promise to think before we open our mouths and try not to keep hurting each other."

"I'd be happy to go along with that, if you will."

"I will," he vowed solemnly, and sketched an X across his chest. "Cross my heart."

If only she could count on him remembering that promise for longer than a minute, she thought wistfully. Harlan Patrick always said what was in his heart. It was a blessing and a curse. She never had to sort through lies and evasions, but she also had to shield herself from the sometimes brutally painful honesty.

She studied his face intently, saw the sincerity in his eyes. "I promise, too," she said just as Harlan Adams spotted her.

"Laurie, my girl, come over here and sit beside me. We have some catching up to do."

"Badgering more than likely," Harlan Patrick murmured.

She grinned. "I can handle your grandfather," she assured him, then winked. "Can you?"

"Doubtful," Harlan Patrick conceded. "Let me know how it turns out."

"Oh, no, you low-down, sneaky cowboy. This reunion was your idea. You can come along and share the heat."

"Now, that sounds downright fascinating."

"I didn't mean it that way."

"You sure? Sometimes a slip of the tongue can be very telling."

She regarded him impatiently. "Try to drag your mind out of the gutter for two seconds and come with me. I am not facing your grandfather alone."

"I thought you said you could handle him."

"I can, but I want backup."

"Sorry. I left my shotgun at home."

"I doubt guns will be called for. Just use that inimitable charm of yours to steer the conversation in some other direction if he starts asking about our intentions."

Harlan Patrick gave her a worrisome grin. "Why would I want to do that? I'm mighty interested in what you have to say on that subject myself."

"Watch your step," Laurie warned. "Or I'll tell him you'll be lucky if you're not dead by the time I head out of here tomorrow."

On that note she headed across the room leaving Harlan Patrick to amble after her. She knew he'd come, if only to protect his own hide.

"Sit right down here," Harlan Adams said, patting the place beside him on the sofa. "Boy, you can drag over one of those chairs since you evidently don't trust me to have a private conversation with your girl here."

When Harlan Patrick was settled, his grandfather turned to her. "Young lady, I have a bone to pick with you."

Laurie tensed. "What's that?"

"When you called here a few days ago, why didn't you say a word about that pretty little baby of yours?"

She breathed a sigh of relief. That was an easy one. "I wasn't sure how much you knew, or how much Harlan Patrick knew, for that matter. I figured you'd say something if you'd seen the tabloid and put two and two together."

He nodded knowingly. "That's why you called, then? You were pumping me for information?"

"Afraid so," she admitted. "I wanted to know if Harlan Patrick had seen the picture and if so, what his mood was. You told me all I needed to know when you said he'd taken off for parts unknown."

"You could have told me the truth, you know," Harlan Adams scolded.

"I didn't think it was my place," Laurie insisted. "I figured it was Harlan Patrick's news to share with his family when he saw fit."

"I suppose you're right," he agreed, then looked at his grandson. "So why didn't you tell me before you left town to go chasing after her?"

"When I left here, I was fit to be tied. All I was interested in was finding Laurie and getting at the truth myself," Harlan Patrick responded. "That's all water under the bridge now, Grandpa. The important thing is that Laurie and Amy Lynn are here now."

"For how long?"

"Until tomorrow," Laurie said, her chin lifted combatively.

"Tomorrow!" Harlan Adams exploded. "Why, that's no time at all."

"I'm in the middle of a concert tour. I wouldn't be here now if it weren't for the fact that your grandson virtually kidnapped me. I have a concert date tomorrow night in Ohio."

"And then?" the older man persisted. "Will you be back then?"

Laurie sighed. "No. There are a few more dates after that, and then I have to get back to Nashville to work on the next album."

Harlan Adams looked troubled. "I see. Your mama must be disappointed by that as much as I am."

"She's just pleased we got this unexpected chance to visit," Laurie said pointedly. "She wasn't well enough to travel when I had Amy Lynn, and since then I've been on the road so much, there was no point in dragging her along from city to city."

Harlan Patrick grinned. "And we should be grateful for stealing a few unexpected minutes with you, too, right?"

"Yes," she said succinctly.

"I have an idea," Harlan Adams said with a worrisome glint in his eyes.

"What's that, sir?"

"Why don't you leave Amy Lynn right here while you're off running around? It'll give us a chance to get to know her, and you'll have some peace of mind knowing she's well cared for while you're working."

Laurie was on her feet at once, trembling. "No, absolutely not," she said backing away. "Amy Lynn stays with me. She is my daughter. Dammit, I knew this would happen. I knew it." She glared at Harlan Patrick. "You put him up to this. I know you did."

She turned her back on the two men, crossed the room in quick, angry strides, plucked Amy Lynn off the floor and headed outside. After basking in all the attention, Amy Lynn was furious at the disruption. She began to wail as Laurie raced from the house with her clutched tightly in her arms.

Not until she was outside by the car, breathing hard, did she finally stop. Forcing back her own hysteria, she tried to soothe her daughter.

"Shh. It's okay. I'm sorry, baby. I know you were having fun. I didn't mean to scare you."

She sensed Harlan Patrick behind her even before he spoke.

"You didn't have to take off like that, you know. A simple no would have sufficed."

"Really?" she asked, whirling on him. "When has a simple no ever meant anything to an Adams? You all scramble, scratch, claw, manipulate, whatever it takes to get your way. Just like I said in there, for all I know, you put your grandfather up to that."

Despite her vow to herself that she wouldn't cry, she felt the salty sting of tears in her eyes, even as fury and frustration mounted.

"You won't get her away from me, Harlan Patrick. You won't."

"I haven't tried, have I?" he asked reasonably. "That was Grandpa Harlan's idea, not mine."

"But you'd jump at the chance to keep her here if I'd go for it, wouldn't you?"

"Well, of course I would. She's my daughter, and I barely know her. What would a few days matter, Laurie? You could pick her up after the tour ends, or I could bring her back to you in Nashville."

"No," she said again, just as forcefully.

"Why not?"

"Because…"

She looked into the eyes of this man she had known practically her whole life, a man she had loved almost that long, and tried to gauge his intentions. She couldn't, not entirely, and because of that she voiced her greatest fear.

"Because I don't know if you'd ever give her back."

Ten

As Laurie's words cut through him, Harlan Patrick had to fight the urge to shake her. How could she ever imagine that he would talk her into leaving Amy Lynn with him and then refuse to give their daughter back? How could she accuse him of even contemplating such an under-handed thing? Did she think he was capable of pulling a low-down, dirty stunt like that? Did she think he would sink to her level? That was what she had done, after all. She had kept his daughter from him. He should have thrown that in her face just to see how she liked it.

Instead, because she was holding his daughter in her arms, he battled with himself until his temper was under control, then said evenly, "If I say I will bring her back to you, then that's what I will do, Laurie. Have you ever known me to go back on my word?"

Her cheeks flushed. "No," she conceded. "But the cir-cumstances have never been like this before, either. I guess what I'm saying is that I almost wouldn't blame you if that's what you did. Isn't that exactly what I did to you?"

He was surprised by her admission, reassured somehow that she recognized the irony of the accusation she had leveled at him.

"Yes," he said mildly. "But the time for casting blame and getting even is over. What we have to do now is figure out the future and what's best for Amy Lynn."

She seemed to clutch their daughter a little more tightly. "What's best for Amy Lynn is not to have her life disrupted. She's always been with me. What would she think if I just vanished, even for a few days? I don't want her thinking I abandoned her. I know what that's like all too well."

"Let Val stay, too. That would give Amy Lynn a sense of continuity. It might also reassure you that I won't be able to get away with stealing her right out from under you. Val would have my hide first."

"I can't," she protested. "I need Val with me. There are endless details she needs to see to when I'm on tour. I'd be lost without her."

It was this intransigence that had kept them apart all these years. "Come on, Laurie. Work with me. Compromise. Val is the queen of long distance. She can make things happen from anywhere. She doesn't have to be glued to your side."

He could see from her expression that she was struggling with herself, wanting to do what was right and fair, but terrified of choosing wrong.

"I'll think about it," she said finally. "That's the best I can do."

"Talk to Val. See what she says," he urged.

"This isn't about Val, dammit. It's about Amy Lynn," she said as she struggled to hang on to the increasingly restless baby.

Harlan Patrick forced a smile for his whimpering, frustrated daughter, then met Laurie's gaze evenly. "It's also about trust, isn't it? It's about whether or not you really trust me to keep my word."

"Yes," she agreed.

"I never broke my word," he reminded her. "You did."

And then he turned and walked away before he said a whole lot more, before he lashed out with bitter words he might never be able to take back.

Gently bouncing Amy Lynn in her arms, Laurie stayed where she was and watched Harlan Patrick leave. Funny, she hadn't realized just how badly it hurt to be left behind, to have the person she loved turn his back on her. Sure, this was only an argument, a faint blip on the canvas of their relationship, but she felt as empty and lost as if he'd gone for good.

Was that how he'd felt when she'd gone? Or had it been a thousand times worse, knowing that she had no intention of coming back again? She realized suddenly that it hadn't been the same for her. Though she had missed Harlan Patrick desperately, especially in the first months after leaving, she had been excited by the future, challenged just to survive. She had been moving on, while he had stayed behind.

"Everything okay?" a feminine voice asked gently.

Laurie turned from the direction in which Harlan Patrick had gone to find his mother standing quietly behind her.

Melissa Adams was a fiercely protective woman who loved her husband and children with all her heart. She had also been strong enough to stand up to Cody Adams years earlier and refuse to marry him even though she had his child—Sharon Lynn—until she knew for sure that Cody truly loved her. In some ways her circumstances back then were not unlike Laurie's now. The difference was that Cody was the one who'd left Texas not knowing that he was about to become a father, while Laurie had walked away from Harlan Patrick.

"I suppose it depends on your definition of *okay*," Laurie said wearily. "He's furious with me."

"Because you don't want to leave your daughter behind tomorrow when you go?"

"That, and because I left in the first place, because I wouldn't marry him years ago and settle down as a rancher's wife."

"You did what you had to do," Melissa Adams stated.

Laurie stared at her in surprise. "You can see that?"

"Well, of course I can," she said with a hint of impatience. "He put you in a terrible position by forcing you to choose."

"I never wanted to make that choice," Laurie added. "It was like having to decide whether to keep my right arm or my left."

Melissa smiled at the analogy. "I imagine it was."

"I always thought we could work it out. Foolish me," Laurie said. "I knew the man was stubborn, but I also thought he loved me enough to want what was best for me."

"Come over here and sit with me," Melissa said, leading her to a grouping of chairs in the shade of a tree. "You have to understand something about Harlan Patrick. As hard as his daddy and I tried to avoid it, he grew up knowing that the world was his for the asking. You can thank his granddaddy for that. Harlan thinks the sun rises and sets on his family. It doesn't mean he doesn't see their flaws. Goodness knows, he does. He just leads each and every one of them to believe he can have it all. When it doesn't work out that way, it's always a huge surprise."

She chuckled. "You should have seen Cody's face the

first time I told him no. You'd have thought I hit him with a two-by-four."

Laurie found herself grinning. "I can imagine."

"Harlan Patrick took it even worse when you said no," Melissa said quietly. "It came close to breaking my heart to see him hurting so. I hated you for that, but that doesn't mean I couldn't see that you were doing what you needed to do. You have a gift from God with that voice of yours. It's your right, maybe even your duty, to do what you can with it, to see how far it can take you."

"I need to sing," Laurie said, grateful for even this much understanding. She tried to explain why that need was a match for her love for Melissa Adams's son. "I need to know that I'm good enough, that I can stand on my own two feet. My mother never had that. Once my father walked out, every single day of her life was a struggle. I never wanted to be that dependent on anyone. Music seemed to be the answer. If I hadn't had a decent voice, I would have chosen something else, but I would have had a career of my own."

"Have you ever explained that to my son?"

Laurie paused thoughtfully, realizing that she'd always just assumed he knew. "Not in so many words, no."

"Maybe you should."

"It wouldn't change anything. I'd still have to go, and he'd still have to stay."

"But at least he'd understand that you're not just leaving him. Tell him, Laurie. Don't let him go on thinking that he's the one who's not good enough."

Laurie was shocked by Melissa's words. "Not good enough? How could he possibly believe that?"

"Because you left him behind." She regarded Laurie sympathetically. "If you go again and take his daughter, you'll just be adding to his sense of failure. You'll be telling him you don't think he's good enough to be a daddy, either. Please, Laurie, talk to him. Do whatever you think is right about Amy Lynn, but talk to Harlan Patrick."

Laurie squeezed the older woman's hand. "I will. I promise. It was never my intention to make him think he wasn't good enough. It was about me and what I needed."

"Let me take Amy Lynn back inside, then, and you go find him," Melissa suggested. "The two of you need some time alone together to make peace."

After a moment's hesitation, Laurie shifted Amy Lynn into Melissa's waiting arms.

"Take all the time you need," the older woman said. "She'll be fine with us." She gazed straight into Laurie's eyes. "And she'll be right here whenever you come looking for her. I promise."

"Thank you," Laurie whispered in a choked voice. "Not just for taking Amy Lynn. For this talk, for understanding, for everything."

"You're more than welcome. Remember, it's my son's happiness that's at stake here, too. I have a vested interest in the outcome."

Melissa headed toward the house, then turned back. "I suspect you'll find him down by the creek. It's where he always goes when he needs to think."

Laurie smiled. "I remember."

The creek was close enough to walk to, far enough away to give her time to think. Unfortunately it could have been at the ends of the earth and it wouldn't have been far enough for her to reach any conclusions about what she should do about the future or even about leaving Amy Lynn behind for a few days.

She'd spotted Val out by the paddock, engaging in a one-sided conversation with the rodeo star. Amused, she had concluded that her assistant very well might not mind being left behind along with Amy Lynn. She could use a new challenge in her life, a personal challenge, rather than the logistical kind Laurie presented her with every day. It was evident from her nonstop chatter in the face of his unsmiling demeanor that Val considered the cowboy a challenge.

Even so, Laurie wasn't sure she could walk away from her baby even for the few days remaining in the tour.

So, she concluded, she would continue to weigh the option, just as she had promised Harlan Patrick she would. In less than twenty-four hours she would have to make her decision. Something told her it wouldn't come any sooner, either.

As she reached the stand of cottonwoods along the edge of the creek, she spotted Harlan Patrick, leaning back against the trunk of one of them, his Stetson tilted down over his eyes. Even in repose, there was a tension evident in the set of his shoulders, in the grim line of his mouth.

She eased up beside him and settled down on the ground just inches away.

"You asleep?" she inquired when he didn't move so much as a muscle.

"No."

"Thinking?"

"Not if I can help it."

"What, then?"

"Trying to blank it all out, trying to pretend that you and I haven't come to this."

"Pretending doesn't help much, does it?"

"It might if it worked," he grumbled. "Can't say it's ever worked for me."

She thought of what his mother had said and made up her mind to tell him everything that had driven her away from Los Piños, away from Texas, away from him.

"Can I tell you something?"

He tilted his hat brim up and slanted a look at her. "I'm not going anywhere."

She tried to find a starting point, but had to go back a long way to find it. "Do you remember when my daddy left?"

He regarded her with surprise. "Your daddy? No, I can't say that I do."

"I do, Harlan Patrick. I remember it as vividly as if it were yesterday, and I was only four years old at the time. He and my mama fought that night. I could hear them from my room, the loud, angry voices, bitter accusations that I couldn't understand. To this day I don't know what the fight was about, just that it ended everything. When it was over, the front door slammed and, just like that, he was gone right out of our lives. He never came back." Hot tears welled up, then spilled down her cheeks. "He never even said goodbye."

Even now the memory was enough to make her ache inside. Loneliness and fear all but swamped her, but as bad as it was, all these years later it was only a sad echo of how terrible it had been back then.

"I'm sorry," Harlan Patrick said. "You never talked much about him."

"I couldn't. It hurt too much." Swiping angrily at the tears, she glanced over and met his gaze. "But you know what hurt even more?"

"What?"

"Watching what it did to my mama, what it did to our lives. We never had a secure day after that, not financially, not emotionally. I was always terrified that she would leave the same way he did, out of the blue, when I least expected it. I was scared that we'd run out of money and be thrown out of our home. And you know what else that did to me? I vowed then and there that I would never, ever be in that position."

"You had me, Laurie. You knew I would never desert you, that you'd always have everything you ever wanted."

"That was later. Besides, don't you see, my mama thought that about my daddy once, too. Look what happened to them. To me that meant that the only person you could really count on was yourself. That's why I went to Nashville. That's why I fought so hard to make it as a singer. I didn't leave you, Harlan Patrick. I went after the dream of what I could be, what I *needed* to be to make the fears go away."

He reached for her then, gathered her into his arms. "Oh, baby, why didn't you ever tell me this before?"

"I did. At least, I thought I had. I thought you knew everything there was to know about me. It wasn't until today that I realized that it wasn't a fair assumption."

"I should have known," he agreed softly with her head tucked against his shoulder. "I should have been able to see into your heart."

"Maybe neither one of us understood that even between the closest of friends, sometimes you have to say the words and not leave anything to chance." She reached up and touched his face, tracing the familiar angles and planes. "I love you, Harlan Patrick. Please, don't ever doubt that. I loved you then and I love you now."

As she spoke, she felt the splash of a teardrop against her fingers and realized that her brave, fiercely strong cowboy was crying. "Oh, Harlan Patrick," she whispered brokenly. "Don't. Please, don't cry over me."

"Darlin', I never cry," he said, his voice husky.

Smiling at the predictable denial, she rose to her knees and knelt facing him. She cupped his cheeks in her hands, then brushed her lips across the salty dampness on his skin. When she claimed his mouth, he moaned softly, then dragged her against him, his hands swift and sure as they roved intimately over her.

Like a summer brushfire, need exploded between them. Memories that needed refreshing responded to each caress as if it were new. His touch was impatient, inflaming her with its urgency. With her breath already coming in ragged gasps and her blood racing, she clasped his hands and held them tightly.

"Wait," she pleaded.

He stilled at once, but there was torment in his eyes as they clashed with hers. "Wait?"

"Slow down. That's all. Just slow down. It's been a long time, Harlan Patrick. I want to savor every second."

He grinned and reached for her again. "Couldn't we hurry now and savor later?"

"Oh, no," she said, slapping away his hands, then reaching for the buttons on his shirt. "You just sit still and leave this to me."

That drew a spark of interest. "Leave it to you, huh? Sounds fascinating." He locked his hands behind his neck and relaxed back against the tree. "Do your worst, woman."

She chuckled. "Oh, I promise you, it will be very clever and it will be my best, not my worst." The first button on his shirt popped free, exposing a V of bare flesh with just a hint of wiry dark hair. She pressed a kiss to the spot, noticing that his skin was feverishly hot already. The pulse at the base of his neck leaped.

"Promising," she assessed, grinning at him.

The next button opened and then the next, exposing more and more of that wide, sexy chest for her increasingly inventive kisses. Oh, how she had missed this. She had missed the tenderness, the laughter and intimacy, the sensual games that only two people who loved and trusted could play.

When she reached the last button above his belt buckle, she tugged the remainder of the shirt free, then dropped a daring kiss on the bared skin where dark hair arrowed down toward the evidence of his arousal. He jolted at that and clasped her shoulders tightly.

"Careful, sweetheart. You're starting to take risks."

"I thought you were a man who liked to live on the edge."

"Not me. I'm just a stay-at-home, old-fashioned kind of guy."

With her fingers already at work on his buckle, she hesitated at the description. It cut a little too close to reality, when she was trying to recapture the fantasy.

"Need some help with that?" he asked, obviously unaware of the alarms his words had set off.

She drew in a deep breath, then shook her head. "Nope. I've done this before, you see."

"Not with anyone else, I trust," he said lightly.

She lifted her gaze to meet his and realized that despite the joking tone, the question was dead serious. "Never with anyone else," she said softly. "Only with you, Harlan Patrick."

There were plenty of men in her new world, record-company executives, fans, actors. She had thought about some of them, wished she could fall in love with one of them, wished she could want them as she wanted the man she'd left behind in Texas, but Harlan Patrick had always been right there in her head and in her heart. She sang about one-and-only loves a lot, because she had found hers years ago.

"Only with you," she repeated as she slowly slid down the zipper of his jeans and reached for him.

At the glide of her fingers across his arousal, he gasped and reached for her wrists, cuffing them with a grip that stilled any movement.

"Okay, darlin', you've had your fun," he said. "Now it's my turn."

"But I was just getting started," she protested, laughing at his refusal to leave her in control.

"And now I am," he countered.

Before she knew it, he had flipped her over until she rested beneath him on the soft, sweet grass. Somehow he managed to keep her hands neatly immobilized above her head, while his free hand began its own magical journey over fabric, resulting in chafing caresses that left her skin sensitive and burning. He didn't waste time on finesse. When he wanted to touch bare skin, buttons popped, scattering everywhere. Her bra clasp was dismissed as easily, and then his tongue was soothing the very skin he'd inflamed only seconds before.

Her nipples ached with the pleasure of it, and that was even before he took each one into his mouth and sucked, sending waves of delight rippling through her. Her hips, pinned to the ground by the weight of him, bucked ever so slightly, causing yet another delicious friction.

"We've still got on too damned many clothes," Harlan Patrick murmured in frustration, freeing her hands so he could use both of his to dispense first with his own clothes and then hers.

When she was naked, the soft, sultry breeze kissed her skin and made her nipples pucker just as his touches had.

"You are the most gorgeous creature God ever made,"

Harlan Patrick said, his heated gaze studying her as if she were brand-new to him.

"I have stretch marks," she protested.

"From carrying my baby," he said, touching the faint white marks on her belly with gentle reverence. "That only makes you more beautiful."

She grinned. "How could any woman not love you? You always know the right thing to say."

"I always tell the truth," he insisted.

"Truth or the view through rose-colored glasses, I appreciate it," she said.

Even though she was the one who'd urged a slower pace, she reached out to stroke him in a gesture guaranteed to shock him into action.

"Now who's impatient?" he taunted.

"Please, Harlan Patrick, make love to me. Make love to me now."

"With pleasure, darlin'. With pleasure."

With the wicked skill of someone who knew her body intimately, he skimmed touches over perspiration-slick flesh, then dipped into the moist folds at the apex of her thighs, finding the tiny nub that sent her off into rippling waves of ecstasy.

Only then, when she was still trembling in the aftershocks, did he part her legs and ever so slowly enter her. The reunion was a stunningly sweet reminder of the past, a swirl of present-tense sensations and then an urgent journey into the future.

Past, present, future—love was there for all of it, making the throbbing tension and exquisite release seem unique to this moment, even as it echoed a haunting familiarity and held the promise of unending repetition.

Curved securely into Harlan Patrick's arms, Laurie

wanted to believe in now and forever. She wanted the fantasy to last, but in no time at all reality intruded.

"Marry me," Harlan Patrick whispered, his hand resting against the curve of her breast, his voice thick with need. "Marry me, Laurie."

This time it was her tears that fell, splashing against his bare skin as her heart split in two yet again.

"I can't," she said, her voice choked. "Haven't you heard anything I've said? It wouldn't work."

"How can you say that? We're perfect together. We've always belonged together."

Icy cold and trembling, she pulled away and began frantically gathering her clothes, yanking them on with haphazard abandon until she was dressed, but still quivering in front of him. When she couldn't get her blouse closed because of the missing buttons, he silently handed her his shirt. She put it on, then tied the ends with trembling fingers.

"Explain it to me, Laurie. Tell me why it won't work, when we're so good together."

"Like this, we're perfect together," she agreed. "But the rest?" She gave an impatient, all-encompassing wave of her hand. "It hasn't changed, Harlan Patrick. I'm going back on tour tomorrow and you're staying here."

His mouth firmed into a grim line. "I'll get used to being separated."

"You won't."

"Then I'll come along."

"You'd hate that even more. And before too long, you'd hate me, too." She bent down and touched his lips one last time. "You know I'm right. In your heart, you know it."

Scooping up clothes, she left before he could counter that, but she'd gone only a few paces when she realized that he hadn't even tried.

Eleven

Harlan Patrick was mad enough to tear the whole blasted ranch apart, to say nothing of what he'd like to do to Laurie. How could the woman make sweet, passionate love to him one second and then walk away from him the next? It was insulting, demeaning.

Then again, he ought to be used to it. She'd done it often enough to be downright skilled at it, and he ought to be smart enough by now not to be taken by surprise.

While he wrestled with the black mood she'd left him in, he took his time walking back to the main house. Even though he had no desire to face Laurie again anytime soon, he had every intention of sticking as close as possible to his daughter. If Laurie refused to relent and leave Amy Lynn at White Pines while she finished her concert tour, then he was going right back on the road with her. It gave him a great deal of satisfaction to know that she was really, really going to hate that.

He was almost back to the main house when he crossed paths with one very surly, out-of-sorts Slade Sutton.

"Keep that woman away from me," the hand said, squaring off in front of him defiantly.

Even with his own problems fresh in his mind, Harlan Patrick couldn't stop the grin that tugged at his mouth. "Problems with Val?"

"She never shuts up." Slade scowled. "Next time you invite somebody out here who needs baby-sitting, get somebody else. I'm here to work with the horses. You decide to change the job description, I'm outta here."

There was little doubt he was serious about it, too, Harlan Patrick concluded. Val must have proved herself to be a real handful. Trying not to let his enjoyment of the situation show, he said, "I figured you'd be so used to breaking fractious horses that one little old filly wouldn't give you a moment's trouble."

"She's not a horse. She's a blasted nuisance," Slade growled, and stalked away.

Harlan Patrick hooted as he watched him go. "Made quite an impression, did she?" he commented under his breath. "I'll have to see what I can do about getting her back here."

He chuckled at the devious schemes already forming in his mind and concluded that there was a whole lot more of his granddaddy in him than he had ever realized. Matching the cantankerous former rodeo star with Val had been a stroke of genius. In fact, it might be the only good thing to come out of this whole damnable trip to White Pines.

In the midst of his laughter, he paused thoughtfully. If Val had a reason to want to spend more time in Texas, she was exactly the kind of woman who'd find a way to make it work. And if *Val* could make it work, wouldn't Laurie begin to see the possibilities, as well? It was something that bore thinking about, he concluded, and he would do just that, right after he made sure she hadn't stolen his pickup and hauled his daughter back into town or straight on up to Ohio and her next concert date.

To his relief he found Laurie inside, Amy Lynn sound asleep in her arms. The two of them were still surrounded by family. Val had joined them at last but was sitting by herself on the fringes, clearly trying to remain unobtrusive. Harlan Patrick went over and pulled a chair up beside her.

"How'd your tour of the ranch go?" he inquired innocently.

She shot him a wry look. "What tour? I could tell you exactly how long it takes to clean a horse's hooves. I could tell you exactly what shade of red Slade Sutton's neck turns when he's given a compliment. I could even tell you how much feed each horse gets. All of this is from my own personal observation, by the way. Mr. Sutton doesn't have a lot to say. And beyond the stables, this place remains a mystery."

That was pretty much what Harlan Patrick had expected. "And Slade?" he inquired.

"What about him?" she asked with a telltale touch of color in her cheeks.

"Does he remain a mystery?"

"Pretty much." She slanted a curious look at him. "What do you know about him?"

"Probably not much more than you."

"He works for you. Didn't he come with a resumé?"

"Of course, but believe me, it was very succinct and focused almost exclusively on what he knows about horses. In the end those were the only qualifications we cared about."

"How'd he get the limp?"

"A rodeo accident, I suppose. As long as he can do the

job, I saw no point in probing into how it happened. Besides he's made it clear he doesn't want to talk about it."

She grinned at that. "He doesn't want to talk about anything."

"You didn't let a little thing like that put you off, did you?"

"Of course not. I considered it my duty to try to get one entire sentence out of him, something beyond *yup* and *nope*, that is."

"And did you?"

"Eventually."

"What did he say?"

"'I'm going to the bunkhouse now,'" she reported, then sighed. "Not exactly what I'd hoped for."

Harlan Patrick chuckled. "He didn't invite you along, did he?"

"Oh, no. He all but shoved me toward the main house." Her eyes sparkled with indignation. "I could have been insulted."

"But you weren't?"

She shrugged. "It takes a lot more than that to rattle my chains. It just made me more curious."

"Too bad you don't have longer to try to figure out what makes him tick," Harlan Patrick suggested slyly.

She gave him an amused, knowing look. "Oh, something tells me I'll be back here before too long. And when I am, Slade Sutton doesn't stand a chance. I haven't run across a challenge like that man in a very long time."

Bingo, Harlan Patrick thought triumphantly. He glanced over toward Laurie and found her gaze on him. She looked away at once, but not before he caught the bleak expression in her eyes.

What on earth was she thinking? he wondered, then

realized he'd caught her looking at him just that way on
the tour bus when he and Val had been huddled together
making the plans for this trip. Was it possible that she was
jealous of the friendship he and her assistant were forming? Surely not.

Then again, if she was, if she didn't grasp even now
how totally and thoroughly committed he was to her,
maybe he could make the insecurity work to his advantage, too.

He settled back and pondered how to go about it. Maybe
he should make a point of inviting Val back to White Pines
for a visit in Laurie's hearing. Val wouldn't mistake the
invitation for anything other than another chance to try
to unravel the mystery of Slade Sutton, but Laurie? Who
knew what she might make of it? Maybe it would shake
her if she thought there was a chance she was going to lose
him to a woman who had no hesitations at all about making the same choice that Laurie herself refused to make.

Was the plan devious? Of course. Would anybody get
hurt? No one he could think of. Was it risky? Wasn't just
about everything?

But on the chance it could work, it was a gamble he
was more than willing to take. He intended to get Laurie
to realize that they were meant to be together, no matter
what it took, no matter how many obstacles had to be over-
come. He just prayed his imagination was up to the task.

Tired of the pointed questions being asked about her
plans for the future, Laurie broke free from her conversation with Sharon Lynn and went in search of Harlan
Patrick, praying she wouldn't find him off somewhere
with Val. She had no idea what sort of bond those two
had formed, but she wasn't crazy about it. They'd already

hatched up one kidnapping scheme. Who knew what they would come up with next.

She found Harlan Patrick outside—alone, thankfully—and joined him.

"I'd like to get back into town," she said stiffly. "I want to spend a little more time with my mother before we leave tomorrow."

He slanted a skeptical look at her. "Is that it? Or are you just anxious to get away from my family? Are they getting to you, Laurie? Are you beginning to feel guilty about keeping Amy Lynn from them and from me?"

"I've always felt guilty about that," she retorted candidly. "But I did what I thought was best at the time and, frankly, I'm sick to death of apologizing for it. What's done is done, Harlan Patrick. I can't change it, and I won't let you use it to blackmail me into giving you your way."

"Is that what I'm doing?"

"Of course it is. You tried threats and that didn't work. You tried charm, and that didn't work either. You've even tried sex. Now you're letting your whole family gang up on me. I'm sick to death of it." Tears threatened, but she refused to shed them, blinking rapidly to keep her eyes dry.

He looked about ready to explode. "Do you honestly think that's why I made love to you?" He threw up his hands. "Forget it. Let's say that I did. Have you even once considered that I am trying all those things because this is too important for me not to use every weapon I can think of to get your attention?"

"It's not a war, dammit."

His gaze, as serious as she'd ever seen it, met hers evenly. "It is to me. I'm fighting to hold on to my family."

She swallowed hard at that, but she didn't relent. She couldn't. "We're not your family, Harlan Patrick."

"Like it or not, darlin', Amy Lynn is my daughter. Around here that's about as close a family tie as you can have. I'll do whatever I have to, Laurie. My first choice would be to marry you, but you don't seem to want anything to do with that. Since that's the case, I have to consider my other options."

She regarded him worriedly. "What options?"

"I haven't settled on any yet. When I do, you'll be the first to know."

"Is that a threat of some kind?"

"You can take it any way you like."

She studied his intractable expression and sighed. "Have we really come to this?"

"Apparently," he said with evident regret. "Just remember one thing, Laurie. It was your choice, not mine."

She started to argue, but there seemed to be little point to going another round with him. He had his opinion about where the fault lay. She had hers. In the end it probably didn't even matter. All that really counted was that they were at an impasse. Again.

"Will you drive us back to town now? Or should I ask Justin? He and Patsy don't live all that far from my mom. I'm sure he'd love to have twenty uninterrupted minutes to get his two cents in. He's been scowling at me ever since he got here. Seeing that gun strapped to his waist and that badge of his gives me the jitters."

Harlan Patrick actually grinned at that. "It pretty much had the same effect on me at first, but I'm getting used to it. I'm starting to enjoy tormenting him. As for giving you a lift, I'm sure he'd be delighted to, but there's no need. When the time comes, I'll take you."

He started to reach out, almost tangled his fingers in her hair, in fact, but then to her relief he drew back.

"We'll go right after dinner."

She balked at the delay. "I said I wanted to go now."

"We don't always get what we want in life, do we? You've certainly made up your mind to see that I don't."

"And this is payback?"

"Oh, no, darlin'. When payback comes, you'll recognize it right off. This is about my grandfather and the fact that he's already got the grill fired up and he's planning a big ol' barbecue to welcome you back into the fold. I don't want him to be disappointed."

If it was a ruse, it was a clever one. He knew she would never do anything to openly defy his grandfather's wishes. Harlan Adams had been too kind to her over the years.

"Fine," she said tightly. "After dinner, then."

"And just to show you that I am a reasonable man, I will have someone pick up your mom and bring her out here to join us. How about that?"

Relieved at the prospect of having an ally at last, she nodded. "That would be wonderful. Thank you."

"I'll go and make the arrangements, then."

She watched him go, hating that there was such tension and bitterness between them. Conversations were either stiff and awkward or they rapidly disintegrated into fights. Once they had shared everything, talked for hours, laughed together over the silliest things.

It had almost been easier before they'd made love. Now, knowing that the chemistry hadn't died, it was more difficult than ever to accept that love just wasn't enough.

"You still love him, don't you?" Val asked, joining her on the porch. "I can see it in your eyes."

"No, of course not," Laurie denied. "It was over a long time ago."

"Right. That explains why you came back here wearing

his shirt and without a single button on your blouse. I saw it all knotted up and stuffed in your bag. That story about falling in the creek didn't quite ring true since your pants weren't the least little bit damp. I like the little midriff effect you tried so it wouldn't look quite so much like Harlan Patrick's shirt. Some people might never guess what happened. Of course, none of those people are inside."

Laurie groaned. "They know?"

"They're not blind. If the blouse hadn't been a dead giveaway, the color in your cheeks would have been." She studied Laurie intently. "Are you crazy? The man worships you. Why are you making things so difficult for him? Is there something I'm missing?"

"How many times do I have to explain that this isn't about Harlan Patrick? For that matter, why do I have to explain anything to you? You work for me."

The color drained out of Val's face. "I thought I was also your friend," she said quietly. "My mistake."

She started to leave, but before she could go, Laurie caught her arm. "I'm sorry. I didn't mean that the way it sounded. You know you're more than an employee. I don't know what I'd have done without you the last couple of years. You're the best friend a woman could ever have."

"May I make a suggestion, then?"

"Of course."

"You might want to get a lawyer."

Shocked, Laurie stared at her. She could feel the blood draining out of her face. "Why do you say that?"

"My impression of this family is that they fight fair, but they fight to win. Unless you and Harlan Patrick reach some sort of compromise about your daughter, I'd guess that he'll have you in court so fast, it'll make your head swim."

"Has he said that?" Laurie demanded. "Is that what the two of you have been huddling about? Has he been making threats?"

"No, our conversations have been about Slade mostly."

"Then why would you say something like that? How did he get you on his side?"

"I'm not on his side," Val said patiently. "But Laurie, wake up. Face facts. You're keeping his daughter away from him. He's suggested you let her stay here while you finish your tour. You said no. He's asked you to marry him. You've said no."

"How do you know all that?"

"I listen. In this crowd it doesn't take long for word to get around." She regarded Laurie intently. "How long do you think it's going to be before he tires of taking no for an answer and sets his own agenda?"

The truth was he had already hinted at it more than once. She'd even asked him about veiled threats earlier, but he'd denied he was making any. "What should I do?"

"Work it out. Be reasonable. Now, personally, if it were me and I had a guy like him that crazy about me, I'd be at the courthouse taking out a wedding license, but that's me."

"He knows why I can't marry him," Laurie said defensively.

"No, he knows why you won't marry him," Val corrected. "If you wanted to make it work, you could."

When Laurie started to protest, Val held up her hand. "Never mind. It's between the two of you. I'm butting out."

"That'll be a first."

"Well, it may not last, so be grateful for now." She grinned. "As for me, I think I'll take a little stroll down by the bunkhouse."

Laurie regarded her with amusement. "Slade wouldn't be down there, by any chance?"

"Could be."

"Since when do you go chasing after a man?"

"Believe me," Val said ruefully, "this one will not come chasing after me. I'm compromising. You might want to watch. It's easier than you think."

"Very amusing."

"I meant it to be instructive."

Val had walked about ten yards when Laurie realized that she was no longer wearing the sneakers she'd borrowed and put on earlier. She'd changed back to a more typical pair of slinky, totally inappropriate high heels. Laurie was pretty sure she knew why.

"Hey, Val, be careful. You're wobbling," she taunted.

"I am not wobbling. I've been walking in heels my entire life," Val called back.

"Not on a ranch. What happened to your sneakers?"

Val grinned. "They don't do nearly as much for my legs."

"I hope he's worth breaking your neck for."

"That remains to be seen."

Laurie watched her go, struggling between amusement and wistfulness. There had been a time when she had been just as giddy, just as eager to impress Harlan Patrick. For a little while earlier, she had recaptured that feeling by being in his arms again. All of those old yearnings had rushed through her, reminding her that once there had been a period of innocent belief that they could conquer anything.

As she walked back toward the house, she saw her mother emerging from a car along with Justin's wife, Patsy, and her son, Billy. Billy went racing off on sturdy little legs to join the other children crowding around their great-grandfather on the patio. Laurie went to meet her mother.

"Hey, Mom, I'm glad you came."

As Laurie linked arms with her mother, she smiled at Patsy, who appeared to be about fifteen months pregnant. "Thanks for bringing my mom out." Gesturing toward Patsy's huge belly, she asked, "When are you due?"

"Any day now, thank God. I'm not sure I'll be able to haul myself up out of a chair if I get any bigger. Justin's threatened to keep the town tow truck handy in case I get too big for him to manage."

"You should have seen me at nine months," Laurie said. "I felt like a blimp. I knew no baby on earth could weigh that much, which meant I was going to have a devil of a time losing the excess weight. Staying in seclusion meant I had way too much time on my hands to eat."

Laurie's mother interrupted. "I'm going to leave you two girls to talk about babies. I want to say hello to Harlan and Janet and thank them for including me."

She left before Laurie could protest. She glanced at Patsy, who was studying her enviously. She expected some sort of remark about her choice to stay in seclusion to keep her pregnancy a secret from Harlan Patrick.

Instead, Patsy said, "Obviously you didn't have any trouble with getting the weight off again. You're gorgeous. Practically skinny, in fact. How'd you do it?"

"I brought in a personal trainer and set up a gym. The man had no mercy."

Patsy sighed. "Well, I'm afraid a trainer's out of the question on our budget. I guess I'll have to get back in shape the old-fashioned way, by chasing after the kids and starving myself to death."

Laurie decided then and there that she would send her

trainer on an extended trip to Los Piños as her baby present to Patsy. The man could work miracles in a month. Faster if he hated being stuck in what he was likely to consider the middle of nowhere.

"Don't worry about a thing," she told Patsy, making a mental note to have Val call the trainer in the morning and make the arrangements. "You'll do just fine. You did after Billy was born, didn't you?"

"I never got this huge with Billy. Will wasn't around the way Justin has been. Justin hovers. If I don't have a glass of milk in my hand and snacks in front of me, he's certain the baby will be undernourished. The man is driving me crazy."

"Better you than me," Laurie murmured.

Patsy grinned. "I heard that. Has he been giving you a rough time?"

"No more than anyone else around here. I can't blame them, though. They just care about Harlan Patrick."

"And about you and Amy Lynn," Patsy insisted. "That's the way this family is. They take everyone in if they know that a family member cares about them. They did with me."

"But I'm not playing by the rules. I'm leaving again."

"Doesn't matter," Patsy insisted. "You're the mother of a great-grandbaby." She gave Laurie's hand a squeeze. "Around here that's all that counts."

"There you are," Justin said, walking toward them with a plate of appetizers in his hand. Pretty much ignoring Laurie, he shoved the plate under his wife's nose. "Try a little of this. It's your favorite cheese."

Patsy gave Laurie a weary grin. "See what I mean." She ignored the plate and started away from him. "Justin, I'm not hungry. I'm saving room for steak."

"One little bite," he encouraged, trailing after her.

Laurie's gaze followed them wistfully. She would have given anything to have had Harlan Patrick doting on her during her pregnancy.

But she had handled that time on her own, too. It had proved once and for all that she could cope with any curves life tossed her way, reassuring her that she would always be in control of her own destiny.

It was ironic, she supposed. She had proved to herself that she needed no one to survive, even to thrive, but rather than feeling triumphant, all she could think about these days was how very lonely she had been before Harlan Patrick had reappeared in that Montana nightclub.

Twelve

The barbecue was pure torment. Harlan Patrick retreated to the paddock with a cigarette he'd bummed from Slade. To his surprise the hand had been coaxed into joining the family—apparently by the very woman he'd protested vehemently that he wanted nowhere near him. Val had been looking especially pleased with herself all evening. Harlan Patrick was glad somebody's romance looked promising.

He hitched himself up on the split-rail fence and tried not to light the cigarette or to think about Laurie. The last time he'd seen her she'd been telling stories about the country music business and the sometimes overzealous fans. She'd looked so alive, almost as alive as she'd been in his arms down by the creek that afternoon.

How could he even think about asking her to give up something that obviously brought her so much joy? How could he compete at all with the adulation of millions of fans? He was just one cowboy out of thousands who fantasized about her.

As he sat on the railing, he heard someone begin to strum a guitar. It might even have been his father, who professed to have musical talents, but sure as heck couldn't carry a tune. Harlan Patrick's heart clenched in anticipation. He knew it wouldn't take long once the music started for someone to coax Laurie into singing.

Sure enough, that low, sexy voice of hers caught on a breeze and carried to where he sat. It was a new song, one he hadn't heard before, and it was gut-wrenching, another surefire hit. Despite his instincts for self-preservation, he tossed aside the still unlit cigarette in disgust and began moving back toward the patio where everyone was gathered.

A security floodlight at the end of the patio bathed Laurie in a silvery glow as flattering as any spotlight. She had the guitar now, and her eyes were closed as she sang about lost love and past mistakes. Harlan Patrick had the feeling she was singing about the two of them, which made it all the harder to bear when the lovers in the song parted one last time.

As the last notes died, he was drawn to her side.

"That was beautiful," he said in a quiet voice not meant to be heard over the family's enthusiastic applause and catcalls. "A new song?"

Her gaze met his, and the rest of the crowd seemed to disappear.

"I've been working on it for a while now."

"That ending's a real tearjerker."

She shot him a knowing look. "It's the way it had to be."

His heart seemed to slow to a stop. "Then you don't see any way to change it?"

"Not offhand. Do you?"

He held out his hand. "Dance with me."

She glanced around. "There's no music."

"I can fix that. Come with me." When she hesitated, he grinned. "Dare you."

Her eyes sparkled with a hundred shared memories of

the mischief those two words had gotten them into. After another moment's hesitation, she slipped her hand trustingly into his and went with him. He picked one of her CDs from a whole stack inside and slid it into the player, then turned the volume down low. This was for the two of them and no one else.

"We're not going back outside?" she asked.

"Scared to be alone with me, Laurie?"

"Of course not."

He tugged her gently into his arms. "Good. 'Cause I want you all to myself right now. Just you and me and this music that's so all-fired important to you."

She started to pull away, but he held her close. "That wasn't a put-down."

"It sounded like one."

"You know me, darlin'—sometimes I'm not as good with words as you are."

"Oh, please," she retorted impatiently. "Nobody in Texas is better at a turn of phrase than you, Harlan Patrick. That's why women fall all over themselves chasing after you."

"Maybe I should try my hand at writing songs, then," he suggested in jest.

She regarded him evenly, clearly taking the idea far more seriously than he'd intended. "Maybe you should."

"I'd be lousy at it."

"Why do you say that?"

"Because I'd be writing them with happy endings."

She sighed and rested her head against his chest. "You're right. You are the ultimate romantic."

He was amused by the wistful note in her voice. "Why is it that I have to fall for the only woman on earth who'd consider that a bad thing?"

"It's not a bad thing. It's just not very practical, especially in my line of work. Nothing sells better than a good ol' song about love gone wrong."

He pulled back and regarded her curiously. "Is that why you're so dead set on keeping us apart? Are you afraid if you and I have a happy ending, you'll lose your touch?"

She stared at him, clearly shocked by the suggestion. "Don't be ridiculous. I'm not turning myself inside out just so I can be inspired to write another song with a sad ending. People write about all sorts of things without having to live them. A decent mystery writer doesn't have to gun somebody down to write about it."

"You sound a little defensive. Are you so sure you're not just the teensiest bit worried that loving me will ruin your way with a lovesick turn of phrase?" he asked, because the more he thought about it, the more sense it made to him. "You're afraid to be happy, Laurie. You think that well of misery that you draw on for your music will dry up if you're not careful."

"That is the most absurd notion you've ever expressed, Harlan Patrick. I don't want to be miserable. I don't want to make you miserable."

"Then do something to change it. Take a chance on us, Laurie. Come back here after your tour. If you won't marry me, live with me for a while. See what kind of balancing act we can come up with."

"No," she said practically before the words were out of his mouth.

Pulse pounding with fury, he backed away from her. "You didn't even think about it."

"I don't have to think about it. I will not bring Amy Lynn to live here with you. It'll only confuse her when it's time for us to go."

He slammed a fist into the wall, scraping his knuckles. "Dammit, you won't even try, will you? I don't even matter that much to you."

"You do matter," she insisted. "But—"

"But what?"

"You'll overwhelm me, Harlan Patrick. If I do as you ask, it will be too easy to settle in and stay."

"What the hell is wrong with that?"

"You know what's wrong with it," she insisted, tears streaming. "I've told you. You just haven't been listening, as usual."

"Because of your father?" he asked incredulously. "This is all because of a man who left you when you were four?"

"Yes," she said, regarding him defiantly. "Because the first man I loved, the one who was supposed to love me forever, walked out and there was nothing I could do to stop him."

He could hear the anguish in her voice and knew that her reasoning made perfect sense to her, even if it made next to none to him. He cupped her tear-streaked face in his hands.

"Sweetheart, I am nothing like your father. I'm not going to leave you. Not ever. We've been apart for years now, yet I'm still right here, waiting. Doesn't that prove anything at all to you?"

"That you're stubborn mostly," she said with a rueful expression. "You can't guarantee feelings. I could drive you away. I wouldn't mean to, but it could happen."

Finally he began to understand the real cause of her anguish. "Is that what you think happened with your dad? You think your mother did something to drive him away?"

"That must have been it."

He regarded her incredulously. "This is something that's so important to you that you're shutting me out because of it and you've never asked your mother what really happened?"

She shook her head. "I couldn't. I could see how she was hurting. She never mentioned him again, so neither did I."

"Then I think it's time you did."

"No. I can't."

"What are you really afraid of?" he asked, startled to think of the brave, adventurous woman who'd once taken any dare being scared of anything. He studied her intently, saw the shadows in her eyes and realized suddenly what it was. It was the nightmare of every child of divorced parents. Why hadn't he seen it sooner?

"You're afraid it was something you did that made him go, aren't you?" he asked quietly but insistently.

"Of course not. I was a kid, a baby, practically."

"That's right. You were a kid, and whatever happened was between grown-ups," he reminded her. "Laurie, you have to talk to your mom. Until you know for sure, until you lay that to rest, you will never let any man into your life. Do you want to spend the rest of your life alone?"

"I'm not alone," she said with a defiant thrust of her chin. "I have Amy Lynn and Val and the band. I'm surrounded by people."

"You can't make Amy Lynn your entire world," he argued. "It's too big a burden to put on a little girl. As for the others, there are no guarantees they'll stay, either."

"They will," she insisted.

Rather than arguing with her about the uncertainty of the future, he settled for forcing her to take a long hard look at the present. "Are they there when you get scared in the middle of the night? Can they keep you warm when it's cold? Can they kiss away your tears?"

He saw her struggling with the truth.

"No," she admitted finally, "but—"

"You deserve more, Laurie. You deserve someone who'll be there, someone who knows you inside and out, someone who's not just drawing a paycheck." He held up a hand before she could protest. "I know they care about you, but it's not the same." He gazed into her eyes. "Is it?"

She drew in a shuddering breath. "No," she conceded, her expression bleak. "It's not. But it's all I have."

"It doesn't have to be."

"Yes, it does," she insisted. "I can't risk any more."

He knew then that he was losing her all over again. "Talk to your mother," he pleaded again. "Please, Laurie. For us. For Amy Lynn. Find out what happened all those years ago."

Laurie was silent all the way back into town, struggling with herself. A part of her knew that Harlan Patrick was right. Her whole future, whether with him or someone else, rested on finding out the truth about what had happened all those years ago. She'd been hiding from the need to do it for years now, pretending that the long-ago hurt wasn't affecting every choice she made.

In fact, she had to wonder if her father wasn't the real reason she had remained so stubbornly determined to spend her life on the road, cramming in concert appearances in tiny, out-of-the-way places, hoping that one day she would glimpse a familiar face in the crowd. Even as the thought occurred to her, she knew that she had finally grasped something that had been eluding her for years.

"Oh, my God," she murmured.

Three startled faces turned to her in the car.

"What?" Harlan Patrick asked.

"Nothing," she said at once.

"Laurie, is everything okay?" her mother asked from the back seat.

She glanced over her shoulder and forced a smile for her mother and for an equally concerned Val. "Fine. I just remembered something, that's all."

Her gaze came to rest on her sleeping daughter, buckled securely into her car seat. Would Amy Lynn grow up with the same terrible insecurities if Laurie kept Harlan Patrick out of her life? Was she dooming her precious baby to the same sort of future she faced?

Never! She resolved then and there to begin looking for answers and she would start first thing in the morning, before she left for Ohio. As soon as she'd made the decision, she felt better, more at peace than she had in years. And she owed it to Harlan Patrick and his persistent refusal to take no for an answer. He had prodded her into heavy-duty soul-searching.

When they got to the house, she let the others go inside, lingering beside him in the car.

"Thank you," she said quietly.

"For what?"

"For forcing me to face the past."

"Have you really done that?"

She shrugged. "Not exactly, but I'm getting there. I'm going to have that long-overdue talk with my mom in the morning. You could do me a huge favor if you'd come and take Amy Lynn and Val out for breakfast."

"Gladly. I'll take 'em over to Dolan's. Sharon Lynn will love introducing another Adams to her cooking. The rest of us are proof that you can survive it."

"You know perfectly well she makes the best hotcakes around."

"When her mind's on it," he agreed with a grin. "Lately, with little Ashley getting ready for preschool, she's been listening to her biological clock ticking and she tends to get a little distracted. With Amy Lynn there for her to fuss over, I'm liable to have to do the cooking myself."

"I'll warn Val," she promised.

He tucked a finger under her chin and turned her head to face him. "I'm glad you're going to do this."

"I just pray I won't regret it."

"You should never regret asking for the truth. It's living with lies and secrets and guesswork that'll do you in."

"I suppose so."

He leaned over and pressed a kiss against her forehead. "Sure you don't want me to be here when you talk to your mom?"

"No. I have to do this on my own." She rested her palm against his cheek. "Have I mentioned lately how much I love you?"

He smiled. "Every now and again, but I never tire of hearing it. That's what keeps me hanging in here."

"I wish things weren't so complicated."

"Hey, darlin', what would be the challenge in that? Life's full of complications. Surviving them is what makes a person stronger."

"Then I guess I've done my bit to see that you're as tough as Hercules."

He winked at her. "Want to feel my muscles?"

"You wish. Don't start something you're not prepared to finish, cowboy."

"Oh, I am always prepared when I'm around you." He brushed a kiss across her lips, then lingered.

Laurie felt the slow rise of heat in her blood, the tug of desire building low in her belly. It took so little for her to want him, so little to set her heart to racing. She backed away and drew in a deep breath.

"Hold that thought," she pleaded.

"Forever, if I have to."

"Not that long," she promised, then slid out of the car. "I'll see you in the morning."

"Bright and early," he agreed. "Sleep tight, darlin', and dream of me."

He was already pulling away when she whispered, "I always do."

Dreaming of Harlan Patrick was what would give her the courage to confront her mother in the morning. Imagining that confrontation was what kept her awake most of the night. She was already in the kitchen with the coffee going when Val wandered down at the crack of dawn.

"Coffee?" she murmured, yawning.

Laurie poured her a mug. "Would you do me a favor this morning?"

"Sure, anything."

"When Harlan Patrick comes by in a little while, will you take the baby and go out to breakfast with him? I need to have a talk with my mom."

"Of course," Val said, then studied her worriedly. "Is everything okay?"

"It will be," Laurie said grimly. "It has to be."

Val reached over and squeezed her hand. "I'll go get ready now. The baby should be awake, too. We'll be all set when Harlan Patrick gets here."

"Thanks. And thanks for not asking a lot of questions."

"You'll tell me what you can, when you can. Until then, I'll do whatever I can to help."

Alone again, Laurie sipped her second cup of coffee and tried to find the words she would need to ask her mother about what had happened all those years ago. She couldn't just blurt it out, not after all these years of polite silence. She had no idea what her mother's reaction would be. She'd been devastated back then, unable to hide the sorrow that had left deep shadows under her eyes and wiped the color from her cheeks.

Fortunately Harlan Patrick arrived and spirited Val and Amy Lynn away before her mother came downstairs.

"You here all alone?" she asked Laurie with evident surprise when she wandered into the kitchen just after eight. "I thought I heard Val and the baby stirring."

"Harlan Patrick took them to Dolan's to breakfast."

Her mother regarded her worriedly. "And you didn't want to go along? You and Harlan Patrick haven't fought again, have you?"

"No. I just wanted some time alone with you. Can I fix you something to eat?"

"Absolutely not. You stay where you are. I'll just have some cereal."

She poured cornflakes into a bowl as she had practically every day of her life that Laurie could remember. She added milk and sat down opposite Laurie. She stirred the cereal in the bowl, but didn't take a bite. Finally she lifted her gaze to clash with Laurie's.

"Okay, girl, what's on your mind? You didn't chase everybody out of here just so you and I could catch up, did you?"

"Not exactly."

"What then?"

Laurie drew in a deep breath. Feeling as if she were on the edge of a precipice, she finally forced herself to dive off. "I want to know about Dad."

The spoon slipped from her mother's grasp and clattered against the bowl. "Your father? Why on earth would you bring him up after all these years?"

"Because Harlan Patrick thinks he's the reason I won't make a commitment, and I've finally concluded he could be right."

"That's ridiculous. You barely even knew your father. He's been gone for more than twenty years now, and you've never asked about him once."

"That's why I'm asking now. I need to know everything, Mom. I need to know why he left. Was it something I did? Something you did? Have you ever heard from him again? Do you know where he is?"

"Well, I never..." Clearly agitated, her mother refused to meet her gaze.

Laurie reached across the table and clasped her mother's icy hand. "Please, Mom, it's important. Did I do something wrong? Is that why he left?"

"Don't be ridiculous. You were a child. He adored you."

"How can you say that? He walked away without ever looking back. He never sent so much as a card at Christmas or for my birthday."

Her comments were greeted with guilty silence. "Mom, he didn't, did he?" She stared at her mother in stunned horror. "He did send me something and you kept it from me. Why, Mom? Why would you do something like that?"

"You never asked about him," her mother retorted defensively. "I saw no need to go stirring things up."

"What did he send?"

With a look of utter defeat on her face, her mother stood

up shakily and left the room. Laurie didn't try to stop her because something told her that at long last her mother wasn't running away from the past. She was going after it.

With her heart in her throat, Laurie waited. Her mother came back into the room a few minutes later with a huge cardboard box in her arms.

"I should have thrown these away, I suppose," she murmured as she set the box in front of Laurie. "But I couldn't. I think I always knew this day would come."

Laurie stood and peered into the box that had been taped shut and labeled Old Bills, all but ensuring she would never open it. There were postcards and letters and greeting cards, all addressed in a firm, masculine handwriting. There were even a few small gifts, still wrapped in Christmas and birthday paper.

"Oh, sweet heaven," she murmured as tears filled her eyes and flowed down her cheeks.

"I'll leave you to go through this," her mother said.

"No," Laurie snapped. "Before you go, I want to know why. I want to know why he left."

"It was simple, really," her mother said wearily. "He didn't love me anymore."

"Falling out of love is never simple. Something must have happened. I heard you arguing that night. It must have been about something."

"Oh, baby, you have so much to learn about marriage. Even when both people love each other with all their hearts, it takes work and commitment to stay together, to have a relationship that grows stronger year after year. Your dad was tired of the struggle to make ends meet. He was tired of having to account for the money he spent or where he spent his time. He was tired of coming home to the same bed every night."

"He had an affair?"

"No, not that I knew about, but he was bored with me, with marriage. And when he tired of it all, he left. My love wasn't enough to keep him here."

She heard the raw pain in her mother's voice even after all these times and felt guilty for stirring it up again. "Oh, Mom, I'm sorry."

"Don't be. I accepted it long ago."

"Did you really?" Laurie wondered aloud. "You kept all this from me."

"Maybe I worried that if you knew he wanted to see you, you would choose him over me. I hope that's not why, but it might have been. I told myself I was doing what was best for you, keeping you with somebody who would always love you, who wouldn't turn away no matter what." She regarded Laurie sadly. "Was I so very wrong to do that?"

"I should have had a choice," Laurie whispered. "It was my choice to make."

"You were four years old," her mother retorted sharply.

"If not then, later. When I was eight or ten or even seventeen."

"By then it was too late."

Laurie's heart thudded dully. "He's dead?"

"No, I just lost track of him. The cards and packages stopped when you were barely ten. I guess he gave up."

Laurie vowed then and there to find him. If he was still alive, she would find her father again and get his side of the story. Maybe even after all this time, they could try to build some sort of relationship with each other. Maybe he would be someone she would want in her life. Maybe he wouldn't be, but this time she would have the chance to choose.

And then, at last, maybe she would find the peace that had eluded her for so many years.

Thirteen

When Harlan Patrick walked back into the Jensen kitchen two hours later, he found Laurie still seated at the kitchen table, surrounded by papers. Her face was streaked with tears, her eyes puffy. She was holding an unopened package, its bright red Santa wrapping paper incongruous on the hot summer day.

"I can't open it," she told him quietly, not looking up. "I can't take my eyes off of it, but I can't open it."

He guessed at once who had sent the gift, and how very long ago. "It's from your father."

She nodded. "My mother saved it." She gestured toward the postcards and birthday cards littering the table. "All of this, and I never knew."

"He must have missed you very much."

"He said he did," she said in a soft, disbelieving voice. She set the package on the table and reached for a postcard. "See here, he says he loves me, that he wishes I were with him."

Harlan Patrick noted that the card was from Dallas. Laurie chose another one, from California.

"He said it here, too," she told him. "He was at the

beach." She met Harlan Patrick's gaze with tear-swollen eyes. "Did you know I'd never been to the beach, not until my first concert stop in Los Angeles? That was the first time I saw the ocean. He could have been right there, and I would never have known it."

"Are other things postmarked from Los Angeles?"

Startled, she stared at him. "I don't know. I only read the messages."

He held out his hand. "Let me see." He watched her closely. "That is if you're interested in finding him."

"You know I am," she said vehemently. "I have to."

"Then I'll help."

Her eyes brightened for the first time. "You will?"

"Of course I will. We'll find him together, Laurie. That's a promise."

"And you always keep your promises."

"If I can."

"No," she said, suddenly angry. "Always, Harlan Patrick. You have to say it."

Startled by her burst of fury, he could only guess at the cause. "Your mom's been telling you that promises don't mean much, hasn't she?"

She sighed wearily. "Pretty much."

"Mine do." He glanced at the package on the table. "Why don't you open that now, darlin'?"

"No," she said, tucking the tiny package into her pocket. "I think I'll save it and open it when we find him."

Harlan Patrick knew then that his whole future rested on finding Laurie's father and putting the past to rest once and for all. The sooner he could make that happen, the better. Fortunately he had a cousin who was a sheriff. Justin ought to be able to get the ball rolling before the day was out.

But if Justin ran into a dead end, there were private investigators. Hell, he'd go chasing after the man himself, if that's what it took.

Anxious to get started, he stood up and dropped a quick kiss on Laurie's forehead. "You get your things together, sweetheart. We'll take off for Ohio in a couple of hours. Meantime I have some things I need to do."

"What things?"

"Odds and ends," he said evasively, refusing to get her hopes up until he'd had a talk with Justin about just how difficult this search was likely to be. "Be ready when I get back, okay?"

"Sure," she said distractedly, already lost in another of her father's letters.

"Maybe I'll turn the packing over to Val," he murmured as he left the room. Laurie's mind clearly wasn't likely to be on anything except her daddy for some time to come.

A few minutes later he sat in Justin's office and pleaded his case.

"You want me to track down Laurie's father?" Justin repeated.

"As a favor to me. She needs to put an end to all the wondering."

"Any idea where I might start this search?"

"California. The last cards and letters he sent came from a little town just north of Los Angeles."

"And when was that?"

"About ten, maybe fifteen years ago, judging by the postmarks. I don't think there was anything more recent than that. I suppose he just gave up when he never heard back from her."

"Do you honestly think he's been staying put all this time?"

"Maybe not, but it's a starting point. Surely a bright law-enforcement officer such as yourself can be clever enough to follow his trail after that."

"Flattery won't help."

"Bribery, then? Blackmail?"

Justin regarded him with indignation. "You'd resort to that, wouldn't you?"

Harlan Patrick grinned. "Oh, yeah, and who knows all your sins better than me?"

Justin didn't flinch at the threat. In fact, he seemed to be considering it thoughtfully. "Okay, then. Let's concentrate on the bribery for a second."

His straight-arrow cousin was open to bribery, actually soliciting it? Harlan Patrick couldn't wait to hear what he had in mind. "Okay. What'll it take?"

"Patsy and I want to build a new house on that land granddaddy intends to leave me out at White Pines."

Harlan Patrick's gaze narrowed. He wasn't sure he liked where this was heading. Justin had always been very sneaky about tricking him into hard work, then taking off for parts unknown. "Exactly what does that have to do with me?" he asked suspiciously.

"We need labor. We need a strong back and lots of sweat. We want to do this ourselves."

"Excuse me, but I see a slight contradiction here. If you want to build this all by your little lonesomes, why am I involved?"

"Because Patsy's pregnant, in case you haven't noticed. She might be able to hold a hammer, but it's doubtful she could get close enough to actually hit a nail."

"You'd better not let her hear you say that," Harlan Patrick warned. "I'm told women are very sensitive on the subject of their waistlines, especially this late in a pregnancy. Besides, she won't be pregnant forever. Isn't the baby due any minute now?"

"True, but I'd like to have the frame of the house up as a surprise on the day we bring the baby home from the hospital."

"Maybe you ought to go for walls, too, or were you intending to sell her on the idea of open-air living?"

"Very funny. I'm not planning on making her live there yet. I just want to show her it's under way. Can I count on you?"

In exchange for a future with Laurie? He didn't even hesitate. "I'll give you twenty-four hours a day as soon as I get Laurie up to Ohio." He regarded Justin evenly. "What about you, then? Can I count on you?"

Justin grinned. "Was there ever any doubt? I'm a cop. Nobody loves a good mystery more than me."

"Thanks. I owe you."

"Oh, yeah, and I intend to start collecting first thing tomorrow."

"Tomorrow? I was thinking of spending one day in Ohio before I came back."

"Tomorrow," Justin repeated. "I can't count on this baby waiting around much longer. Patsy looks as if she's about to pop."

"I'll be back tonight," Harlan Patrick agreed with regret. He'd hoped for a long night with Laurie back in his arms. Maybe this was just as well, though. When they were together the next time, he wanted her full attention and he seriously doubted he would have it until she'd finally found her daddy.

Laurie was startled when they got to her hotel in Columbus and Harlan Patrick stayed outside the room, rather than following her inside. She'd also been a bit bemused by his lack of persistence when it came to keeping Amy Lynn with him for the next couple of weeks, but she'd been so grateful that she hadn't questioned that.

"You're not coming in?"

He shook his head. "I've got to get right back to Texas."

"But I thought—"

"I'll be back before you know it, darlin'."

Conflicting emotions tore through her. She'd expected him to stay, to plague her about coming home, to be in her face for the next two weeks. It should have been a relief to know that he was leaving. It wasn't. He was standing right next to her, and already she felt alone and abandoned.

"Why?" she asked, because she'd never gotten a chance to ask another man that very question. "Why are you leaving?"

"You're going to be very busy the next couple of weeks, and I have some things to do. You won't even have time to miss me."

She missed him already.

He tilted her chin up. "I will be back. I promised Justin I'd help him with something, a surprise for Patsy. It'll take a few days, maybe a week or two."

"Fine. You do what you have to do," she said finally, ungraciously.

He chuckled. "A man could almost get the idea that you're not anxious to see me leave."

She drew herself up and resorted to her haughtiest demeanor. "Don't be silly. I never wanted you trailing after me in the first place."

"When did you change your mind?" he asked, bending closer. "Was it when I did this?"

His mouth settled over hers, and his tongue slid between her lips. Laurie eased into the kiss as naturally as breathing.

"Or this?" he inquired, his hand doing a slow sweep over her hip before finally coming to rest just below her breast.

Her pulse raced.

He leaned back and gazed into her eyes. His own eyes were the deep, mysterious blue of dawn with the promise of excitement to come. His hand closed over her breast, and his thumb scraped over the nipple until she gasped with the wicked sweetness of the sensation.

"Could it be that?" he asked, laughter in his eyes now.

"If you have any other alternatives you intend to demonstrate, perhaps we ought to take this inside," she suggested breathlessly.

"Oh, you'd like that, wouldn't you?" he taunted. "Knowing that you could keep me here and have your way with me?"

Laurie felt a grin spreading across her face. "You bet." Her smile broadened. "Dare you."

Before she realized what he intended, he scooped her into his arms, walked into the room and kicked the door shut behind them.

"Darlin', don't you know better than to dare a man like me?"

She chuckled at his predictability and at the fire that made his skin burn to her touch. "Got you," she taunted.

"Oh, no," he said, heading for the suite's bedroom. "I've got you."

And in case she had any doubts about that, he spent the next several hours proving it.

It was dawn before he left, sneaking from the bed that

smelled of perfume and sex. He bent over to drop a kiss against her cheek.

"I'll be back before you know it," he promised. "Unless Justin murders me for being late this morning."

"Love you," she told him with a yawn.

"Remember that when you wake up," he teased, and then he was gone.

Laurie's eyes flew open at the sound of the door clicking softly closed. "I'll never forget it again," she whispered. "Never."

Just as he had predicted, that day and the next she was so busy that she hardly had a second to spare. Val had lined up newspaper and television interviews, along with drop-in visits to a couple of country-music radio stations. At night there were her appearances at the Ohio State Fair, where the temperatures were wickedly hot, the air still and muggy. The wildly enthusiastic crowds more than made up for the discomfort.

It was only late at night that Laurie realized that she hadn't heard a word from Harlan Patrick, but by then it was too late to call and morning brought a new and demanding round of commitments.

From Columbus the tour moved on to Cleveland, then west to Indianapolis, then south to Louisville. She was getting closer to home again, but for some reason she didn't care to explore too closely the allure of Nashville wasn't what it once had been. Something inside her knew that that brief visit to Los Piños had reminded her that her real home was in Texas and always would be.

Back in her dressing room after another wildly successful concert, she sorted through the stack of messages Val had left for her, hoping for one from Harlan Patrick.

Nothing. She told herself she wasn't disappointed, but the truth was that she felt let down and scared. It was as if he, too, had vanished from her life.

Val wandered into the dressing room carrying Amy Lynn.

"I thought you were taking her to the hotel," Laurie said, reaching for her wide-awake daughter.

"Your daughter woke up about an hour ago and started fussing. Nothing I could do seemed to settle her down, so I figured we'd come on over here and see if seeing her mama could help."

Laurie looked into those wide blue eyes, shimmering with unshed tears, and thought of other blue eyes she'd like to be staring into about now. How had she gone for so long without Harlan Patrick around? Could she ever do it again? She took the baby from Val.

"What's wrong, darling girl? Are you missing your daddy?"

Amy Lynn stared back at her. "Da?" she said wistfully.

Laurie grinned. "Val, did you hear that? She said her first word. She said, 'Da.'"

"Are you going to call Harlan Patrick and tell him that?"

"I can't. It's nearly midnight. He's probably been asleep for hours. Ranchers get up at the crack of dawn."

Val grinned. "Something tells me he wouldn't mind losing a little sleep for this news. Besides, you've been missing him like crazy. Call. Maybe then both you and the little one here would actually get a good night's rest."

Laurie thought it over, then nodded. "You're right." She reached for the phone and punched in Harlan Patrick's number. It seemed like an eternity before he answered, his voice thick with sleep.

"Yeah, what?"

Laurie held the phone up to Amy Lynn's mouth. "Say it," she whispered. "It's your daddy."

Amy Lynn studied the phone quizzically, then said loudly, "Da?"

Laurie heard Harlan Patrick's hoot even before she put the receiver back to her own ear. "You heard?"

"She said 'Daddy,' didn't she?"

"Close enough," Laurie agreed. "Isn't she the most brilliant child on the face of the earth?"

"Absolutely. Just one question, though. What's she doing up at this hour?"

"She was missing you." Her voice dropped a notch. "So was I."

"The same goes for me."

"You haven't called."

"That's because I'm working for a slave driver. Once Justin gets a notion in his head, he pulls out all the stops."

"Exactly what are the two of you up to?"

"Justin's not up to much, if you ask me. I'm doing all the physical labor. He seems to have designated himself as supervisor. The man has no shame at all. He's blatantly using me."

"And what does he have you doing?"

"Building a house for him and Patsy out here at White Pines. It won't even be close to finished before the baby's born, but he wants to surprise her with the frame at least."

"I had no idea you knew how to build a house."

"Actually I'm not so sure I'd want to live in any house I built, but I can swing a hammer and follow directions. Besides, it was a fair trade for what I want from Justin."

"Which is?"

"He's doing a little research for me."

Laurie's heart climbed into her throat. "He's looking for my father, isn't he?"

"He's trying," Harlan Patrick admitted slowly. "Don't get your hopes up, though. So far, all he's run into are dead ends."

"At least he's trying," she whispered. "Thank you."

"I told you I'd do what I could. Now tell me about the tour. Is it going well? I saw the piece on TV the other night. Mom called me when she heard the promotion for it. I think that show's ratings probably went through the roof here in Los Piños. Grandpa Harlan called right afterward. Then Sharon Lynn called. The consensus was that you looked beautiful and sounded brilliant."

She laughed. "You all aren't biased, by any chance?"

"Maybe just a little," he agreed, then yawned. "Sorry."

"No, it's late and I'd better let you go. I just wanted you to know that your daughter and I were thinking about you."

"Are you at the hotel?"

"No, we're still in my dressing room. I'm heading back there now."

"Sleep well, darlin'."

"You, too. I miss you."

"Not half as much as I miss you. Give my girl a kiss for me."

"You want to tell her good-night?"

"Absolutely."

Laurie took Amy Lynn back from Val and held the phone to her ear. "Here she is," she told Harlan Patrick.

She could hear the low hum of his voice as he talked to Amy Lynn, saw her puzzled frown and then a gurgle of delight as she realized once again that it was her daddy.

"Da," she repeated joyously, patting the phone. "Da!"

When Laurie tried to take the phone away, Amy Lynn's face screwed up. "Da," she echoed piteously.

"Tell him bye-bye," Laurie coached.

Amy Lynn waved instead.

"She's waving," Laurie told him.

"I don't want to miss any more firsts," Harlan Patrick said. "I want to be there."

Laurie sighed. She understood his longing. "I know."

"I'll see you both soon," he promised.

"Good night, Harlan Patrick."

"Night, darlin'."

Neither of them seemed to have the will to sever the connection. Finally, with a sigh, Laurie placed the receiver back on the hook.

"Feel better?" Val asked.

"No."

"Hearing his voice doesn't do it for you?"

"It only made me miss him more." She regarded her assistant and admitted the painful truth. "This is why it won't work, you know. It hurts too much to be apart. We'll just end up making each other miserable."

"Did it hurt any less when you thought you'd never see him again?"

Startled by the question, Laurie paused thoughtfully. "No," she conceded finally.

"Then isn't it better to know that you will be together again, that this misery is just temporary?"

"You're right," she said, excited by the discovery. "I hadn't looked at it that way." She gave her assistant a hug. "Thank you."

"That's why you pay me the big bucks," Val said.

"Do I pay you big bucks?"

"Not big enough," Val retorted, then added with confidence, "But you will."

"Yes, I imagine I will," Laurie agreed. "And whenever I start wallowing in self-pity, remind me again of the alternative."

"It's a deal."

"How many more days on this tour?"

"Seven more days, six more concerts, then back to Nashville."

"Back to Texas," Laurie corrected.

"But—"

"Make it happen, Val. Whatever you have to do."

Val grinned. "In return for those big bucks you're going to start paying me, consider it as good as done."

Fourteen

Three days after that middle-of-the-night call from Laurie, Harlan Patrick was hammering the last nail home in the frame for Justin's new house when his cousin drove up.

"Excellent timing," he called down to him from his perch on the skeletal rooftop. "Have you actually put up one board in this place?"

Justin shifted his Stetson back on his head and stared up through reflective sunglasses. "No need. You're doing just fine."

"What brings you by, since it's obviously not to help out?"

"I found Buzz Jensen."

Harlan Patrick felt his heart begin to thud. "Alive?"

"Oh, yeah."

He didn't like the sound of that.

"I'll be right down."

He climbed down the ladder braced against what would eventually be the kitchen wall and headed for a cooler he'd filled with ice and soft drinks. Regretting that it wasn't a beer, he popped the top on one can, took a long swallow, then met his cousin's gaze.

"Okay, give it to me. Is he in jail or something?"

"No, but he is married again."

Harlan Patrick took that news in stride. "I suppose that's to be expected. He left Laurie's mom a long time ago."

Justin stirred uncomfortably. "But the way I understand it, he never divorced her because she didn't believe in divorce."

"You're kidding me, right?"

"No. I checked it out myself. Mary Jensen told me she'd refused to give him a divorce."

"That means the man's a bigamist," Harlan Patrick said.

"With a happy new family in California, none of whom apparently have a clue about his past in Texas," Justin confirmed. "Unless he found some way around the legal system that I can't figure out."

"Well, hell," Harlan Patrick muttered. "This is a wrinkle I hadn't counted on. What am I supposed to do now?"

"I don't see that you have any choice. You promised Laurie you'd find her father for her. You've done that and you're going to have to tell her."

"How's she going to take it when she finds out he's got this whole new family? Hell's bells, how are they going to take it when they discover that he's been living a lie? What kind of can of worms are we opening here?"

"That's the trouble with searching for the truth," Justin noted. "Sometimes you find out a whole lot more than you ever wanted to know."

"Maybe you're wrong," Harlan Patrick said. "Maybe Buzz Jensen did get a divorce."

"Without Mary knowing about it?"

"It's possible," Harlan Patrick persisted.

"Doubtful," his cousin countered. He removed his sunglasses and met Harlan Patrick's gaze. "What are you going to do?"

"What do you think? I'm going to California."

"With Laurie?"

"Not on your life. I'm going on my own to check things out first. I'm not taking her there until we know the whole story."

"And then?"

He raked a hand through his hair. "I wish to hell I knew."

Five hours later, just past dinnertime, he was driving up to a small ranch-style house on a hillside just north of Los Angeles. The lawn was well tended, window boxes were filled with brightly colored flowers and toys and bicycles were scattered across the yard. A sedan that needed a paint job and a newer pickup sat in the driveway. Evidence of normal, everyday people just trying to get by, he concluded.

With a sigh of regret, Harlan Patrick climbed out of his car and walked toward the house. If this hadn't been the only way to get the answers Laurie needed, he wasn't sure he could have brought himself into these people's lives to tear apart their tidy little world.

When he rang the bell, the door was answered by a teenage girl who bore such a striking resemblance to Laurie that it almost took his breath away. He'd always assumed Laurie had inherited her looks from her mother, but it was clear now that she had a good bit of her father in her, too.

"Hi," she said with the same flirtatious, infectious grin that Laurie had used to captivate him years earlier. "Who're you?"

"Harlan Patrick Adams."

"Well, hey, Harlan Patrick. I'm Tess. What can I do for you?"

He had to hide a grin at the blatant suggestiveness she managed to put into those few little words. "I'd like to see your father if he's at home."

"Sure," she said at once. "Would you like to come in?"

Her open, trusting nature made him feel like a heel. This was going to be tough enough without going inside. "No, thanks," he said with a smile. "I'll wait right here."

"Hey, Dad," she bellowed. "Somebody here to see you." She regarded Harlan Patrick with interest as they waited. "I could get you something to drink if you like. Maybe a soda?"

"Nothing, thanks."

A middle-aged man came from the back of the house. He gave the girl a stern look. "How many times have I asked you not to shout all the way through the house? You could have come and told me we had company."

"I didn't want to leave him standing on the doorstep all by himself," she said. She gave Harlan Patrick a last wistful look. "See you."

"Bye. Thanks for your help."

After she'd gone, Buzz Jensen faced him. "What can I do for you?"

"I'm Harlan Patrick Adams," he said quietly. "From Los Piños."

As he mentioned the name of the town, he saw the man's shoulders sag with defeat. Dread spread across his face. He came out onto the front stoop and closed the door behind him.

"Why are you here? What do you want?"

"Just to talk, if you don't mind."

"Is it Mary? Has something happened to her?" There was genuine concern in his tone, that and a hint of panic.

"No. It's about Laurie."

The man staggered visibly. "Nothing's happened to her, has it? I would have heard. It would have been on TV."

Worried by the man's sudden pallor, Harlan Patrick

took his arm and guided him to a lawn chair. "Are you okay?"

"Just surprised, that's all. Tell me what's happened."

"Laurie's fine."

He shook his head as if to clear it. "Then why are you here?"

"She's been asking a lot of questions lately. She's been thinking about you, wondering why you left all those years ago." Harlan Patrick looked the older man straight in the eye. "I love her, sir, but, you see, she's afraid I'll leave her the way you did. She needs to understand what happened back then before she can trust me or any other man."

"Hasn't she asked her mother?"

"She has, but it's not enough. There's a bond between a father and daughter. I'm only beginning to realize it myself." He met the older man's gaze evenly. "You see, Laurie and I have a baby girl."

He seemed startled by that. "You're the one, then. I saw that tabloid picture of her and the baby. I wondered who was responsible for getting her into trouble."

"I never knew about the baby, not until that picture. You have to believe that. There is no way I wouldn't have been there for her if I'd known."

Buzz Jensen nodded in sudden understanding. "You're one of those Adamses, aren't you? I should have guessed it straight off. Named after your granddaddy. Honor's a big thing with an Adams."

"Yes, sir. So is family."

"Is that why you're here, instead of Laurie. You want to buy me off or something?"

"No. I wanted to see you, talk to you, make sure that arranging for Laurie to see you wouldn't lead to more hurt for her."

"I would never hurt her," he said indignantly.

"You already have," Harlan Patrick reminded him quietly. "That's the problem."

Buzz Jensen uttered a sigh of acknowledgment. "I suppose you're right."

"What about your family? Do they know about Laurie? Will they be hurt by all of this when the whole story comes out?"

"My wife knows," he acknowledged.

Harlan Patrick hesitated, then forced himself to ask, "Does she know you never divorced Laurie's mother?"

He nodded. "She accepted that we couldn't be married."

Harlan Patrick was relieved to know the man wasn't a bigamist, after all. That didn't make the situation a whole lot less complicated, though. "What about your kids?"

"They don't know about it." His expression turned defiant. "I don't want them to."

"I don't see how you can avoid it," Harlan Patrick countered. "Not if you see Laurie. They'll have questions."

"You can't bring her here," he said adamantly. "It's as simple as that."

Harlan Patrick was shocked by the decision. "You won't see her? Not even after what I've told you? How can you do that to her?"

"I didn't say I wouldn't see her. I said she couldn't come here. If you want to set up a meeting for somewhere else, I'll go." His eyes filled with tears. "I never thought I'd have the chance to see my baby girl again. I thought I'd go to my grave knowing that I'd failed her and that she'd never forgiven me."

There was so much pain and sincerity in his voice that Harlan Patrick had no choice but to believe him. "She never knew about the cards and letters," he told him then. "Her mother kept them from her until recently."

Buzz Jensen's hands shook as he reached over to clasp Harlan Patrick's hand and relief washed over his face. "Thank you for telling me that. You don't know how hard I prayed that it was something like that. I didn't want to believe she'd just forgotten all about me."

"No, sir, Laurie never forgot." He stared straight into the older man's eyes. "But the time has come to help her let go."

"Just tell me what you want me to do."

"If you can leave first thing in the morning, I'll take you to her."

He nodded. "I'll make the arrangements."

"Seven o'clock, then. I'll pick you up."

"I'll be waiting," Buzz Jensen promised, his expression eager despite the questions the people inside were likely to have about the stranger who'd come calling.

Later, alone in a nearby motel, Harlan Patrick thought back over the meeting and tried to reassure himself that it was all going to work out. Or was he just setting a whole lot of people up for heartache?

As she left the stage after the last Louisville concert, Laurie was totally, thoroughly drained. All she wanted was to take a long hot shower and crawl into bed. Before she could do that, though, she had a group of VIP fans waiting to meet her backstage.

Val arranged these meet-and-greet sessions at the behest of local radio stations. When she wasn't so tired, Laurie actually enjoyed them. Tonight, though, she could barely keep her eyes open. An idea for a new song had come to her the night before right at bedtime, and she'd stayed awake most of the night fiddling with it. A half-hour nap before tonight's show hadn't made up for the lost sleep.

As she walked into the green room where drinks and hors d'oeuvres had been set up, she forced a smile and moved from one cluster of people to another, making small talk, thanking the DJs who played her music, flattering their wives and sponsors. For a solid hour she played the part of gracious hostess, before Val whipped in and whispered in her ear.

"What?" she asked, staring at her assistant incredulously.

"Harlan Patrick's here," Val repeated. "He's in your dressing room."

"Why didn't you bring him in here?"

"He wanted to wait there," Val said. "I'll make your excuses. Go."

Laurie didn't have to be urged twice. She flew down the hall and threw open the dressing-room door, but instead of Harlan Patrick, there was a stranger waiting, an older man who looked vaguely, disturbingly familiar. Her breath lodged in her throat.

The man stood slowly, took a hesitant step toward her, then stopped. "Hi, baby."

"Oh, my God," she murmured, thunderstruck. "It's you."

"It's your daddy," he confirmed.

Filled with wonder, she stepped closer, reached up with trembling fingers and touched his lined cheek, traced the deeper grooves that fanned out from the corners of his eyes—lines that hadn't been there the last time she'd seen him.

But the scent of his aftershave was the same, tantalizing her with the memory of being lifted high in strong arms, then cuddled against a broad chest.

"It really is you," she said in amazement. "But how did you get here?"

"Harlan Patrick found me. He came to California and brought me here."

She realized then that he was in the room, too, standing to the side, watching intently as if ready to intercede the instant the meeting started to sour. She rushed into his arms. "Thank you," she said, peppering his face with kisses. "Thank you."

"You're okay?" he asked, searching her face.

"Better than okay," she said, tears flowing freely down her cheeks.

"Why don't we get out of here, then?" he suggested. "You two could use someplace private to get reacquainted. I've already talked to the sitter about staying with Amy Lynn till I get there."

"Yes, of course. The hotel, then." She gazed at her father. "I'll get you a room, next to mine if possible."

"Already done," Harlan Patrick said.

"He doesn't miss much, this fellow of yours," her father said with evident admiration.

"No," she agreed. "He doesn't miss much."

At the hotel Harlan Patrick retreated to the adjoining suite while she and her father sat opposite each other. Suddenly she was as tongue-tied as a four-year-old confronted with a stranger.

"I don't know what to say to you, what to ask," she admitted eventually.

"Would it help if I told you I was pretty much at a loss, too?"

"Some," she said with a smile that came and went. Finally she blurted out the only question that really mattered, the one that had tormented her for all these years. "Why, Daddy? Why did you go?"

"What has your mother told you?"

"Just that you were bored, that you needed to move on."

He regarded her with regret. "Sad to say, that's probably as close to the truth as I could tell you. I was immature and irresponsible back then. I wasn't ready to be tied down. I tried—for five years I did the best I could—and then I just had to go."

The glib explanation filled her with anger. "You make it sound so simple, as if you were walking away from a business deal that wasn't to your advantage. Didn't I matter to you at all?"

He seemed stung by the accusation. "Of course you did. I regretted leaving you more than anything, but I couldn't see any other way to figure out what kind of man I was. I suppose I thought I'd come back one day or that you'd come and visit me, but then this and that happened and I just stayed away, built a new life. When I never heard a word from either of you, I figured you and your mama had done the same."

"I just found out about the postcards, the letters, everything you sent back then."

"That's what Harlan Patrick told me. I'm sorry, baby. I didn't know your mother would keep them from you. After a while, when I knew you were old enough to answer and you didn't, I figured it didn't matter to you anymore."

"You were my father," she said angrily. "How could you not matter to me?"

"I'd been gone a long time."

"But you were my father," she repeated.

"I'm sorry, baby."

He opened his arms and after a long hesitation, Laurie moved into them. "But I'm back in your life now and this time I'll be a part of it for as much or as little as you want."

"Are you still in California?"

He hesitated, then nodded. "Yes."

"I'll come to visit," she said at once. "And bring Amy Lynn. Wait until you see her. She's beautiful."

"I saw the picture in the tabloid. I couldn't believe I was really a granddaddy." He met her gaze, then glanced away, his expression guilty. "You can't come there, Laurie. Much as I want you to, you can't."

Her whole body seemed to go cold at his words. "Why?"

"Because I have a new family now, a boy and a girl. They…" He looked as if he might weep. "They don't know about you."

She stared at him in shock. "But you and Mama—"

"That's right. We never divorced, so you see why I can't let you come. They're too young to understand what I've done to them. Their mother knows, but we've protected the kids. My girl's a teenager. She's at that impressionable age when this could tear her world apart."

"You have another daughter," she repeated, her voice flat as she envisioned a girl who'd grown up with her father's love and attention the way she should have, the way she'd never had a chance to.

"How could you?" she asked, her emotions raging. "How could you do that to them? To me? What kind of man would do that?"

"One who's weak," he said at once. "A strong man would have stayed in Texas, made his marriage work, but I wasn't strong then and I wasn't strong when I settled down with Lucille in California, but she knew the truth. That's how I justified it."

"There is no justification," Laurie all but shouted as she saw her happy ending slipping away.

He sighed deeply. "You're right. There is no justification."

"So this is it, then? You drop in, say hi and then run

back to the life you've built on a lie? I'm supposed to wait around for you to sneak away for an occasional visit with me, an unfortunate reminder of the past you left behind." She stood up and glowered down at him. "Well, thanks, but no thanks. As of this moment, I no longer have a father. I no longer need one in my life."

She reached for her purse, fumbled inside until she found the package she'd been carrying with her ever since its discovery. She took one last look at the bright paper, then flung it in her father's face. "Give this to your other daughter, the one who matters."

"Laurie," he whispered, reaching for her.

"No," she said furiously, backing away and opening the door. She took one last look at her father's haggard face, his shattered expression, and then she walked out and quietly closed the door behind her.

When she walked into the room next door, Harlan Patrick was waiting. He looked up at her entrance, studied her face, then opened his arms. She ran into them and burst into tears.

"He still won't let me be a part of his life," she whispered brokenly. "He still doesn't want me."

"You know that's not true," he consoled her. "It's complicated. There are other people to consider. Maybe one day he'll find a way to tell them everything. In the meantime can't you accept that he does love you? He dropped everything and came here the minute I contacted him. Isn't that proof of how he feels?"

She wished it were, but it wasn't. Not when the bottom line was that he would be walking out again and leaving her behind.

Fifteen

Laurie was inconsolable. By morning she had retreated into a bleak silence that tore Harlan Patrick's soul in two. No matter what he said to her, no matter how he pleaded with her to make allowances for her father's new circumstances, she saw only that she was being essentially abandoned all over again.

"But I'm not leaving," he reminded her. "I'm right here."

"I know," she said quietly. "And I'm grateful. I really am."

"I don't want your gratitude, Laurie. I love you. This is where I want to be."

"No," she said with a shake of her head, her expression sad. "You want to be back in Texas, where you belong."

Harlan Patrick sighed. "Okay, yes, I want to be at White Pines, but I want you and Amy Lynn with me. You're the two people I love most in this world."

But no matter what he said, it wasn't enough. She had convinced herself that her father's decision to keep her and his new family apart meant she was somehow unworthy of his love, that no man would ever be able to love her.

"Dammit, Laurie, can't you see that he's the one who's losing here? This is costing him the love of a woman who's beautiful, talented, generous and kindhearted. Blame him. Hell, hate him if you want, but don't turn this back on yourself. Don't start thinking that you're the one who's unlovable again. I'm here to tell you it's not true. Doesn't my opinion count for anything?"

She regarded him with eyes dulled by hurt. "Of course, but—"

"But I'm not your father," he supplied, defeated.

"I'm sorry."

"You don't have to be sorry, dammit!" He raked his hand through his hair and tried to think of some way to get through to her, some way to bring back her spirit. She should have been spitting mad now, not resigned, but nothing he could think of to say or do even touched her.

Two days later he was at his wit's end. So was everyone else around her. She'd insisted Val cancel half a dozen interviews. Her concert performances had been lackluster, the reviews damning. She was dying inside and killing her career in the process. Watching her do it to herself was excruciating for Harlan Patrick.

"You have to do something," Val said, blasting into Laurie's hotel suite with a handful of clippings in her hand. "I just got off the phone with Nick. He's getting rumblings about promoters wanting to back out of concert dates scheduled for the fall. She's destroying herself."

"I know," he said quietly. "I can see it, but I have no idea what to do. I can't get through to her. Other than when she's with Amy Lynn, it's as if she's just going through the motions of living."

"I'm scared for her," Val said. "I've never seen her like this before, not even when she found out she was pregnant and refused to tell you about it. I know she felt very much alone then, but expecting your baby gave her a reason to keep going. Her whole focus was on Amy Lynn and her music. Now she's about to lose her music, and it doesn't even seem to matter to her."

Harlan Patrick heard every word Val said, and an idea began to take shape in his mind. It was drastic and very, very risky. Laurie might never forgive him for it. In the end he could lose her; he could lose everything.

But if it worked, if it got her attention and made her start to live again, it would be worth it, he concluded.

"I know what I have to do," he said finally.

"What?"

"Just leave it to me. It'll be better if you don't know ahead of time." He clasped Val's shoulders and leveled a look into her eyes. "Just remember that I am doing this for Laurie, not to hurt her, okay? Remember that."

"Harlan Patrick," she began worriedly.

"It'll be fine," he reassured her as he grabbed his bag and packed his belongings.

"You're leaving?" she asked, clearly shocked.

He nodded. "I'm going back to Texas. Tell Laurie that and tell her she'll be hearing from me any day now. Tell her I've had enough."

"Enough?" she echoed. "What does that mean? Harlan Patrick, what are you planning?"

He dropped a kiss on her cheek. "Keep an eye on her for me. She's going to need you."

"Oh, my God," she whispered as he reached the door. "You're going to file for custody of Amy Lynn, aren't you? Aren't you?"

He nodded.

"Are you sure about this?"

"I can't think of any other way to make her fight, can you?"

"No, but what if she doesn't? What if she's not strong enough to fight you?"

Harlan Patrick refused to consider that. He knew that she would never let her daughter go, would never let Amy Lynn feel the pain of abandonment Laurie had felt her whole life long.

"Oh, she'll fight," he said with confidence. "I'm anticipating gale-force winds when she figures out what I'm up to."

"I hope to God you're right."

"I have to be," he said simply. "Her future, *our* future depends on it."

Harlan Patrick was gone. Laurie came back to the room after taking Amy Lynn for a walk to find her own clothes neatly hung in the closet and his gone. Val watched as she made the discovery, her expression uneasy.

"What do you know about this?" she demanded.

"About what?" Val asked.

"About Harlan Patrick leaving? Did he leave a note?"

"No. He said you'd be hearing from him, though."

"Oh," Laurie said, wearily. "I suppose he got tired of my moping around here. I can't say that I blame him. I just don't seem to have the energy to do anything anymore."

"Then it's a good thing that there's only one more concert to do. You'll be able to get down to Texas and get some rest."

"I don't think I'll be going to Texas, after all," Laurie said. "There doesn't seem to be much point to it now."

Val looked as if she wanted to argue with her, but she said only, "Well, Nick will be happy to hear about the change in plans. He's anxious to see you. He's been worried about you."

"Why?"

Val hesitated. "The reviews haven't been what he hoped for the last couple of cities. You know Nick—he starts imagining that the sky is falling."

She couldn't seem to make herself care about it. "I was off a couple of nights. I know that," she admitted. "I'll do better tonight, I'm sure."

"I'm sure you will, too," Val enthused. "You always knock 'em right out of their seats at the final concert on a tour."

But somehow Laurie couldn't work up any enthusiasm for that final show. She knew that she was letting the audience down. She even apologized for it, but there was no mistaking the sense of disappointment that pervaded the concert hall at the end of the evening. The posttour celebration at the hotel fizzled out when not one of the band members could bear to look her in the eye.

"I'm sorry," she said, and fled.

Upstairs as she approached her room a man stepped out of the shadows.

"Laurie Jensen?"

It was less a question than a statement. There wasn't even time to panic before he was slapping an envelope into her hands and heading for the elevator.

"Wait! What is this?" she called after him, but he was already stepping on the elevator.

Her hand shook as she tried to get her key into the lock. Inside the room, Val was curled up on the sofa, chatting quietly on the phone. When she saw Laurie, she murmured something and hung up.

"What's that?" she asked, spotting the papers in Laurie's hand.

"I'm not sure. A man in the hallway handed them to me, then vanished."

"Legal papers?" Val suggested.

Laurie stared at the envelope. "Legal papers? What kind of legal papers would I be getting?"

"There's only one way to find out."

"Yes, I suppose you're right," Laurie agreed, but her fingers shook as she tried to rip open the envelope.

She unfolded the thick sheaf of papers and began to read. After the first few sentences, the words began to blur.

"No," she whispered, and sank down on the sofa. The papers fell to the floor. "He can't do this. He can't."

"Who can't do what?"

"Harlan Patrick," she said bleakly. "He's suing me for custody of Amy Lynn."

"Can he do that?" Val asked, her expression shocked.

"Well, of course he can. He's an Adams, isn't he?" She shot back to her feet and began to pace. "But he's not going to get away with it—I can tell you that. If he thinks he's going to steal my baby away from me, he's out of his mind."

"You're going to fight him, then?"

She stared at her assistant. "Well, of course I'm going to fight him. Get on the phone and make arrangements for me to get to Texas first thing in the morning. Harlan Patrick isn't going to get away with this. He might be rich and powerful, but I'm Amy Lynn's mother and I've got rights. I've got a little money and influence of my own, by God. I'm a match for any Adams."

"Of course you are," Val soothed.

She turned away, but not before Laurie detected the beginnings of a smile. "What are you grinning about?"

"Nothing."

"Val?"

"Nothing."

"Do you know something about this?"

"Of course not. Harlan Patrick doesn't confide in me."

"Oh, really," Laurie said wryly. "You two certainly had your heads together often enough."

"Not about this," Val insisted.

"Well, I hope you're telling me the truth, because if you're not, you can kiss this job goodbye."

Val did grin at that. "In the meantime I'll make the reservations."

"Forget reservations. Charter a damned plane."

Laurie listened as Val called and booked a charter flight for three. "I gather you're coming along," she said when Val had hung up.

"Are you kidding? I wouldn't miss this for the world."

Laurie was so furious, so terrified, she had Amy Lynn and Val up at dawn and at the airport by seven. A few hours later they were in Los Piños with a rental car waiting at the local airstrip.

"Are we going by your mom's?" Val asked.

"No," Laurie said, aiming straight for White Pines. "You wanted to be in the thick of things, didn't you? Well, strap on your seat belt, honey, 'cause it's gonna get downright bumpy."

As if to emphasize the point, she hit a bump in the road that just about bounced them through the roof. She still hadn't calmed down by the time they reached the ranch.

Still, her manners hadn't completely deserted her.

She managed to make small talk with Melissa and Cody Adams as she deposited Amy Lynn with them and finally shuttled Val off in search of Slade Sutton. She noted that it didn't take much urging to get her assistant to go, despite her protestations that she was here to watch the fireworks.

"Where is he?" she demanded, her gaze fixed on Cody.

"Harlan Patrick?" he inquired innocently.

"No, the blasted tooth fairy. Where is he?"

"I believe he's working on his house."

"Building a new addition," Melissa chimed in.

It wasn't until she was climbing the hill to Harlan Patrick's house that the significance of Melissa's words began to sink in. He was building a room for his daughter, in anticipation of gaining custody of her. The sneaky, conniving devil. She wondered if she could bring the whole thing tumbling down and prayed for the chance to try.

She heard the hammering first, then spotted a barechested Harlan Patrick on the roof. Good, it would be a nice long drop from up there when she clobbered him. She found the ladder around back and climbed up, nimbly scrambling over the roof until she could stare him in the face. The bare expanse of gleaming chest made it difficult to concentrate, but she forced herself.

"How could you do this?" she demanded.

He glanced up as if he'd just noticed her arrival, which had to be a crock since he had a 360-degree view of the surrounding area from up here.

"Hey, Laurie. What brings you by?"

"Don't you put on that innocent act for me, Harlan Patrick Adams. What the hell do you think you're doing?"

"Building an addition to my house."

She grabbed the hammer out of his hand, only barely

resisting the urge to use it to pound some sense into his thick skull.

"I am not talking about right this second, you idiot. I am talking about those papers you had served last night."

He feigned sudden understanding. "Ah, those."

"Yes, those. What were you thinking?"

He shrugged. "I couldn't see any other way to get your attention."

"Oh, you have my attention, all right. I'm so mad I could tear you limb from limb right now."

He grinned. "I can see that."

"Don't you dare laugh at me. This is important, Harlan Patrick. Amy Lynn's future is not some game."

His expression sobered at once. "No, it's not a game," he agreed.

"Then why did you do it? Why did you file for custody?"

"Because I want her here with me. I don't want her to ever have the same doubts about her daddy's love that you've had about yours." He reached over and tucked a stray curl behind her ear. "I want you here, too, Laurie. Always have."

She'd heard the words before, but for some reason they seemed to take her by surprise. She studied him with bemusement. "Is this your peculiar idea of a proposal, then?"

"That depends."

"On?"

"What you intend to do with that hammer." He gestured toward the tool she was thumping repeatedly into the palm of her hand.

"This?" She paused thoughtfully. "I'm tempted to use it to get your attention."

"How about kissing me instead?" he suggested with a wicked gleam in his eyes.

Before she could respond, he leaned over and took her mouth with an urgency that left her breathless and reeling. She clasped his shoulders to steady herself. That was a mistake, because his skin burned beneath her touch, sending shock waves of desire cascading through her.

She sighed when he released her. "Harlan Patrick, that's never been the problem between us. That's what muddies the waters."

He gazed into her eyes. "Be honest with me, Laurie. Can you do that?"

Something told her that she didn't have a choice. Whatever she said now was going to make all the difference in how the future turned out.

"I'll tell you whatever you want to know," she agreed.

"How do you feel right now?"

"Besides panicked?"

His smile was grim. "Besides that. Being back here, how does it make you feel?"

"I love it here. You know that. I just can't *stay* here."

"Could you stay here some of the time, say, between concert tours and recording sessions?"

Her gaze locked with his, and her heart began to pound. "What are you suggesting?"

"Something I should have insisted on long ago. It's a genuine compromise, darlin'. It's hardly any wonder that neither of us recognize it. Bottom line, we make this our home. You go to Nashville when you need to, go on tour when you have to, but you come back here. Amy Lynn and I'll be waiting and maybe a few more kids when we can fit the baby-making into your busy schedule."

She searched his face, desperate to see if he could truly

live with this solution. "Are you sure? Can you really accept having a part-time wife?"

"As long as it's you," he assured her. "It took me long enough to grasp the truth, but I figure having you half the time will be better than having a poor substitute all the time."

She grinned at him. "Harlan Patrick, you do have a romantic way with words."

"I'm not the wordsmith in the family. You are."

"You know," she said slyly, "you can carry a tune pretty good for a cowboy. Maybe you could come along and sing with me once in a while."

"No way, darlin'. The bright lights and glamour are all yours."

Suddenly it all fell into place for her. She had no idea why she'd fought him so long. This was where she belonged, right here, in Harlan Patrick's arms. He'd been steadfast in his love practically forever. Unlike her father, he knew his own heart and was willing to make whatever sacrifices were necessary to keep her in his life.

As for her singing, the acclaim, well, it was all just icing on the cake. He was offering her the chance to have that cake and eat it, too. How could she possibly say no to that when it was what she'd dreamed of practically forever.

"This room you're building, is it going to be a nursery?"

He shook his head. "A whole new master-bedroom suite with a music room right alongside it, so you can write your songs and rehearse right here at home."

"Really?"

"Yes. You see, I've been counting on you coming home."

"Just how far along is this room?"

He grinned. "Not far enough along for what you've got in mind, but it will be by the time we say I do."

Laurie looked into his eyes and saw the love there, understood finally the risk he had taken to bring her back from despair. He knew her inside and out and he wanted her.

"I love you, Harlan Patrick Adams."

"I know that."

"I always have."

"I know that, too."

"And you?"

"Darlin', you and our family and White Pines are all I'll ever need to make me a happy man."

She threw her arms around him then, recklessly wrapped her legs around his waist, regardless of their precarious perch on the roof. After all, she was a woman who liked to live dangerously.

"Then prepare yourself to be ecstatic, cowboy," she said, her gaze locked with his. "I'm coming home."

* * * * *

SUDDENLY,
ANNIE'S FATHER

One

Slade Sutton knew a whole lot about horses, but he didn't know a blasted thing about females. The only woman with whom he'd ever risked his heart had damn near killed him in a car crash, then divorced him when he could not longer win rodeo championships. Worse, she'd left him with a daughter who was a total mystery to him.

Annie was ten-going-on-thirty, wise beyond her years, clever as the dickens and the prettiest little girl he'd ever seen, even if he was a mite biased on the subject. While he'd been on the circuit, they'd been apart more than they'd been together, which had left both of them as wary as if they'd been strangers.

Ever since the accident and Suzanne's desertion, Annie had been living with his parents, but he knew the time was fast approaching when he would no longer be able to shirk his responsibilities. He'd begun dreading every phone call, knowing that most spelled trouble. Annie had a knack for it, and his parents' level of tolerance was slipping. He could hear it in their tired voices. He'd been making excuses for weeks now for not going home for a visit. He'd half feared they'd sneak Annie into his truck on his way out of town. Every night he prayed she'd stay out of mischief just a little longer, just until he could get his bearings in this new job.

Of course, he'd been working for Harlan and Cody Adams for nearly a year now at White Pines, caring for their horses, setting up a breeding program, breaking the yearlings. He could hardly claim he was still getting settled, but he dreaded the day when his parents called him on it.

He studied the picture of Annie that he kept on his bedside table and shook his head in wonder. How had he had any part in producing a child so beautiful, so delicately feminine? He lived in a rough-and-tumble world. She looked like a fairy-tale princess, a little angel.

Judging from the reports he'd been receiving, however, looks could be deceiving. Annie was as spirited as any bronco he'd ever ridden. She charged at life full throttle and, like him, she didn't know the meaning of fear.

The phone on the bunkhouse wall rang, cutting into his wandering thoughts. Hardy Jones grabbed for it. Hardy had more women chasing after him than a Hollywood movie star. It had become a joke around the ranch. No one saw much use to Hardy's pretense of living in the bunkhouse, when he never spent a night in his bed there. And no one besides Hardy ever jumped for the phone.

"Hey, Slade, it's for you," the cowboy called out, looking disappointed.

Trepidation stirred in Slade's gut as he crossed the room. It had to be trouble. Annie had been too much on his mind today. That was a surefire sign that something was going on over in Wilder's Glen, Texas.

Sure enough, it was his father, sounding grim.

"Dadgumit, Slade, you're going to have to come and

get your daughter," Harold Sutton decreed without wasting much time on idle chitchat.

Much as he wanted to ignore it, even Slade could hear the desperation in his father's voice. He sighed. "What's Annie done now?"

"Aside from falling out of a tree and breaking her wrist, climbing on the roof and darn near bringing down the chimney, I suppose you could say she's having a right peaceful summer," his father said. "But she's a handful, Son, and your mama and I just can't cope with her anymore. We've been talking it over for a while now. We're too dadgum old for this. We don't have the kind of energy it takes to keep up with her."

Slade's father was an ex-marine and had his own garage. He put in ten hours a day there and played golf every chance he got. His mother gardened, canned vegetables, made quilts and belonged to every single organization in Wilder's Glen. Slade wasn't buying the idea that they couldn't keep up with a ten-year-old. Annie had just stretched their patience, that was all. It had to be.

"Look, whatever she's done, I'm sure she didn't mean to. I'll talk to her, get her to settle down a little."

"This isn't just about settling her down," his father countered. "She needs you."

The last thing Slade wanted was to be needed by anyone, especially a ten-year-old girl. Between the aches and pains that reminded him every second of the accident that had cost him his career and very nearly his life, and the anger at the woman responsible, it was all he could do to get through the day on his own. He was grateful every single minute of it, though, that his parents had been willing to take Annie in when he hadn't been up to it. She'd been better off with them than she would have been with him. He'd been too bitter, too filled with resentment toward her mama to be any kind of example for an impressionable kid.

"You know I'm grateful," he began.

"We don't want your thanks," his father said, cutting him off. "We love Annie and we love you. We know the jam you were in after the accident. We understood you needed some time to get back on your feet."

"But—"

"Let me finish now. Your mama and I aren't up to raising Annie the way the girl ought to be raised. We had a houseful of boys. Girls just aren't the same, even though Annie seems bent on being the toughest little tomboy in the whole town. Besides that, times have changed since you and your brothers were kids. The world's a different place."

"Not in Wilder's Glen," Slade protested. "It's perfect for Annie. It's a small town. She'll be as safe there as she could be anywhere."

"Her safety's not the only issue. Even if it were, she'll be just as safe in Los Piños. No, indeed, there's a more important issue, and you know it. She misses you. She belongs with you. We were glad enough to fill in for a while, but it's time for you to take over now and that's that. Otherwise the child will be scarred for life, thinking that her own daddy didn't want her any more than her mama did."

"But—"

"No buts, and you can forget coming after her. We'll bring her to you this weekend," Harold announced decisively, as if he no longer trusted Slade to show up for her.

Slade sighed heavily. The sorry truth was he wouldn't have, not even with a deadline staring him in the face. He would have called at the last minute with some excuse or another, and counted on his parents to hang in with Annie a little longer.

Hearing a date and time for assuming responsibility for his daughter all but made Slade's skin crawl. Much as he loved Annie, he wasn't cut out to be a parent to her. His experience with her mother was pretty much evidence of his lack of understanding of the female mind. He was also flat-out terrified that the resentment he felt toward Suzanne would carry over to their daughter in some way he wouldn't be able to control. No kid deserved that.

Annie was the spitting image of his ex-wife in every way, from her gloriously thick hair to her green-as-emerald eyes, from the dusting of freckles on her nose to her stubborn chin. Apparently she had her mama's wicked ways about her, too. She'd caused more trouble in the last year than any child he'd ever known. She'd topped his own imaginative forms of rebellion by a mile and she hadn't even hit puberty yet. What on earth would her teenage years hold? To be fair, he couldn't blame his parents for not wanting to find out.

"Are you sure?" he asked, his own voice desperate now. "I don't think it's such a good idea for her to come here. She's comfortable there with you. She's starting to think of that as home. She spent the school year there. She's made friends. Uprooting her all over again won't be good for her. Besides that, the Adamses don't even know I have a daughter. I'm living in a bunkhouse. Some days I don't get to bed till midnight and I'm back up again at dawn."

He'd ticked off a half-dozen excuses before he was done, most of them flat-out lies. He knew that a staunch family man like Harlan Adams would never object to Slade bringing his daughter to the ranch. If anything, he'd be furious Slade hadn't brought her to be with him before now.

As for the living arrangements, Harlan Adams would make adjustments for that, too. It had been Slade's choice to live in the bunkhouse, rather than one of the other homes dotted across Adams land. He'd wanted to stay close to the horses that were his responsibility. Horses were something he understood.

He tried one last panicked ploy. "I could get you some help," he offered. "Maybe a housekeeper."

"This isn't about cooking and cleaning," his father scoffed. "It's about a little girl needing her daddy. We're coming Sunday and that's that."

There was a finality to his tone with which Slade was all too familiar. Just to emphasize his point, Harold hung up before Slade could think of a single argument to convince him to keep Annie with them.

"Looks like it's time to face the music, bud," he muttered under his breath. Way past time, some would say.

Resigned to his fate, first thing in the morning he arranged to sit down with Cody Adams to discuss his housing situation.

"If there's no place available, I can call my folks back and tell them to give me more time to work it out," he told Cody, praying for a reprieve.

"Absolutely not," Cody said at once, then grinned at Slade's heavy sigh. "Uh-oh, were you counting on me to bail you out of this?"

"I suppose I was," Slade admitted. "Annie and I haven't spent a lot of time together. I'm not sure how good I'll be at this parent thing."

"Then you're lucky you're here. Anytime you're at a loss, just ask one of us for help." The rancher's expression turned sly. "I know one woman who'd be glad to step in and do a little mothering if Annie needs it."

An image of Val Harding came to mind without Cody even having to mention her name. A petite whirlwind with a nonstop mouth, she had set her sights on Slade during a visit to the ranch a few months back. She hadn't let up since. Thankfully, she was in Nashville right now with her boss, country music superstar Laurie Jensen, who was married to Cody's son.

"Thanks all the same," Slade said curtly. "Last I heard Val was out of town."

Cody's grin spread. "Got back last night. The way I hear it from Harlan Patrick, Laurie's going to take a break for a while. She'll be working on the songs for her next album. Val should have plenty of time on her hands."

"I just hope she finds a way to spend it besides pestering me," Slade muttered.

"What was that?"

"Nothing."

Thankfully, Cody let the subject drop. He held out a key. "Check out that house down by the creek. It's been vacant since Joe and his wife left. It's probably a little dusty, but it should be fine for the two of you once it's aired out and had a good cleaning. If it needs anything—dishes, extra blankets, whatever—let me know. I'll get somebody to handle the horses today. You get the place ready. Call up to the main house. One of Maritza's helpers can come down to give you a hand."

"No need," Slade said. "I'll take care of whatever needs to be done. Thanks, Cody. I owe you."

Cody regarded him speculatively. "Family counts for a lot around here. We'll welcome Annie as if she were one of us. You can rest easy on that score."

Slade knew he meant it, too. The Adamses were good people. Maybe they would be able to make up for whatever he lacked.

He took the key Cody offered and headed toward the small house made of rough-hewn wood. It wasn't fancy, but there was a certain charm to it, he supposed. Pots of bright red geraniums bloomed on the porch and a big old cottonwood tree shaded the yard. The creek flowed past just beyond.

The house had been closed up since the last tenant had left, a married hand who'd retired and moved to Arizona. A cursory glance around the small rooms told Slade it had everything he and Annie could need, including a small TV that had been hooked up to cable. The kitchen was well stocked with dishes and pots and pans. Fortunately, the refrigerator had a good-size freezer, big enough to accommodate all the prepared meals he and Annie were likely to consume. His cooking skills ran to cold cereal and boiled eggs.

The closets revealed a supply of linens for the beds, a small one in what would be Annie's room, and a big brass bed with a feather mattress in what was clearly the master bedroom. Staring at that mattress was disconcerting. All sorts of wicked images came to mind, images of being tangled up with a woman again. One particular woman, he conceded with some dismay. He could all but feel her breath on his chest and sense the weight of her head tucked under his chin. It had been a long time since he'd allowed himself to indulge in the fantasy, much less the reality.

"Quite a bed, isn't it?" an all-too-familiar voice inquired with a seductive purr.

Slade scowled at the intrusion by the pesky woman

whose image had just flitted through his mind. "You ever heard of knocking?" he asked.

Val didn't flinch at his impatient tone. "I wasn't sure anyone was in here. Nobody's been living here and the front door was standing open. I was afraid someone had broken in."

Slade regarded her incredulously. "So you decided to do what—wander in and talk them to death? Didn't it occur to you that if a robber was in here, you could get hurt?"

She grinned, looking smug. "Worried about me, cowboy? That's progress."

She slipped past him into the room, leaving a cloud of perfume in her wake. Slade tried not to let the scent stir him the way it usually did. Sometimes he thought he smelled that soft, flowery aroma in the middle of the night. Those were the nights he tossed and turned till dawn and cursed the day Val had come to live at White Pines and taken an interest in him.

"Nice view," she observed, gazing out at the creek. "What are you doing here, by the way?"

"Moving in," he said, backing out of the room before his body could get any ideas about tossing her onto that feather mattress to see if it—and she—were as soft as he imagined.

She turned slowly. "Alone?"

"No."

Something that might have been disappointment flared briefly in her eyes. "I see."

Guilt over that look had him admitting the truth. "My daughter's coming to stay with me." He tested the words aloud and found they didn't cause quite so much panic since his talk with Cody. Knowing he'd have backup had eased his mind. Maybe Annie could survive having a father as inept as him, after all.

Val's expression brightened with curiosity. She seized on the tidbit as if he'd tossed her the hottest piece of gossip since the world had discovered that singer Laurie Jensen had a secret baby by the man who was now her husband.

"You have a daughter?" she asked. "How old? What's she like? Where's she been all this time? What about her mother?"

Slade grinned despite himself. "You care to try those one at a time?"

"Oh, just tell me everything and save us both the aggravation," she retorted. "I wouldn't have to pester you so if you'd open up in the first place."

"Is that so? And here I thought you enjoyed pestering me."

"Getting you to talk is a challenge," she admitted. "And you know how we women react to a challenge."

He regarded her intently. "So, if I just blab away, you'll go away eventually?"

She grinned. "Maybe. Try it and see."

"Sorry. I'm too busy right now. Maybe another time."

The dismissal didn't even faze her. "Busy doing what? Looked to me like you were daydreaming when I came in."

"Which is why it's all the more important for me to get started with the work around here now," he said, and headed for the kitchen again. He'd seen cleaning supplies in there on his first stop. He snatched up a broom, a vacuum, dust cloths and furniture polish. He figured he could give the place a decent once-over in an hour and be back on the job before noon.

Val reached for the broom. "Give me that. I'll help."

Slade held tight. "There's no need. You'll ruin your clothes."

The woman always dressed as if she were about to meet with the press or go out for cocktails. He doubted she owned a pair of jeans or sneakers, much less boots. In fact, today was one of the rare occasions when she wasn't wearing those ridiculous high heels she paraded around in. He had to admit those shoes did a lot for her legs. It was almost a disappointment when she traded them for flats, as she had today.

In flats, she barely came up to his chin, reminding him of just how fragile and utterly feminine a creature she was. It brought out the protective instincts in him, despite the fact that there wasn't a doubt in his mind that Val Harding could look out for herself. Heaven knew, she protected Laurie with a ferocity that was daunting. No one got anywhere close to the singer without Val's approval. Slade secretly admired that kind of loyalty. Too bad Suzanne hadn't possessed even a quarter as much. They might have stayed married.

"Oh, for heaven's sakes, give me the broom," Val said. "A little dust never hurt anything. You'll get finished that much sooner if you let me help. Otherwise, I'll just trail around after you asking more questions you don't want to answer."

She had a point about that. It wasn't likely she'd respond to his dismissal and just go away. Reluctantly, Slade relinquished the broom and watched as she went to work with a vengeance on the wide-plank oak floors in the living room. She attacked the job with the same cheerfulness and efficiency with which she ran Laurie's professional life.

When she glanced up and caught Slade staring at her,

she grinned. "Get to work. I said I'd help, not do the whole job."

"Yes, ma'am," he said at once, and turned on the vacuum. As he ran it over the carpet in the bedrooms, he could hear her singing with wildly off-key enthusiasm. He wondered if Laurie had ever heard one of her country music hits murdered quite the way Val was doing it.

With her help, he had the house tidied up in no time. Fresh air was drifting through the rooms and filling them with the sweet scent of recently cut grass and a hint of Janet's roses from the gardens at the main house.

An odd sensation came over him as he stood in the living room and gazed about, listening to Val stirring around in the kitchen. The place felt like home, like some place a man could put down roots. For a man who'd spent most of his adult life on the road, it was a terrifying sensation.

Slade Sutton was the most exasperating, frustrating man on the face of the earth. Val watched him take off without so much as a thank-you. He looked as if he were being chased by demons as he fled the house. The limp from his accident was more exaggerated as he tried to move quickly. She knew his expression, if she'd been able to see his face, would be filled with annoyance over his ungainly gait and, most of all, over her.

Of course, he had that look a lot when he was trying to get away from her, she admitted with a sigh. It had been months since she'd first met him, and she could honestly say that she didn't know him one bit better now than she had when she'd paid her first visit to White Pines.

No, that wasn't quite true. Today she'd learned he had a daughter. Amazing. How could anyone keep a secret like that, especially around the Adamses, who made her look like an amateur when it came to nosing into other people's lives? Laurie had tried to keep Harlan Patrick's baby a secret from him and that had lasted less than six months. Of course, the tabloids had had a hand in leaking that news and sending Harlan Patrick chasing after Laurie.

A lot of women would have given up if they'd had the same reception from Slade that Val had had. Why go through the torment of rejection after rejection? Why poke and prod and get nothing but a shrug or a grunted acknowledgment for her persistence? She'd asked herself that a hundred times while she'd been in Nashville this last time. She'd hoped that a little distance from the ranch would give her some perspective, maybe dull the attraction she felt for him. After all, Slade Sutton wasn't the last man on earth.

But he was the only one in years who'd intrigued her, the only one who hadn't been using her to get closer to Laurie. In fact, he was the only man she knew who barely spared a glance for the gorgeous superstar. Val had caught him looking at her, though, sneaking glances when he thought she wasn't aware of him. Maybe that hint of interest, reluctant as it was, was what kept her going.

Or maybe it had something to do with how incredibly male he was. Handsome as sin, a little rough around the edges, he had eyes a woman could drown in. She'd discovered that when he finally took off his sunglasses long enough to allow anyone to catch a glimpse of them. A dimple flirted at the corner of his mouth on the rare occasions when he smiled. His jaw looked as if it had been carved from granite. In fact, he was all hard angles and solid muscle, the kind of man whose strength wasn't obtained in a gym, but just from living.

Bottom line? He made her mouth water. She sometimes

thought that if he didn't kiss her soon, she was going to have to take matters into her own hands.

Then again, she preferred to think she wasn't quite so shallow. That it wasn't all about lust and sex. Maybe she just liked a good mystery.

Slade was certainly that. He'd told the Adamses no more than he had to to get hired. He'd told her even less. There'd been times in the last six months when she'd found that so thoroughly frustrating she'd been tempted to hire a private investigator to fill in the gaps, but that would have spoiled the game. She wanted to unearth his secrets all on her own. It was turning out to be a time-consuming task. At the rate of one revelation every few months, she'd be at it for a lifetime.

It was a good thing her daddy had taught her about grit. Nobody on the face of the earth was more determined or more persistent than she was. She'd used those lessons to get the job she wanted in Nashville, pestering Laurie's agent until he'd made the introduction just to get her out of his office. Now she was personal assistant to the hottest country music star in the country. Those same lessons made her the best at what she did.

Now they were going to help her get Slade Sutton, too.

She watched him hightail it back toward the barn and his precious horses. She grinned, understanding fully for the first time that she made him nervous. He was every bit as skittish as one of those new colts he found to be such a challenge. That was good. It was a vast improvement over indifference.

Yes, indeed, he could run, but he couldn't hide, she concluded with satisfaction. Laurie was home for a much-deserved breather, and Val had a whole lot of time on her hands. Slade didn't stand a chance.

Two

Sunday morning dawned with a sudden storm that rivaled the turmoil churning in Slade's gut. Lightning and thunder split the air. From inside the house, he could see the creek rising rapidly, though it was not yet in danger of overflowing its banks as it had on a few terrifying occasions in past summers. Just a few years ago, he'd been told, it had flooded out this house, destroying most of the previous tenants' belongings and washing away a lifetime of memories. In the tenacious manner of the Adamses and everyone around them, they had cleaned it up without complaint and started over.

He shuddered at another crack of thunder, though his unease had more to do with the next few hours than with the storm. Annie would be here all too soon. He had no idea how she felt about him these days. On his few visits to Wilder's Glen, she had been withdrawn, clearly blaming him for the changes in her life.

As for him, he was nowhere near ready to deal with the changes her arrival would bring to his life. Oh, he'd made a few preparations. He'd moved his things over to their house. He'd gone into town and picked up enough frozen dinners to last for a month. The freezer was so crowded with them, there wasn't even room for ice cubes.

He'd even gone into a toy store and impulsively bought a huge stuffed bear to sit in the middle of Annie's bed. When she was little, he'd bought her a stuffed toy or a doll every time he'd come home. She's always loved them then. Her eyes had lit up with unabashed joy and she'd crawled into his lap, hugging the latest toy tightly in her arms. Her smile had wiped away the guilt he'd always felt at leaving her behind. Maybe it would work one more time.

He trudged over to the barn through the pouring rain, finished up his chores, regretting the fact that they didn't take longer. When he was through, he went back to the house to shower and wait. That gave him way too much time to think, to remember the way his life had been not so long ago.

He'd been a celebrity of sorts, a champion, whose whole identity had been wrapped up in winning rodeos. He'd had plenty of money in the bank. He'd had a beautiful, headstrong wife who could turn him on with a glance, and a daughter who awed and amazed him. Life was exciting, a never-ending round of facing the unexpected. There'd been media attention and applause and physical challenges.

What did he have now? A decent-paying job working at one of the best ranches in Texas. It was steady employment, no surprises. That's what he'd told himself he wanted after Suzanne had walked out. Routine and boredom had seemed attractive after the turbulence of their last few weeks together. No emotional entanglements, not even with his own kid. He sighed heavily as he considered the selfishness of that.

He'd pay for it now, no doubt about it. Annie was no

longer the joyous, carefree sprite she'd been a year ago. Suzanne was to blame for some of that, but he had to shoulder the rest. It was up to him to make up for the fact that Annie's mother had walked out on both of them. If he'd been neglectful in the months since, Suzanne had been cruel. He knew for a fact she hadn't written or called in all that time.

Rainwater dripped from the roof as he watched and waited. The summer storm finally ended almost as quickly as it had begun, leaving the air steamy and the dirt driveway a sea of mud. Dirt splattered every which way when his father's car finally came barreling in just after one o'clock. Slade grinned at the sight. His father was driving the way he always did, as if he were ten minutes late for a military dress parade. The marine in him had never fully died.

Slade stepped off the porch and went to greet them, wrapping his mother in a bear hug that had her laughing. Only when he'd released her did he notice the exhaustion in her eyes, the tired lines around her mouth. Surely she hadn't looked that old the last time he'd seen her. Knowing the toll Annie had taken on her was just one more thing for him to feel guilty about.

He studied his father intently as he shook his hand. He didn't see any noticeable changes in Harold Sutton's appearance. His close-cropped hair had been gray for years, so Slade couldn't blame that on Annie. His grip was as strong as ever, his manner as brusque and hearty. He didn't look like the kind of man who'd let a child get the better of him. Slade had to wonder if that hadn't just been an excuse to force him to take Annie back into his life.

"Good to see you, Son."

"You, too, Dad."

"Annie, girl, get on out here and say hello to your daddy," Harold Sutton commanded in a booming voice left from his days as a marine drill sergeant. None of his sons had ever dared to ignore one of his orders. Punishments for disobedience had been doled out swiftly. For a minute, though, Slade thought that Annie might. She stared out at them from the back seat, her expression mulish.

Eventually, though, she slipped out of the car with obvious reluctance and stood there awkwardly, refusing to come closer. It was all Slade could do not to gape when he saw her.

How the devil had his daughter gone from being a little angel in frilly dresses to *this*? he wondered, staring at the ripped jeans, baggy T-shirt and filthy sneakers Annie was wearing. He'd been prepared for the cast on her arm, but not for the fact that it appeared she'd been rolling in mud wearing it.

And what the dickens had happened to her curls? The last time he'd seen her, she'd had pretty, chestnut-colored hair, braided neatly and tied with bows. Now it looked as if someone had taken a pair of dull scissors and whacked it off about two inches from her scalp.

Annie regarded him with a sullen expression, while he tried to figure out what to say to her.

"You look real good," he managed finally.

Annie didn't even waste her breath replying to the blatant lie. She just continued to stare at him with a defiant tilt to her chin and a heartbreaking mix of hurt and anger in her eyes. He might have responded to that, if his mother hadn't latched onto his arm and pulled him aside.

"I'll explain to you about that later," she muttered under her breath, her gaze pointedly focused on Annie's hairstyle. "Please don't say anything about her hair. She's very self-conscious about it."

"She darned well ought to be," Slade retorted. "What were you thinking?"

"It wasn't me," she snapped. "When she found out we were bringing her over here, she did it herself."

He shot a bewildered glance toward his daughter. "But why?"

"I have no idea. She's a mystery, Slade. Keeps everything bottled up inside. It comes out in these daredevil acts of hers. I never know what kind of trouble she's going to get herself into. She's a smart girl, but you saw her report cards. She got through the school year by the skin of her teeth. I'm pretty sure her principal will throw a party when she hears Annie's transferring to another school district."

She gestured toward the three suitcases his father had lined up on the porch. "That's everything she has. Your dad and I will be going now," she said, as if she couldn't wait to get away, to get some peace and quiet back into her life.

Slade stared at her in shock. "You can't leave," he protested. The nastiest bull on the circuit had never set off such panic deep inside him.

"It's a long way back home. Tomorrow's a workday for your daddy. Besides, you two need time to settle in."

"But you've driven all this way. I thought we'd go into town for a nice dinner or something," he said, trying to delay the inevitable moment when he and his daughter would be left on their own.

His mother gave him a sympathetic pat. "Everything's going to work out just fine, Son. She's your own flesh and blood, after all. All the girl needs is a little love and attention from her daddy. You remember how she used to worship the ground you walked on. She was a daddy's girl, no doubt about it. She never mentions her mama, but I catch her staring at the pictures we have of you on the mantel."

Love and attention, Slade thought, staring at Annie uneasily after his parents had driven away. Too bad those were the two things likely to be in very short supply coming from him.

Val stood in the office Harlan Patrick had built for her just off her boss's music room and stared at the scene outside. It was like watching an accident unfold in slow motion, horrifying and tragic. Slade Sutton was regarding his daughter as if she were a rattler he considered capable of striking at any second. His wariness was downright pathetic, but then Slade seemed to be wary of most females.

Watching him with his daughter, she couldn't hear what was being said, but it was all too evident that neither of them had conversational skills worth a hill of beans. The few feet between them might as well have been a mile.

Hug her, Val coached silently. Neither of them budged. Slade's hands were jammed into his pockets. His daughter's were jammed into her own. It was as if they both feared reaching out. Val wondered if Slade even realized that the girl was mimicking his mannerisms.

Abruptly he turned and stalked away. As the girl stared after him, her chin wobbled as if she might cry, but then she, too, turned and stalked off, in the opposite direction. Her suitcases stayed where they'd been left, right on the porch. He hadn't even bothered to take her inside and show her where she'd be living.

"They're a sorry pair, aren't they?" Laurie asked, coming to stand beside her. "I was watching from upstairs.

I guess it's true what I heard, that they'd been estranged for months now. I wonder why."

"The why's not important. Somebody needs to see to that poor child," Val said, her indignation rising. "Slade's obviously not going to do it."

"Why don't you go?" Laurie suggested, regarding her with amusement. "You know you want to. You've been itching to find out more about Slade's daughter ever since you discovered he had one."

Val shook her head and reluctantly turned away from the window. "I don't want to meddle."

Laurie grinned. "That'll be a first. When it comes to meddling, you could rival Grandpa Harlan. If I didn't know better, I'd swear you were an Adams. My relationship with Harlan Patrick wasn't any of your business, either, but that didn't keep you from teaming up with him."

"That was different. You two belonged together. You were just too stubborn to admit it. You needed a little push."

"Maybe that's all those two need."

"Forget it. You know how Slade is. He'll be furious if I go sticking my nose into his business," she said, fighting the temptation to meddle anyway. Another glance at that downcast child and she'd let her heart overrule her common sense.

"Since when did his moods bother you?" Laurie asked. "Besides, I thought you took great satisfaction in provoking him."

Laurie was right about that. Val did like getting Slade Sutton all stirred up. Every now and again the fire she managed to spark in his eyes struck her as very promising. So far, he'd carefully avoided indulging in anything remotely close to a passionate response. In fact, he made it a point to steer clear of her whenever he could. Yesterday had been one of those rare occasions when running hadn't been an option.

One day, though, she was going to catch him alone when he didn't have chores to tend to. She would seize the chance to deliberately push him over the edge. Then she'd finally discover if all this chemistry she'd been feeling for the past few months was one-sided or not.

Now was not the time, however, and Annie was not the best subject to use to provoke a response from him. There were too many complicated emotions at work here that Val didn't understand.

After she thought for a minute about the scene she'd just witnessed, it occurred to her that for once Slade might be grateful to have her step in. Clearly he was out of his depth, though why that should be eluded her.

She, on the other hand, liked kids. All sorts of maternal feelings washed through her every time she held Laurie's baby. Now that Amy Lynn was beginning to toddle around on unsteady legs, Val enjoyed chasing after her almost as much as she liked setting up interviews and keeping Laurie's life on track. She might not have signed on as a babysitter, but it was one of the duties she took on willingly.

"Okay, okay," she agreed finally, giving in to Laurie's urging and her own desire to get involved. "I'm going." She said it as if she were caving in to pressure, just to preserve the illusion of reluctance. The truth was she was eager to meet Slade's daughter, just as Laurie had said.

Outside, she strolled casually in the direction in which she'd seen the child go. Surprisingly, she found her near the stables. Apparently she'd gravitated back toward where she knew her father would be, after all. Slade was nowhere in sight, but Val assumed he was inside the barn doing those endless chores he found so fascinating.

"Hi," Val said, coming up to the corral railing to stand beside her. "I'm Val."

The girl kept her gaze focused on the horses.

"You must be Annie," Val continued, as if she hadn't been totally ignored. Apparently father and child shared a disdain for polite responses. "I've been hearing a lot about you."

"Not from my dad, I'll bet," Annie responded, giving her a sullen glance.

"Actually, that's not true. Your dad is the one who told me you were coming. Then I heard about you again from my boss, Laurie Jensen."

The mention of Laurie's name was bound to catch the attention of anyone who'd ever listened to country music. Laurie's albums were at the top of the charts. Annie Sutton proved to be no exception. She regarded Val suspiciously.

"Yeah, right. Like you actually know Laurie Jensen."

"Like I said, I work for her." She gestured vaguely toward Harlan Patrick's house, which wasn't visible from where they stood. "She lives about a quarter mile down the road, not too far from your dad's house. Surely he's mentioned that to you."

Annie shrugged. "Me and my dad don't talk too much." She focused her attention on the horses for a while, then asked, "So, how come Laurie Jensen lives here?"

"She's married to Harlan Patrick Adams, who's one of the owners of this ranch."

There was a flash of interest in eyes that had been way too bored for any typically inquisitive ten-year-old. "No way."

"It's true."

Her expression brightened visibly. "And you said Laurie Jensen actually knew my name?"

Val grinned at her astonishment. "She did."

"Awesome."

Relieved to have caught the child's interest, Val decided to capitalize on it. Maybe she could forge a bond with Annie more easily than she'd imagined. "Maybe you could come by sometime and meet her, listen to her working on songs for her next album. If your dad doesn't mind, that is."

Annie's excited expression faded. "Oh, he won't care. He doesn't want me here, anyway."

Even though she'd suspected as much, Val was still shocked by the words, angered by the fact that Slade had let his feelings show so plainly. "I'm sure that's not true."

"Yes, it is. He hates me."

"Why on earth would he hate you? You're his daughter," Val protested, unwilling to believe there could be any truth to the accusation.

"It's because of my mom. She almost got him killed when she drove his car into a ditch, and then she left us," she said matter-of-factly. "I guess I don't blame him for hating me. Everybody says I look just like her. I heard Grandma tell one of her friends that if I'm not careful I'll turn out just like her, too. Nothing but trouble, that's what she said."

Val was stunned. This was more than she'd ever learned from Slade, and it went a long way toward explaining his attitude toward women. Still, his problems with his ex-wife were no excuse for treating his daughter the way he'd been doing. And her grandmother should have watched her tongue. Val couldn't see that it served any useful purpose to go knocking her former daughter-in-law where Annie could overhear her.

"Your mom's leaving must have hurt you both very much," Val said, treading carefully. "Sometimes grown-ups don't get over something like that very easily."

"Like kids do?" Annie retorted. She sighed heavily, as if resigned to the fact that no adult could ever understand what she was going through.

"Of course not," Val agreed, "but—"

Annie faced her squarely. "Look, you don't have to be nice to me. I'm just a kid and I'm used to being on my own. My grandma and grandpa pretty much left me alone, except when I did something wrong."

"I'll bet you got into trouble a lot then, didn't you?" Val guessed.

Annie stared at her with obvious surprise. "How'd you know that?" She sighed once again. "Never mind. I suppose *he* told you. He probably warned you about me."

Val decided not to tell her it was predictable. Annie probably thought she was the only kid who'd ever used that technique to get the attention of the adults around her. "Nope. Lucky guess," she said instead. She glanced toward the horses. "Do you like horses as much as your dad does?"

Annie shrugged. "I suppose. My grandma and grandpa lived in town, so we didn't have horses."

"But you must have been around them when your dad was on the rodeo circuit."

"Me and my mom didn't go with him all that much after I started school. I guess we did when I was real little, but I don't remember that. My mom said it was my fault he left us behind all the time."

Val hid her dismay. What kind of mother openly blamed

her child for the problems that were clearly between her and her husband? And what kind of father allowed it to happen? She wanted to reach out and hug this sad, neglected child, but Annie's defensive posture told her she wouldn't welcome the gesture, much less trust that it was genuine.

"You're going to really love living here," Val told her instead. "There are lots of kids around. The Adamses are wonderful people. They'll throw a party at the drop of a hat. You'll fit in in no time."

Annie looked skeptical. "They probably won't invite my dad and me. He just works here."

"I work here, too, but they always include me."

"You're a grown-up," Annie said, but she couldn't hide the wistful look that crossed her face.

"Maybe so, but I was hoping maybe we could be friends. I haven't been here all that long myself. Maybe we could go into town one day. I could show you around while your dad's working."

Annie regarded her skeptically. "Yeah, well, if you're doing it so my dad'll notice you, you're wasting your time. He hates girls, because of my mom. My grandma says he'd be a recluse if he could."

Apparently Grandma had one very loose tongue. "Well, you're here now, so being a recluse is not an option," Val said briskly, giving Annie's shoulder a reassuring squeeze. "He may not know it yet, but having you here is going to be very good for him. I can tell that already."

Despite Annie's conviction about how little her father thought of her, she gave Val a hopeful look that almost broke her heart.

"Do you think so?" she asked.

"I know so," Val assured her. If she had to knock Slade Sutton upside the head herself, she was going to see to it.

Three

Val had a giant-size calendar spread out on the floor in Laurie's music room, while her boss sprawled on the sofa, idly picking out a tune on her guitar.

"This song is terrible," Laurie concluded, eyeing the instrument as if it were at fault. "I haven't been able to write worth a lick since Harlan Patrick and I got married."

"Stop putting so much pressure on yourself," Val advised. She'd been listening to the same complaint for weeks now. If Laurie wasn't careful, she was going to talk herself straight into a writer's block, even though on her worst days she was better than half the songwriters out there. "Take time out to count your blessings. You have a handsome, sexy husband who adores you. You have a gorgeous daughter who is absolutely brilliant for someone barely a year old."

Laurie managed a ghost of a smile at the reminders. "Okay, yes, I am very lucky."

"Concentrate on that for a few days. After all, you only need two more songs for the new album," she reminded her boss. "The studio time's not booked for two more months."

The faint smile faded at once. "Why two months?" Laurie grumbled, picking out the notes of her last hit on the guitar. "I should be in Nashville now. If I don't get back to work soon, my fans will forget all about me."

Val rolled her eyes heavenward. Laurie had been a wreck ever since she had agreed to take a break from her usual hectic recording and concert pace. She blamed her agent, Val and Harlan Patrick for talking her into it. Most of all, she blamed herself for caving in. The forced idleness was making her crazy, especially since her husband was as busy as ever running the ranch and couldn't devote himself full-time to keeping her occupied.

"No one is going to forget about you," Val soothed. "Nick and I have that covered. There will be plenty of items in the media. I've booked you on at least one of the entertainment shows every single month until the album's due to be released. There are fresh angles for every story. Besides, I thought you had enough media coverage to last a lifetime when they were chasing after the story of your secret baby."

Laurie didn't look pacified. "What if Harlan Patrick was right?"

"About what?"

"What if I refused to marry him for so long because I knew once I was completely happy I wouldn't be able to write another song?"

"Oh, for heaven's sakes, that is the most ridiculous thing I've ever heard. You don't have to be wallowing in heartbreak to know what it's like. Draw on old memories. For that matter, write something upbeat for a change." She gave Laurie a wicked smile. "Write about having babies."

Laurie's scowl deepened. "Now you sound exactly like Harlan Patrick. He wants me barefoot and pregnant."

"Maybe that's because he missed seeing you pregnant with Amy Lynn. Maybe he just wants to be in on the next pregnancy from start to finish. Maybe it's not some evil scheme to see you trapped down here on the ranch."

Laurie sighed. "I suppose."

"You know what I think?"

"What?"

"I think you're already pregnant."

Laurie's idle strumming screeched into something wildly discordant. "Oh, God. Bite your tongue."

"Stop it," Val chided. "This is exactly the mood you were in when you were carrying Amy Lynn. To be honest, you were unbearable. Of course, then it was understandable. You had to hide out so Harlan Patrick wouldn't find out about the baby. There's no need to hide out now. You can go on the road. You can do anything you'd do if you weren't pregnant. It wouldn't be a calamity, Laurie. And Harlan Patrick and the rest of the family would be over the moon at the news."

"I suppose," Laurie conceded, clearly unconvinced. She glanced down at the calendar Val had been working on. "What are you doing?"

"Trying to finalize next spring's concert tour."

Laurie's expression brightened. "Let me see," she said, putting the guitar aside to kneel down beside Val. "Dallas, Tucson, San Antonio, Phoenix, Albuquerque, Denver. Why is everything in the Southwest? Does Nick know something I don't? Am I losing fans in the South?"

"No, you are not losing fans anywhere. The schedule won't be like this when Nick is finished with the bookings," Val assured her, then grinned. "We both just thought you'd prefer to be close to home around the time the baby's due."

"I am not pregnant," Laurie repeated with a stubborn jut of her chin.

"Saying it won't make it true," Val taunted. "See a doctor, Laurie. Take a home pregnancy test. Do something before you drive both of us nuts."

She glanced up just then and spotted Annie standing hesitantly on the deck outside.

"Is it okay?" Annie whispered, her awestruck gaze fixed on Laurie, though the question was directed to Val.

"Of course it's okay," Val said. "Laurie, this is Annie Sutton."

"Hi," Annie said shyly, not budging from outside. "My dad said not to bother you, if you were busy."

"We're not busy," Laurie said. "More's the pity."

"You were singing before," Annie said. "I heard you. I hope that's okay."

Val wondered how much more Annie had heard before she'd made her presence known. Her expression, however, was totally innocent. Maybe she'd been so captivated just being near Laurie that she hadn't been paying any attention to the rest.

Laurie grinned at her. "What did you think of the song? Tell the truth. I can take it."

"I thought it was awesome, not as sad as what you usually do," Annie said, creeping inside. "Is it finished?"

"Not yet. I can't decide if I like it." Laurie studied Annie intently. "You really liked it, huh?"

Annie nodded. "Especially the part about finding someone new inside. I feel like that sometimes, as if I'm not who I was anymore, but I don't know yet who I am."

Val saw the sudden inspiration flare to life in Laurie's eyes. She grabbed her guitar off the sofa and began to toy with the lyrics that she'd been struggling with earlier.

Annie crept closer and sat down to listen, her rapt gaze never leaving Laurie's face.

Time seemed to stand still as Laurie captured what Annie had so eloquently expressed, and turned it into the beginnings of a song. As the first words flowed, Val grabbed a pad and jotted them down. She knew from experience that Laurie would want to see them in black and white later. For now, she was too caught up in the creative process to take the time to make sure the words weren't lost as soon as they were uttered.

When the last notes faded away, Annie looked as if she'd been given a precious gift. "That's what I said," she whispered. "You sang what I said."

Laurie grinned. "You inspired it, all right. Thank you. I was stuck until you came in here."

"You mean I helped? I really helped?"

"More than you'll know," Val told her fervently. Maybe now Laurie would realize that the only block to her continued success was in her own mental attitude toward the future. "Now let's get out of here and let Laurie work in peace. She won't be happy until every note's perfect."

"I thought it sounded perfect just the way it was," Annie told her.

"Not yet," Laurie said. "But thanks to you, it's getting there."

Annie followed Val to the door with obvious reluctance. Just as they were about to go out, she turned back. "What's it called?"

"'Where'd I Go?'" Laurie told her. "But I'm going to think of it as Annie's song. And whenever I sing it, I'll tell the audience about the young lady who helped me write it."

"Oh, wow!" Annie murmured, eyes shining. "Wait till

my dad hears about this." Outside, she gazed up at Val. "Do you think she really meant it? Will she put that song on an album? Will she really tell people about me?"

"She'll have to run it past some people, but I'd say yes. Laurie usually knows a hit when she hears it." Unwittingly, Annie had captured Laurie's own mood with her words. She'd given her an excuse for writing about the changes that scared Laurie to death. The meeting had been good for both of them. "As for telling her fans about you, Laurie always gives credit where it's due."

Val grinned down at Annie. "How about you and I go into town and celebrate? I'll buy you the biggest sundae they serve at Dolan's. Remember? That's the place I told you about. If we're lucky, Sharon Lynn will have her new baby there with her."

"Really? You can go now? You don't have to work or something?"

"I can go. Let's see if your dad says it's okay for you to come along."

Some of the light in Annie's eyes faded. "He won't care. He's working. I haven't seen him all day. He told me to stick close to home and not get into trouble."

"Ask him anyway," Val insisted. "He's probably at the stables. I'll wait at the car."

Annie gave her a put-upon look, but she scampered off dutifully. Val resisted the temptation to follow and make sure she actually talked to Slade. Annie needed to have someone trust her, and Val needed to learn to resist the urge to make excuses to catch a glimpse of Slade. It was way past time to try out a new strategy. Straightforward hadn't cut it. Maybe the old-fashioned way—playing elusive and hard-to-get—would work.

Annie came back waving a five-dollar bill. "He said okay, but he's treating."

Val was oddly pleased by the gesture. It could hardly be counted as a date, since he wasn't even coming along, but it would be the first thing Slade had ever given her. Too bad she couldn't preserve an ice cream sundae as a souvenir. Maybe she'd tuck that five-dollar bill into a scrapbook, instead.

Seeing Annie and Val with their heads together was enough to send goosebumps sliding down Slade's back. It had been occurring with distressing regularity ever since Annie's arrival earlier in the week.

Over dinner on Annie's first night, all Slade had heard was "Val said this" and "Val said that." He probably should have been grateful that Annie was talking to him at all, but all he could think about was the topic. He had enough trouble keeping his mind off Val without her name coming up every two seconds. Still, he'd gritted his teeth and listened to every word Annie had to say about this new friend she'd acquired.

"And she said she'd take me into town tomorrow," she'd said, her eyes bright with excitement. "There's this place, Dolan's, that has ice cream and hamburgers. It's owned by a lady named Sharon Lynn. You probably know her. Her dad's your boss or something. Anyway, Val said Dolan's is *the* place to go in Los Piños. Or she said we could go for pizza. It's not like one of those national chains. It's made by a real Italian family. I think they came from Rome way back even. Anyway, she said it's my choice. So, what do you think?"

What Slade thought was that the woman was as pesky as flies at a picnic. There hadn't been a single day since she'd first turned up at White Pines that she'd minded her own business. If she got it into her head to befriend Annie, it could only mean trouble. It would start with ice cream and pizza, but who knew where it would lead? Still, he couldn't bring himself to put a damper on Annie's enthusiasm by saying no.

"If you want to go, it's fine," he'd said. "Just don't take advantage. I'll give you the money for your food."

"No, it's her treat. She said so."

But when Annie had come to him for permission, he'd insisted on giving her the money for ice cream. A gentleman didn't let a lady pay. The lesson had been drilled into him by his mother and echoed by his father. It had stuck, which he supposed made him some kind of an old-fashioned oddity in this day and age of dutch treat and ladies doing the asking for dates. On the circuit he'd been astounded by just how brazen some women were, even once they knew he was married.

Annie and Val went for ice cream and burgers on Monday. They had pizza on Tuesday. Val planned a swim in the creek and a picnic on Wednesday. The two of them were thick as thieves. Yes, indeed, it made his skin crawl. Annie needed a new friend, one who wasn't old enough and sexy enough to make her daddy's heart pump quite so hard.

Kids her own age would be good, he concluded, and the ranch was crawling with them. Was it possible to arrange some sort of play date at Annie's age? He could talk to Cody about it. Or should he just pray that the kids found each other before hearing about Val drove him nuts?

The thought had barely occurred to him when he spotted Val striding toward him with a purposeful gleam in her eyes. Watching her walk was a thoroughly entertaining experience. The woman's hips swayed provocatively enough to make a man's blood steam, especially when she got the notion to wear a pair of kick-ass heels that made her legs look long and willowy, despite the fact that she was just a little bitty thing. She'd worn those heels today as if she knew the effect they had on him.

He indulged in a moment of purely masculine appreciation before he reminded himself that that expression on her face spelled upheaval.

"Whatever it is, the answer is no," he announced emphatically when she was several yards away. He turned his attention back to the horse he'd been grooming before he'd caught sight of Val.

When she remained silent for way too long, he risked a glance up. She gave him one of her irrepressible grins. "Good. I have your attention. Just for the record, I haven't asked for anything yet."

"But you will," he muttered. "You always do."

She laughed. "See, we are making progress. You already know me very well."

"That is not a blessing." he retorted.

"Oh, hush, and hear me out," she said, clearly undaunted. "I was thinking we ought to plan a little get-together in Annie's honor. She should get to know all the kids in the family. Not that I don't enjoy her company, because I do, but she needs to have friends her own age. I'm sure she has to be missing the ones she left behind."

Slade wanted to resist the idea just because it had come from Val, but she was right. He'd been thinking precisely the same thing not minutes ago, albeit for very different reasons. Like Val, though, he could see how much it would mean to his daughter to make some friends. Maybe they could fill in the gaps in her life that he couldn't. He couldn't go on relying on Val to keep Annie occupied indefinitely.

"Fine," he said grudgingly, relieved that she seemed to have some sort of a plan in mind. "Do whatever you want. I'll pay for it."

"Oh, no, you don't," she retorted. "Not me. *You and me*," she said with emphasis. "This is a joint venture. I'll do the inviting, if you like, but you have to put out a little effort, too."

He regarded her warily. "Such as?"

"Make arrangements with Harlan to use the barbecue and pool up at the main house, plan a menu with Annie, then pick up the food from town. It'll mean the world to Annie that you want to do this for her."

He supposed she had a point. Gestures probably mattered to females of all ages. Suzanne had certainly counted on them. She'd expected flowers, candy or jewelry every time he'd walked through the door.

"Okay, I'll talk to Harlan," he agreed. "But I don't know a damn thing about planning a menu. I'm lucky if I get a frozen meal on the table for dinner without nuking it to death. Besides, in case you haven't noticed, Anne and I don't communicate real well."

Val regarded him with impatience. "Oh, for goodness sakes, how hard can it be for the two of you to put your heads together and come up with a standard barbecue menu? Steaks, burgers, potato salad, coleslaw, baked beans, dessert. How complicated is that?"

He grinned despite himself. If there was one thing he'd learned about Val Harding, it was that she was frighteningly efficient. "Sounds to me like you've got it all worked out. We'll go with that."

She looked as if she might argue, but she nodded instead. "Okay, then. You set the date with Harlan, and then the three of us will go shopping. We'll make a day of it."

He sighed, thinking of the number of Adamses involved and the likely expense. He had money in the bank from his rodeo days—at least what was left after Suzanne had taken a healthy share of his winnings. He'd been stashing away most of his salary to buy his own ranch sometime down the road. He intended to buy the best horses in Texas, then breed and train them. This little party clearly would put a serious crimp in that plan. The kind of blowout Val was describing cost big bucks. For something that lasted a few hours, it seemed like a waste of good money.

"Maybe we should think about hot dogs, instead. And kids like chips. Maybe some homemade ice cream." His enthusiasm mounted. "Yeah, that would work."

One look at Val's expression killed the idea.

"No way, Sutton. When it comes to entertaining, I believe in going all out. Bring your wallet. I only buy the best."

"I was afraid of that," he said resignedly.

"Don't look so terrified. It'll only hurt for a little while." She winked. "And if you play your cards right, I'll kiss you and make it better."

Now there was a prospect that could take a man's mind off the agony of having his budget blown to smithereens. Unfortunately, it also conjured up images that made mincemeat out of all that restraint he'd been working so hard to hang on to.

"Maybe I should just write you a blank check and let you go for it," he suggested hopefully.

She gave him an amused, knowing look. "The prospect of spending the day in town with me doesn't scare you, does it?"

"Falling off the back of a two-thousand-pound, mean-spirited bull scares me. Getting trampled by a bucking bronc gives me pause. You…" he gave her a pointed look "…you're just a pesky little annoyance."

For an instant he thought he caught a flash of hurt in her eyes and regretted that he'd been the cause of it. He ignored the temptation to apologize, though. If he could get her to write him off as a jerk, maybe he'd finally get some peace.

Of course, then he'd also be all on his own with Annie. *That* was more terrifying than the bull, the bronc and Val all rolled into one.

"Sorry," he muttered halfheartedly.

"For what?" she said, her eyes shining a little too brightly. "Being honest? No one can fault you for that."

"Still, I should have kept my mouth shut. You've been good to my daughter. I owe you."

"Now that's where you're wrong. Around here people look out for one another, no thanks necessary."

"And where I come from, you don't lash out at someone who's done you a kindness."

A faint smile tugged at her lips. "Are we going to argue about this, too?"

Slade shrugged. He figured arguing was a whole lot safer than the kissing he was seriously tempted to do. "More than likely."

"Maybe we could call a truce," she suggested. "For Annie's sake."

"Won't work," he said succinctly.

"Why on earth not?"

"Well, now, the way I see it, you and I are destined to butt heads."

"Because that's the way you want it," she accused.

Slade grinned. "No, because you're a woman and I'm a man. Simple as that."

"Tell me something I didn't know. Why does that mean we have to fight?"

"Human nature."

"Sweetheart, if that were human nature, the population would dwindle down to nothing."

He gazed directly into her eyes, then quaked inside at the impact of that. Still, he managed to keep his voice steady. "Now, you see, *sweetheart,* that's where God steps in. He set it up so all that commotion would be counter-balanced by making up. Bingo, you've got babies."

Val listened to him, her eyes sparkling with growing amusement. When he'd finished, she grinned at him. "Seems to me like you've just given me something to look forward to, cowboy. Let me know anytime you're ready to start making up."

She turned then and sashayed off, leaving Slade to stare after her in openmouthed astonishment. Just when he thought he finally had her on the ropes, dadgumit, she won another round.

Four

Slade was just starting to check out a prized new stallion that had been delivered when he glanced up and saw Harlan Adams waiting just outside the stall, his gnarled hands curved over the top rail.

"Something I can do for you?" he asked the rancher. Slade had to wonder if this had something to do with the party. They'd already discussed it, and Harlan had embraced the idea with the expected enthusiasm.

Harlan Adams might have relinquished the day-to-day running of White Pines to Cody and Harlan Patrick, but no one who knew anything about him doubted the influence he still held over the place. Even in his eighties, his mind was sharp as a tack. Only the physical limitations of aging kept him from doing everything his son and grandson did. Slade always tried to grant him the respect he was due, even when the man hadn't just done him a huge favor.

"Just came down to get a look at that horse you and Cody spent a fortune of my hard-earned money on," he replied, his gaze moving over Black Knight as if he expected the horse to be nothing less than solid gold.

"We'll get some excellent foals for you in a year or

two," Slade said. Even though Harlan's grumbling remark about the stallion's cost had been made good-naturedly, Slade was unable to keep a hint of defensiveness out of his own voice. "He was worth every penny."

"Oh, he's a beauty, all right," Harlan agreed readily. "Don't get all lathered up, Son. I trust your judgment. Cody carried on so, I just wanted to see him for myself. Thought it might give us a chance to talk some more, too. You were in too big a hurry when you stopped by the house to ask about the party."

The casual announcement set off alarms. Harlan Adams never came out to the stables merely to chat. He came when he wanted to poke and pry into matters that were none of his concern. Slade waited warily to hear what was on his mind.

Harlan found a stool and dragged it over so he could observe as Slade expertly went over the horse. Not used to having anyone watch his every move—except when he'd been in the rodeo ring—Slade was unsettled by the intense scrutiny. His nervousness promptly communicated itself to the powerful stallion. Black Knight turned skittish, prancing dangerously close to the walls of his stall. Slade smoothed a hand over his flank and murmured to him until he settled down.

"You've got a way with these animals, don't you?" Harlan observed with apparent admiration. "Cody claims he's never seen anyone better."

Slade shrugged, though he was pleased by the compliment. "I suppose. I just treat 'em like the magnificent creatures they are."

"The way a man treats his stock says a lot about him, if you ask me." The rancher paused, then asked with disconcerting directness, "You as good with your daughter?"

Startled by the abrupt shift in subject to something so personal, Slade snapped his head up. Defensiveness had his stomach clenching again. "Meaning?"

Seemingly oblivious to the tension in Slade's voice, the old man pointed out, "You kept her hidden away long enough. Didn't even mention her when you applied for work. Never knew a man to hide the fact that he had family, especially a daughter as clever as your Annie. Why was that?"

"With all due respect, sir, I think that's my business."

Harlan Adams regarded him unrepentantly. "Well, of course it is. That doesn't mean I can't ask about it, does it? Around here, we like to think of the people working for us as part of the family. You've been here long enough to know when it comes to family, we tend to meddle. It's second nature to us."

Slade managed a halfhearted grin at that. "So I've heard." He just hadn't expected to become a target of it. It made him damned uncomfortable having to answer to his boss about his relationship with Annie. He doubted an outsider would understand all the complicated emotions at work.

"Well, then, tell me about your girl," Harlan prodded again, clearly not intending to let the matter drop. "She made a real good impression when I met her. Val brought her by the house for a visit the other day."

"What can I say, sir? She's a handful." A worrisome thought struck him. "She hasn't gotten into some sort of mischief around here already, has she?"

'Of course not," Harlan said, dismissing that worry. "We're glad to have her. She reminds me of my Jenny, the way she was when her mama and I first started going out. Whoo-ee, that girl was a hellion back then. Gave her mama and me fits. Not a one of my boys was as much trouble, and believe me, they weren't saints."

"Is that so?" Slade doubted Jenny Adams had ever gotten into the kind of mischief Annie could pull off.

"Stole my truck, for starters," Harlan told him.

Slade stared, thinking of the beautiful, self-possessed young woman he'd met at ranch gatherings. He could think of a lot of ways to describe Jenny, but car thief wouldn't have been among them. She'd been an activist for Native American affairs. Now she taught school and was darn good at it, from what he'd heard. A bit unconventional, perhaps, but effective.

"You're kidding me," he said, sure the old man had to be pulling his leg to make him feel better about Annie's misdeeds.

"No, indeed. Girl was just fourteen, too. Smacked the truck straight into a tree." He almost sounded proud of her accomplishment.

"I take it she wasn't hurt," Slade said.

"No, thank the Lord. When I caught up with her, she was cursing a blue streak, like the car was to blame. I brought her back into town to face the music. That's how I met her mama. Janet had just opened up her law practice here in town. Jenny was none too pleased about her mama's divorce or about being uprooted from New York. She was mad at the world. I brought her out here and put her to work. She tended to be mischievous like your Annie, to put a generous spin on it." A grin spread across his face. "Took a paintbrush to some of the buildings around here, too. I never saw such a mess."

Slade shook his head, baffled by Harlan's amused expression as he told the story. "And you and Janet still got married? Amazing."

"Nothing amazing about it. Janet and I were suited. I could see that right from the start, though it took a little longer to bring her around to my way of thinking," he said. "As for Jenny, she came around, too, once she knew I'd go on loving her no matter what she did. Persistence, that's the ticket. Something you ought to remember. It's a trait to value."

Slade didn't ask why. He was afraid he knew, and it didn't have a thing to do with his relationship with Annie. An image of Val flitted through his mind. That woman could write the book on persistence.

Harlan clearly wasn't through doling out advice. "You know, Son, a little spirit in a girl's a good thing, especially in this day and age. A woman needs to know how to stand up for herself. How else is she supposed to learn that without testing her wings as a kid?"

He grinned. "Besides, most always what goes around, comes around. Being reminded of that gets you through the bad times. Jenny certainly got her comeuppance in due time. She's a teacher now and a stepmom to a little hellion herself. She's getting all that trouble back in spades. Knows how to handle it, though, because she's been there herself."

"Maybe I should send Annie over to you to raise," Slade said, only partly in jest. "You sound far better equipped to cope with her than I am."

"Oh, I suspect you'll get the hang of it soon enough. In the meantime, you've got a pretty little stand-in," he said, his expression sly. "Val seems to be taking quite an interest in Annie. In you, too, from what I've observed."

Slade had no intention in discussing his love life—or lack thereof—with Harlan Adams. In addition to meddling for the sheer pleasure of it, the man was the sneaki-est matchmaker in Texas. Prided himself on it, in fact.

"Val's been very kind to Annie," Slade agreed, and left it at that. "So have you. Thank you again for agree-ing to this party. It'll go a long way toward making her feel more at home here."

"That's what a ranch like this is meant for," Harlan said. "What's the fun in living to a ripe old age, if you can't surround yourself with family and lots of young people? I'm looking forward to seeing 'em all splashing around in that big old pool out back. Plus it gives me a chance to hear Laurie sing. Nobody has a voice like Harlan Patrick's wife. Millions of folks pay to hear her concerts, but I can usually coax her into singing a song or two just for fam-ily. Gives me pleasure."

"I'm sure it does."

"I heard she wrote a song for Annie."

Slade was taken aback by that. "Are you sure about that?"

"First day they met, the way I hear it. Annie gave her the inspiration."

"Imagine that," Slade murmured. Annie must have been over the moon, but she hadn't said a word.

Or maybe—as happened all too often—he just hadn't been listening.

As Harlan Adams headed back up to the main house, Slade stared after him, then sighed. He had a feeling this was one time when the old man had been just as clever about passing along advice as he usually was about dig-ging out secrets or meddling in affairs of the heart. He'd probably be keeping a close eye out to see just how well Slade followed it.

* * *

Val was in her element pulling the party together. Nothing gave her a sense of accomplishment like making lists and checking off every little chore. She'd helped Laurie with enough entertaining that it was second nature to her. This party would be smaller and less formal than something Laurie would have thrown in Nashville, but the details were essentially the same.

She enlisted Annie's help, thoroughly enjoying the child's wry sense of humor, which came out at the most unexpected moments, shattering that tough, sullen facade she wore the rest of the time. Then there were the rare moments of vulnerability that tore at Val's heart.

"What if the kids don't like me?" Annie asked for the millionth time a few days before the barbecue.

"They'll like you," Val reassured her. "Dani's twins are about your age, but most of the others are younger. You'll be like a big sister to them. They'll look up to you. Look how well you get along with Amy Lynn. She toddles around after you like a puppy."

"What does she know?" Annie scoffed. "She's just a baby."

"The point is, she likes you just fine. So will all the others."

"They'll make fun of me."

"Why on earth would they make fun of you?" Val asked.

"For one thing, my hair's a mess."

"The cut is a little uneven, that's all," Val insisted in what had to be the most massive understatement she'd ever made in the name of kindness. She'd gathered that Annie had done the style herself in a fit of anger over being sent to live with her father. "I could try to trim it a little more evenly, if you like."

Annie's eyes brightened. "Could you?"

"I'll take a shot at it, unless you'd prefer to get it cut in town."

Annie shook her head. "My dad would never pay for it. He'd say it was a waste of money to fix something I did to myself in the first place."

Val had a feeling they had already had exactly that discussion. She couldn't honestly say she blamed Slade. Still, Annie had probably suffered long enough for her ill-conceived moment of rebellion.

"I'll get the scissors. You go and wash your hair," she told Annie. Beyond shaving the child's head, she doubted there was anything she could do that could possibly make her hairstyle worse than it was.

Fortunately, Annie had a little curl to her hair and the delicately shaped face of a pixie. Val snipped and trimmed until her hair was short as a boy's. The curl softened the effect, feathering against her cheek and drawing attention to her lovely green eyes. Val stood back and surveyed the results.

"I think you look beautiful, if I do say so myself," she said, handing Annie a mirror. "You have the perfect face for a style this short. Those gorgeous eyes of yours look huge. You are going to be a heartbreaker one of these days, young lady."

"No way," Annie said, then took the mirror Val held out. She gazed into it, then up at Val. "I'm almost pretty," she whispered in an awestruck voice.

"Well, of course you're pretty," Val said, glad she'd been able to take away one of Annie's worries.

"But what will I wear?" Annie moaned now. "All I have

is a ratty old bathing suit that's too small. You saw it the day we went to the creek. I can't wear that."

Val had to concede it no longer fit and had been faded by too much sun and chlorine from the town pool in Wilder's Glen. "I'll bet if you explain that to your dad, he'll let you get a new one."

Annie looked defeated. "He won't go for it." She glanced up at Val hopefully. "Maybe you could ask him. He'll listen to you."

"No," Val insisted. "You discuss it with him."

"He doesn't listen to a word I say," Annie grumbled. "Did you know I told him about Laurie writing a song for me? He mumbled something that sounded like 'that's nice,' then went right on reading a bunch of old horse magazines."

"Obviously you picked a bad time."

"It's *always* a bad time," Annie complained. "I'm always interrupting something more important."

Val vowed to speak to Slade about paying more attention when his daughter tried to have a conversation with him.

"I wish I were your daughter," Annie said with a heavy sigh. "You listen to me all the time."

"That's because when you and I are together, you have my undivided attention. If you tried to talk to me when I'm working, I probably would be every bit as distracted as your dad. Lesson one, kiddo, if you want something from someone, make sure it's a good time before you ask, otherwise the answer will be no for sure."

"How can you tell?"

"Instinct."

"I don't think I have that," Annie said glumly.

Val chuckled. "You will. It takes time to develop.

You're only ten. It just means being more sensitive to other people's moods."

"Like if my dad's worried about some old horse or something, I shouldn't ask him for something," Annie said, her expression thoughtful.

"Exactly. Either leave him alone or ask about the horse. Sympathize with him."

"Okay, I get it." She jumped off the kitchen chair and headed for the door. "Bye. Thanks for the haircut."

"You're welcome. Where are you off to?"

"I'm going to see if my dad's in a good mood or not so I can ask about the bathing suit." Her step faltered. "If he's in a bad mood, do you think you could help me bake him chocolate chip cookies? Those are his favorites. He's bound to listen to me after that."

"See if you can't pull it off using your wits," Val said. "But, yes, if all else fails, I'll help with the cookies."

So, she thought after Annie was gone, chocolate was the way to Slade's heart. She just happened to have a recipe for a chocolate cake that had been known to bring grown men to their knees. It might be just the dessert to serve at Annie's party. She would personally see to it that Slade got a very large slice.

Slade gave Val a pleading look on Friday afternoon when she turned up at the stables to remind him they had to go into town to shop for the party. He reached into his pocket and started to peel off a wad of bills.

"Can't you and Annie go? I've got work to do." He held out the cash.

Val ignored it and met his gaze evenly. "No."

Slade blinked. "No? Just like that? You won't even consider it?"

"No," she repeated. "Just like that. Annie and I have done all the planning up until now. The deal was that we would all go shopping. I'm not letting you renege."

"I told her she could buy a bathing suit if you helped to pick it out," he said, as if that might convince her of his honorable intentions.

He could have saved his breath. Val had an agenda here and she didn't intend to be deterred. "That's very generous of you. She really needs one." She grinned. "But you're not getting off the hook by throwing more money our way. She needs to spend time with you, too."

"I guarantee she'd have more fun if the two of you went without me," Slade said.

"Could be," Val agreed readily. "Unless you work really hard at getting through to her."

He gave her a sour look. "Lady, you drive a really hard bargain."

She nodded unrepentently. "That's why Laurie pays me the big bucks. And just so you know, thanks to her, I have lots of practice at getting my way." She winked at him. "Five minutes, cowboy. We'll meet you at the car."

Slade turned up five minutes later, still looking none too pleased. After a disconcerted glance at Val, who was already behind the wheel, he climbed into the passenger seat with obvious reluctance.

"Everybody belted up?" Val inquired pointedly.

Slade heaved a sigh and put on his seat belt.

She grinned at him. "Thank you."

"No problem."

She had already made a mental list of possible topics to try to get Slade and Annie talking. By the time they reached town, she had exhausted most of them, right along with her nerves. It had been the most frustrating half hour of her life. Slade answered in monosyllables. Apparently picking up on her father's mood, Annie retreated into sullen silence.

"What shall we do first?" Val asked when she'd parked on the main street in Los Piños. She turned to Annie. "Shall we try to find a bathing suit?"

"Whatever," Annie said.

Undaunted, Val led her scowling companions to the general store, one of the few places in town that carried clothes and the only one that carried bathing suits. The selection wouldn't be the greatest, but she doubted she could have coerced Slade or Annie into going over to Garden City instead. They obviously didn't want to spend one more minute in each other's company than they had to.

Because Annie was dragging her feet and Slade looked as uncomfortable as if she'd coaxed him unwittingly into a lingerie shop, Val seized the initiative. She selected several bathing suits in various styles from the rack and held them up for Annie's inspection.

"That one, I guess," Annie said without enthusiasm, pointing at a bright red one-piece suit.

Val held it up for Slade's approval. "What do you think?"

"Whatever Annie wants."

Val wanted to shake the pair of them. "Well, I like the green," she said instead. "It's the color of your eyes. Try them both on," she instructed, handing them to Annie.

When the girl had gone off to the dressing room, Val whirled on Slade. "Could you possibly manage to show just a little enthusiasm? You're acting as if this is a worse chore than mucking out stalls."

Something that might have been guilt flickered in his

eyes. He sighed. "Okay, you're right. I'm being a pain in the butt."

"Any particular reason or is this just your general nature?"

"Shopping's not my thing, okay? I don't know what she should get."

"Then, unless it is totally inappropriate, let her pick what she likes."

"How am I supposed to know that? She looked pretty miserable no matter which one you held up."

"That's because she's reacting to your mood. Now when she comes back out here, give her a compliment. Tell her she looks great. Tell her she looks grown-up. Just show some enthusiasm. Fake it, if you have to."

He regarded her with unexpected amusement. "You're recommending that I lie to my daughter? You, the queen of directness, are suggesting that I fib?"

"As a general rule, a lie is not the answer, but some situations call for drastic measures," she retorted. She glanced up and saw Annie standing hesitantly just outside the curtain of the dressing room. The red suit that Annie had liked best was clearly intended for someone who actually had a bust. Val swallowed hard at the sight, then muttered so only Slade could hear, "This is one of them."

She could see him struggling with a smile, but he managed to say cheerfully, "That suit's real bright, honey. Is it the one you want?"

Annie's gaze faltered. "I'm not so sure. It's kinda big." She gestured. "Up here."

"Too big," Val said decisively, greatly relieved that Annie had voiced it first. "Try the other one."

When Annie had retreated to the dressing room, Slade

glanced over at Val. "So, tell me, what happened to the little white lie?"

"You gave her moral support. I gave her the truth," she replied. "It balances out."

"You could give her both and I could keep my mouth shut," Slade suggested. "I don't seem to be getting the rules. Or is it that you keep changing them?"

Val frowned at him. "You really don't have much instinct for this sort of thing, do you?"

"Not a bit," he agreed without remorse.

"Well, you're just going to have to learn," she said decisively. "And now's your chance."

Annie reappeared in the green bathing suit. It was a perfect fit. "How about this one?" she asked, glancing hopefully straight at her father.

He surveyed her intently, then gestured for her to turn around. She did a slow pirouette and then he nodded. "Real flattering," he said at last, the compliment all the more meaningful because he had clearly struggled for it. "You'll glide through the water like a little fish in that."

As compliments went, it wasn't all that pretty, and he looked awkward as the dickens as he said it, but Val had to give him points for trying. As for Annie, she looked as if he'd just told her she looked like a princess.

"You used to say that to me a long time ago, didn't you?" she asked shyly. "That I could swim like a fish?"

Slade appeared startled, then a slow smile spread across his face. "You couldn't have been much more than a baby back then. I took you down to the pool when we were on a visit to your grandmama's." He regarded her with amazement. "You actually remember that?"

"I remember a lot," she said, her eyes suddenly glistening with unshed tears. Then she spun away and ran to the dressing room.

Slade gazed helplessly at Val. "What did I say wrong?"

She reached up and touched a hand to his cheek. "Nothing. For once, I think you got it just right."

"But she's crying."

"Because you connected with her. You shared a memory, made her see that there was a time in the past when something you did together was as special to you as it was to her."

Slade shook his head, still staring after Annie, his expression miserable. "I never could stand to see her cry."

Val tucked that little tidbit away right next to his secret addiction to chocolate. She was beginning to discover that despite his gruff, tough exterior, Slade Sutton was an old softie, after all. It made her more determined than ever to snag him for herself.

Five

When Annie finally reappeared, clutching the green bathing suit, her eyes were puffy from crying. Slade's first instinct was to gather her in his arms as he would have when she was a toddler. It had been so long, though, that he was afraid she'd rebuff the gesture.

"Let's pay for this and get some lunch," he suggested instead. "I vote for pizza."

He was rewarded with the faintest glimmer of a smile on Annie's face. He grinned back at her. "Still your favorite?"

"With pepperoni and sausage," she said.

"What about anchovies?" he teased.

"No way you're putting little fishies on my pizza. If you want 'em, get your own."

He turned to Val. "And you? Can I talk you into anchovies?"

"Not a chance."

He feigned a disappointed sigh. "I guess I'll just have to make the sacrifice and go with pepperoni and sausage."

Annie regarded him wisely. "You never get anchovies. I don't think you really like them."

"Well, of course I do," he insisted. "Biggest sacrifice of my life, giving up those little fishies."

"Then get your own pizza," Val suggested, winking at Annie. "She and I can share."

"Yeah, Daddy. Why don't you get your own and have it just the way you like it?"

"Nope. Can't eat a whole one. I'll just have what you guys are having."

Val gave Annie a knowing look. "Yep, you're right. He's faking it."

Just to prove them wrong, he ordered anchovies on two slices of their large pizza and forced himself not to gag while he took the first bite.

"Best I ever had," he claimed as he finished the first piece.

Annie watched him intently, then reached for the second slice. "Let me try it." She bit into it, then grimaced. "Oh, yuck. How can you eat that?"

"Because we all but dared him to," Val said. "Some men will do anything if they're challenged."

"Is that it, Daddy?" Annie asked skeptically. "Was it just because we dared you?"

"Okay, yes," he said finally, his gaze locked with Val's. "You caught me."

Annie grinned, apparently satisfied that her first instincts about the anchovies had been accurate. "You don't have to eat the other slice. You can have some of ours."

"Oh, I don't know about that," Val chimed in, a wicked gleam in her eyes. "I think he should finish what he started. Wasting good food's a crime, when so many people around the world are starving."

"I'll mail the leftover slice of pizza to anyone you care to suggest," he responded, already reaching for one of the more appetizing wedges. Val snagged his wrist in a grip that suggested, for a pipsqueak, she'd been doing some strength training in Laurie's home gym. "I take it you object."

"Oh, yes," she said. "That pizza has my name on it."

He leaned over and pretended to study it intently. "I can't see it. Can you, Annie?"

His daughter stood up and glanced at the slice carefully. "It's Val's, all right," she said at last.

His head snapped up. "You took her side," he said, genuinely bemused by it. "What kind of kid takes the side of a stranger over her own father?"

Though he'd said it in jest, as soon as the words were out of his mouth, he could see Annie's expression clouding over. He'd done it again—spoiled the mood for reasons that escaped him.

"Annie?" he prodded gently. "What did I say?"

"Nothing," she mumbled. "May I be excused?"

Slade noticed that she addressed the question to Val.

Looking troubled, Val asked, "Where will you be?"

"Outside, I guess."

"Slade?" Val said, turning to him.

"Fine, go," he said tersely. When Annie had left, he scowled at Val. "Okay, I blew it again. Mind telling me how?"

"You all but told her that, for siding with me, she wasn't a good kid," she said. "I know you were teasing, but she took it to heart."

"Are you telling me that every time I open my mouth, I'm going to be walking through a minefield?"

She nodded. "Pretty much."

"Which one of us do you think is going to crack first?" he asked.

"My money's on you, unless you can learn to roll with it. Think about this," she said with a certain amount of glee. "Puberty's going to be much, much worse."

Slade held up a hand. "Don't even say it."

"People survive it," Val assured him. "Kids and their parents."

"Maybe if there are two parents, who can bolster each other's spirits," he said.

"Oh, no, single moms survive it, too. Mine did."

Startled, he studied her face, saw the unexpected shadows in eyes that usually glinted with good humor. "Where was your dad?"

"He died when I was eight."

Which explained why she empathized with Annie, why she was fighting like a tigress to see that the lines of communications between him and his daughter were opened. No doubt it pained her to see a child with a perfectly good, healthy father going through life as if she had none.

"I'm sorry," Slade said. "That must have been tough."

"It was." Her expression turned from sad to thoughtful. "Funny, I've lived most of my life without him, yet I still miss him. I can still remember the scent of his pipe tobacco, the way it felt when he scooped me up and hugged me. I felt such a sense of security, as if no harm could ever come to me. After that, there were just years and years of uncertainty, even though my mom was terrific and worked her butt off for us."

She shook her head, as if clearing it of unwanted memories. "Sorry. We were talking about you and Annie."

Slade nodded. "Yes. I think we were. That's why you care so deeply what happens between her and me, isn't it?"

She seemed surprised by the suggestion. "I hadn't

thought about it, but, yes, I suppose it's one reason. I wouldn't have expected you to pick up on that."

"Because I'm just an insensitive jerk?"

"Some of the time," she agreed bluntly.

Her gaze met his with that directness he sometimes found so disconcerting.

"Other times you can be…surprising," she added.

"You said your past might be only one of the reasons my relationship with my daughter matters to you. What's another?"

"Maybe I'm just a sucker for a happy ending."

Slade had the feeling that it was a whole lot more complicated than that, more personal. He'd known from the beginning that she was attracted to him, but he'd figured his refusal to get involved had only turned him into a challenge. Now he wondered if he'd been wrong. Could she be developing real feelings for him? He hoped not. He could have told her he was a bad bet. Hell, she could surely see that for herself after all these months.

Finally, he dragged his gaze away from hers, tried to ignore the rock-hard arousal that long, lingering glance had stirred. If he'd been a different kind of man or she'd been a different kind of woman, maybe they could have done something about it. As it was, she was off-limits.

"We should probably be going," he said, his voice gruffer than he intended. He busied himself with calling for the bill, carefully counting out the money, taking enough time to assure that his body settled down.

When he finally risked another look at Val, the color was still high in her cheeks, as if she were embarrassed at unwittingly revealing some innermost secret.

"Ready?" he asked.

"Sure," she said, her controlled facade slipping neatly

back into place. She moved briskly from the restaurant, allowing him no more than a glimpse of that swaying walk of hers. Just outside the door, she halted abruptly.

"What's wrong?" Slade asked.

Val glanced up and down the street. "I don't see any sign of Annie. She promised to stay right out here and she's gone."

"She's probably just popped into one of the stores," Slade said, stepping out onto the sidewalk to see for himself. "Come on, let's check Dolan's. She seems to have developed a real fondness for the ice cream there. She's probably trying to talk Sharon Lynn into giving her a cone right now."

But Annie wasn't at the drugstore soda fountain and Sharon Lynn said she hadn't seen her.

"I had a bad feeling when she asked to go outside," Val said. "She was upset. I should have stopped her."

"What about me? I'm her father. I didn't think she'd take off. Let's take a minute and think about this. It's a small town," he said, as much to reassure himself as Val. "How far could she have gone? It's been less than a half hour since she left the restaurant."

He thought of the tale Harlan Adams had told him about Jenny. Surely he hadn't shared the same story with Annie. If so, was she impetuous enough to have tried the same stunt herself?

"Is the car still where we parked it?" he asked, peering down the street.

"Well, of course," Val said, without even looking. "She can't drive, Slade." She dangled the keys in front of him. "I have these."

He breathed a sigh of relief. It was one less thing to worry about. He doubted Annie's skills ran to hot-wiring a car, unless she'd been hanging out at his father's garage. Still, he couldn't prevent the gut-sick sense of dread that washed through him when he realized that Annie was definitely missing.

Even though he'd just let her off the hook—and rightly so—he still wanted to rail at Val for getting them into this fix in the first place. If they hadn't been planning a party, if they hadn't come into town, if, if, if…

Bottom line, though, he had to find his daughter, and when he did, he was going to tan her hide, no matter what the so-called experts had to say about spanking these days.

For the next twenty minutes, he and Val searched high and low, but there was no sign of Annie in any of the likely places.

"You don't suppose she's gone to the bus station?" he asked Val, not quite able to bring himself to believe that his daughter was upset enough to truly run away. Had she decided to go back to his parents in Wilder's Glen? Could she possibly have enough money in her pocket for the ticket?

Val gave his hand a reassuring squeeze. "Stop it right this minute. That child adores you. She's not going to run away. All she really wants is your attention. She learned that misbehaving guaranteed that somebody would take notice. She's going to test you the same way she did her grandparents."

"That all sounds very logical, but she's a kid. Do you really think she's plotting this out in a reasonable manner?"

"No. It's instinctive with her. The best way to make sure you pay attention is to infuriate you."

Slade regarded her with impatience. "Didn't you tell me not a half hour ago that she ran out because I hinted she wasn't a good kid? Why would she deliberately do something to prove just how bad she can be?"

"Because any attention is better than none."

"I've just spent the whole blasted day with her," Slade all but shouted in frustration.

Val touched his arm in a soothing gesture. "Slade, she's ten. It doesn't have to make sense. Come on. This is no time to panic. Let's settle down and think about this for a second. Where would she go?"

"We've looked at Dolan's. You've already looked at the pet shop, the toy store and the general store. I've been to the bookstore and the hardware store."

Val stared at him. "Why on earth would you think to look in a hardware store?"

"She likes tools." He shrugged. "Don't ask me why."

"Could be she's trying to be like you," Val said thoughtfully. "In which case, what about the feed and grain store? Did you look there?"

"She's never lived on a ranch before. Why would she go to a feed and grain store?"

"For the same reason she'd go to the hardware store—because it's something that interests you."

Slade didn't believe for an instant that they would find Annie standing amid bags of oats, but by golly, there she was, and she was rubbing her hand over a saddle with a look of pure longing on her face.

"Don't you dare yell at her," Val warned.

"I wasn't going to yell," Slade insisted, though he very likely would have if Val hadn't grabbed his arm and slowed him down. He took a deep breath, then shot a look at Val that apparently reassured her. She released his arm. He slowly crossed the store to stand beside his daughter.

"Hey, short stuff, we've been looking everywhere for you."

Her expression guilty, Annie snatched her hand away from the saddle. "I just figured you'd turn up here sooner or later," she said defensively.

"You could have said something to us before you took off," he suggested mildly. "You promised to wait just outside the restaurant."

"I guess I forgot about it." She gave him a defiant look. "Sort of like you broke your promise and didn't think to say goodbye when you took off and left me at Grandma's."

Slade was shocked by the accusation, especially since she'd obviously kept it bottled up inside for months now. "Of course I said goodbye. And we talked about you staying there while I went to look for work."

She shook her head. "You talked. I never agreed. When I got up in the morning, you were gone."

He thought back to that time and how little clear thinking he had been doing, and realized it was entirely possible that it had happened just that way. "I'm sorry."

She shrugged. "Yeah, well, it doesn't matter."

He hunkered down and took her by the shoulders. "Yes, it does matter, and I am sorry. I never meant to hurt you. I thought staying with Grandma would be the best thing for you."

"And you're the grown-up, so I guess that means you were right." She shrugged away from him. "Never mind. You found me now. Is it time to go home?"

Slade directed a helpless look in Val's direction and she immediately stepped in.

"We still have to buy food for the party," she reminded them. "That's why we came into town, remember?"

"I don't care about the party," Annie replied.

Slade was losing his fragile grip on his patience. "Fine," he said tightly. "We can always cancel."

Annie's alarmed gaze shot to his. "We can't call everyone and tell them to stay home."

He softened his tone. "Why not?"

"It would be rude." She turned to Val. "Wouldn't it?"

"Very rude," she agreed.

Relieved to see Annie's spirit returning, he nodded. "Then, by all means, let's go shopping."

The trip through the grocery store was an adventure. Slade should have known Val would come prepared. She had a mile-long list, organized precisely according to the aisles of the store. He was relegated to pushing the cart, while she and Annie made their selections with as much care as if they were choosing lifelong mates. Deciding which mustard to buy took on the significance of selecting the perfect present. He would have chosen the cheapest of everything and been out of the store in ten minutes. Annie and Val seemed to have very definite—and often diametrically opposed—opinions. They'd been debating white sweet corn versus yellow for the past five minutes.

"Slade, what do you think?"

"Corn's corn," he said.

"No, Daddy. Silver Queen is the best. Grandma says so."

"And I've always liked sweet yellow corn," Val said.

"Get some of each."

"A compromise," Val said, beaming at him as if he'd single-handedly brought peace to the Middle East. "What a novel idea."

"How much longer is this going to take?" he grumbled. "I have chores to do."

"Harlan Patrick said not to worry about the chores," Val informed him. "He said he'd take care of them."

Slade scowled. "You asked Harlan Patrick to take on my chores?"

"Settle down, cowboy. He volunteered. He knew we were going to be getting ready for the party. If you're going to follow us around with a scowl on your face, you might as well wait in the car."

He stared hard at her. She was serious. She was dismissing him as if he were an unruly kid.

"Can't do it. You need me to pay for all of this."

"I'll pay," she said, facing him stubbornly. "You can pay me back."

"If I'm forking out all this money, I want to see what I'm getting," he insisted.

"Fine. Suit yourself."

"I will."

Annie watched them intently, then sighed. "It's my fault, isn't it?"

"What's your fault?" he and Val demanded in a shocked chorus.

"That you're fighting. You probably never fought till I came."

"We barely spoke till you came," Val said with sincerity. "Don't worry about it, Annie. Your father and I are used to it. This is the way we communicate."

She tucked Annie's arm through hers. "Let's check out the steaks. I want really thick ones. How about you?"

"Daddy likes thick steaks, too," Annie said, as if trying to convince Val of their compatibility.

"Give it up, sweetie. Making peace between us is not your job," Val assured her, then leaned down to whisper something that had Annie grinning.

They moved off to the meat section, giggling. Slade watched them with their heads together and sighed heavily. Would he ever have that kind of easy relationship with Annie again? Or had he ruined it forever by abandoning her at her grandparents?

She and Val were still laughing when he found them loading up on steaks. As he got closer, he realized they were talking about dresses, of all things. Judging from Annie's recent wardrobe choices, he hadn't imagined she knew what a dress was. Val gave him a wink.

"Your daughter and I were just discussing whether or not we should get new outfits for the party. After all, we can't spend the whole day in bathing suits. What do you think?"

What he thought was that his entire life savings were going into this party. But even he was smart enough not to say that.

"I say go for it, if it's what you want."

"Will you help us pick them out?" Val inquired with a glint in her eyes that made him very uneasy.

"Me? In a dress shop? I don't know." The quest for a bathing suit had been disconcerting enough. He'd reduced his daughter to tears over that.

"Maybe I should just wait in the car," he suggested. "And you can't take too long because we'll have all this food. It'll spoil in this heat."

"Come on, Daddy. Please?" Annie said.

It was the first time in a long time that she'd actually asked him for anything. After what she'd said earlier about him running out on her, how could he refuse?

Which was why he ended up spending the most unnerving two hours of his life sitting on a puffy yellow ottoman surrounded by frills and watching two females parade around in silk and satin that was more suited to a formal event than a barbecue. He got the feeling that they were just having fun playing dress-up.

Watching his daughter was one thing. Watching Val was something else entirely. The woman made very sure that she ratcheted his temperature up to white-hot before she showed an ounce of mercy. One of these days he'd make her pay for that, and he was getting some fascinating ideas about how.

"Have you two decided yet?" he asked eventually. "The steaks will be barbecued in the car pretty soon."

"One more dress," Annie pleaded.

"One more," he agreed.

When she came out of the dressing room this time she was wearing a yellow gingham sundress. She twirled around and made the skirt spin. "I like this one, Daddy. What do you think?"

"I think you'll be the prettiest girl at the party," he said, earning a beaming smile from Val, who'd already paid for her own selection.

He told himself that his effort to say the right thing had been made on Annie's behalf, but Val's approval touched something deep inside him. It had been a long time since what anyone thought had mattered. Maybe he was going to survive Suzanne's betrayal whether he wanted to or not.

Six

It never ceased to amaze Val how many members of the Adams family could be assembled at the drop of a hat. At the mention of a party, they swarmed to White Pines like ants getting word of a particularly tasty picnic. Even Luke and Jessie, who lived across the state, and their daughter Angela, who lived in Montana with her family, made it to White Pines for most events.

Harlan Adams was in his element presiding over this latest party. His grandchildren and great-grandchildren gravitated to him, not just because he was the family patriarch, but because of the love that flowed from him as tangibly as water splashing from a fountain.

It broke Val's heart to see Annie standing on the fringes, looking left out. She knew if she'd been a little closer, she would have been able to detect the sheen of unshed tears in her eyes. Harlan, ever the thoughtful host, apparently spotted her about the same time.

"Well, there she is," he said, smiling warmly and beckoning to her. "Annie, my girl, come over here and meet the rest of these hellions. This is your party. You can't be standing on the sidelines."

Annie's expression brightened at once as she was introduced to various Adams cousins. Within minutes she and Jenny's stepson had teamed up against Dani's twin stepsons for a boisterous game of Marco Polo in the pool.

"She looks happy," Slade observed, sneaking up beside Val.

She turned and caught his sober expression. "She does, doesn't she?"

"Thank you for that."

"I didn't do anything."

"Don't be so modest," he chided. "You dreamed up this party and badgered me into it. You planned the guest list. You saw to it that Annie had the right things to wear. You bought the groceries."

"It's just a party, Slade," she said, reluctant to take too much credit for instigating such a simple thing.

He shook his head. "It's more than that, and you know it. It's a chance for Annie to make friends. You cared about her feelings, Val. I'm still not entirely certain why, but you did, and I'm grateful."

For some reason she couldn't explain, his thanks irked her. She told herself that he'd say the same if she'd been a hired caterer whose cheese puffs were especially tasty. "I don't want your gratitude," she said, though she was unable to explain just what she did want.

"A gracious woman would accept it, though." He grinned knowingly. "Any particular reason you're not? Are you holding out for something more?"

He had her pegged, she realized unhappily. Maybe what she wanted was as simple—or as monumental—as recognition that she could make a difference in his family, that she could fit in. She wanted him to see her in a new light, to realize what she could bring to his life.

Okay, she really wanted him to fall madly in love with her. And all because she'd helped him buy some clothes for his kid, and picked out some steaks. Was she crazy or what? Relationships didn't blossom based on a grand gesture.

"I'm sorry," she murmured. "I'm glad you're pleased with the way this turned out."

"I'd be even more pleased if you'd come eat with me," he said.

Val was astonished. It was rare for Slade to seek out her company. She usually had to throw herself at him. "Why?" she asked, regarding him warily.

"Why not?" he said, as if he uttered similar invitations all the time. "If you turn me down, I'll just end up talking horses all afternoon with Cody or Harlan Patrick. I can do that anytime."

She grinned. "I thought you liked nothing better than talking about horses."

"No, darlin', even I get tired of hearing my own voice on that topic sometimes. Besides, only a fool would rather talk to a bunch of cowboys instead of a beautiful woman."

She gazed into his eyes and saw a glimmer of amusement that was as rare as the invitation. "Are you actually flirting with me?" she asked, not bothering to hide her astonishment.

He leaned down to whisper in her ear. "To tell the truth, it's been so long, I can't say for sure."

The soft sigh of his breath across her cheek was almost as heady as a kiss. It made Val want to move an inch or two closer, to coax his arms around her. She'd been wanting him to kiss her for so long now she was just about ready to make it happen and damn the consequences.

"Maybe if you have a little food, you'll know for sure,"

she said, turning and leading the way to the buffet that she had helped the housekeeper set out earlier. "Do you want the whole meal now or just an appetizer?" She turned to find his gaze locked on her.

"An appetizer," he said quietly. "Some things shouldn't be rushed."

He really was flirting with her, she concluded. What she couldn't figure out was why. Not twenty-four hours ago he couldn't get away from her fast enough. Was it the party atmosphere? She hadn't noticed that his personality changed all that much at past parties. She regarded him suspiciously.

"What's really going on here, Slade?"

He looked as innocent as a newborn. "I have no idea what you mean. I thought we'd grab some food, find a place away from the ruckus and enjoy some quiet conversation. Does that bother you for some reason?"

"Of course it doesn't bother me," she retorted. "It's just so…out of character."

"Maybe I've reformed."

"Overnight?"

"They say the love of a good woman can do amazing things to change a man."

She plunked down her plate. "Okay, that's it. Who said anything about love?" Her gaze narrowed. "Has Laurie said something to you?"

"About?"

"Me, dammit."

Laughter danced in his eyes. "Can't say that I've talked to Laurie recently."

As her temper lathered up, his grew cooler, Val noticed. It was very irksome. She tried to match his calm, even tone. "Harlan Patrick, then."

He grinned. "Val, I don't know why you're making such a fuss about sneaking off to a corner to chat. For weeks now you've been pestering me with a million questions. Now when I'm ready to talk, the cat's got your tongue. Why is that?"

"Because it doesn't make sense. Neither does that comment about the love of a good woman. I think you're making fun of me, Slade Sutton."

He set his plate down and cupped her face in his hands, hands that were just a little rough from hard work. Hands capable of incredible tenderness, she discovered.

"Maybe I'm just waking up," he said, his gaze fixed on her mouth. "I'd like to kiss you, Val. You going to turn skittish if I do?"

Her breath caught in her throat. Finally, after all these months, he was going to kiss her. It was what she'd been praying for. She'd imagined his lips on hers a thousand times. She'd ached to have him wake up and notice her.

Because she couldn't have gotten a word past the lump in her throat if she'd tried, she simply shook her head.

Slade smiled. "Okay, then."

He lowered his head until there was little more than a sliver of air between his mouth and hers, and there he stopped. Anticipation shimmered through Val. It required all of her willpower to simply wait, when she wanted so desperately to close that distance and finally discover if he tasted half as wonderful as she'd imagined. Her heart pounded at the prospect. Her nerves rioted.

"Daddy!"

Annie's shrill, excited voice cut through the air. Slade jerked away so quickly, Val very nearly cried out at the loss.

"Hey, Daddy, look at me! I can dive off the board."

Slade glanced down into Val's eyes with mute apology. "Let's see, angel," he called out. He took Val's hand and urged her to come with him as he moved back toward the pool.

Sure enough, Annie executed a perfect dive off the low board. She swam to the edge of the pool and stared up at them hopefully.

"What did you think?"

"Awesome," Slade said. "How long have you been doing that?"

"Since a few minutes ago. Zack taught me."

"Then you're a natural," he praised. "Maybe we should see about getting you some diving lessons this summer, if it's something you'd like to do."

Her eyes shone. "Could I? Zack says there's a lady in town who gives lessons. She was in the Olympics once. She's really, really amazing. So, do you think we could call and find out if she'd take me?"

"First thing on Monday," he agreed. "Be sure you get her number from Zack."

She swam away happily to tell the twins what he'd agreed to.

"I can't believe she's that good," he said, staring after her, obviously awestruck.

"She has a real talent for it, that's for sure," Val agreed. "You handled that really well, you know."

Slade shrugged. "I just told her the truth."

"You did it instinctively. Seems to me you're getting your fatherhood legs back under you."

"I'll admit, I've been walking on eggshells since she got here. I guess for a minute there I forgot all the problems we've had and just reacted to her excitement."

"See how easy it is when you stop thinking so hard and worrying about every little thing?"

He gave her a rueful look. "Great advice, but if you ask me, it's easier said than done."

"Just keep trying," Val advised. "It'll get easier."

"I hope so," he said fervently.

"By the way, I'd be happy to drive her in for her lessons, if you can't get away. Laurie doesn't need me much these days, so I'm at loose ends."

Slade shook his head. "I can't ask you to do that."

"You didn't ask. I offered."

"Still, it's my responsibility."

"Which means it's up to you to make sure she gets there, right?"

He nodded cautiously, as if sensing a trap.

"And you've already found me to take her." She patted his arm. "Good job, Dad."

He frowned. "I think we ought to talk about me relying on you so much to help with Annie. It's not right."

"I'd much rather get back to that kiss that almost happened," Val countered.

He suddenly looked uncomfortable, as if she'd brought up a long-ago indiscretion that he regretted. "That was probably a mistake," he said.

"Why?"

To her irritation, he was acting as if she were trying to pin him down to set a wedding date. He wouldn't even meet her gaze.

"It just was, okay? Think of it as a momentary lapse in judgment."

She stared at him for a full minute and realized he was dead serious. He was dismissing all of that sizzling tension between them as if it had been no more than an unwanted fluke.

Furious, she lashed out. "Well, believe me, cowboy, it won't happen again."

She whirled around and walked away before he could see the humiliating tears that were stinging her eyes.

"Val."

She ignored the command in his voice and kept right on walking. She didn't stop until she'd reached the creek. Then she sat down in the shade of a tree and let the tears flow.

"Damned fool," she muttered, not certain whether she was thinking of herself or Slade when she said it. It probably didn't much matter. The label fit both of them just as neatly.

"Fool," Slade muttered under his breath as he watched Val storm off. He was forced to admit that she was justifiably furious.

He'd messed up good this time. He'd lost his head earlier, when he'd seen her in a skimpy little bathing suit barely covered by some sheer, floating material that purported to be some sort of robe. He'd reacted with a purely male surge of testosterone, rather than the caution that usually characterized his encounters with her. No wonder she'd been so baffled at first.

Oh, he'd been flirting all right. Walking straight down a very dangerous path. The only thing that had prevented him from making the mistake of a lifetime was Annie's interruption. He owed the kid diving lessons and a whole lot more for that. If only she'd been a little quicker, perhaps he could have avoided hurting Val's feelings, too.

"Where's Val?" Laurie asked, clearly undaunted by the scowl he shot at anyone who'd come close since Val's departure.

"Heading toward the creek last time I saw her," he said, trying not to squirm under her knowing gaze.

"Did you two have a fight?"

"What would your assistant and I have to fight about?"

"I can't imagine," she said lightly. "But it must have been something significant for her to run out on a party she pulled together for *your* daughter."

He glared at her, stung by the pointed reminder that he should be grateful to Val, rather than mistreating her. "Are you trying to make me feel even more guilty than I do?"

"Yes," she said without the least sign of contrition. "Val's a wonderful woman and you treat her abominably. If you're not interested, just tell her to back off."

"I have, on more than one occasion, as a matter of fact. She doesn't listen. Maybe you should recommend to her that she steer clear of me," he suggested.

"Believe me, I've tried. She seems to have the crazy idea that you need saving from yourself. She's also very fond of Annie. So am I, for that matter."

Relieved by the chance to change the subject, he seized the opening. "I hear you wrote a song for Annie."

Her expression brightened as it always did when she talked about her music. "As a matter of fact, I did. I was struggling with some lyrics and she said something that brought them into focus. I give her full credit."

"You going to sing it today?"

"Maybe." She gave him a look every bit as sly as one of Harlan's. "If Val's around to hear it. I always like to get her reaction when I'm still fiddling with a new song."

"In other words, if I go find her and drag her back, you'll sing Annie's song."

"You're very quick for a cowboy."

"Whatever that means."

She patted his cheek. "For the record, I don't think you'll have to drag her back. Just be nice. Be honest. When you think about it, it's really not so terribly much to ask."

Slade put aside his plate of food for the second time that afternoon. At this rate, he wasn't even going to get a taste of the extravagant spread he'd paid for.

"Keep an eye on Annie for me," he said to Laurie.

"Not a problem."

He headed for the creek, debating all the way whether he had any business getting anywhere near Val. However, when he saw her sitting on a rock, shoulders slumped, staring despondently at the water, he knew he'd been right to come. He was the one who'd ruined the day for her.

He stopped several feet away. "I'm sorry," he said quietly.

She didn't look up, but her shoulders visibly stiffened. "For?"

"Starting something I shouldn't have. Saying what I did. Take your pick."

"How about for being a jerk?"

He grinned, accepting the judgment as fair. "That, too." He settled down on the huge boulder next to her.

"Why'd you do it?" she asked without turning her head.

"Which part?"

"Start something?"

"Because I took one look at you in that outfit and I wanted to be sure that no other man at the party started getting ideas." The words came out before he had a chance to censor them.

Her head swiveled toward him at that. Fire flashed in her eyes. "You were branding me?"

He winced at her indignant tone. "It wasn't like it was a conscious thing, but in a manner of speaking, yes, I suppose I was."

The answer clearly riled her. "If that is not the most egotistical, presumptuous thing I have ever heard in all my life."

"Guilty," he agreed. "I apologize again. I've got to say in my own defense, it took me by surprise, too, wanting you that badly."

She seemed startled by the admission and more than a little pleased. "You wanted me?"

"Oh, yeah," he said softly, his gaze traveling once more over the bathing suit that wasn't even partially concealed by that ridiculously flimsy cover-up.

"How about now?"

He struggled with the urge to show her, then finally resisted. He couldn't silence a heartfelt admission, though. "Oh, yeah," he murmured.

She nodded with satisfaction. "Good," she said, and stood up in a graceful, fluid move that practically had Slade's tongue hanging out. "I'm ready to go back now."

Great. He was so stirred up he was ready to throw her on the ground and make passionate love to her, and she was ready to return to the party.

All for the best, he told himself over and over as she sashayed past. Wasn't that exactly why he had come down here? Wasn't his only mission to get her back to the party? Hadn't he sworn not to get carried away again?

Oh, sure. Like it had never once crossed his mind on the way down here that he might just finish that kiss, after all. Liar, liar, liar! He was pathetic.

"Coming?" she inquired sweetly, amusement flashing in her eyes.

"You know, darlin', you're a little like TNT."

"Oh?"

"Small, but very volatile."

She gave a little nod of satisfaction, clearly pleased by

the analogy. "Remember that the next time you get any crazy ideas about starting something you're not prepared to finish, cowboy."

"Oh, I'll remember it, believe me," he said fervently. In fact, he figured it would take a month of ice-cold showers to get this afternoon's little game out of his mind.

He managed to get through the rest of the afternoon without doing anything else crazy, but when evening came and the music began, he couldn't resist when Harlan Patrick all but shoved Val into his arms.

"Take over for me, pal. I'm going to find my wife," Harlan Patrick claimed. "Thanks for the dance, Val."

"Anytime," she said, her gaze fixed on Slade. "Well?"

Trapped, he held out a hand. "Would you care to dance?"

"Thank you," she said, moving into his arms as if she belonged there.

Holding her loosely, he stared down into her eyes. "You might want to reconsider this. Since my leg got banged up, I'm not so light on my feet."

Her gaze clung to his. "It's a slow song, Slade."

"So it is," he said, tightening his embrace until her head was tucked under his chin, her breasts pressed against his chest.

Big mistake, he concluded, when she was snuggled next to him. His blood heated to about one degree past boiling. Her rose-garden scent surrounded him, teasing at his senses.

It had been a long time since he'd held a woman this close, longer still since he'd wanted one with this aching neediness. Thank heaven she'd changed out of that provocative bathing suit. If he'd felt silky, bare skin beneath his touch, he'd have been lost.

Not that the sundress she wore was much of an improvement. Every time his hand slid up her back, his fingers brushed across soft, feminine flesh. And each time that happened, he could feel the shiver that washed over her. It was precisely the sort of responsiveness that made a man crave more. He was tempted to explore, to make the next caress more brazen and the one after that downright intimate.

He knew with everything in him that Val would be willing, even eager. A deeply ingrained sense of honor had him holding back. She was the kind of woman who deserved more than he had to give. She deserved pretty words and heartfelt whispers. She deserved happily ever after. He couldn't say for sure what tomorrow would bring, much less the day after that.

He realized with a start that she was staring at him, her expression troubled.

"Why so serious?" she asked.

"Counting the beats in the music," he lied. "If I don't, I'll stumble all over my feet and yours."

"Liar," she accused softly. "You were thinking too hard again, only this time it was about me, wasn't it?"

Her uncanny knack for reading his mind was disconcerting. "Maybe."

"I'll repeat what I said earlier. Sometimes it's smarter to go with your instincts."

He shook his head, wishing it were that simple. "A boy goes with his instincts, Val. A man—especially a man with a daughter to raise—has to stop to consider the consequences."

"So it was Annie on your mind just now?"

"No," he said firmly. "It was you. Only you."

"But you said—"

"I only meant that I can't just rush in and take what I want. It wouldn't be fair to you. It wouldn't be fair to Annie. I don't want her getting ideas about the two of us."

"That's very noble," Val said softly, but an increasingly familiar flash of fire in her eyes belied the quiet tone. "It's also bull."

He stumbled. "Excuse me. Did I hear you correctly?"

"You did. You're scared, Slade. That's what this is really about. You're terrified that if you let your guard down for one single second, you might actually have to deal with real emotions. You're terrified that whatever you start with me won't begin and end with sex."

He supposed there was a certain amount of truth in that. He'd let his emotions get the upper hand once and look where that had gotten him. Suzanne had ripped his heart in two.

"Maybe," he agreed, clearly surprising her.

"You're admitting it?"

"Sweetheart, I'm not oblivious to the truth. But saying it aloud doesn't change anything."

"Of course it does. Once you recognize the problem, you can start to move on."

He grinned at the simplicity of that. "Just like that, huh?"

"Exactly like that."

"You're forgetting one thing."

"What?"

"First, you have to want to move on."

She tripped. He steadied her, then met her gaze evenly. "I don't," he said succinctly.

"Well, of course you do," she said. "You can't want to go through life all alone."

"I'm not alone. I have Annie. I have my work. I have friends, including you, I hope."

"Friends? You and me?" She said it as incredulously as if he'd asked her to muck stalls with him.

"Why not?"

"Because…" she blustered, then stopped.

"Well?"

"Because it would never work."

"Why not? We're two intelligent adults. Surely we can keep our hands off each other, if we decide that's the sensible thing to do."

Her gaze locked with his. "What if I don't want to be sensible? What if I want to make a huge, glorious mistake by jumping into bed with you?"

"Then you'll be disappointed," he said firmly. "Because it isn't going to happen, Val. Not tonight. Not ever."

For some reason he couldn't fathom, she seemed to find his declaration amusing. "Is that so?"

"You can count on it."

"If you say so," she agreed mildly.

"We have an understanding then?" he asked, feeling it was somehow vital to get that nailed down.

"Oh, yes," she replied, with what could only be described as a silky purr.

Slade regarded her uneasily. She'd capitulated too easily. She'd said all the right things, all the things he wanted to hear. So why didn't he believe a word of it?

Maybe it was because even as she'd said the words, her gaze had been locked on his lips as if she'd never seen a more fascinating, more desirable mouth. Naturally that avid speculation had made him want to kiss her all over again.

Well, hell, he thought, as he took a decisive step back. This was going to be a whole lot harder than he'd anticipated. And Val, he predicted, wasn't going to do one single thing to make it any easier.

Seven

"The party was totally awesome," Annie declared as she walked home with her father afterward. She gazed up at him slyly. "I saw you dancing with Val. You were holding her real close. You like her, don't you?"

"She's a very nice woman," Slade said, hedging. This was exactly what he'd been afraid of—that Annie would start imagining a relationship where none existed.

Annie was having none of that. "Dad! You know what I mean. You really like her."

He scowled and put it more plainly. "Annie, don't go getting any ideas. Val and I are just friends, nothing more."

"I think she likes you," she added, as if he hadn't spoken. "She gets this funny look on her face when she sees you, kinda like she's got a fever or something."

Slade wondered how Val would feel about *that* description. She'd probably welcome it, declare Annie to be a very bright, intuitive child. Which she was, of course, even if it was irksome.

"What makes you think this look she gets on her face has anything to do with me?" he asked, curious about a ten-year-old's reasoning when it came to romance. Maybe if he understood it, he could nip these crazy ideas in the bud.

Annie regarded him as if he were dense. "Because she only looks that way when she sees you, silly."

"And you think it's because she likes me? Why?" he persisted.

"Because it's the way Laurie looks at Harlan Patrick, and she loves him, right? So it must mean that Val at least likes you a little."

Ah, Slade thought, *that* look. Laurie and Harlan Patrick did stare at each other like a couple of lovesick calves most of the time. To Slade's surprise, not even marriage had wiped that expression off their faces. Maybe they were still in the honeymoon stage.

Come to think of it, though, most of the Adamses wore that look when they spotted their mates. Even Harlan and Janet, who'd been married for years, brightened when they saw each other. Slade hadn't thought such infatuation could last past the marriage vows, but in this family it had. He still thought it was probably an anomaly, something all but impossible for an outsider to obtain.

"Look, kiddo, I meant what I said. Don't go getting any ideas about me and Val, okay? I'm not looking to get married again."

"What about a mom, though? I could really use one," Annie declared in a wistful way guaranteed to snatch the rug out from under him.

"I'm sorry," he said sympathetically. "I'm afraid it's not in the cards. But I think Val would very much like to be your friend."

Annie sighed heavily. "It's not the same."

Slade sighed, too. "I know, darlin'." Even though he'd

declared that to be his own goal earlier, having Val for a friend didn't seem likely to measure up for him, either.

"You look pleased with yourself," Laurie said, when she found Val sitting at the kitchen table with a cup of tea the next morning. "Basking in your success?"

"Which success would that be?"

"I was thinking of the party. What about you?"

Val gave her a grin. "I was thinking about the fact that I very nearly provoked Slade into forgetting all about those rigid principles of his. Of course, he dredged them up at the last second and spoiled things, but it was promising."

Laurie poured herself a cup of tea and sat down opposite her, her expression suddenly serious. "I thought principles were a rare thing in a man, so rare that they should be treasured when we stumble across them."

"They are," Val agreed. "Up to a point."

"In other words, the man still refuses to let you seduce him."

"So far," Val said, undaunted. "I think he's weakening, though."

"What happens if he does?" Laurie asked pointedly. "What happens if you finally succeed in getting him into bed, maybe just one time, and that's as far as it goes? Would you be satisfied with that?"

Val scowled. "No," she admitted. "I'm in this for the long haul."

"Then isn't it better that one of you is exercising some restraint?"

She considered Laurie's reasoning. "Okay, yes, but I really hate it when you're right," she grumbled.

Laurie chuckled. "I'm sure. Harlan Patrick complains about it, too."

Val reached for one of the homemade cinnamon buns that the housekeeper at White Pines had brought down still warm from the oven. It was scant consolation for reining in her longing to make some significant progress with Slade, but it would do. All that sugar was guaranteed to give her a rush.

"Do you have any real work for me to do today?" she asked Laurie hopefully. She desperately needed something to occupy her mind, to keep it off of Slade.

"Sorry, I can't help you," Laurie said without genuine regret. "We're on vacation, remember? If hanging around here is getting to you, you could always take a trip. Maybe some time away would help you to put things in perspective. Go on up to Nashville and go out with some of those men who are always hanging around when we're in town."

Val considered the idea and dismissed it. Being idle at White Pines with Slade nearby was still a vast improvement over anything else she could think of to do, even if she did spend every day all hot and bothered with no relief in sight. As for the men who'd pursued her over the years in Nashville, not a one fascinated her as Slade did.

"Maybe I'll just go and see what Annie's up to."

"I suspect you're going to have to find a playmate your own age now," Laurie teased. "Your party accomplished exactly what you set out for it to do. Annie's made new friends."

"Maybe I'll just round up a whole bunch of them and take them to a movie in Garden City," she said, recognizing that Laurie was probably right again.

"Or you could call Nick and see if he has work for you to do. You know my agent—he never takes a vacation."

"I'd rather go to a movie," Val said. Maybe, if she was

very clever about how she went about it, she could get Slade to come along.

As she stood up to leave, Laurie shot her a knowing look. "I imagine you'll find Slade in the new corral working with that stallion he and Harlan Patrick just bought."

"I never said anything about going to look for Slade."

"Didn't have to," Laurie said. "You're very predictable. Have been ever since you laid eyes on him."

Val paused thoughtfully. "Maybe that's my problem. Maybe I'm too predictable."

"Oh, no," Laurie said, regarding her worriedly. "I don't like that gleam in your eyes. What are you up to, Val?"

"Just coming up with a new plan," she said innocently. "Nothing drastic. I won't embarrass you."

Laurie waved off that concern. "You couldn't embarrass me if you tried. I just don't want to see you get hurt."

"Hey, no risk, no glory," she said blithely, and went in search of Annie.

Contrary to her original scheme, she did not try to manipulate things so that Slade would go along with her to chaperone a bunch of kids at the movies. In fact, she avoided him altogether, leaving it to Annie to get his permission for the outing.

When Annie mentioned that her diving lesson had been scheduled for the next day, Val volunteered to drive her. Afterward, they went out for the pizza Annie never tired of. Back at the ranch, Val dropped Annie off in front of her house, then drove on to Laurie's.

That was the pattern they fell into for the next couple of weeks. She rarely caught more than a glimpse of Slade. She gave him a casual wave and moved on, hoping that it was driving him to distraction the same way it was her.

At the end of the second week, after one of her diving lessons, Annie said, "Dad wants me home for dinner tonight." She wrinkled her nose when she said it.

Val tried not to let her disappointment show. "Oh? Does he have something special planned?"

"No. He says I'm taking advantage of you. He says he is perfectly capable of feeding me," she said, probably quoting him verbatim.

Val barely resisted the urge to smile. "I'm sure he is."

"That's what you think," Annie said with obvious disgust. "His idea of food is a frozen dinner he's nuked beyond recognition. He went shopping the other day and came home with five different versions of macaroni and cheese and six different versions of fried chicken and mashed potatoes. They all taste like burned rubber when he's done."

It was hardly news that Slade couldn't cook. He'd admitted as much himself. Val just hadn't realized precisely how bad he was.

Fortunately, she could offer a solution. She loved to cook, though she rarely had an opportunity when Laurie was on the road and going from hotel to hotel. Even here Val never had a chance to spend time in the kitchen. Laurie enjoyed showing off her domestic skills for her new husband, and Val was always invited along. Even when she begged off, it was only to eat in town or have a sandwich in her room.

She considered the best way to handle this. She doubted Slade would respond to any hints she offered about teaching him to cook, but Annie was likely to be a more than willing student. She was clearly sick to death of frozen dinners.

"I could help out," she suggested carefully.

Annie's expression brightened. "Would you? I mean,

Daddy would probably say no," she said, echoing Val's own assessment. "But maybe he wouldn't have to find out about it. Not at first, anyway."

"We can't lie to your father," Val objected, though probably not as strenuously as she should have.

"It wouldn't be lying. Not really," Annie insisted. "You could just come over in the afternoon and give me cooking lessons. By the time he gets home, dinner will be on the table. He won't know I didn't do it all myself."

"Honey, I think he'll suspect that something's going on. It's not like you can suddenly start fixing perfect pot roast overnight."

"I'll buy a cookbook and tell him I'm learning a new recipe every day. If you can read, you can cook, right? Once he tastes something that actually has real flavor to it, he won't complain," Annie said persuasively. "Please."

Val debated the wisdom of allowing Annie to deceive her father, of actually being a party to that deception. She weighed that against the old adage that the way to a man's heart was through his stomach.

"We'll try it tomorrow and see how it goes," she said finally. "If your father gets the least bit suspicious, you tell him the truth. You do not lie to him. Understood?"

Annie nodded eagerly. "Can we really do pot roast? Grandma made awesome pot roast. I really miss it."

"I'll pick up the ingredients in town in the morning. I'll meet you at your house at two. Okay?"

"Perfect. Daddy never gets home before five-thirty or six. Is that long enough?"

"Perfect," Val agreed. Whether he knew it or not, Slade was about to be treated to the way his life could be if he'd just wake up and allow her into it.

* * *

Slade smelled the aroma of pot roast wafting from his house before he got within ten feet of it. His mouth watered. His suspicions kicked in, right along with a stirring of anticipation he didn't like one bit.

But when he walked inside, he found Annie at the stove lifting the lid on a huge pot. Half expecting to find Val, he was torn between disappointment and relief. She'd been avoiding him lately and he hadn't been nearly as grateful as he should have been. For a minute when he'd sniffed that pot roast, he'd been hoping that she was the one responsible. Maybe the housekeeper at White Pines had sent it down.

"What's that?" he asked, venturing close.

"Pot roast," Annie said proudly. "Doesn't it smell awesome?"

His gaze narrowed. "Who made it?"

"I did." She gestured toward a book that lay open on the counter. "It wasn't so hard. I just followed the directions."

He stepped up to the stove and peered into the pot. A roast indeed had been cooked to perfection. It was surrounded by carrots, onions and little potatoes, all perfectly done and seasoned with herbs.

"You did this?"

She nodded. "Are you hungry?"

"Starved," he admitted, deciding he'd pursue the issue of Annie's cooking after he'd had a chance to taste dinner. If it tasted half as good as it smelled, he doubted he'd have the heart to scold her.

"You wash up and I'll get it on the table," she said.

He noticed she had already set the small oak table with real dishes and place mats. She'd even plunked a vase of wildflowers in the middle. His little tomboy turning domestic? He wasn't buying it for a minute. Then again, maybe she was as sick of those frozen meals as he was. Maybe she'd been desperate for something edible. He wouldn't put it past her to take matters into her own hands. She was a lot like Val in that.

He took a quick shower, pulled on clean jeans and a T-shirt, then settled at the table. A steaming plate of food awaited him. Annie watched him expectantly. He cut a bite of the pot roast and tasted it. The meat almost melted in his mouth. It was even better than his mother's, and it was her specialty.

"Well?" Annie demanded eagerly. "How is it?"

"Better than Grandma's," he said candidly.

Her face lit up. "Really?"

"Taste it and see."

She took a bite, then beamed. "Oh, wow! I did it. I really did it."

After that, Slade didn't have the heart to question whether she'd done it entirely on her own. She was too darn pleased with herself. He told himself that was the only reason he let it pass.

The next night, when he found real southern fried chicken on the table, along with genuine mashed potatoes and gravy, he didn't want to spoil her obvious pleasure by getting into an argument.

He kept quiet the next night, too, when he found home-made spaghetti waiting for him, accompanied by a zesty garlic bread and a fresh green salad.

When the desserts started turning up, he could no longer ignore his suspicions. He'd long since detected Val's hand in the increasingly elaborate meals, but his stomach had won out over his honor.

"The cake's real good, honey," he said as he savored

the rich, moist chocolate with a frosting that might as well have been fudge, it was so thick.

"I know chocolate's your favorite. I told…" She stopped herself and a guilty flush climbed into her cheeks.

"Who'd you tell?" he demanded, seizing the opening.

"Val," she confessed in a whisper.

"Did she make the cake?"

"No," Annie said adamantly. "I did."

He leveled a gaze straight at her and waited.

"She just told me how," she said finally.

"And the rest? Did she help with all of it?"

"She wanted to," Annie said with a defiant lift of her chin. "It was her idea."

"And whose idea was it not to tell me?"

"Mine."

"Why?"

"Because I figured you'd get mad. You said I was taking advantage of her, even though I knew it wasn't true. She likes to help."

Slade sighed. "I'm sure she does, Annie, but it's more complicated than that."

"How?"

"Val and I are just friends," he repeated for the hundredth time. "It's not right to take advantage of a friend."

"But she said—"

"I don't care what she said," Slade said, his voice climbing. "This is going to stop."

"We'll starve to death," Annie muttered.

"We are not going to starve," he snapped in frustration. "There's nothing wrong with eating frozen dinners. Millions of people do."

"It's not the same as real food," Annie protested. "Especially after you've ruined it, anyway."

"Then we'll go into town to eat."

She jumped up then, practically quivering with outrage. "You do what you want. I'm going to live with Val."

She flew out the door before he could think to stop her. "Well, hell," he muttered, staring after her.

He waited a few minutes until his temper settled down, then went to look for her. He found her on the porch at Harlan Patrick's, sobbing in Val's arms. Val regarded him helplessly.

"What is this about?" she mouthed silently.

Slade sighed. "Dinner," he mouthed back.

Val's eyes filled with understanding. She stepped back and clasped Annie's shoulders, as she gazed into her eyes. "Why don't you take a walk down by the creek? I always feel better when I go there."

"What are you going to do?" she asked, not once glancing toward Slade.

"Your father and I are going to have a talk."

Annie turned toward him, then studied them both worriedly. "You're not going to fight, are you?"

"No," Slade said.

Val regarded him ruefully. "We might," she contradicted. "But we'll work it out, because that is what grown-ups do."

He supposed the comment was meant to effectively put him in his place. It succeeded.

He waited until after Annie had gone before he stepped onto the porch himself. He chose the swing and set it to swaying as Val moved into a rocking chair.

"I suppose I ought to start by thanking you for all the meals," he said stiffly.

She nodded. "That would be a good place to start."

"You shouldn't have, though."

"Why not?"

"Because—"

"Because you are too stiff-necked to accept help when it's offered?"

"Now wait a minute," he protested.

"Because you're scared I'm going to worm my way into your life?"

"Val—"

"Because you'd rather eat sawdust than something I enjoyed fixing for you?"

He moved quickly, scooping her out of the chair and clamping his mouth over hers before she could wind up and hit him with another accusation. The taste of her exploded inside him. The feel of her in his arms shattered the last of his restraint.

He gulped for air, then went back for more, sure that she was more potent than any female who'd ever crossed his path before. He'd never had a kiss shoot him straight to the moon. He'd never had the soft moan of a willing female fill him with such tenderness.

"Bad idea," he murmured, stepping away.

"No," she said, wrapping her arms around his neck and dragging him back.

With that single word, she dismissed all of his objections, all of his sound, rational thoughts and honorable intentions. With her mouth locked to his, he couldn't think at all, could barely even stand.

"Sweet heaven," he murmured, when she finally paused for breath.

"I can't believe I just did that," she whispered, her cheeks flaming. "I'm so sorry. I don't know what came over me. You've made it clear this wasn't what you wanted, and then you kissed me, and I guess I just went a little nuts. Sorry."

Smiling, he touched a finger to her lips. "Don't be. It was a long time coming. It was bound to happen."

"I thought you swore it would never happen."

"That was before you started chattering nonsense and I couldn't think of any other way to shut you up."

"It was effective, I'll give you that." She tilted her head and studied him. "What now?"

"Now we sit down and have a rational discussion about why it is all wrong for you to go on cooking for me."

She looked as if he'd slapped her. "No," she said. "That is precisely what we do not do. I will not have that conversation with you. Not tonight."

"Val—"

"I won't."

"We have to talk about it."

"Not tonight," she all but shouted.

"Okay," he soothed. "What do you want to talk about?"

A faint smile touched her lips. "I don't want to talk at all."

The subtly sensuous implications rocked him all over again. "Anything else is not an option," he said, his voice ragged. He took a few steps away from her. He grabbed the porch railing and stared out into the gathering darkness. "Did Annie tell you she intended to move in with you?"

"What?"

He heard the incredulous note in her voice and smiled. "She thinks she'll starve if I refuse to let you go on cooking for us."

"Could be she's right," Val said. "But I'll talk to her. I'm sure deep down she knows she can't live with me."

He felt her slip up to the railing beside him, standing just close enough to tantalize him with that flowery scent.

"Slade?"

"Yes."

"Other than your stubborn pride, why is it so wrong for me to help out?"

"It's not wrong," he said, raking his hand through his hair in a gesture of frustration. "It's just..." He couldn't come up with a better word.

"You're not taking advantage of me. Laurie's on vacation. That means I have very little to do. I'm bored. I love to cook. It seems to me it works out well all the way around."

She sounded so quietly reasonable, so sincere. He felt like a heel for robbing her of a chance to do something she enjoyed. "I'll pay you, then."

"Don't insult me."

He winced at the sharp tone. "Okay, then, I pay for the groceries, all of them, going back to when this started."

"That's fair enough."

"And you start sharing the meals with us."

Her head snapped around at that. "Are you serious?"

"Yes," he said, smiling at her shock.

"Won't that make you crazy?"

"Yes," he said. "But not a minute passes that you don't make me crazy, so I might as well get the pleasure of a good meal and some adult conversation out of it." He tucked a finger under her chin and forced her to face him. "That's it, though. Food and conversation."

A spark of amusement lit her eyes. "Food and conversation," she echoed dutifully.

And trouble, he thought to himself. Let's not forget about the trouble. He knew with every fiber of his being that he was asking for it.

Eight

"Haven't seen much of Val lately," Harlan Patrick said, the casual tone belied by the wicked glint in his eyes. "Any idea what she's been up to?"

Slade muttered a response he hoped would end the subject, though his boss wasn't known for taking a hint.

"What was that?" Harlan Patrick asked, his expression innocent.

Slade looked up and met his gaze evenly. "I said go to hell."

Harlan Patrick hooted, obviously undaunted by Slade's bad temper. "Now is that any way to treat your boss and the man who brought Val into your life?" he taunted.

"Probably no way to treat the boss," Slade agreed. "As for the other, I probably ought to kick your butt from here to Dallas for inflicting that woman on me. From the minute you suggested I entertain her while you and Laurie dealt with your own family crisis, she's been pestering me to death."

"Which bothers you so much that you've started having dinner with her every night, just so you can keep an eye on her," Harlan Patrick teased. "Yep, you never know what a woman like Val might be up to. Gotta keep a close eye on her." He grinned. "Real close, I'd say."

"Like I said—"

"I know. I know. None of my business." Harlan Patrick's gaze turned serious. "Of course, Val and Laurie are more than business associates. They're friends. I'm right fond of Val myself. She helped me out when I was chasing after Laurie and trying to convince her to marry me. I'd feel real badly if anyone were to hurt her."

Slade regarded him evenly, accepting the fierce protectiveness that was typical of an Adams when one of their own was endangered. It extended to anyone they cared about. "Message received."

"Good," Harlan Patrick said with a sigh of relief. "Now I've done my duty. Maybe Laurie will get off my back."

Slade grinned. "So it was your wife who put you up to bugging me about this?"

"She's nesting," Harlan Patrick said. "I'm told it's natural with pregnant women. They want everyone around them settled down and happy."

Slade regarded him with surprise. "Laurie's pregnant?"

Harlan Patrick grinned, looking pleased as punch. "Yep. She found out yesterday, though Val told her she was weeks ago. I guess she recognized the signs from last time."

He said the last without rancor, though Slade knew for a fact it had been a very sore point that Laurie had kept his baby from him. If it hadn't been for a front-page picture in a tabloid, Harlan Patrick might never have known about his daughter, might never have made one last-ditch effort to get Laurie to marry him.

"Congratulations," Slade said, pumping his boss's hand. "I guess that means she won't be doing any concert tours for a while, then. That must make you happy." He also knew that Laurie's music and the traveling it required had been a real bone of contention between them before they'd married. The battles over it had been legendary until someone had finally taught the two the meaning of compromise. They were still struggling to get the knack of it, though, from what Slade had observed.

"Actually, the tour's still on," Harlan Patrick said with an air of resignation. "She claims she's healthy as a horse and there's no reason not to go ahead with her plans. I made her promise not to be on the road for at least two weeks before the baby's due. I'm not having my second child born in some other state with me nowhere to be found. I intend to be right by Laurie's side this time."

"You know, Harlan Patrick, sometimes Mother Nature has a mind of her own," Slade pointed out. "The baby might not stick to your timetable."

"Which is why I'm going on the road with her for the last two weeks of the tour. I'm not taking any chances on missing this kid's arrival." He studied Slade. "What about you? Were you there when Annie was born?"

Slade concentrated on cleaning Black Knight's shoe. "Nope. I was on the circuit up in Wyoming then. Suzanne was back here in Texas. She never forgave me for it, either. My mama was at the hospital. She said Suzanne cursed me so loudly in the delivery room, it was a wonder I didn't hear it all the way up in Cheyenne."

"I think we get the blame most of the time when women are in labor," Harlan Patrick said. "I've been at the hospital on a few occasions waiting for various kids in this family to be born. Most of the men got cursed out to their faces. Ten minutes after they held the baby, though, it had all blown over."

"Yeah, but with Suzanne and me, it was the beginning of the end. When I think back, it's probably a wonder our marriage lasted as long as it did after Annie came along. Suzanne was the kind of woman who required a lot of attention. I wasn't around to give it to her, and once Annie started school, they couldn't stay on the road with me."

"That's a concern you'd never have with Val," Harlan Patrick noted, as if it were only an idle observation. "Woman's as independent as they come."

"So I've noticed," Slade said, and let it go at that. Val might claim to be interested in him, might even turn up at his table for dinner most nights, but she could vanish without a trace for hours on end. She didn't need him, not really. He was still struggling with himself over whether that was good or bad. Sometimes he found it more annoying than he cared to admit.

"Does that bother you?" Harlan Patrick asked, zeroing in on his thoughts as if able to read them.

"Of course not. She's entitled to a life of her own. It has nothing to do with me."

"Is that so?" Harlan Patrick inquired, his voice laced with skepticism. He grinned. "You are in such deep denial, it's pitiful."

Slade's head shot up. "Denial about what?"

"The way that woman gets to you."

"Don't go getting any ideas," he said, much as he did to Annie almost daily.

The trouble was, he was the one getting ideas. Some had to do with getting Val from the dinner table straight into his bed. Some had to do with the kind of permanence that scared him to death. Generally speaking, he figured it was better not to think about her at all. Unfortunately, ever since she'd taken over his kitchen, that had proved to be next to impossible.

Even on those occasions when she disappeared before he got home in the evening, her scent was everywhere. So was her touch. The table always had a bouquet of flowers on it. She and Annie had made curtains for the windows, sheer things that reminded him all too vividly of that provocative cover-up she'd worn at Annie's party. The magazines he'd tossed on the floor late at night sat in a neat little pile on a table.

A few weeks ago he might have accused her of trying to take over his life. Now he saw it as taking care of him…and Annie, of course. Instead of blind panic, a warm feeling settled over him as a result of her subtle improvements in his living conditions. The house suddenly felt a lot like a home, the kind he remembered from his childhood, not the kind he and Suzanne had shared on the rare occasions when he was there. The ever-present tension between him and his wife had robbed their home of any warmth or affection. Val made sure there was plenty of both. Sometimes her casual, innocent touches just about drove him to the brink.

The whole thing was worrisome, though. He was getting used to these feelings of being settled, getting used to *her*. Defenses rock-solid a few weeks ago were crumbling now. If he wasn't very, very careful he was going to forget all about his resolve to keep his distance—emotionally and physically.

With Harlan Patrick's warning still ringing in his ears, he reminded himself that that could be very risky in more ways than one.

Her plan to insinuate herself into Slade's life wasn't going the way she'd planned at all, Val concluded after several weeks of staring at him across the dinner table.

They chatted politely. They laughed. They even exchanged long, heated looks once Annie left the table.

But when the dishes were done and Annie had retreated to her room, Slade all but escorted her out the door. He'd come close to slamming it in her face a couple of times. If he hadn't looked so panicked, she might have taken offense. Clearly the man didn't trust himself to be alone with her. His obvious skittishness, which was increasing almost daily, should have been reward enough, but she wanted more. A lot more.

Steering clear of Slade had worked the last time. Maybe it was time to return to that strategy. Sometimes even more drastic measures were called for. Maybe she needed to up the ante by bringing some competition into the mix. Slade had thrived on challenges once. He'd had a fiercely competitive career. She doubted that sort of spirit had faded just because he was no longer fighting for rodeo championships. Maybe he needed to be lured into fighting for her.

"Laurie, a lot of your songs are just about ready to go," she mentioned casually one morning as Laurie sipped some herbal tea to get her perpetually queasy stomach settled. "Why don't you get the band down here for a few days and rehearse? See how they sound with all the pieces in place?"

"Any particular reason you want the band to come?" Laurie shot her a knowing look. "You aren't, by any chance, thinking that a little attention from another man might make Slade jealous?"

"It could work," Val said defensively, not even trying to hide her motives from her best friend. "He doesn't have to know that none of the guys have ever looked at me twice."

"It's risky," Laurie warned, looking worried. "He might

just conclude that you really have something going with one of the guys, that he was just a stand-in while you were stuck down here with me. If his pride kicks in, you'll be worse off than you are now."

Val considered that, then decided it was still worth the risk. "I don't think I could be any worse off. Besides, I'm desperate to get him to wake up. Nothing else I've tried has worked."

"Ever heard of the word *patience*?"

"I've been patient," Val countered.

"Not by my standards, but okay." Laurie shrugged. "If it will stop you from moping around here, I'll do it," she agreed. "Call Nick and have him set it up."

Val grinned and reached for the phone. "I'll have them here by the weekend."

"Have you decided which of the men is going to be your secret admirer? I'm sure any one of them would be happy to volunteer. Contrary to what you believe, they have all looked at you twice. Sometimes more. None of them pursued it, because you made it very clear that you thought of them as business colleagues and nothing more." Laurie waved a finger under Val's nose. "See to it none of them get hurt. I've seen this kind of thing split up a band and I won't have it happening with mine, not because of some game you're bent on playing."

"I'll lay it all out up front," Val promised, chagrined by the understanding of what she was asking of Laurie, of the lengths her friend was willing to go to on her behalf.

When the band arrived on Friday, Val met them at the airport. On the drive to the ranch, she zeroed in on the drummer, who had a shy smile and sexy eyes. She knew from past experience that men grew very competitive when he was around. He was also engaged to be married, which ought to make it safe enough to ask him to be part of her plot.

"Would you mind flirting outrageously with me for the next three or four days?" she asked him as the others unloaded their bags at the hotel. "Nothing serious. It's just to get someone's attention. I know it's a huge favor. I'll understand if you say no."

Paul studied her intently. "You know I'd do anything in the world for you, but you're going to have to clue me in. Are you trying to snag this man or run him off?"

"Snag him," she admitted.

He nodded, his expression serious. "Point him out and I'll get to work. But if you ever tell Tracy about this, I'm a dead man. She won't care that the flirting's not for real. She always thought I had a thing for you."

Val hesitated, remembering what Laurie had said about some of the band having been interested in her. "Maybe this is a bad idea, then. You and Tracy have something special. I don't want to start trouble."

"You won't," Paul assured her. "I know the score. This is nothing personal. Just don't kiss me like you mean it in front of the guys. They're the biggest blabbermouths I've ever run across." He winked. "Of course, if you want to kiss me in private, that's another story."

"If this goes the way I hope, I won't be kissing you at all," she said, then patted his cheek. "Don't look so disappointed. It's for the best."

At Val's instigation, Laurie invited Slade and Annie to the rehearsal on Saturday evening, along with most of the Adamses. Annie dragged Slade over to sit next to Val on the crowded sofa. They were crushed together, thigh-to-thigh. Val could feel his heat burning into her. Unless she was very much mistaken, his temperature had climbed several degrees when he'd realized he couldn't squirm away from her without causing a scene. To her amusement, he'd settled back stoically.

"I'm so excited," Annie confided. "Do you think Laurie's going to sing the song I helped her write? I know she did it at my party and all, but this is with the whole band, like it would be on the album."

Val grinned. "I think you can count on it."

Slade's gaze locked with hers. "You haven't been around much the last couple of days."

"Did you miss me?"

"Missed your cooking," he claimed, though the look in his eyes said it was more than that.

"I've been busy helping Laurie set up this rehearsal. I wanted to spend some time with the guys, too. You know, catching up." She allowed her gaze to drift to Paul, who winked at her. She felt the heat rise in her cheeks.

"Who is that?" Slade asked, his tone suddenly testy.

"Paul McDaniels. He's been with Laurie from the beginning. He's a great drummer. A nice man, too."

Paul came over then, standing close and resting his hand on her shoulder in a familiar, possessive gesture. Val introduced him to Slade and tried not to chuckle at Slade's sour expression when Paul bent down to brush a kiss across her cheek before he went back to join the band.

"You two seem close," Slade said tightly.

"Old friends," she said simply, keeping her gaze on Paul as she said it. She managed to imbue her words with a significance that indicated the relationship went well beyond friendship.

"I see."

The tension radiating from Slade was almost palpable as the rehearsal got underway. He stared at Paul and scowled, as Laurie sang song after song. Only when the first strains of Annie's song filled the air did he manage to drag his attention away from the band to focus on Laurie.

"That's it, Daddy," Annie said, bouncing beside him. "That's my song. Listen."

He grinned at her enthusiasm. As Laurie sang about second chances and new self-discovery, his expression turned thoughtful. When the song ended, he leaned down and gave Annie a kiss.

"You should be real proud, angel. That was a beautiful song." He gazed at Val. "Thank you for giving her the chance to be a part of it."

He stood up then. "I think I'll be going now. I've got an early day tomorrow. Have to get to Fort Worth. Annie'll be staying with Dani and her kids while I'm gone. That should give you plenty of time to visit with your old friend."

Val barely managed to conceal her disappointment, then and over the next few days, during which Slade remained out of town. By the time he came back, the band had returned to Nashville.

As near as she could tell, her scheme had been a bust. For lack of anything more interesting to do, she saw no reason not to go back to the old pattern of cooking for Slade and Annie. For the next couple of weeks, she deliberately breezed in and out of their lives, leaving a trail of perfume and the aroma of freshly baked apple pie, Slade's favorite after her decadent chocolate cake.

However, somewhere along the way, she had concluded that tactical retreat was still her best bet. She made sure she was never there to share the meals she and Annie prepared. Maybe he'd actually miss her—eventually.

She was slipping out the door on a Friday night when Slade managed to catch her.

"Well, well, if it isn't the elusive homemaker," he said, amusement threading through his voice. "What are you up to?"

"Just seeing that the two of you don't starve to death, as usual." She ducked under his arm. "See ya. Gotta run."

He snagged her arm. "Oh, no, you don't."

"Slade," she began, but the protest died on her lips. The glint in his eyes was worrisome. "Slade?"

"You brought enough dinner for two?" he asked.

Because her lips were suddenly too dry for her to speak, she nodded.

"Then you'll have to stay and share. Annie's gone for the evening. A slumber party."

"Oh, really." Annie hadn't said a word to her when she'd left the house a little earlier. She'd made some excuse about running up to the main house. She'd even begged Val to wait until she got back.

"You didn't know?" he asked, sounding genuinely surprised. "I thought you two were thick as thieves."

"I guess she forgot to mention it," Val said, recalling the evasiveness Annie had displayed earlier. The little schemer had set her up.

"So, will you stay?"

"Are you sure you want me to?"

"I suppose that depends on how dangerously you like to live." His gaze settled on her mouth, lingered, then rose to meet her eyes. "Or how involved you are with the drummer."

"I told you, Paul and I are friends."

"Good," he said succinctly. "That leaves us with deciding how much of a risk-taker you are."

"Risk-taker?" she echoed. She was cool, calm, dependable Val. She never took risks unless they were carefully calculated.

He nodded and lowered his head until his lips were almost touching hers. She held her breath and waited, almost certain she would die if he didn't close that infinitesimal gap Instead, he pulled back and grinned.

"Like I said, Val, it's time to decide just how dangerously you want to live."

She had a feeling he was toying with her, pushing her to admit that she had deliberately tried to make him jealous by flirting outrageously with Paul right in front of him. For all she knew, he'd asked Laurie, or even Paul, if there was really anything for him to be jealous about.

Impulsively, she reached up and threaded her fingers through his hair. "Paul who?"

She kissed Slade until she felt him tremble, then pulled away, forcing her expression into a deliberately nonchalant mask. "Still up for this, cowboy?"

As it turned out, Slade was very much up for it…and then some.

Nine

Carrying Val off to his bedroom struck Slade as being both the smartest and the dumbest thing he'd ever considered. She was the kind of woman any man would count himself lucky to have in his bed. He knew there was a sizzling passion between them just waiting to explode. He sensed she would be every bit as generous in bed as she was in other ways.

At the same time, he also knew that he wouldn't walk away from the experience unscathed. He'd already become addicted to setting off those sparks in her eyes, to seeing her mouth curve into a slow smile. What would happen when he'd experienced the most intimate caresses? When her body had welcomed him?

Worse, he was taking advantage of her, taking what she offered without being willing to offer her anything in return except what they shared in bed. He was setting himself up for guilt and her up for heartache.

Knowing that, he actually managed to get himself to halt at the door to his room.

"You can call it quits now," he said, his voice husky. "No harm, no foul."

"Not a chance, cowboy."

The sparkle of anticipation in her eyes was as bright as a star. Gazing into her eyes, he knew there wasn't a chance in hell he could turn back now. He wanted it all, needed her in ways he'd sworn never to need a woman again. Sex was one thing. This was something else entirely, no matter how hard he tried to convince himself otherwise.

It was barely dusk outside and the room was in shadows. Slade wanted it that way. As desperately as he wanted to see every inch of Val, he was just as desperate to keep her from getting a good look at the scars from the accident. His leg wasn't a pretty picture. Suzanne had made it clear more than once that the crisscrossing of stitches disgusted her. He had to assume that most women would feel the same.

As Val's fingers lightly touched his cheek, his attention snapped back to the here and now, back to a touch so tender it set off longing right along with fireworks. He pushed all thoughts of his ex-wife from his head and concentrated on the woman who could make him weak-kneed with a glance.

He settled her on the edge of the bed, then sat next to her. When she reached for the buttons on his shirt, he stilled her hand. "Slowly, darlin'. We have all the time in the world."

She gave him a faint smile. "I keep thinking you'll change your mind. You have before. And dinner is on the table."

"Dinner can wait."

"It'll be ruined," she lamented.

"It can be heated up again. You seem to forget that I was used to ruined before you came along."

She touched a hand to his cheek once more. "So this is it then? You're not going to back out?"

"Not this time," he assured her. "Remember something. We've never gotten to this point before, and for good reason. I knew once we did, I'd never be able to stop." He smiled slowly. "Now let's get back to where we were before I brought you in here."

"You mean this?" Val asked, touching his lips with her own in a kiss so light he might have only imagined it.

"More like this," he said, taking her mouth with a hungry urgency that had them both quivering with need.

This time he was the one reaching for buttons, fumbling with them until her blouse was stripped away. Her bra—no more than a tantalizing scrap of lace—followed. His breath caught in his throat at the sight of her.

"You are…" Words failed him, as they often did when he was struck by her beauty.

"So are you," she teased, working her hands under his shirt and skimming nails over his chest, and then lower, until he had to swallow hard and slow their progress.

"Magnificent," she whispered, supplying the word that had eluded him.

He captured her attention with kisses that ventured from lips to neck to breasts and then, as he skimmed her slacks down, to far more intimate places. She gasped and writhed at his increasingly clever caresses.

"Not yet," she pleaded, when he clearly had her at the edge. "I…want…you…with…me." The words came out as a choked cry of need.

With the room in darkness now, Slade didn't hesitate. "I will be, darlin'," he promised, shucking his jeans and entering her just as she reached the peak and tumbled over.

She was still trembling in the aftermath of that first

sweet climax, when he began to move inside her. He saw her eyes widen, then darken with pleasure as he rode her to the top again. He held back, counted to a hundred, blanked out everything in an effort to make the moment when they both shattered together even sweeter.

His body ached with the effort, but it was the kind of torment that men prayed for.

"Oh, Slade, don't," she begged, only to change her mind when he slowed. "No, please, more."

He lifted her hips off the bed and drove into her, one last, deep plunge that ripped a moan from low in her throat and had him screaming out her name as skyrockets went off inside him.

It was a long time before he could catch his breath, longer still before he could think of what to say.

"Sweet heaven, I think you've destroyed me," he murmured, pressing a kiss to her brow, then collapsing back against the pillows.

She gave him a smile of purely feminine satisfaction. "Is that so?"

"You seem pleased about it."

"If it means you won't soon forget about me, I am."

"Darlin', I couldn't forget about you if I tried. I know that from experience," he said ruefully. If it had been difficult before, it was going to be downright impossible now that he knew the wonder of being with her like this.

Maybe he didn't have to forget about her. Maybe there was an answer that would work for both of them. As Val lay curled contentedly against him, he began to toy with a notion that he had dismissed on more than one occasion before tonight.

Tonight had changed things. There was no going back. Maybe his solution would take them forward. Now all he had to do was work up the courage to bring it up and hope for the right words to explain it.

In the meantime, he was stunned to discover that he wanted her again, that once hadn't been nearly enough. He reached for her, only to have her slip beyond his touch and flip on the light.

"No," he said harshly, shoving past her to turn it off again.

She stilled as if he'd slapped her. "Slade?" Her voice was filled with questions. There was no mistaking the fact that his reaction had hurt her.

"Sorry. There's no need for light."

"Why? What are you afraid of?"

"Who says I'm afraid?"

"You must be. I know you like looking at me. I could see it in your eyes before. Why won't you let me see you?"

He lay back against the pillow, silently cursing her quick mind and his own scars.

"I'm not going to let it rest until you tell me, so you might as well stop stalling," she said, as briskly as she might have handled some business associate who wasn't fulfilling a promise.

Slade drew in a deep breath. Better to admit the truth and gauge her reaction, especially if he intended to go through with his impulsive plan. He couldn't spend the rest of his life hiding in the dark, not around a woman like Val. She'd never allow it.

"There are scars," he said finally.

"From the accident?"

He nodded, then realized she couldn't see. "Yes," he said more curtly than he'd intended.

"You never talk about what happened."

"Why talk about it? It's over with."

"Tell me anyway. Annie says it was your wife's fault and that it robbed you of your career."

His daughter's insight stunned him. "She knows all that?"

"She says that's why you don't like her much, because she reminds you of her mother."

He muttered a harsh expletive. "I had no idea she thought that."

"Is it true? Does she remind you of her mother?"

"She looks like her, that's true enough, but that's where it ends. Annie's always been my treasure. From the first moment I laid eyes on her, I was in awe that I could have created something so beautiful." He sighed. "I guess somewhere in the past year or so, I stopped reminding her of that."

"She needs to hear it," Val said gently.

"Yes," he agreed.

When he fell silent and stayed that way, Val prompted, "You were going to tell me about the accident."

He smiled ruefully in the darkness. "Was I now?"

"Oh, yes," she insisted.

"I was back in Wilder's Glen to see Suzanne and Annie. Suzanne hated it there. It was too small-town for her. She missed being on the road with me, but Annie needed to be settled. She needed to be in school. I didn't know it at the time, but Suzanne took every opportunity to dump Annie with my parents so she could go chasing around, having the same kind of fun she assumed I was having on the road and denying her."

He expected some reaction, but Val remained absolutely silent. Instead, she simply reached for his hand and linked her fingers with his. Oddly, the gesture brought him a measure of peace he rarely felt when he thought back to that tumultuous time.

"Suzanne wanted to go out," he said, recalling the argument they'd had about it. "I'd barely walked in the door. I wanted to stay at home, spend some time with my daughter and my wife in private. Still, I could see her point. I thought she'd been trapped at home while I was away, and deserved a break from it. We went out for dinner, even danced a little, though I was aching from the last rodeo."

He grimaced at the understatement. He'd grown used to aches and pains over the years, but it had been worse that night. He'd lost his concentration in the ring and been tossed off the back of a bull. It had been a miracle he hadn't been trampled.

"We finally left the bar after midnight. I was so exhausted, Suzanne volunteered to drive. She wasn't drunk. Hadn't even had a beer, for that matter. On the way home, she started in on me again about being left behind all the time, about being stuck in Wilder's Glen where my parents could watch her every move. We argued."

He could still hear her voice echoing in his head. "It was the same old thing, a fight we'd had a million times before, but she was driving too fast, paying too little attention to the road. There was a sharp curve and she missed it. We slammed head-on into a tree."

Val gasped softly.

Slade kept his voice dispassionate, even though he could still hear the grinding of the metal, feel the searing pain. "The damage was mostly on the passenger side. My leg was crushed. For a while the doctors thought I'd lose it, but I fought them every step of the way. Eventually it healed, just not well enough for me to go back to the rodeo. Being married to a rodeo star had been enough for Suzanne, enough to compensate for being left behind to raise our daughter. Without that, with me scarred, she saw no reason to stay. As soon as the verdict was in on my future, she took off. She filed for divorce a week later. She didn't even fight me for custody of Annie. She seemed almost glad to be rid of her."

"What a horrible person," Val said indignantly. "I thought for better or for worse was supposed to mean something."

She moved swiftly, too swiftly for him to stop her. Before he could guess her intentions, her hand was on his damaged leg.

"No," he said curtly, trying to grab her hand.

She shook him off, then began to trace his scars with a touch so gentle it took his breath away. His injuries had healed long ago, but not his soul. Val's touch did that. When her lips brushed over each and every ridge of scar tissue, the protective shield around his heart shattered.

He knew in that instant that his earlier decision had been a sound one. She was the one woman in the world with whom he could build a future.

"That was a long time coming," Slade noted when they finally got around to dinner sometime in the middle of the night. Even reheated, the food was a whole lot better than anything he'd ever fixed.

"Are you referring to our meal?" Val inquired.

He held back the desire to grin at her testy tone. "You know I'm not."

She put down her fork and met his gaze evenly. "What now, Slade? Are we going to talk about what's next?"

Leave it to Val to be direct. He decided to see what she was thinking before laying out his own ideas. "You tell me. You seem to be the planner in the room." He watched her struggle with that for a minute, but Val wasn't easily caught off guard.

"I say we give it six months and see how it goes," she said briskly. "That ought to tell us if this is some sort of a fluke."

The response irked him. He'd mentally moved way past a trial run. "Oh, really?" he said irritably. "Six months? And how do we explain our relationship to my daughter during that time? Or do we sneak around the way her mama did? That would certainly keep the excitement alive."

"I was under the impression that you didn't bother to explain much to Annie," Val said, matching his sarcasm.

He put a hand to his chest. *"Wham! A direct hit."*

She winced guiltily, then sighed. "Okay, I was being glib. And unfair. You're right that Annie is at an impressionable age. We can't carry on right under her nose and get her hopes up. Any suggestions?"

This was it, Slade thought. The opening he'd been waiting for. He'd made his decision. It was time to put all his cards on the table.

"She adores you. You and I get along okay." He watched her expression closely, then added, "Why not just go for broke and get married?"

Val looked momentarily taken aback, but she recovered quickly. There was very strong evidence from the clatter of her silverware hitting her plate that the fire in her eyes was not sparked by passion.

"Now there's a proposal that will make a girl's heart go pitter-pat," she said with cool disdain.

Slade promptly took offense. He'd asked her to marry him, hadn't he? "If you were expecting hearts and flowers, you picked the wrong guy. I don't believe in romance or love or happily ever after. I thought you knew that."

"Then what are we talking about here?" she demanded with rising indignation. "A mother for Annie? You'll make the ultimate sacrifice to see to it she has a real home?"

He squirmed uncomfortably. "More or less."

"And now that you've tested the sex and discovered it's terrific, that's just a bonus for you?"

This wasn't going well. He didn't have to be hit upside the head with an iron skillet to get that. The idea had popped into his mind weeks ago, sometime between the instant he'd first caught a whiff of her apple pie and the time all-too-recently when he'd lost himself inside her. The latter probably hadn't been the best time to reach any life-altering decisions.

"Maybe we should think about it some more," he suggested.

Val stood up and tossed her napkin in his face. "No need for that, cowboy. I'll marry you when hell freezes over."

Naturally, the second she flounced out the door, Slade realized that he'd actually done the one thing he'd never expected. He'd gone and fallen in love with the woman.

Watching her walk out on him left him with a sick feeling in the pit of his stomach.

"Well, that went well," he muttered. If it had gone any better, she'd probably be quitting her job and moving back to Nashville first thing in the morning.

"I think I'll take that vacation you suggested," Val said to Laurie in the morning. On the walk back from Slade's, she'd cursed a blue streak in the night air, then reached a decision. It was time to get away from temptation.

Her friend's gaze shot up. "Vacation? Why? I thought things were going better with Slade."

"Not so that you'd notice," she said, reluctant to admit just how far things had gone the night before, and even more reluctant to explain how they'd ended.

Laurie studied her intently and seemed to come to her own conclusions. "Well, you can't leave now," she said emphatically. "The recording sessions start in less than a month. We have to start kicking things into high gear. I need you."

"I can do the work in Nashville, then. It'll be even better. Nick and I can be in closer contact."

"You're my assistant, not Nick's," Laurie said firmly. "And I need you here." Her gaze narrowed. "As your friend, though, I'm asking if that's going to be a problem."

"No," Val said with a sigh. Her job was too important to her to give it up because she had made a huge mistake falling in love with Slade. "I'll make it work."

"For what it's worth, I'm sorry you're having a rough time. I could get Harlan Patrick to beat Slade up for you."

Val grinned despite herself. "No, but thanks."

"The offer's good anytime, if you change your mind."

"I won't," Val assured her. "Now what do you need me to do today? Should I start finalizing the media plan?"

"That can wait," Laurie said. "Nick's supposed to send down the final schedule today or tomorrow. When we have it, you can start lining up interviews. We'll do radio shows in every city, so they'll push the tickets."

"Pushing tickets is not an issue," Val said. "You're already sold out in every city Nick has booked."

"Oh," Laurie said, looking genuinely surprised.

She still underestimated her own popularity. It was one of her charms, Val thought. She doubted Laurie would ever think of herself as the superstar she was. It wasn't in her nature to get a swelled head or to pull any prima donna stunts.

"I'll do the interviews anyway," she said, proving exactly what Val had been thinking. "I owe those guys for the airtime my songs get."

"I'll take care of it," Val promised.

"In the meantime, why don't you go for a walk? Or drive over to Garden City and go shopping?" She gave Val a sly look. "A new pair of sexy heels might make you feel better."

Val stuck her foot out and stared at it despondently. "See? Boots. You've turned me into a cowgirl."

"I know. That's why I suggested the heels. They might remind you of who you are."

Val wasn't sure if that was good or bad, but for lack of anything better to do, she nodded in agreement. "A shopping trip sounds good. Want to come?"

Laurie shook her head. "I have everything I need."

"Not baby clothes," she said. "Or wallpaper for the new nursery."

"The old nursery is just fine," Laurie said, but she was clearly tempted. "Harlan Patrick pulled out all the stops when he built it."

"But that's Amy Lynn's room. You know you're going to want something new for the baby. You'll be on the road the final months of your pregnancy. You won't have time to do this then."

"I could just leave it to my husband. He did okay last time."

"But you want a say in it," Val teased. "You know you do."

Laurie held up her hands in a gesture of surrender.

"Okay, okay, let's do it. I'll get my charge cards and warn Harlan Patrick that I'm going on a spending spree."

"He'll probably suggest we fly to Dallas and invade Neiman-Marcus," Val said, more than a little intrigued by that idea herself.

"Why not?" Laurie said, getting into the spirit of it. "I'll tell him he can come along, if he'll fly us over. Give me an hour to persuade him."

Val chuckled at her determined expression. "An hour, huh? You must be good."

"I am," Laurie said with pride.

In fact, it took her little more than a half hour to find her husband and talk him into playing hooky for the day to go shopping for baby things.

"It's a good thing Granddaddy doesn't know where we're going or he'd insist on coming along," he said as they boarded his uncle's company jet. "Nothing he likes better than stocking a new nursery."

A few minutes later, he glanced back from the cockpit. "You guys all set back there?"

"Ready to go, Captain," Laurie said. She glanced over at Val. "Are you okay with this? It's not exactly a girls' day out with Harlan Patrick along."

"Having your husband along is fine with me, but he is probably the only man I could tolerate right now. As a gender, I've pretty much concluded they're dense as granite."

"As a gender?" Laurie teased. "Or just one particular man?"

"Okay, Slade. There, I've said his name. I don't want to hear it again for the rest of the day." She thought about it for a second, then added fervently, "Maybe even for the rest of my life."

Beside her, Laurie chuckled.

Val glared. "It is not a laughing matter."

"Oh, but it is," Laurie said. "I seem to remember someone all but laughing her head off when Harlan Patrick was
giving me fits. Turnabout's fair play."

"Is this what I did to you?" Val asked.

"Pretty much."

"How annoying."

"It was," Laurie agreed. "But I forgave you, because
I knew your heart was in the right place. Harlan Patrick
and I belonged together."

"Yes, well, Slade and I don't."

"If you say so."

"I do," she said firmly. Maybe if she said it often
enough, she'd finally start to believe it.

Ten

"So, how'd it go with Val last night?" Annie inquired when she caught up with Slade at midday.

He scowled. "None of your business."

For most of the morning, he'd been dreading Annie's return and the likelihood she'd be asking a question just like this one. He knew he'd gone about things all wrong, but he hadn't anticipated Val's violent reaction. After the way she'd chased him for months, after the way she'd taken Annie under her wing, he'd foolishly been convinced that she'd jump at the opportunity to marry him and become a mom to Annie. Her fiercely negative response just proved how little he knew about women.

Annie's expression fell at his blunt words. "Oh, no, Daddy. What did you do?"

"Who says I did anything?" he asked defensively. "Shouldn't you still be sound asleep at the slumber party or something?"

"Nobody sleeps at a slumber party," she pointed out. "That would ruin it."

Yet another example of the illogic of the female mind, he supposed. "Why don't you go on up to the house and read?" he suggested, grasping at straws to get some peace and quiet and avoid his daughter's judgmental gaze. "You got a whole armful of books from the library the other day."

"I was bored the other day. Now I'm not. I'll read them later." She faced him with a defiant tilt to her chin and her hands jammed into her pockets. "I thought maybe I could help you today."

He was in no mood to have her hanging around pestering him, asking more questions about Val that he didn't want to answer. Besides that, he couldn't imagine what a ten-year-old girl could do to help. She knew nothing about ranch work and next to nothing about horses. She was so skinny, she looked as if a stiff wind could blow her away.

"Not today," he said in a clipped tone. "Aren't some of the other kids around here someplace?"

He could read the hurt in her expression, but she squared her shoulders as if the dismissal didn't bother her in the least. He could practically see the pride kicking in.

"Never mind," she said stiffly. "You don't need to worry about me. I'll find something to do."

He watched her walk away, saw her shoulders slump dejectedly, and felt like kicking himself. What kind of rotten louse took out his frustrations on a little girl who was only trying to help? For an instant he was tempted to call her back, but it didn't take much to convince himself that she was better off finding one of the Adams kids to play with. Sticking around him in his present mood sure wouldn't be a lot of laughs. He was sick of his own company.

An hour later he was putting Black Knight through his paces when Hardy Jones came down to the paddock and propped his elbows on the rail. He watched the workout for a minute, then said, "As soon as you can take a break with that, I think you'd better come with me."

The usually jovial hand's grim tone set off alarms. "What's happened?" Slade demanded. "Is it Annie? Is she hurt? Or Val? Has something happened to Val?"

"No, no, they're both fine," Hardy said soothingly. "Sorry. I should have said that straight out. But there is a problem and it does involve Annie."

Only then did Slade notice the spark of amusement in the younger man's eyes that he was struggling unsuccessfully to hide. It was a look that went with mischief, not calamity.

"Oh, no," Slade muttered. "I'm really going to hate this, aren't I?"

"More than likely," Hardy agreed cheerfully. "Just remember, it's not the end of the world. From what I've heard since I started working here, there have been worse stunts over the years. Our boss and Justin were behind a few of them. Harlan Patrick survived to take charge, and Justin turned into a straight-arrow. I'm sure Annie will outlive this as well."

Being reminded of Harlan Patrick's and Justin's legendary exploits was not at all reassuring. "Maybe you'd better just tell me. That way I'll be prepared for the shock."

"Not a chance," Hardy said. "Why should I ruin the opportunity to see your face when you find out what Annie's been up to."

Slade scowled. "You are a diabolical man. One of these days one of those ladies you like to flirt with is going to snag you, but good. Personally, I can't wait to see it."

The notorious womanizer merely grinned. "Never happen," he said with the total confidence of a man destined to take a serious fall.

A tight knot formed in Slade's belly as they headed up the road toward his house. What the devil had Annie done? Had she burned the place down? He sniffed the air, fully expecting to smell smoke. To his relief, none was discernible.

As they rounded a curve in the road and his house appeared, his mouth gaped.

"What the dickens has she done?" he murmured, staring at the fresh coat of bright pink paint that decorated the lower half of the house and most of Annie. She was sitting on the front steps, arms folded protectively across her middle, a stubborn jut to her chin.

"Quite a picture, isn't it?" Hardy inquired, laughter lacing his voice.

"Where in God's name did she find paint that color?"

"Mixed it herself, from what I hear. There was a can of white paint and a can of red in the storage shed. I give her credit for ingenuity. Of course, it was indoor paint, but she didn't know the difference."

"I'll call Harlan and Cody right away, make sure they know not to worry," Slade said, his expression grim. "I'll have the house painted white again by tomorrow."

"I'm not worried," Harlan assured him, picking that precise moment to pay a call. Obviously the news of Annie's adventure had traveled fast. His eyes glittered with amusement. "You should have seen the multihued shed Jenny created in an act of pure rebellion years back. This is downright sedate by comparison."

"I don't suppose you related that story to Annie," Slade said, beginning to understand where Annie might have gotten the idea to do something so outrageous.

"I suppose it could have come up," Harlan admitted

without the slightest hint of guilt. "I enjoy telling tales about my family."

Slade got the distinct impression he found the stories highly entertaining in retrospect. Slade wondered if the rancher had taken them in the same spirit when they happened. Probably so. That was the kind of man Harlan Adams was—tolerant to a fault.

"Are you sure you don't pass along these stories just to put ideas into the heads of your great-grandchildren?" he asked the old man. "Is that your way of getting even for what your children and grandchildren did years ago?"

"It might have crossed my mind that they deserved a little payback for past misdeeds," he admitted unrepentantly.

"I can't decide which of you to strangle first," Slade muttered. "Though I suppose you're pretty much off-limits."

"Pretty much," Harlan agreed. "And my sympathy is with Annie. After all, the girl was just indulging in a little self-expression. In fact, if she hadn't run out of paint, I might have helped her finish the job."

"Thank goodness for small favors," Slade said fervently. He glanced at Hardy, who was observing the exchange with evident fascination. "Thanks for bringing this to my attention. I'll take it from here."

Still grinning, Hardy took off for the bunkhouse. Harlan seemed less inclined to go.

"Don't you be too hard on the girl," he warned.

"Believe me, she'll get no more than she deserves," Slade said tersely.

After Harlan had gone, Slade strode up to the porch and scowled down at his daughter. "Mind explaining what the hell you were thinking of?" he all but shouted.

Annie's eyes blinked wide. "Daddy, you cussed."

"This isn't about my language," he said. "It's about this." He waved his hand in a gesture that encompassed the half-painted house. "Why, Annie?"

Her eyes blazed with self-righteous anger. "Because I needed something to do and I thought it would look pretty."

"I thought you hated pink," he said, as bemused by the color choice as by the painting itself.

"It's a girl color," she said, as if that explained it.

Slade was mystified. "So?"

"I've tried and tried to do stuff you like," she said with evident frustration. "But you won't let me, so I figured maybe if I did girl stuff, you'd like me better."

She sounded so utterly sincere, so lost and lonely, that it came close to breaking his heart.

"Oh, Annie," Slade whispered, and sank down on the step beside her. When he opened his arms, she scrambled into them.

"I'm sorry, Daddy," she whispered. "I thought it would be pretty, but it's not." Her voice caught on a sob. "It's awful. And then Hardy came along and saw it and he started laughing."

Slade was surprised to find that he was chuckling himself. "I imagine he did."

She pulled away. "You're laughing, too. Does that mean you're not mad at me?"

"Oh, yes, I am mad at you," he corrected. "But as someone pointed out to me very recently, it's not the end of the world. We'll buy some white paint and fix it up in our spare time."

"You'll help?" she asked. "Even though I'm the one who made the mess?"

"I'll help. But you're going to do your share, young

lady. And you're going to be grounded for a week. You will not leave the house while I'm at work. That'll give you a chance to do some thinking."

"Can I watch TV?"

Slade thought of the soap operas and talk shows that made up a huge percentage of daytime TV. "Nope. You can read those library books." He caught a hint of something in her face and realized she was already reaching the same conclusion that he was—that no one would be around to see to it that she abided by the rules.

"Forget it," he said.

"Forget what?" she asked innocently.

"You can't sneak behind my back. I'll know."

"How?"

"Fatherly instinct."

"Do you really have that?" Annie asked skeptically.

Her response was more on target than Slade would have liked. "Okay, I'll get someone to stay here with you. That's how I'll know."

"Who?" she scoffed. "I'm too big for a baby-sitter."

He thought of Val and wondered if she was too furious with him to be called on in an emergency.

Annie's eyes glinted knowingly. "What about Val?"

"We'll see," he said.

"I could go over to Laurie's, so I wouldn't be any trouble," she suggested.

Slade shook his head. "No way. That would be too much like a treat. This is supposed to be punishment. Don't worry about it. I'll work it out."

"Okay, Daddy," she said meekly.

A little too meekly, Slade thought, casting a suspicious look at his daughter. Was it possible that this was exactly the outcome she'd been counting on? Was she that determined to see that something happened between him and Val? More than likely, he realized. Caught between two clever, sneaky females, a man didn't stand a chance.

After he'd finished work for the day, showered and changed, Slade turned up at Val's, hat in hand, at least figuratively speaking. Her greeting couldn't exactly be described as warm.

"Yes?" she said, not even stepping aside to let him in. She acted as if he were a peddler coming to sell vacuums.

"Could we talk for a minute?" he asked. Seeing Harlan Patrick and Laurie in the background, their expressions fascinated, he added, "Outside?"

"We're having dinner."

"I'll wait."

"I don't think so. I'm tired. I've been shopping in Dallas all day with Laurie."

"It won't take long."

Val sighed heavily. "Fine. Let's get it over with." She stepped outside and closed the door firmly behind her.

"This won't take a minute," Slade promised again, fighting the desire to sweep her into his arms and kiss her until that stern, unapproachable set to her lips disappeared.

"Maybe you should sit down," he suggested.

"You said it wouldn't take long."

Oh, she was still furious with him, all right. She had no intention of making this easy. And why should she? He'd insulted her. That was plain enough. He began to pace, trying to find the words to convince her to help him out of the jam in which he'd found himself.

"Okay, it's about Annie," he said finally. "I know I have no right to ask this, but I need someone to stay with her for a few days."

"Oh?"

"I suppose you heard what she did?"

Her expression softened and something that might have been the beginnings of a smile tugged at the corners of her mouth. "Oh, yes. It was the first thing we saw when we got back from our trip. It certainly is a cheerful color. It doesn't suit you at all."

Slade let the deliberate jab pass. "Well, I can't let her get away with it, of course. I've grounded her for a week, but I can't very well stop working to stay with her and see that she abides by the rules."

Val stiffened as if she'd already guessed what was coming next. "No."

"I haven't even asked yet."

"I'm not going to stay with her. She's your daughter, Slade, not mine. Hire a baby-sitter."

"She'd run roughshod over a babysitter. She needs someone she respects to keep her in line."

"And that's me?"

"You know it is. Look, if I could think of some other way, believe me, I'd grab it. I know how you feel about the two of us."

She gave him a penetrating look. "Do you really?"

"Yes. I suppose you like Annie well enough, but you're fit to be tied with me. Rightfully so, from your perspective."

"And from yours?"

"Okay, I have to admit, I don't entirely get it," he said. "I know you have feelings for me and, like I just said, you care about Annie. Was it so wrong to suggest we get married?"

"Yes," she said succinctly. "But I am not going to discuss it with a man as dense as you apparently are. It would be a waste of my breath."

"Try me."

She almost did. He could see that she was tempted to try to spell it all out for him, but at the last second, she apparently changed her mind. "I'll look out for Annie the next few days, but let's be clear on one thing. I am doing it for her sake, not yours."

Slade concluded now was not the time to press her about the rest. And at the moment, he was willing to accept her help on whatever terms she set. "Thank you."

"Don't thank me. Spending time with Annie is my pleasure. I wish you felt the same way."

Before he could respond to that, she'd whirled away and gone back inside, slamming the door in his face.

If Laurie and Harlan Patrick hadn't been right inside, he would have gone after her and kissed her silly, he told himself. As it was, he just sighed and wondered if he could manage to dig the hole he was in any deeper.

"How come things didn't go so good with you and Daddy the other night?" Annie asked within five minutes of Val's arrival the next morning.

Val noticed that Slade had already made himself scarce. She told herself that was for the best, but deep down she knew she'd been hoping to catch at least a glimpse of him. Dumb, dumb, dumb! Hadn't she learned anything the past few days?

"So," Annie persisted. "What happened?"

"Who says anything happened?" she asked.

Annie gave her a pitying look. "I can tell. He's been mean as a snake and you haven't been around."

"Well, it's between your father and me."

Annie shook her head. "No, it's not. I live here, too, remember? I'm just a kid. Somebody ought to fill me in so I don't feel left out. Did you know that scars from childhood can last an entire lifetime?"

Val held back a grin. "Is that so? Where did you hear that?"

"On *Oprah*."

"I thought you weren't supposed to be watching TV."

"Oh, this was a long time ago," Annie assured her. "Weeks and weeks ago at least. It was probably while I was still at Grandma's."

Val thought she was protesting a little too vehemently, but let it pass. "Well, right now, you are a kid who's in very big trouble. Let's concentrate on that instead of whatever deep psychological scars you think you might get from being left out of the loop."

Annie shrugged. "Whatever."

"Suppose you tell me what possessed you to paint the house."

"It seemed like a good idea at the time. Besides, it worked, didn't it?"

Val studied Annie intently. "Meaning?"

Annie suddenly seemed just a little too fascinated with her cereal. Val doubted she was counting the little *o*s still floating in her bowl.

"Okay, kiddo, what are you up to?"

"Nothing, I swear it," Annie said, her expression totally innocent.

"I don't believe that for a minute."

"It's true. I just thought the house was a boring color, that's all." She wrinkled her nose. "Daddy wants to paint it back to white."

"And you don't?"

"Nope. I was thinking maybe yellow," she said, her gaze on Val, her expression serious. "What do you think? It's your favorite color, isn't it?"

"Yes," Val agreed. "I do like yellow, not that that should have anything to do with what color you decide to paint your house."

"Why not? I mean, if it were yellow, you'd want to be here more, right?"

Val set her coffee carefully on the table. "Okay, that's it. We need to talk, young lady."

"About what?"

"Whatever it is that's going on in your head. You cannot plot and scheme to get your father and me together." Never mind that she'd done her own share of plotting. It had all been to no avail.

"Why not?" Annie asked, sounding far more curious than daunted.

"Because that's not the way human emotions work. Grown-ups either care about each other or they don't. You can't make things happen just because you'd like them to." Val could have attested to that firsthand.

"But Daddy really likes you. I know he does. And you like him. So why can't it work out? Why should we all be miserable, when it would be so easy to be happy?"

Val had wondered the same thing herself until she'd heard Slade proposing marriage solely for the sake of his daughter. They had made love for most of the night. She had experienced a level of passion she had never even known existed. She had honestly thought Slade had, too. Then she'd discovered that she had only convinced him that they'd be compatible enough if he were to marry her for Annie's sake. It was a wonder she hadn't plunged a knife into his heart on the spot.

"It just can't work out," she told Annie very firmly, because it was what she'd finally forced herself to accept.
She couldn't spend her whole life with a man who was
so insensitive that he didn't even see how deeply he'd insulted her.

"Well, I don't buy it," Annie said stubbornly.

"You don't have to," Val told her. "All that matters is
that it's what your father and I both believe."

"Then you're both dumb," Annie proclaimed. She
flounced out of her chair and ran to her room.

That was the last Val saw of her until lunchtime. She
fixed tuna salad sandwiches, put them on the table and
then went to call Annie. She got no response.

Val's stomach knotted. Surely Annie hadn't crawled
out a window and run away. She knocked and called out
again, then opened the door. Annie was curled up in bed,
her back to the door.

Val crossed the room and gazed down at her. She was
sound asleep, but her cheeks were still damp with tears.

"Oh, baby," Val whispered and sank onto the edge of
the bed. She touched a hand to Annie's cheek.

"Go away," Annie muttered, still half-asleep.

"Lunch is ready."

"I'm not hungry."

"Tuna salad sandwiches and chips," Val said, trying to
tempt her. "And I baked cookies. Your favorites." Slade's,
too, though she'd sworn as she emptied the bag of chocolate chips into the dough that she was fixing them only
for Annie's sake.

"I don't care."

Val bit back a sigh. "Look, sweetie, I know you're unhappy that things aren't going the way you'd hoped, but
sometimes we all have disappointments in life."

"Is that all it is to you?" Annie demanded, suddenly quivering with outrage. "A disappointment? Like not getting ice cream for dessert or something? It's my life! I don't have anybody who loves me, not really. Daddy tolerates me because he has to. Grandma and Grandpa dumped me. I thought you were my friend, but you don't care."

"I do care," Val insisted.

"Like I believe that."

"Believe it or not, it's true. Otherwise why do you think I'd be here today?"

"Because Daddy asked you to. He probably paid you."

"Your father is not paying me," she assured the child. "And we both know I'm not very happy with him at the moment, so obviously I'm not doing it for him. So why am I here?"

Annie studied her face. "Because of me," she whispered hesitantly.

"Because of you," Val agreed. "You're a wonderful girl, Annie. You're bright and funny and unpredictable. If I had a little girl, I'd want her to be exactly like you."

"Really?" she asked, hope shining in her eyes.

"Absolutely."

Annie seemed to consider her response for several minutes before her expression brightened. "Okay, then, here's what we do."

Something in her voice alerted Val that she'd blundered in some way she had yet to understand. "Do?" she repeated cautiously.

"Yes," Annie said very firmly. "So you can adopt me and I can be your little girl for real."

Eleven

For days after Annie's calm declaration that she wanted Val to adopt her, Val couldn't shake the storm of emotions that roared through her. At the time, she'd tried to explain very carefully to Annie why that was impossible, but the conversation continued to nag at her.

Annie had been so serious, so terribly vulnerable. And a part of Val had wanted to say yes. She couldn't deny it. She had come to love Annie already as if she were her own. She blamed Slade's stubborn streak for making that impossible. If only he could have told her he loved her when he'd asked her to marry him, if only it hadn't sounded more like he was striking a bargain than proposing marriage, maybe she would have said yes. Then Annie truly would have been her little girl and Slade would have been her husband. Instead, none of them had what they wanted or needed.

"What do I do?" she asked Laurie. "Do I tell Slade? I mean, this is way beyond her saying she wants to run away from home. She's actually picked out the home she wants to run to."

Laurie regarded her knowingly. "You're flattered, aren't you?"

"Don't be ridiculous."

"You are. A part of you is glad that Annie chose you over Slade. You see it as proof that he's a terrible parent and that you'd be a better one."

"It's not a competition, dammit!"

"No," Laurie agreed mildly. "It's not. Or at least it shouldn't be. You and Slade both want the same thing here. You both want Annie to feel loved and secure."

"That's certainly what I want," Val said. "That's why I've stepped in—to fill in the gaps in her life."

"Oh, really?" Laurie said. "I thought that was more about using Annie to get Slade's attention."

Val stared at her friend. "That's a rotten thing to say."

"Is it?"

Instead of snapping back an answer, Val considered the accusation. "Okay," she admitted reluctantly, "at the beginning, I suppose there might have been some truth to that, but no more. I care about Annie."

"Good. Now we're getting somewhere. And the truth is that Slade's been using you, because he's at a loss about how to handle his daughter. Correct?"

"Yes," Val said, not liking the picture that was emerging of two selfish adults with a ten-year-old caught in the middle.

"Don't look so glum. It's not all bad," Laurie said. "Annie is getting the attention she needs and you and Slade care more about each other than either of you wants to admit."

"Oh, I'll admit it," Val said. "He just doesn't want to hear it." He just wanted a practical marriage of convenience with no messy emotions involved.

"Then back off," Laurie suggested. "Give him time to miss you."

"I thought that was what I was doing," Val said. "Then he came over here and begged me to stay with Annie."

"Obviously this arrangement is way too convenient for him and it's sending very mixed messages to Annie," Laurie said, her expression thoughtful. "I think maybe I was wrong when I said you shouldn't go back to Nashville for a while. I think maybe it's a good idea, after all."

A gut-sick feeling washed over Val. "You're sending me away?"

"Don't look so put out. It was your idea, remember? And it's not Siberia."

"But why now? You just finished telling me a few days ago that you couldn't spare me."

"I was wrong," Laurie said succinctly. "Besides, I think both you and Slade need to remember who you are. You're a career woman, Val. You're the best personal assistant I've ever run across. I know a dozen people who'd snap you up in a heartbeat if I ever let you get away. The last few weeks haven't been typical at all. You've had time on your hands to cater to Slade's every whim and to Annie's." She nodded decisively. "Yes, I think it's for the best. I'm putting you back to work."

Val opened her mouth to argue, then realized that Laurie was probably right. She needed to gain some perspective on everything that had gone on the past few weeks. She'd settled into some sort of fake domesticity, complete with a ready-made family. She needed to weigh that against the life she'd had before Laurie had married Harlan Patrick and they'd started spending most of their time at White Pines.

Could she really juggle both a family and a career and be fair to both? She'd always assumed she could. She'd been instrumental in making Laurie see that she could have it all. Val didn't want to accept it, but maybe the reality was that she would have to choose.

"I'll call the airlines and make the arrangements," she told Laurie. "Then I'll check in with Nick so he can list everything that needs doing to finalize the recording sessions."

"You can take that mountain of fan mail back to Nashville with you, too," Laurie said. "Have the staff there get busy answering it. You've got more important things to do."

More important than being used by a man to play surrogate mother to his lonely little girl, Val told herself firmly. But when the time came to get on the plane, she wasn't nearly as certain that she believed that. Annie had stolen her heart. As for Slade, she was very much afraid that he had captured her soul.

When Annie discovered that Val had gone to Nashville, she was inconsolable. Slade found her huddled in the rocker on the front porch sobbing her eyes out. He guessed she'd already heard the disconcerting news that had reached him just an hour or so earlier. In case he was wrong, he approached the subject cautiously.

"Baby, what's wrong? What happened?" he asked, hunkering down in front of her.

"It's Val," she whispered, sniffing loudly. "I did something wrong and now she's gone away and left me."

Slade had heard all about Val's abrupt departure from Harlan Patrick. His boss seemed to take great pleasure in breaking the news that she'd gone off to Nashville. Nowhere in that discussion had Annie's name come up. Neither had Slade's. In fact, it sounded as if she'd left without giving a thought to either of them.

"Honey, she had work to do. You know she helps Laurie. Sometimes that means she has to go away. It wasn't about you."

"Yes, it was. It's because of what I said."

Slade regarded her with puzzlement. "What did you say that could possibly make Val leave?"

"I told her I wanted her to adopt me," she mumbled, so low he could barely hear the words.

Even so, once they sank in, Slade felt as if the wind had been knocked out of him. He pulled the other rocker close and sat down so he and Annie would be at eye level.

"Tell me exactly what happened."

"I told you. It happened when I was grounded. I said I wanted her to be my mom. She'd said she really liked me, so I figured she'd go for it."

Slade had been through a similar misjudgment all too recently. Apparently neither he nor Annie was good at gauging Val's likely reactions. "Where did I fit into this?" he asked, fearing he knew that answer, too.

Annie gazed down at the floor. "You didn't." Her chin jutted up. "You were mad at me, anyway. I figured you wouldn't care."

"Well, I do," he said forcefully. He reached over and tucked a finger under her chin, forcing her to meet his gaze. "You're my little girl, okay? I know I'm not the best dad in the whole world. I know I've made a lot of mistakes since your mom went away. But I love you, Annie. I wouldn't let you go for anything. I certainly wouldn't let somebody else adopt you and take you away from me, not even Val."

"But she'd be such a great mom," Annie said plaintively.

"I know, baby. I think so, too. But right now it's just you and me. We're stuck with each other. Think we can make it work?" He realized as soon as the words were out just how fearful he was that she'd say no.

"I suppose," she said finally, the lackluster response accompanied by a heavy sigh of resignation.

"How about going into town for ice cream to celebrate?"

"What do we have to celebrate?"

"The fact that we're starting over, that we're a family, just you and me."

Her expression brightened ever so slightly. "Don't you have work to do?"

"It can wait," he said, standing up. "This is more important."

As if she sensed that she had the upper hand for now, she regarded him slyly. "Hot fudge?"

"If that's what you want."

She stood on tiptoe and wrapped her arms around his waist. "I love you, Daddy. I never really wanted to leave you."

"I know, baby. I love you, too." He resolved then and there to make sure she always knew that, no matter what it cost him in time or effort or words. No child of his was ever again going to feel so neglected that she'd rather be adopted than stay with him.

In town, they went straight to Dolan's, where Sharon Lynn greeted them with a look of astonishment. "Playing hooky, Slade?"

He grinned. "Yep, it's a special occasion. I'm out with my best girl."

He knew that for once he'd said the right thing, because Annie's eyes sparkled.

"Well, if it's a celebration, that must call for hot fudge sundaes. Am I right?"

"You bet," Annie said, scrambling onto a stool at the counter.

"You, too, Slade?"

"Why not?"

"So, I hear Val's gone off to Nashville to work on the last-minute details of Laurie's next album. How's my little brother taking the idea of letting his wife go back to Tennessee for recording sessions and then on the road?"

"Haven't heard a complaint out of him," Slade said honestly. "I think your little brother has made his own plans for this tour."

"Such as?"

"You'll have to ask him," he said, not sure if Harlan Patrick had told the whole family the news about Laurie's pregnancy and his intentions to spend the last part of her tour on the road with her.

Sharon Lynn regarded him slyly. "And how are you doing without Val around?"

"We miss her," Annie said. "Real bad. Don't we, Daddy?"

"I know you do," he agreed, and let it go at that. Sharon Lynn's expression suggested she knew perfectly well that he missed Val, too.

"Where's Ashley?" Annie demanded. "I thought she usually came to the store with you."

"She's in the back room taking her nap." She glanced up at the clock. "She'll probably be awake any minute, if you want to check on her."

"Great," Annie said, sliding off her stool. "Ashley's

the best, Daddy. She's real smart. It's almost like having a little sister. Do you think maybe one day—"

"If you're going to check on her, go," he said gruffly, cutting her off. He did not want to get into a discussion of babies with Annie, not with a very interested Sharon Lynn listening in. Whatever he said would be all over White Pines by nightfall. Val would hear it right after that.

Sharon Lynn regarded him with sympathy. "Getting a lot of pressure from all sides lately, aren't you?"

"You can say that again." The irony was it was Val they ought to be bugging, not him. He'd asked her to marry him, after all, though he doubted she'd mentioned that to a soul. Everyone clearly thought he was the holdout.

"I'm an Adams, so I can say this—we're a family of meddlers. Don't let us push you into something."

"Not likely," he said curtly.

She laughed. "You say that like you think you'll see the clever wiles and sneaky meddling coming, but, believe me, you won't. Grandpa, particularly, can score a direct hit before you even realize he's in the game."

"I've noticed that," he said. "I'm not worried."

"You're made of tougher stuff, right?" she asked with amusement.

Slade scowled. "Yes."

She patted his hand. "That's what you think."

She slid his sundae in front of him, then went to check on Annie and her own little girl.

Slade took a bite of the ice cream and thick fudge sauce, then sighed and pushed it aside. The only thing sweet he really wanted right now was one of Val's kisses. The best sundae in the world couldn't hold a candle to that. How he was going to convince her of that, though, was beyond him.

* * *

A few days after the debacle with the paint and the adoption scheme, when Annie asked Slade if she could help him, he was more open to the idea. Not that he could imagine her being of much assistance, but at least he'd know firsthand what she was up to. He also knew she was feeling very much at loose ends since Val had left town.

"I'm getting ready to muck out the stalls," he informed her, figuring that would put her desire to be like him to the ultimate test. "Are you sure you want to help?"

To his astonishment, her eyes brightened. "You'll really let me?"

He hesitated, then shrugged. "Sure. Why not?" He gave her terse directions, then stood back and watched as she threw herself into the task with energetic enthusiasm. She was a constant source of amazement to him.

"Hey, Dad," she called after she had thoroughly cleaned two stalls and left them spotless.

"What?"

"Do you suppose you could teach me to ride sometime?" she asked hesitantly. The wary expression in her eyes suggested she was prepared to be rebuffed, and the tilt of her chin hinted that she wouldn't take it lightly.

He considered the out-of-the-blue request and wondered what had brought it on. "You were never interested in riding before," he noted.

She stood in front of him, her expression serious. "But you love it, don't you? I mean, even after the accident and all, you still love the horses. You didn't, like, go off and become a mechanic like Grandpa or something."

Slade cringed at the very idea of an indoor job. His father might think engines were every bit as fascinating as an animal, but he didn't. "No way."

"Well, then, I figure, if you like horses so much, I should, too. It's gotta be in my genes, right?"

Slade considered Val's assessment weeks ago that his daughter was interested in tools because he was. Then he thought back to the saddle he'd seen Annie admiring and wondered if that was part of the same phenomenon. Was Annie reaching out to him in the only ways she knew how? Was she struggling to fit into his life by doing the things he did, so they could share in the enjoyment? And if that was it, wasn't it way past time he met her halfway?

"Put down that rake and come with me," he said.

Her eyes widened. "Why?"

He grinned. "Because you're about to have your first riding lesson, young lady."

"On Black Knight?" she asked hopefully. "He's so awesome."

"Nope. I think he's a little too feisty for you. We'll start with Aunt Sadie."

"But she's old," Annie protested, obviously disappointed.

"She's gentle," Slade corrected. "That's what matters. She won't dump you in the dust the first time you get on."

Annie actually looked as if she wouldn't mind being bounced from the saddle if it meant getting to ride a more challenging horse than the old mare, but Slade remained firm. He brought Aunt Sadie out of her stall and showed Annie how to saddle her and put on her bridle.

When the horse was ready, Annie led her out of the barn and into the corral.

"I'll give you a boost up," Slade said, linking his hands for Annie to step into. She mounted the horse as smoothly as if she'd done it many times. "Are you sure you've never been on a horse before?"

"Never," she said. "But I used to climb onto the fence rail at Grandma's and pretend it was a horse. I got pretty good at getting on."

Amused, Slade nodded. "You're good, all right. Now let's see how you are at riding the real thing."

He took the lead and moved around the corral in a slow circle. "How does it feel?"

"Boring," Annie said. "I want to ride fast."

"First things first." He handed her the reins. "Let's see you get her to start and stop."

Aunt Sadie had a very docile nature, so there was almost nothing Annie could have done to get her riled up enough to throw off her rider. But somewhere in the back of the old mare's mind must have lurked a memory of a time when she'd run as fast as the wind. At Annie's urging, she broke into a full gallop before Slade realized what was going on.

As the horse tore past him, he shouted at Annie, "Pull on the reins, sweetie! Get her to stop."

Either Annie didn't hear him or chose to ignore the command—more likely the latter. Her face was split with a grin as she sailed past for the second time.

"Annie Sutton, you're going to spend a month in your room if you don't ride that horse over here and get off of it right now," he yelled.

He wasn't sure when he finally realized that something was wrong. Maybe it was when Aunt Sadie broke toward the open gate at the back of the corral. Maybe it was when he caught Annie's smile fading and panic settling onto her face.

"Daddy!" she squealed. "I can't make her stop."

Slade broke into a run, but with his bum leg he was no

match for the horse, who'd sensed a kindred spirit and was intent on showing Annie what she was made of.

"Whoa!" Annie shouted to no avail. "Daddy! Help!"

"Pull slowly on the reins," Slade advised, trying to remain calm.

Annie did as he said, but she was so panicked that she was digging her heels into the horse's sides at the same time, sending Aunt Sadie a mixed message. The horse made her own decision about which message to listen to.

When she reached the gate, Aunt Sadie bolted through and took off for open pastures, Annie clinging to her back. Her sobs carried on the breeze, filling Slade with a terrible sense of helplessness and dread.

Harlan Patrick heard the commotion and came running. He took in the situation at a glance, grabbed Black Knight's mane and threw himself onto the horse bareback. Slade realized that's what he should have done, but everything had unfolded so quickly he hadn't had time to think. He cursed the injuries that made his reflexes too slow to have done what Harlan Patrick was able to do without thought.

He watched the huge black stallion eat up the ground between him and Aunt Sadie. When he was close enough, Harlan Patrick grabbed the reins of the runaway horse and slowed her down. The instant Aunt Sadie halted, he reached over and gathered Annie into his arms and brought her back.

"Thank you," Slade said, taking Annie from him. Still sobbing, she clung to Slade's neck and wrapped her legs around his waist.

"I'll see to the horses," Harlan Patrick said. "She'll be fine, Slade. It happens to every kid at some point. Don't beat yourself up."

"She could have been killed," Slade said grimly.

"But she wasn't. That's what matters. She's fine. The horses are fine. No harm done."

Except to Slade's pride. He felt like he'd failed his daughter one more time. Her first ride, which should have been a wonderful memory, would probably haunt her now.

He realized then that Annie had grown silent. He turned his head and met her gaze.

"I'm sorry, Daddy."

"It wasn't your fault."

"It must have been. You said she was gentle. I must have done something wrong."

"No, baby. Sometimes horses just get an idea into their heads. That's why you have to take it easy and learn how to control them. Next time will be better."

Eyes shimmering with tears suddenly filled with hope. "You'll let me ride again?"

Much as he wanted to deny her the chance and keep her from risk, he nodded. "If you want to."

"Oh, yes," she breathed, her face lit with excitement. "Up until I couldn't get her to stop, it was awesome."

Slade shook his head. "I guess you were right about those genes of mine being part of your makeup. I never took a spill so bad that I didn't want to get right back on and try it again."

"See, Daddy? We *are* alike."

As humbled as he was by how obviously thrilled Annie was by the comparison, Slade couldn't honestly say if he thought the assessment was good or bad.

Twelve

Back in Nashville Val worked from dawn to way past dusk, driven by a need to fill every hour with so much work that there wouldn't be a single second when her thoughts could stray to an impossible cowboy and his tomboy daughter. The tactic worked reasonably effectively, though Nick had taken to steering clear of her because she snapped his head off at the slightest provocation.

"If you're so damn miserable, go back to Texas," Laurie's agent told her at one point. "I don't know what it is about the men down there, but neither you nor Laurie seem to have a lick of common sense when they're involved."

"There's work to be done here," she'd retorted, ignoring his analysis of the potent impact of Texas males. "Laurie thought it would be best if I helped you out for a while and that's exactly what I'm doing."

"Fine," he'd said, relenting. "Far be it from me to question the wisdom of my biggest star, but if you ask me, we'd all be happier if you'd just give in and work things out with the cowboy. She certainly was."

"Nobody asked you."

Nick had shrugged, then gone back into his office and

slammed the door. Val had no doubt that if it had been up to him, he'd have sent her packing. He'd never been crazy about the influence she had over his superstar. Nor had he liked the fact that she'd helped Laurie keep the secret of her first pregnancy from him. He had told them both in no uncertain terms that if they kept him in the dark on anything that important ever again, he'd cut his professional ties with Laurie. Val's present mood only added to the ongoing friction.

The days passed, filled with brusque encounters with Nick and a million and one details to be handled. Slade never—well, hardly ever—entered her thoughts.

But there was nothing Val could do to prevent Slade from haunting her dreams. She was having an especially sweet one when the ringing of the phone woke her.

"Hey, sleepyhead, I thought you'd be up with the chickens," Laurie said cheerfully.

"You're the one on the farm," Val grumbled, burying her head in the pillow.

"It's a ranch."

"Same difference."

"Not exactly, but we'll let that pass."

"Why are you calling at this hour?" she muttered. "It's still dark out."

"Something's happened," Laurie said, her tone suddenly sobering. "Harlan Patrick and I debated whether to tell you, but I thought you'd want to know. And since I was up anyway, I figured I'd try to catch you at home."

Heart pounding, Val sat upright at once. "Is it Slade?" she asked, instantly alert. "Has he been hurt?"

"No, though I find it interesting that you're so worried about a man you'd vowed to put out of your mind."

"If it's not Slade, then it has to be Annie," Val said, ig-

noring the taunt. "What's happened, Laurie? Spit it out.
She hasn't run away again, has she?"

"Okay, yes, it's Annie. And, no, she hasn't run away.
She is not hurt, either, but she had a few terrifying moments." She went on to describe the riding lesson that had
gone awry. "I'm not sure which one of them was more
shaken, Annie or Slade. He's absolutely beside himself
that it was Harlan Patrick who thought to jump on Black
Knight and go after her. Harlan Patrick's worried about
him. He told me Slade feels like he failed her again."

"That's ridiculous."

"Well, of course it is, but you know Slade. All that
macho pride has kicked in."

"I'm coming back," Val said, making up her mind at
once. "I'll check the flights the second we hang up and
let you know when I'll be there."

"I think a phone call would do the trick," Laurie suggested dryly. "It would mean a lot to Annie to know that
you're concerned about her."

"No," Val said firmly, thinking as much of father as
daughter. A call wouldn't settle anything with Slade. "A
call's not good enough. I need to be there. Those two will
probably retreat into silence again unless somebody's there
to keep them talking."

"They were talking just fine last time I saw them. They
had their heads together planning Annie's next riding lesson. Slade relented and said she could try again, even
though he's obviously not happy about it."

"It might not last," Val said, though her position was
clearly weakened by Laurie's reassurance.

"In other words, your mind is made up and you don't
want me bothering you with facts," Laurie said, chuck-

ling. "You've only been gone a few days. You weren't, by any chance, just waiting for an excuse to come back?"

Maybe she had been, Val admitted to herself, though not to Laurie. Work wasn't nearly as fulfilling as it had once been. And Nashville hadn't felt nearly as much like home as she'd expected when she'd returned. Apparently, for better or for worse, she truly had left her heart in Texas.

"You're not still beating yourself up over Annie's accident, are you?" Harlan Patrick asked when Slade wandered into the barn at midmorning.

Slade hadn't especially wanted to be reminded of the accident or his own guilt-ridden reaction to it. "Nope."

"Because it wasn't your fault." Harlan Patrick went on as if Slade hadn't spoken.

"I know," Slade conceded. "Could have happened to anybody, anytime."

"Exactly," his boss said, as enthusiastically as if Slade had grasped a very tricky concept.

"Did you want something?" Slade asked, hoping to get him to move on.

"Not really," Harlan Patrick said. He turned to leave, then paused. "By the way, did I happen to mention that Val is coming back today? She should be here anytime now."

Slade came very close to gouging a huge chunk of skin out of his hand, when the pick he was using to clean Black Knight's shoes slipped. "Is that so?" he responded, as if the news were of no consequence. After she'd left, he'd half wondered if she would ever set foot in Texas again. He'd had the uncomfortable feeling that he'd driven her away.

"Thought you'd want to know." Harlan Patrick waited expectantly.

"And now I do," Slade said tersely.

Harlan Patrick chuckled. "You are so pitiful. You know you want to ask why she's coming back so fast."

Because he did, Slade continued to pretend indifference. "Do I?"

"It's because of Annie," Harlan Patrick supplied.

Slade's gaze shot up. "Annie didn't go calling her, did she?"

"Nope, you can thank my wife for the phone call. She reported all the details about Annie's accident, including the fact that your daughter is just fine. Val decided she needed to see for herself."

Slade wasn't sure why that aggravated him, but it did. It was more proof that Val cared as deeply as a mother would about his little girl. Yet she refused to make the role official. That meant her rejection of his proposal had everything to do with him.

But, dammit, if he didn't measure up, why hadn't she just said so? Why had she slept with him in the first place? It seemed to him the woman didn't know her own mind. He could have worked up a pretty good head of steam on the subject, but the lady in question came wandering into the barn just then. His pulse started pounding as if he'd been wrestling a bull for an hour.

"Speak of the devil," Harlan Patrick said, sweeping Val off her feet and planting a kiss on her forehead. "Welcome home. We sure did miss you around here, didn't we, Slade?"

Slade grunted a noncommittal response that had Harlan Patrick grinning.

"Guess I'll go on up to the house and check on my wife, unless you two need me to stick around for some reason."

He regarded first Val and then Slade expectantly. "No? I didn't think so. See you two. Play nice."

After he'd gone, Slade muttered, "He is a very annoying man."

"I think he's wonderful," Val said.

"Something else we can fight about, I suppose."

Val sighed. "I didn't come back to fight with you. How's Annie?"

"Annie is just fine. I'm surprised you're not up at my place checking her for bumps and bruises."

She grinned. "I would have been, but she wasn't around." Her expression sobered. "How are you? You must have been terrified when the horse took off."

"I've had better moments," Slade agreed. He sat back on his haunches and surveyed her as intently as if he hadn't seen her in months, rather than days. "I see you're back in your fancy shoes again. Must be the big-city influence. You never did seem real comfortable as a ranch girl."

"Are you deliberately trying to bait me?" she asked, sounding more curious than angry.

"Why would I do that?"

"I have to wonder the same thing. You didn't, by any chance, miss me?"

"Not me. Too much work to do."

"I missed you," she said softly, her voice filled with what might have been regret.

Slade fixed her with a steady gaze. "Is that so? You don't seem especially happy about it."

"Why would I be? We're on different wavelengths, that's plain enough. You seem intent on keeping us that way."

His gaze shot up at the unreasonable accusation. "Not me. I wanted to marry you, remember?"

"Oh, yeah, I remember. That proposal was one of the more memorable moments of my life," she said with unmistakable sarcasm. She headed for the door. "I'd better go."

Slade stood up and took a step toward her. "Val?"

She hesitated.

"Don't go."

She slowly turned back. "Why?"

"Because I did miss you," he confessed, unable to hide the bemusement he felt. It was ridiculous to miss a woman he considered to be little more than a thorn in his side. "And if I wouldn't get a slap for it, I might show you just how much."

She seemed to be weighing that, but as his breath lodged in his throat, she took a step toward him, then halted. "Meet me halfway," she taunted.

Slade stepped closer and took her shoulders in his hands. She was so fragile he feared she'd break, but he knew deep down that she was tougher than he was by a long shot. Gazing into her eyes, he felt his senses spinning out of control. Desire slammed through him, unbidden. Mostly unwanted.

Still, he couldn't keep himself from lowering his head until his mouth found hers. Fire exploded through him at the first touch. To his amazement, she was trembling in his arms, and when he looked, there was a suspicious sheen to her eyes.

"You aren't about to cry, are you?" he asked worriedly.

She blinked rapidly. Her chin jutted up. "Why would I cry over a silly kiss?"

"That's what I'd like to know." He dismissed the fact that she'd just referred to the kiss as silly. Otherwise, he might have been insulted.

"I'm not shedding any tears over you, Slade Sutton," she said with a touch of defiance. "So you can keep that ego of yours in check."

This time when she whirled around to leave, Slade didn't try to stop her. He just stood back and enjoyed the view of her sashaying along on those ridiculously high heels. He'd been telling himself for days now that he didn't give a damn that she'd gone. Now he was forced to admit that he was very glad that she was back. For the last half hour or so, he'd finally felt whole again.

Blasted man, Val thought to herself as she wandered off in search of Annie, after stopping long enough to change back into boots and jeans. Telling her she belonged in the city, that she didn't fit in on a ranch. Well, he could just go to blazes. She had as much right to be here as he did. She had a job here, just like he did. She had friends. She could even learn about cows, if she was of a mind to.

"Val, you're back!"

Annie came racing toward her and all but threw herself into Val's arms. Val stumbled back at the impact, but she couldn't stop the grin that spread across her face at the exuberant welcome. At least one member of the Sutton family knew her own heart and wasn't afraid to let her emotions show.

"Hold still and let me get a good look at you," Val instructed.

"I almost got thrown from a horse," Annie said proudly. "Did you hear?"

"I heard."

"Harlan Patrick saved me."

"I heard that, too."

"Daddy looked like he was going to faint. He was real scared."

"I'm sure he was."

"You know what, though?"

"What?"

"He said it was okay for me to ride again. He's going to give me another lesson this afternoon. Want to watch?" she demanded excitedly. "I'm going to star in a rodeo just like Daddy one day."

Val winced. She doubted Slade was privy to that particular bit of career planning on his daughter's part. "Have you mentioned that to your father yet?"

"Not exactly. I figured I'd better get really good before I tell him. Otherwise, he'll just say no."

"A few weeks ago you wanted to be an Olympic diver. What happened to that?"

"I'm still diving," Annie said, clearly perplexed. "Why can't I do both?"

Val laughed. "I suppose you can, if that's what you want. Of course, you've only been on a horse once. What makes you think you'll really like being in the rodeo?"

"Because Daddy did," she said simply.

"You know, kiddo, you don't have to do everything your dad did."

"But I want to," Annie protested.

"Because you really enjoy it, or because you think it will make him love you more?"

She could see from the look on Annie's face that she hadn't expected anyone else to understand her motivations. Maybe she hadn't even recognized them herself until Val put it into words.

"I want him to see that I'm really like him, not like my mom," Annie said.

"The point is to be Annie," Val said. "That's what he'll love you for. Not for trying to be someone else."

Annie didn't seem convinced by the logic. "Will you come watch me ride or not?"

"I'll come," Val said. That way there'd be two people standing by the corral railing with their hearts in their throats. "What time?"

"Not till five, 'cause Daddy has to finish work first." She bounced up and down excitedly. "That means there's time for us to go into town and have pizza, if you want to. Zack and Josh could meet us, maybe."

"Why not?" Val agreed. "Check with your father first."

Annie ran off, then came back waving money. "He said okay, but he's paying."

Since he wasn't there to argue with, Val nodded. "Let's go, then. Where are Zack and Josh?"

"At the vet clinic with Dani. She's paying them to help out."

"Then we'll go by there."

"Or I could call them on your cell phone," Annie suggested. "I've never used one before."

Val grinned at her enthusiasm. "It's in my purse."

Annie dragged out the phone, followed Val's instructions, then beamed when the call went through. "Hey, Zack, guess what? I'm on Val's cell phone and we're in the car."

Val couldn't hear the boy's response, but assumed from Annie's expression that he was duly impressed. Wouldn't it be wonderful if life could always be so uncomplicated? she thought to herself, listening to one side of the conversation. Instead, grown-ups carried all sorts of baggage that interfered with taking pleasure in the simple things.

Take Slade, for instance. He would never in a million

years admit that being dumped by his ex-wife had scarred him so deeply he was afraid to love again, but that was exactly what was going on. If asked, he'd probably just say Suzanne had been a jerk and that their split had been for the best. Val thought she knew better. He'd really loved her. Otherwise her leaving wouldn't have bothered him half as much as it clearly did after all this time. It wouldn't have left him incapable of admitting how he felt about another woman. The idea that he had been capable of loving so deeply once gave her hope for their own future.

"Hey, Val," Annie said, poking her sharply in the ribs.

"What?" she murmured.

"You just drove past the clinic."

Dragging her attention back to the present, Val realized she'd driven halfway through Los Piños without even noticing. Thinking about Slade had a way of distracting her. She glanced in the rearview mirror and saw the twins standing on the sidewalk in front of the clinic, looking baffled over being passed by.

"Sorry," she murmured, going around the next block and heading back.

"You were thinking about Daddy, weren't you?" Annie inquired, her expression smug.

"What makes you think that?"

"Because you looked all dreamy one minute and mad the next."

Out of the mouths of babes, Val thought wryly. The child had nailed it. That was exactly the way Slade made her feel.

"You know what I think?" Annie asked.

Val was afraid to ask. "What?" she inquired cautiously.

"Since you said you wouldn't adopt me, I think that you and Daddy should get married. Then you could be my mom. It would be great," Annie enthused, obviously sold on the idea. "We get along great and you almost never yell at me. You said you'd like to have a little girl just like me, so why not me, right?"

What was it with the Suttons? Val thought. They both seemed to think marriage was about instant motherhood. Fortunately, she was in front of the clinic and Josh and Zack were scrambling into the back seat.

"We'll discuss it another time," she told Annie firmly.

"But you do think it's a good idea, don't you?" the girl persisted.

"Another time," she repeated.

"What are you talking about?" Zack demanded, his freckled face alight with curiosity.

"And how come you drove right past us before?" Josh asked.

"She was distracted," Annie confided. "She was thinking about Daddy."

Heat flooded Val's face. If she didn't change the subject and fast, this story was going to spread through the Adams clan with the speed and intensity of a wildfire.

"What do you guys want on your pizza?" she asked, figuring that most little boys would rather discuss food than mushy stuff any day. She hadn't counted on the Adams penchant for matchmaking. Obviously it took hold at a very early age and even influenced those connected to the family only by marriage.

"You're in love with Slade?" Josh asked.

"Uh-huh," Annie answered for her.

"Wow, that's neat," Zack said. "You'd be, like, Annie's mom then, huh?"

"Okay, enough," Val said, pulling into a parking space in front of the Italian restaurant. "This is not open for discussion." She scowled first at Annie, then at both boys. "Are we clear?"

Zack looked knowingly at Josh. "She's got it bad, all right. Remember when Dad used that exact same voice to tell us to keep our noses out of his relationship with Dani?"

"That's right," Josh said. "He was always telling us to mind our own business. It was a good thing we didn't, though. Otherwise, they might never had gotten married." He looked at Annie. "Sometimes grown-ups are real slow about stuff like this. You gotta give 'em a push."

Val moaned. "There will be no pushing, no meddling, no discussion," she said flatly. "Otherwise, there will be no pizza."

That finally shut them up. But she could tell from the grins they exchanged that as far as they were concerned, the matter was far from ended.

Thirteen

Val the cowgirl was back with a vengeance. Slade watched her heading toward the corral with a sinking sensation in the pit of his stomach. Her snug jeans gave him almost as many ideas as those heels she'd abandoned in favor of more practical boots. Still feminine to the core, though, she'd knotted her Western-style shirt at the waist. He knew from past observation that if she lifted her arms just a little, the hem of that shirt would glide up and expose a tantalizing few inches of silky skin. His body tightened just anticipating it.

"What bee have you got in your bonnet?" he asked when she neared.

"We have to talk," she declared, in the kind of no-nonsense tone that always had the contradictory effect of making him think of everything except the business that was clearly on her mind.

"About?"

"Annie."

Val began striding up and down in front of him at a dizzying pace. Slade reached out and snagged her arm in an attempt to get her attention.

"Whoa now! Why is it that when I want to talk about what's best for Annie, you act like I'm insulting you? Now you can't wait to bring up the subject."

Val frowned. "There's a problem. Do you want to hear about it or not?" She took up pacing again.

"Experience tells me I'd be better off not knowing, but go ahead."

She paused briefly and declared, "Annie's decided she wants me for a mother."

"No news there," he said. "She wanted you to adopt her not so long ago."

"Are you going to listen or not?"

He held up his hands in a gesture of surrender. "Okay. I'll be quiet as a mouse. Just be sure to cue me when it's my turn. Otherwise I might miss it."

She frowned at his attempt at humor. "Very funny. Now here's what we're up against. She has gotten Josh and Zack on her side. I wouldn't be one bit surprised if they weren't up at the main house plotting with Harlan."

That was actually the best news Slade had had in weeks, but he could see that Val wasn't overjoyed about it. She'd gone back to her agitated pacing.

"And the problem is?" he inquired, just to rile her. He knew perfectly well what the problem was. She was tempted and she really hated it that she was. She'd vowed to resist him till doomsday and she was scared spitless that she was going to cave in long before that.

"She's going to be disappointed," she declared, chin jutted up.

"Is she?"

"You know she is," Val said, scowling at him. "We've already decided it won't work between us. You need to stop her before she has her hopes dashed."

Slade gave her a pitying look. "You know, for a woman who claims to know my daughter better than I do, you really don't have a clue what she's like, do you? She's not going to be put off by anything I say." He paused thoughtfully, then gave Val a pointed look. "She's a lot like you in that respect. She'll pester us both until she gets her way. I say we give in and save ourselves the trouble."

"She is not going to get her way," Val said grimly. "We decided—"

Slade cut her off. "You decided."

"Same difference."

"No, sweetheart, it is not the same difference. You have your agenda. I have mine. Much as I hate to disappoint you, I'm on Annie's side on this one."

She stopped her pacing and stared at him. "You are?"

"Oh, yes."

"But why? We agreed—"

"No," he corrected again. "You refused my proposal. *We* didn't agree about anything. Of course, there's no news there, either. We haven't agreed about much since the day we met. Keeps things interesting."

"Oh, for heaven's sakes, we're playing word games," she snapped irritably. "The point is we're not getting married. Annie shouldn't get her hopes up."

Slade shrugged. "Why not? I have."

Her gaze narrowed. "You have?"

"Sure. In fact, I've found the past few minutes very encouraging."

She regarded him with a baffled expression. "You have? Why?"

"You're fighting me too hard on this. You came running back from Nashville the minute you heard Annie had a little scare. You might as well stop denying it. You're in-volved with us, darlin'. That gives me hope."

"Well, of course I'm involved with you. That's not the point."

"Then what is?"

The simple question silenced her.

"Well?" he prodded.

"If you don't get it, then I am not about to explain it to you," she said with a huff of indignation. "But for the rec-ord, I will not marry you, Slade. That's final."

"We'll see," he retorted mildly. For the first time in ages, he actually thought he might have a chance with her. He just had to be a little patient. Maybe let Annie work on her.

"You're pitiful, Sutton," he said, when Val was out of earshot. "You're counting on a ten-year-old to do your courting for you."

The sorry truth was, though, that Annie was probably a whole lot more adept at it than he was.

"You know, that gal of yours is smart as a whip," Har-lan Adams told Slade when the rancher wandered down to the corral the next morning to watch Black Knight's workout. He'd been stopping by almost daily lately.

"Val?" The name slipped out before Slade could stop it.

The old man chuckled. "I was talking about your daughter, but Val's a bright one, too." He studied Slade intently. "Annie seems to think the two of you would make a good match. How do you feel about that?"

"Truthfully, I've had thoughts along that line myself," Slade surprised himself by admitting. A few months ago he wouldn't have shared personal information with anyone. Now he'd concluded that a little matchmaking expertise from a grand master would be more than welcome.

"Well, what's stopping you, then?" Harlan asked impatiently. "The woman's had eyes for you ever since she set foot on this ranch. Nobody around here's missed that."

Now that he was into the subject, Slade decided to lay all his cards on the table. "To tell you the truth, I made a couple of tactical mistakes. I haven't been able to recover from them yet."

Harlan's eyes took on the excited glint of a man rising to a challenge. He hoisted himself up onto a railing, clearly settling down to listen. "Tell me," he commanded.

Slade described how he'd reached the conclusion that Val would be the perfect mother for Annie.

"And you told her that?"

"Yes."

"And that's when you asked her to marry you?"

Slade nodded, wincing under the old man's incredulous look.

"Whoo-ee, I'm surprised she left you standing."

"To be honest, so am I. She wasn't happy, that's for sure."

"Well, can you blame her? No woman wants to sign on as mother for a kid without getting a little something for herself in the bargain. If raising a child's all she wants, she could hire on as a housekeeper or open a day-care center, and be done with it. That's not Val's style. Any fool could see that."

"Well, I missed it," Slade said defensively. "At least, until it was too late to take the words back."

Harlan subjected him to a penetrating stare. "Is this still all about Annie?"

"No. The minute Val stormed out, I realized I loved her."

Harlan gave a little nod of satisfaction. "Good. Now we're getting somewhere. Why haven't you just flat out told her?"

"After what's happened, she'd never believe me. She'd figure I was saying all the right words, just to get my way."

The rancher's expression turned thoughtful. "You could be right about that. Timing's important in a situation like this. So, if words won't do it, you'll have to take action."

"Such as?"

"Prove to her how much you care. Court her, Son. Flowers, candy, the whole nine yards. I've seen some mighty fine courtships around this ranch in my time. Been party to a few of them. You just have to listen real close and do exactly what I tell you."

"Won't that seem a little obvious?"

"More than likely, at least at first. You'll have to prove you're in it for the long haul. Never let up. Don't give her a second's peace. Sweet-talk her every chance you get. Worked on Janet and she was a tough one, let me tell you."

"I'm afraid sweet talk's not in my nature," Slade objected.

"You'll learn, Son. When the stakes are high enough, a man can do most anything."

"What stakes?" Annie demanded, slipping up behind them, her face alight with curiosity. "Are you gonna play poker? Will you teach me?"

"Poker's a game for grown-ups, young lady," Harlan told her. "But when you're old enough, I'll teach you how to play and win. Right now, though, your daddy and I are talking about something else."

"Val, I'll bet." She grinned up at Harlan. "Thanks."

He reached down and ruffled her hair. "Glad to help out. You here for your riding lesson?"

She nodded. "Want to stay and watch?"

"Afraid not. I've got to get back up to the house before Janet gets home. I might be able to sneak a cup of real coffee and a couple of Maritza's sugar cookies without getting caught." He winked at Slade. "You remember what I told you and keep me posted on what's happening. Sometimes a plan requires a few adjustments before it starts to work."

Slade shook his hand. "Thank you, sir. I won't forget."

"See that you don't. I haven't had a failure yet. I don't aim to start now."

After his boss had headed back to the main house, Slade noticed Annie grinning from ear to ear. "You sent him down here, didn't you?" he demanded.

"What if I did?" she asked defiantly. "Somebody had to do something. If I wait around for you and Val, I'll be too old to even need a mother."

"Thanks," Slade said, clearly catching her by surprise.

Prepared to make her case, she seemed startled by his response. "You're not mad?"

"No, though as a general rule, we don't go around sharing our private business with outsiders."

"Grandpa Harlan's not an outsider."

"He is not your grandfather," Slade pointed out.

"But he said I could call him that, so that makes him practically family, right?"

Annie's convoluted logic silenced him.

"Well?" she prodded.

"Close enough, I guess." Slade waved her toward the barn. "Go on and bring your horse out and saddle her up."

"By myself?" she asked, eyes wide.

"You've got to learn sometime."

"Oh, wow," she said, and took off running.

"Slow down," Slade hollered, but he was wasting his breath. Annie never did anything slower than full throttle.

He realized as he waited for her to return that the two of them were actually settling into a workable routine these days. They were communicating, something he hadn't thought possible a few weeks ago. And though she still occasionally mystified him, he found the unexpected twists her mind took to be fascinating, rather than terrifying. He supposed he had Val to thank for that.

"Daddy, is this okay?" she asked tentatively, bringing out the saddled mare. Aunt Sadie stood docilely beside her.

Slade checked the cinch, tightened it ever so slightly, then gave his daughter's shoulder a squeeze. "Good job."

Her eyes lit up. "Really? I did it right?"

"Just about perfect. Now let's see you mount," he said, holding out his hands to give her a boost up.

"Not bad," he said approvingly. "You're getting better every day."

"Pretty soon you can start teaching me stuff you did in the rodeo," she said.

Slade froze. "No," he said curtly. "The rodeo's not for you."

"Why not? You did it."

"And look how I ended up."

"You didn't get hurt in the rodeo," she said, refusing to back down. "You got hurt in the accident."

"Forget it," Slade snapped. "It's no life for a girl."

Tears welled up in Annie's eyes at his sharp tone. He sighed heavily, then muttered, "Sorry, I didn't mean to yell."

"Why did you?"

"Because the rodeo is dangerous," he explained. "I

want you to do something different with your life, something safe and sensible."

"And boring," she said derisively.

Slade fought to control his temper. Fighting her on this
now would only make her cling to the idea all the tighter.
He could see that she wanted to live up to his example,
mostly because that was the only one she had. That made
it all the more critical to get Val in her life, so she'd realize there were options for women that didn't involve
potentially life-threatening confrontations with nasty-
tempered broncs or bulls. Though he'd known many bril-
liantly skilled women on the rodeo circuit, it wasn't what
he wanted for his daughter.

"We'll discuss it when you're older," he said finally.

"How old?"

"Ninety-seven," he teased, forcing a grin.

"Oh, Daddy," she said, but she grinned back at him.
"I love you."

"I love you, too, angel." Even as the words crossed his
lips, he realized it was one of the very few times he'd told
her since the first few days of her life, when he'd been
overwhelmed with the emotions of being a new father.
Maybe if he practiced saying the words to Annie, they'd
feel more comfortable when the time came to try them
out on Val.

Watching Slade working with Annie, seeing the girl's
eyes shining from all the fatherly attention, Val sighed.

"Your job here is done," Laurie observed, joining her
on the porch. "You've gotten the two of them together."

"They do seem easier around each other, don't they?"

"They've become a family," Laurie said. "Now, then,
what about the two of you? Before you give me some eva-

sive answer, understand that I am not asking about you and Annie, I'm asking about you and Slade."

Val hesitated. "Nothing's changed."

"I don't understand it. The man is obviously crazy about you. Why hasn't he done something about it?"

"Actually, he did ask me to marry him," Val admitted unhappily, finally prepared to spill the whole story. Maybe her friend could explain where it had all gone wrong.

A beaming smile spread across Laurie's face. "That's wonderful." At Val's silence, her expression faltered. "Isn't it? I thought you loved him."

"I do."

Laurie shook her head. "I don't get it."

"He still wants me just for Annie's sake."

"Still?"

"It came up before. I turned him down," she said succinctly. "I told him his proposal was insulting. I haven't changed my mind."

"Are you sure this is all about Annie? The man doesn't strike me as the type who'd saddle himself with a wife he didn't care about just for the sake of his child. Maybe he just doesn't know how to admit he loves you, especially after fighting you so hard. It's a male pride thing."

Val wanted to believe that Laurie was right, but what if she wasn't? "What am I supposed to do?" she demanded. "Take a risk and marry him and pray that he'll get around to admitting it one of these days? Sorry. I don't live that dangerously."

Laurie looked disappointed in her. "I can't believe it. Is this the same woman who was pushing and prodding me into marrying Harlan Patrick and working out the details of our living arrangements later? I guess it's a whole lot easier to dole out advice than it is to take it."

"That was different," Val insisted, not rising to the bait. "You two were wild about each other. You had been practically forever. The details were just that—details. Love—or the lack of it—is the core issue between Slade and me. He claims he doesn't believe in it. He says we're compatible enough and I'll be good for Annie. That's it."

"Forget what he says," Laurie declared impatiently. "You should know by now that actions speak louder. From where I sit, and believe me, I've been on the sidelines through most of this, I say the man loves you. I've watched him these past few months, Val. He never takes his eyes off of you."

"Probably because he's trying to figure out where I'll pop up next so he can avoid being there," she grumbled. "I don't want to spend a lifetime with a man who's not totally committed from the outset. Things get complicated enough during a marriage even when there is a strong basis of love to start with."

"Val," Laurie chided. "I have never known you to resist a challenge. How can you walk away from one that's this important to your whole future?"

Val didn't have an answer for her.

Laurie regarded her with quiet intensity, then asked, "Or have you decided that Slade Sutton is just not worth it?"

Laurie's words echoed in Val's head for days to come, along with Annie's pleas to stop by for another cooking lesson. In fact, both Annie and Laurie seemed to be scheming to throw Val and Slade together as often as possible. Val was having a hard time avoiding all the traps they laid. Even Harlan Adams seemed to be getting in on the act, which terrified her. She knew precisely how relentless he could be when he'd deemed a match to be suitable.

She stubbornly resisted all their efforts. She didn't want to discuss Slade, didn't want to discuss her own cowardice. In fact, she didn't want to do much of anything except stay in her room and mope. That pretty much kept her out of Slade's path as well, which she was convinced was the only way to make him entirely happy.

She was surprised, therefore, when he turned up at Harlan Patrick and Laurie's one night wearing a suit and carrying a bouquet of flowers.

"What are you doing here?" she asked suspiciously, as Laurie and her husband hovered in the background, unrepentantly eavesdropping.

"I've come courting." His expression practically dared her to make something of that.

Her pulse leaped despite her very recent determination to put this man entirely out of her life. "Why?"

He grinned at that. "The usual reasons. You know, man meets woman, man's hormones kick in and the next thing he knows he's doing things that are totally out of character, like dressing up on a week night and buying posies." He held them out to her, looking awkward as a schoolboy on a first date.

"I see," she said, reluctantly accepting the bouquet, which was fragrant with roses from Janet's garden. "You must have missed the all-important lesson about calling and asking for a date."

"Nope," he said without the slightest hint of apology. "I deliberately skipped right on over that part. I figured you might turn me down. Annie says the unexpected could work to my advantage."

Val held back a chuckle. "You're taking courting advice from a ten-year-old?"

He ran a finger inside his collar, as if it were suddenly too tight. Patches of red stained his cheeks. "She seems to have a better grasp of this stuff than I do. It's been a long time since I've played the game. Haven't much wanted to until now."

For some reason—his words, that uncharacteristic blush, something—she was suddenly filled with renewed optimism.

"It's actually not so hard, if you listen to your heart," she suggested quietly.

To her astonishment, Slade tucked a finger under her chin and tilted her head up, then met her lips with his own. Oblivious to the fascinated onlookers, he kissed her silly. When they were both gasping for breath, he eased away.

"Thanks to you, darlin', I just discovered I have one."

Fourteen

The prospect of being officially courted made Val's palms sweat. It looked as if all her efforts were finally paying off. Rather than filling her with triumph, the outcome panicked her.

What if she'd been wrong? What if she and Slade weren't suited at all? What if she'd simply been lured by the fact that he was so stubbornly unobtainable? What if it had only been about lust, rather than love? The chase, rather than forever?

After all, what did she really know about love? She'd witnessed the enduring passion between Laurie and Harlan Patrick. She'd seen the quieter love shining in Janet's eyes whenever she spotted Harlan across a room. But in Val's own family, there had been no such example. After her father's death, her mother had never remarried, never even dated very much. Even so, Val had never sensed that it was because her grand passion had died.

No matter how hard she tried, Val couldn't seem to quiet her doubts. What if, what if, what if…? The unanswerable questions tumbled through her head like errant ping-pong balls.

As usual, she'd jumped in feet first, tackling the project of getting Slade's attention as systematically as she would the logistics for one of Laurie's tours. Now it was time to put up or shut up, time to pay the piper, time to fish or cut bait. The clichés tripped through her brain at a dizzying clip.

She needed time for her emotions to switch directions, time to quiet all the nagging fears. She didn't need a man on her doorstep with a handpicked bouquet of flowers and passion in his eyes. That was serious stuff. She'd just been playing a game, or so she'd tried to convince herself during the endless weeks of rejection. Hadn't Laurie pegged that very thing? Hadn't she been the one to suggest that Val had decided Slade wasn't worth her time or effort?

Of course, if that were the case, she should have told him to take his flowers and stuff them, rather than stand there with her heart racing and a smile tugging at her lips. She should have refused to sit on the porch swing, thigh-to-thigh, her hand tucked in his, while he talked nonstop for the first time since she'd known him.

Thinking back on it, she sighed. It had felt so right being there with him. A curious kind of peace had stolen through her, even as her pulse had skipped to an erotic, when-will-he-kiss-me beat. She hadn't thought there could be so much anticipation between a man and a woman who'd already made love, who'd already discovered the most intimate secrets of each other's bodies. But it had been as if they were starting over fresh, as if they'd met for the first time that night, as if there were a million sensual fantasies still to explore.

And she'd agreed to see him again tonight, this time for a real date, just the two of them. They were going to Garden City for dinner and a movie, assuming they could agree on one, given his fondness for action and hers for comedy. She'd had every piece of clothing she'd brought to Texas spread out on her bed at one time or another since dawn, trying to choose the perfect first-date outfit. Half had made their way back into the closet, deemed unsuitable. Unsatisfied with the choices left, she was now reconsidering.

"Did I miss the tornado that blew through here?" Laurie asked, standing in the doorway, her expression quizzical.

"I'm trying to decide what to wear," Val said, considering a simple silk blouse and raw silk slacks in a matching shade of teal. Too plain, she concluded, and tossed them atop the rest for the second time.

"Would I be nuts to point out that you're already dressed?" Laurie inquired, coming in to perch on a chair well out of the path of clothes flying from closet to bed with barely a hesitation in between.

"For tonight," Val replied succinctly, holding up a favorite dress in seduce-me red. "What do you think of this? Too much?"

"Are we talking Slade?"

Val nodded.

"You'll have him cross-eyed and panting."

"Perfect," Val said, hanging the dress on a hook on the closet door so she could stand back and get the full effect. This dress had served her well in the past when she'd wanted to walk into a room and turn up the heat. That was precisely why she'd dismissed it earlier. She wasn't sure heat was what tonight called for. In fact, she was pretty sure it called for caution and quiet reason. If Slade touched her, though, reason was likely to fly straight out the window. She'd missed those insidious caresses that could carry her to a whole other universe.

"Where are you going?" Laurie asked.

"Dinner and the movies."

Laurie shook her head. "Not in that dress. That dress belongs on a dance floor, where he can see it. If you're in a movie, you could be wearing jeans and a T-shirt and it wouldn't matter."

"Good point. We'll go dancing," she said, all but sold on the dress and hang the nagging voice in her head that called for something more sensible. Being in Slade's arms on a dance floor held too much appeal. Being in Slade's arms at all was practically irresistible.

"Wait a second." Laurie was shaking her head before Val finished the statement. "His leg, remember? He might hate the idea of dancing."

"We've danced at parties here," Val argued.

"Among friends."

"He was a little awkward at first, but after that he was into it," Val insisted. She grinned. "Besides, I'm pretty sure he'll be glad to get his hands on me any way he can. He seems to have crossed the great divide between being pursued and becoming the pursuer."

"And how do you feel being on the other side?" Laurie asked.

She considered the question thoughtfully. "Scared. Giddy. Confused."

"Confused? Because you're not sure of your feelings for him, after all?"

"That, too. More important, though, I have no idea what turned him around." She sank down on the edge of the bed, clutching the heels that matched the red dress. Because it was Laurie asking, she forced herself to dig deep and try to explain her greatest fear. "A week ago, it was all about Annie. Now it seems to be about Slade and me. Did he just wake up one morning and decide he wanted me? Or is this some last-ditch effort to get me for Annie, after all?"

"So you still don't trust his motives?" Laurie asked.

"Would you?"

"Probably not, which is why dating is good. If this is all pretense just to win you over, you'll know soon enough. There's not a man on earth who can actually fake being in love. They just aren't clever enough to fool a woman, not for long, anyway."

"Are you so sure about that?" Val asked, unable to keep a plaintive note out of her voice. "What if I get suckered in, just the way he wants me to, and find out I'm wrong?"

To her dismay, Laurie actually laughed at the question. "Sweetie, the person hasn't been born yet who can fool you for long. You're very intuitive about human nature. You're warm and generous and caring, which is why Slade wants you in Annie's life and his. He might be able to keep up a pretense for an evening or two, but you'll see through it in a heartbeat. Besides, I don't think Slade's capable of long-term deception. Deep down, he's too honest. That's why he put his cards on the table in the first place. If he's playing a different hand now, it's because he wants to."

"I suppose."

Laurie gestured toward the red dress. "I say go for it. Make the man pay for holding out for so long, for making you doubt what you feel for him."

Val grinned. "That dress is meant to make a grown man weep, isn't it?"

"I imagine that depends on whether or not you decide to let him get you out of it," Laurie replied with a wink. "Don't let Harlan Patrick get a glimpse of it. He'll be down at the barn warning Slade that you're in a take-no-prisoners mood. It will ruin the element of surprise."

Slade took one look at Val and almost abandoned his plans to take her to Garden City. The only place he wanted to take her was bed.

He was pretty sure he'd never seen a dress that slithered over a body as cleverly or as seductively as the red silk scrap she was wearing. Worn in winter, it would guarantee frostbite. It bared shoulders and cleavage and legs. In fact, he was hardpressed to decide what it did cover beyond the necessities. He swallowed hard and tried to find his voice.

"That's…you look…"

She twirled around. "You like it?"

He ran a finger under his collar and wished he weren't wearing a jacket. The temperature had to have gone up a good thirty degrees just since she'd opened the door.

"It's, um… Are you sure you want to wear that just to go to the movies?"

"I thought maybe we'd go dancing instead," she said, striding past him with that provocative sway that was devastating enough when she wasn't encased in red silk. Practically overnight she'd turned into the perfect spokeswoman for sin.

For once, at the mention of dancing, his bum leg was the last thing on his mind. His frantic gaze scanned her back, trying to find one single spot where he could put his hand on it in public without risking heart failure. Couldn't be done, he concluded.

Maybe he could talk her out of dancing between soup and dessert, he decided, following her to the car. He held open the door and practically choked as that fancy slip of a dress slid up her thighs as she got in. He caught the quirk of her lips and realized then and there that she knew exactly the effect she was having. Most parts of his body were already hard, but that smug little smile stiffened his resolve.

Let the woman do her worst. He wasn't going to back down or start running scared. In fact, this evening could get downright fascinating if he decided to call her on her game. Unless he counted the one and only time he'd taken Val into his bed, it had been a long time since he'd let a little casual flirting turn serious.

"Dancing it is," he said, as he slid behind the wheel and gave her a slow, thorough once-over that could have melted steel. He almost chuckled at the alarm that flickered in her eyes, right before she blinked and looked away.

He'd been planning dinner in a casual restaurant that was popular with some of the ranch hands, followed by a movie. He'd counted on being able to slip an arm around her shoulders or maybe snuggle her hand in his own while they'd sat in the darkened theater. That dress and her desire to go dancing had thrown his plans into disarray. He wasn't sure he knew of any place in Garden City that could withstand the shock value of that dress. He glanced over at her.

"Did you have someplace special in mind? I'm afraid my visits to Garden City haven't taken me to the kind of place that dress belongs," he admitted.

Amusement flashed in her eyes again. "And what kind of place do you think it belongs?" she inquired in a tone that challenged him to tred diplomatically.

"Someplace fancy. Elegant. You know, where they do the waltz, instead of the two-step." He didn't say he was afraid anything as energetic as the two-step would have her shimmying right out of that dress.

She grinned. "Good answer. Laurie mentioned that the Garden City Hotel has a new dining room that brings in a band on Saturdays."

It would also have beds upstairs. How convenient, Slade thought, already well beyond the last dance in his imagination. Truth be told, he wasn't sure he could hold out past the appetizers.

"Sounds good," he said, his throat tight.

Those were the last words he managed to choke out until they reached the neighboring town and its quaint historic district. The Garden City Hotel was a very old, wooden structure that maintained its image as one of the city's original buildings. It would have suited the set of a Western movie just fine.

Inside, however, was another story. The owners had updated and refurbished the interior to create an elegant ambiance. Slade figured the restaurant was guaranteed to blow his food budget for the month. Val was worth it, though. She was the kind of woman who belonged in a place like this. In fact, she'd probably grown accustomed to luxuries while she was on the road with Laurie. He wondered if she could accept that luxuries like this came along once in a blue moon on a ranch hand's salary.

Heads turned as she sashayed across the lobby to the dining room. Slade credited the dress for the reaction, but the truth was Val in burlap could have made heads turn. She had a kind of presence that no other woman he'd dated had had. The Adams women had it. He'd always figured it came with money, but maybe it had more to do with self-confidence. Val exuded it. A pride and possessiveness he had no right to feel welled up inside him just the same.

The dining room was lit with candles on every table, setting a romantic mood—or trying to keep folks from seeing the prices on the menu, Slade thought cynically. A small band was tuning up on a raised platform at the far end of the room. The dance floor in front of them was large enough to accommodate a dozen couples and no more. The whole ambiance was intimate, suggesting that those lucky enough to be there were part of a very exclusive club.

The maître d' clucked over their lack of a reservation until Slade slipped him a twenty-dollar bill. Amazingly enough a table right beside the dance floor suddenly became available. Val followed the man in his stiff black suit, while Slade brought up the rear and admired the view. He figured if his heart gave out before the night was over, he'd die a happy man.

"Madame," the maître d' said, holding Val's chair. He kept his gaze discreetly averted as she sat down, Slade noticed. Good thing, he thought. He would have hated to have to punch the guy out for ogling her legs.

"Nice place," he said, after they were alone.

Her eyes twinkled merrily. "Do you really like it?"

"What's not to like? The music's promising. The menu weighs a ton and the wine list has enough French on it to guarantee there's a decent champagne on there."

"Champagne?"

"It's not just for celebrations, darlin'. And even if it were, I'd say this occasion calls for it."

"Oh, really? Why is that?"

"It's our first date." He glanced over the wine list, beckoned the wine steward and ordered a bottle of Dom Pérignon.

Val's eyes widened with surprise. "Isn't that a little expensive? A nice, domestic white wine would do."

"Not tonight," he said tersely, determined to prove he

knew how to treat a lady. There'd been a time when he'd swilled down fancy champagne after every rodeo victory. Despite his preference for an occasional beer and a burger, he knew his way around in a place like this. For reasons he couldn't entirely explain, he set out to prove it. "Mind if I order for both of us?"

Val gave him a puzzled look, but nodded.

He ordered escargots, chateaubriand for two, and salads after the meal. "We'll decide on dessert later," he told the waiter.

One glance across the table told him he'd startled her with his choices, with his easy familiarity with the menu.

"Snails?" she whispered in a choked voice.

"Sure. The place is French, isn't it? They're a delicacy."

"If you say so."

He grinned at her reaction, then leaned across the table to confide, "Personally, I stick to dipping the bread in all that garlic butter, but you can do what you want."

Laughter bubbled up and erupted. "Oh, thank God. I was terrified you were actually going to expect me to eat them."

"Nope. We'll just admire them for a while, then send them on their way."

"Won't the waiter wonder about that?"

"Not in a place like this," Slade decreed. "They're paid to keep their thoughts to themselves."

After the champagne had been poured, he held out his hand. "Care to dance?"

Val stood up at once and moved gracefully into his arms. The band had started with something slow and old-fashioned, a Glenn Miller tune, if Slade wasn't mistaken. The tempo made it easy for him to keep time. Holding Val inspired him.

He could hardly tell where soft skin gave way to silky fabric beneath his touch. Her scent rose to fill his head with thoughts of being outdoors in a garden, with her in his arms under the stars. The brush of her thighs against his made his pulse pound and sent blood rushing to a part of his anatomy that had been on the verge of arousal ever since he'd caught his first glimpse of her earlier. Val knew it, too, but instead of pulling away, she tucked herself even closer, snuggling against him in a way that was downright dangerous.

"You're playing with fire, sweetheart," he warned softly.

Wide eyes gazed up at him. "Is that so?"

"Another couple of minutes and we'll miss dinner altogether."

A smile came and went. "It's just snails and steak. We can have that anytime."

Slade gave her a startled look. She'd sounded half-serious. "What are you suggesting? Since you were the one who wanted to go dancing and this is our very first turn around the floor, I think you'd better spell it out for me."

She gave him a brazen look that went with the red dress. "I'm suggesting we grab that bottle of champagne and make a run for it. I hear the rooms have really, really big beds."

Slade's pulse ricocheted wildly. "And if they're all taken?"

"Use your imagination, cowboy. It's been working overtime all night, anyway."

But nothing he'd imagined had involved making love in the front seat of a truck. "You stay put and fend off those snails. I'll get a room," he declared with grim determination.

Ten minutes later, they were upstairs in a room domi-nated by a king-size bed. The heat that had been simmer-ing on low between them all night turned into a bonfire when he discovered that all Val had on under that dress were panties and a red garter belt. He swallowed hard as she stood before him and daintily rolled down her hose to remove them.

"Lady, you are dangerous," he murmured as he touched a fingertip to one nipple and watched it harden. When he touched the same place with his tongue, she gasped and all but came apart.

"Now," she pleaded. "Please, Slade. I want you inside me now."

Her cry was almost his undoing. He slipped inside her moist heat with all the best intentions to take it slow, but she wouldn't allow it. The frantic rise and fall of her hips demanded a pace that tugged him toward oblivion. When her body shattered with a violent climax, she carried him along, then sank back against the pillows with a sigh of pure contentment.

Still trying to catch his breath, he regarded her with amusement. "Pretty pleased with yourself, aren't you?"

"I have no idea what you mean," she claimed, her ex-pression all innocence despite the position of their bodies.

"This evening has gone exactly the way you planned." It sounded more like an accusation than he'd intended.

Her gaze darkened. "Are you complaining?"

"About this? Never," he said. "I'm just a little confused about how we ended up here."

"We're two adults, Slade. If we want to sleep together, we certainly can. We're not hurting anyone."

"So this is just about sex?" he asked, his tone lethal.

"You had some kind of an itch and I happened to be around to scratch it?"

She blinked at the question and something that could have been hurt shadowed her eyes, but she recovered quickly. "That's a little crude, but yes," she said.

Slade rolled to the side of the bed and sat up. He was suddenly so furious it took every ounce of restraint he possessed to keep from yelling at her.

"I think we must have gotten our signals crossed," he said eventually. "You see, when I climbed into this bed, it was with the intention of making love to a woman I care about, just like it was the last time we were together."

"You weren't making love that first night," Val retorted. "You were striking a bargain."

Slade felt as if she'd punched him in the gut. "That's what this was about? Some sort of payback? A signal, maybe, that you're willing to play the game my way?"

"Exactly." Her chin wobbled, but her eyes flashed fire.

"Well, I'm not," he said dully. "The next time you and I make love, it will be on our wedding night."

"And what if I won't marry you?"

"Then this will have to hold us both till hell freezes over," he said, yanking on his clothes.

When he was dressed, he tossed her red silk dress at her. "I think it's time to go home."

Only then did he dare to look at her. A huge tear was rolling down her cheek.

"Don't do that," he said sharply.

"What?"

"Don't cry. Don't act as if I've hurt your feelings. You were the one who wanted to turn this into something cold and impersonal."

"You're wrong," she whispered. "That's not what I wanted at all."

"What then?"

She sighed heavily and began to get dressed.

Slade grabbed her arm and held her still, then waited until she finally gazed into his eyes. "What did you want?"

"I wanted you to admit how you really felt about me," she said. "I guess I know now, don't I?"

"And what do you think you know?"

"That you want me."

"And?"

"That's it," she insisted.

Slade muttered an expletive under his breath, then dragged her back into his arms. Only after he'd kissed her thoroughly did he step back. "Next time think harder."

Fifteen

Nothing about the date had gone the way Val envisioned. She'd wanted to tempt Slade, wanted to drive him a little crazy, but she hadn't meant to lure him straight to a hotel room.

Nor had she intended to insinuate that their relationship was about nothing more than sex. She'd insulted him and cheapened herself.

"Why, why, why?" she moaned as she sipped her first cup of coffee the next morning.

"Why what?" Laurie asked, joining her at the kitchen table.

"Why did you let me wear that red dress?"

"*Let* you?" Laurie echoed. "Could I have stopped you?"

Val heaved a sigh. "No. I suppose not," she conceded. "Did it work?"

"In a manner of speaking. He couldn't wait to get me out of it."

"And your problem with that is?"

Before Val could answer, Laurie glanced up and immediately got to her feet. "Don't mind me," she said with obviously forced cheer. "I think I'll take my decaf into the music room. Lots to do. See you."

Listening to the suddenly inane chattering of her friend, Val followed the direction of Laurie's gaze and found Slade standing on the doorstep, shifting uncomfortably from foot to foot. She should have guessed, should have been prepared for what the sight of him would do to her. She wanted him every bit as badly now as she had the night before when she'd let her hormones drive reason from her mind.

"Mind if I come in?" he asked, when Laurie had gone.

Val shrugged, feigning an indifference she was far from feeling. "Suit yourself."

Rotating his hat in his hands, he sat down across from her and peered at her earnestly. "Look, I don't know exactly what happened last night."

"Oh, really?"

He scowled at her, then at the hat, finally tossing it aside as if it were a distraction. "You know what I mean. It was like we took a giant leap from the first date to the fifth with no stops in between. I want you to know that wasn't what I had in mind when I asked you out."

"What did you have in mind?" she asked, curious about what might have happened if that red dress had stayed in the closet.

"Starting over, just you and me, trying to find out if what we're feeling is just plain crazy or something real."

As if the explanation made him uncomfortable, he got back to his feet and busied himself pouring a cup of coffee before rejoining her.

"Look, you know I made a lot of mistakes with Annie's mom," he began again, that earnest look back in his eyes. "I never intended to get caught up in something like that again. And you and me, well, there are a lot of strikes against us. We're not exactly from the same world."

He was so serious, so determined to set things right, that she couldn't help leaning forward to confide, "I've gotta tell you, if your world contains escargots, we really don't have a lot to talk about."

A half smile came and went at her teasing. "I was trying to impress you, prove I could be the kind of man you're used to. It's not my fault you wore a dress that could make a man forget his own name, much less his intentions."

Val sighed. "That dress was probably a mistake. It was supposed to get your attention, but it was definitely a fifth-date dress."

"I've been doing a lot of thinking since last night. I'd like to try this again," Slade said, studying her worriedly. "Unless you figure we don't stand a chance."

"I've never thought that."

"Good." He rose, grabbed his hat from the chair where it had landed, shoved it onto his head and moved toward the door. He had it open and one foot out, when he turned back. "By the way, have your reached your own conclusions about what happened in that room last night?"

Val held back a grin. "I'm still thinking about it. Could be you'll have to refresh my memory."

He laughed at the taunt. "Fifth date, darlin', and not a minute before."

Val figured they'd better cram dates two, three and four into a very tight timetable, beginning with a picnic by the creek tonight. Just to be sure they didn't skip ahead, maybe she'd invite Annie along.

Of course, that would defeat the purpose of the two of them spending time alone to discover just how suited they might be. She was still debating with herself when Annie inadvertently solved the problem by announcing she was going to watch a swimming and diving meet with her diving instructor and some of the other students.

"We won't be back till real late," she told Val pointedly. "In case you and Daddy want to go somewhere."

Val grinned at the lack of subtlety. "Thank you for letting me know."

"You weren't out very late last night," Annie said, her expression troubled. "How come?"

"We decided to have an early evening. Your dad has to get up before dawn."

"But he doesn't need much sleep. You can stay out as late as you want next time," Annie advised her.

"I'm sure your dad will be pleased to know he doesn't have a curfew," Val said. "Now why don't you get your things together and I'll take you into town, so your instructor doesn't have to drive all the way out here?"

"She won't mind. You should probably take a bubble bath or something."

A few minutes later, as she was sitting in a steaming bath filled with fragrant bubbles, Val concluded that she was in serious trouble if she'd started taking courting advice from a kid.

Still, she felt especially feminine in her sundress and sandals as she waited on Slade's porch with a picnic hamper. It was almost dusk when he finally came dragging up the path, looking beat. His expression brightened ever so slightly at the sight of her.

"What are you doing here?"

"We have a second date tonight," she told him, gesturing toward the hamper. "Nothing fancy. Just a picnic by the creek."

He regarded her with a puzzled expression. "Did we make these plans this morning?"

"Not exactly. I just seized the moment," she admitted. "Annie's gone off for the evening. She informed me she won't be home till late. *Real* late."

A grin tugged at his lips. "Is that so?"

"Do you think a shower will revive you or would you rather do this another night?"

"Let me try the shower and see how it goes."

When he returned, his hair was still damp, but he was freshly shaved and smelled of soap. "If you have fried chicken in that basket, you will make me a happy man."

"With coleslaw and potato salad," she said. "And a couple of cold beers."

"Ah, perfect. Now I'm ecstatic." He held out his hand. "Shall we?"

Gestures like that still surprised her. A few days ago she would have judged it to be totally out of character. Now she sensed that he was literally and figuratively reaching out to her. She hesitated, then tucked her hand in his.

It was cooler down by the creek. Val spread out the blanket she'd brought, then took out their supper. Slade leaned back against the trunk of a tree and accepted a plate. They ate in silence, but Val concluded it was the kind of companionable silence that fell between friends. Used to nonstop conversation, she realized that the quiet had its own rewards, especially when Slade's gaze caught hers and held until her breath clogged in her throat.

There was a dusting of stars across the sky by the time they'd finished eating. A sliver of moon hung in the velvety darkness. Slade stretched out on the blanket and sighed with contentment.

"Never thought much of picnics before now," he said.

"Why?"

"Seemed like a lot of trouble to go to, when you could eat the same food sitting at the kitchen table."

"Has tonight changed your mind?"

"Just about." He gave her a lazy once-over. "I have a hunch if you were to stretch out here beside me and tuck your head on my shoulder, I'd reach a whole different conclusion."

Val leaned down to stare into his eyes. "Second date, remember?"

"Got it," he said, laughter in his eyes. "But don't be surprised if I try to steal a third-date kind of kiss."

She sighed as she settled against him. "I think I'd be disappointed if you didn't."

She felt the soft brush of his lips against her forehead and closed her eyes. Desire spiraled through her, but so did that same sense of peace she'd felt a few nights ago. She was beginning to see that her instincts all those months ago had been right. Slade really was the right man for her.

Val was making him jump through hoops, but Slade supposed he deserved it. First he'd tried to get her to marry him just so Annie would have a mom again. Then he'd dragged her up to a hotel room on their first real date. He hadn't even let her start her dinner, much less finish it. Not that she'd complained. In fact, she'd been as eager as he'd been, but it had been the wrong way to go about getting reacquainted. Now he'd established some weird dating timetable that required him to keep his hands off of her for two more dates.

He supposed they'd go by quickly enough. Val seemed almost as anxious as he was to get them behind her. In the past few days she'd dreamed up a million things she'd always wanted to do, dropping hints the way a bee buzzed around spreading pollen. Then she waited to see if he picked up on them.

She wanted to go dancing again, despite the way the last time had turned out.

"I haven't really gotten the hang of the two-step yet," she said, making it clear that she had an entirely different sort of evening in mind. She didn't seem to care that he had a bum leg, that he was as clumsy as a man could be and still stay on two feet. But he did it, just to get the third date out of the way, or so he told himself. The truth was he had a good time once he got the hang of holding her in his arms and swaying to the music, instead of trying to move around the dance floor. She didn't seem to mind so much that she still didn't know the two-step by the end of the evening.

When Val wasn't dreaming up tortures for him, she was planning little outings for all three of them. There were more picnics, mostly with Annie along, which meant they weren't considered part of their dating schedule. That could have been irksome, but it wasn't once he got the hang of sneaking a kiss whenever Annie wasn't looking. They went to diving meets with Annie and her friends. They took in several movies and ate enough pizza to qualify as honorary Italians.

One night as they finished their meal, several of Annie's friends came into the restaurant. She ran off to talk to them. Slade watched her laughing and felt something deep inside him shift.

"She seems happy," he said cautiously, not quite ready to believe his eyes.

Val regarded him with surprise. "Of course she's happy. Why wouldn't she be?"

"She wasn't when she came to live with me."

"She was scared, Slade. She'd felt abandoned. She didn't believe you wanted her here with you. That's all changed the past couple of months. You're a good father."

He dismissed the praise. "What kind of father abandons his kid in the first place?"

"The kind who's going through a tough time. It's not as if you left her with strangers. She was with her grandparents. They gave her plenty of love and attention."

"But it wasn't the same," he insisted, echoing what Annie had told him on more than one occasion.

"Not the same, but the best you could do for her at the time. Someday she'll understand that. She's already forgiven you. Isn't it time you forgave yourself?"

He was stunned by her words. "Is that what you think I've been doing? Blaming myself? Paying penance?"

Val nodded. "That's certainly the way it looks from here. I even think that's why you asked me to marry you, out of guilt over having failed Annie once before. You decided to give her the one thing you thought she really needed—a mom."

He supposed there was more than a little truth in that. "No wonder you turned me down."

"It was the gesture of a loving father, albeit a misguided one. All Annie really needed was to have her dad back in her life. Look how she's blossomed."

"You're as responsible for that as I am," he insisted.

She grinned. "Okay, we'll share the credit."

He reached for her hand. "You're an incredible woman, Val Harding."

Color flared in her cheeks at the compliment. "Thank you," she whispered in a choked voice.

"Don't you dare cry," he commanded, alarmed by her

reaction. "I'll never be able to say anything nice again, if all it does is make you weepy."

"Weepy's not a bad thing."

"Maybe from where you're sitting," he grumbled. "It makes me crazy. I keep thinking I've gone and ruined things again."

"Hasn't anyone ever explained the difference between happy tears and sad ones?"

"Doesn't matter. They all make me crazy," he repeated. "Suzanne used to turn on the waterworks at the drop of a hat, because she knew she'd get her way."

"Manipulative tears are a whole other ball game," Val said. "It's not a technique I'm fond of."

He studied her intently, then nodded. "No, I don't imagine you've ever had to resort to tears to get what you wanted. You're probably the most direct woman I've ever known."

"Is that good or bad?"

He shrugged. "I haven't decided yet. I always know where I stand, that's for sure."

"And you always will," she assured him. "I can't hide what I'm feeling, Slade. I won't do it, even for you, even if it makes you uncomfortable. That's why I didn't even try to hide my interest in you from the day we met."

Slade thought maybe just this once he could use that disconcerting directness of hers to his advantage, maybe get a reading on just what she was thinking about the two of them these days. He was running out of courting ideas. They'd long since skipped past the fifth date, even if he hadn't tried to get her into his bed again. He was just about ready to pop the big marriage question again, but he didn't want to risk another rejection.

"So," he said, casually. "How do you think this dating thing is going?"

Amusement spread across her face. "Just fine from my perspective. How about yours?"

"Can I be honest?"

"Of course."

"To tell you the truth, it's getting on my nerves."

She went absolutely still. "Oh?"

He recognized that deadly tone with its undercurrent of hurt. "I want more, Val. I'm not a kid. I'm way past dating."

"Maybe I'm not understanding you. What is it you want?"

"I want to take it to the next level."

Her gaze narrowed. "Which is?"

He was about to say marriage, but at the last second his courage failed him. "A relationship," he declared. "I want us to have a relationship."

To his astonishment, she began to laugh.

"What?" he demanded indignantly.

"Oh, Slade, you wonderful, sweet man."

"What?" he repeated.

"What exactly do you think we've been having all these weeks?"

He struggled to find a word, but got lost somewhere between friendship and sex. He figured neither description would earn him any points.

"A relationship?" he suggested cautiously.

"Exactly," she said.

Well, damn, he was better at it than he'd thought. And it wasn't nearly as terrifying as he'd imagined it would be. Maybe he was ready to take that leap to the next level—the highest level—after all.

Just not tonight.

Sixteen

Val had been all but certain that Slade was going to propose the night before. An Italian restaurant wasn't the place she would have chosen for such a momentous occasion, nor would she have had Annie nearby. But that hadn't mattered when she'd seen the glint in his eye and heard him fumbling for words. She'd been sure she knew what was coming.

Her heart had climbed into her throat. Her palms had begun to sweat. She'd looked into his eyes and seen what she thought was love shining there. Hope had blossomed deep inside her.

Then he'd blurted out that he wanted them to have a relationship. What kind of a suggestion was that? She hadn't been able to hold back the laugh, even though she'd seen right away that she'd hurt him. How on earth was she supposed to get *him* to the next level? At this rate, they'd both be confined to rocking chairs on the front porch by the time he got around to asking her to marry him.

"Do you think I should propose to Slade?" she asked idly, while Laurie was rehearsing the last new song for her album.

Laurie's nimble fingers strummed a discordant screech on the guitar. "Excuse me?"

"It wasn't a trick question. Do you think I should propose to Slade?"

"Not in a million years," Laurie said adamantly.

"Why not?"

"For starters, it's the one thing in life that is mostly the man's prerogative."

"Even a man who can't make up his mind?"

"Especially a man who can't make up his mind. Give him time, Val. He'll come around to the idea all on his own. If he doesn't, then it wasn't meant to be. I don't think it's smart to try to shove him off this particular cliff before he's ready."

"What if he's just too scared to spit the words out?"

"Do you think that's Slade's problem?"

"Honestly, yes. I could have sworn he was going to do it last night, but at the last second he shifted gears and said he wanted us to have a relationship."

"That's progress."

"No, it's not," Val said impatiently. "That's what we've been doing all along, having a relationship."

"Perhaps he meant an *intimate* relationship."

Val considered that. "Could be." She winced as she thought of the way the light had died in his eyes at her laughter. "I probably shouldn't have laughed."

Laurie groaned. "You didn't."

"Afraid so."

"That'll do a lot to build up his courage."

"Which brings me back to why I think I should do the proposing. It'll take the pressure off."

Laurie stared at her intently. "You're going to do it no matter what I say, aren't you?"

Val reached a decision and nodded. "Yes. I think I am."

"When?"

"Tonight," she said. "I think I'll take him flowers. Or do you think I should take him a plate of fried chicken? He really likes that."

Laurie sighed. "Just don't take your own engagement ring."

Val regarded her indignantly. "I would never do that. Some things the man has to do."

"I'm relieved you can see that," Laurie said wryly. "Let me know how it turns out."

To Val's chagrin, Laurie didn't exactly sound as if she expected a happy ending.

Slade considered the disaster in the restaurant the night before and wondered how to avoid a repeat. He was tired of this crazy limbo they were in, but for the life of him he couldn't see a way to end it. He wasn't the kind of man who knew how to string pretty words together. Just look at the way he'd blurted out that nonsense about wanting a relationship. No wonder she had laughed. He would have been better off if he'd just shown her the engagement ring he'd bought, and hoped she'd get the message.

He was pretty sure that Val still didn't believe that this was just between the two of them, that he loved her. He wasn't sure he had the words to tell her all that was in his heart. He stood in front of the mirror over the mantel and tried to find some eloquent way of expressing it. Once he'd said her name, he choked.

"Daddy, what are you doing?" Annie said, coming into the room to peer up at him quizzically. "I heard you talking to yourself."

His cheeks turned brick red. "Nothing."

"You said Val's name. I heard it." Her expression filled with sudden understanding. "You're rehearsing, aren't you?"

"Rehearsing what?"

"A proposal," she said excitedly. "You're finally going to ask her to marry you. I found the ring in your pocket and I've been waiting and waiting. What's taking so long?"

"There's a lot to think about."

"Well, just do it. It can't be that hard."

"That's easy for you to say. I tried it last night and blew it."

Annie's eyes widened. "You did? What did you say?"

"Never mind. Let's just say that I didn't get it right."

"Okay, here's what we'll do," she said decisively. "I'll tell you what to say."

"I don't think so."

"Why not? You've got to get it right this time, Daddy. It could be our last chance."

She ran off for a piece of paper and a pencil. Then she laid out a romantic spiel that even he had to admit was better than anything he'd come up with. When he'd finished reading it to himself, she gestured for him to get down on one knee.

"You say it," she said, in the imperious manner of a director determined to coach great theater out of an amateur.

"I feel ridiculous," he told his daughter. "I cannot get down on one knee and say this stuff, especially not to my own daughter."

"I'm not Annie now. I'm Val. Besides, you want her to say yes, don't you?" the ten-year-old matchmaker asked. "Just pretend you're gazing real deep into Val's eyes and say it."

Slade felt like an idiot. He drew in a deep breath and forced himself to read from the paper Annie had given him. "Val, I know I don't have much of a way with words, but you mean the world to me. I never thought I'd fall in love again, but you made it easy. You opened your heart and let me in."

"Us," Annie corrected. "She let us in." She pointed to the page. "See, that's what I wrote."

"This is my proposal, squirt. You can make your own, if you think mine's not good enough."

Annie rolled her eyes. "Daddy, kids don't ask people to marry them. Say it again."

This time Slade managed to get most of the words out without faltering before he realized that the intended bride was actually standing in the doorway, openmouthed and holding a bouquet of flowers in one hand and a foil-covered plate of what smelled like fried chicken in the other. He awkwardly got to his feet, cursing his gimpy leg.

"Guess I stole my own thunder, didn't I?" he asked, gazing into her eyes, which were shimmering with tears. He wished to hell he were better at reading the distinction between happy tears and sad ones. If he lived to be a hundred, he didn't think he'd get it.

The plate wobbled and he grabbed for it. Once it was safely on the table, he said, "I've got a ring around here somewhere, if you'd like me to try it again."

Annie ran off. When she came back, she slipped the ring into his hand, then vanished, though he suspected she hadn't gone out of earshot.

"What you said before—did you mean it?" Val asked.

"That I love you? Yes, Val, I do love you," he said softly. "Annie may have done the coaching, but the sentiments are all mine. I'm sorry it took me so long to recognize the feelings for what they were. I'm sorrier still that it took me so long to tell you."

Her gaze, brimming with more tears, searched his face. "You're sure about that? You're absolutely sure you love me, that you're not being forced into saying this by your daughter?"

"I've never been more sure of anything in my life. Will you marry me?"

"Us," Annie hissed from just outside.

Val chuckled at the intrusion. "Anybody who'd take the two of you on must like living dangerously."

"I have it on the best authority that you do," he pointed out. "Why else would a born-and-bred city slicker turn in her heels for a pair of boots?"

A smile spread slowly across her face and he knew then that it was going to be all right.

"Yes," she said, moving into his arms. "Yes, I will marry you."

As her arms came around his neck, the bouquet fell to the floor, strewing it with rose petals.

After he'd kissed her thoroughly and slipped the ring on her finger, he stood back and studied her face. "So what was with the flowers and the food?"

She blushed furiously. "Oh, just a little peace offering."

Slade didn't believe it for a minute. "Val?"

"I think it's better if we just leave it at that," she insisted, kissing him in a blatant effort to distract him.

It might have worked, too, if it hadn't been for that guilty gleam in her eyes. Suddenly he knew. "You were going to propose, weren't you?"

"Never," she said, as if shocked by the idea.

"You were."

"I was not."

"I would have said yes," he teased. "But you already knew that, didn't you?"

"Okay, I was hoping," she admitted finally. She touched a finger to his lips. "But I'm so glad you said the words first. I'd have hated telling our grandchildren that I had to talk their granddaddy into marrying me."

"What grandchildren?" Annie demanded, coming out from hiding. "All you've got is me."

"Believe me," Slade said, ruffling her hair, "you are the best start to our family we could possibly have."

"Start?" Val mouthed.

"I figure a couple more wouldn't hurt. Now that I'm getting the hang of this fatherhood thing, I'd like to put it to use."

"No boys," Annie insisted. "I want sisters."

"I'm not sure you'll have any say in the matter," Slade informed her. "Mother Nature has her own way of deciding what's right."

"Well, if I can't pick sisters, can I at least pick when the wedding's going to be?"

Val grinned at her enthusiasm. "What did you have in mind?"

"Christmas," she said at once.

"Why Christmas?" Slade asked.

"Because it's still a long ways away and you can't get married till my hair grows out. I ain't looking like a boy in all the pictures."

Slade and Val exchanged a glance.

"I think a Christmas wedding sounds just about perfect," Val said, eyes shining.

"It's one way to guarantee I won't forget our anniversary." Slade teased.

"Oh, Daddy," Annie moaned. "That's not romantic."

"No," Val agreed. "Your father could use a little help in that regard." She winked at him. "But we're working on it."

Slade Sutton and Val Harding had a Christmas wedding that was perfect down to the last detail. Val saw to it with her usual brisk efficiency. Or would have if she hadn't been such a nervous wreck. A very pregnant Laurie picked up the slack and saw to it that nothing was overlooked.

The church was the same one where generations of Adamses had been married. Already decorated for the season, it was filled with white poinsettias and lit by candles for the evening ceremony.

The bride wore white satin and very high heels, even though no one could see just what they did for her legs. She knew from experience that Slade's imagination was vivid enough to get the picture. She figured one glimpse of those heels and he'd haul her off on their honeymoon even before they cut the cake.

The groom wore a Western-cut tuxedo.

The maid of honor was resplendent in a green velvet gown she insisted made her look like a very ripe watermelon. The best man thought otherwise. He thought she was the most beautiful pregnant woman he had ever seen.

And the bridesmaid—to everyone's astonishment—wore a red velvet dress trimmed in satin, and had her hair fixed up in curls. To her amazement everyone said she was the prettiest girl in the church.

She knew better, though. Annie knew the prettiest woman there was her new mom.

* * * * *

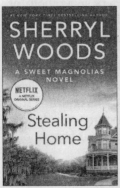  

Get 4 FREE REWARDS!

We'll send you 2 FREE Books plus 2 FREE Mystery Gifts.

FREE
Value Over
$20

Both the **Romance** and **Suspense** collections feature compelling novels written by many of today's bestselling authors.